Emperor and Hierophant

BOOK THREE, ARCANA ORACLE SERIES

EMPEROR AND HIEROPHANT

SUSAN WANDS

Published by SparkPress, a BookSparks imprint,
A division of SparkPoint Studio, LLC
Phoenix, Arizona, USA, 85007
www.gosparkpress.com

Published 2025
Printed in the United States of America
Print ISBN: 978-1-68463-302-9
E-ISBN: 978-1-68463-303-6
Library of Congress Control Number: 2024927611

Interior design by Tabitha Lahr

This book is dedicated to Pamela Colman Smith:
painter, illustrator, designer, costumer, teacher,
author, publisher, performer, and seer

PART I

Scuttling

CHAPTER ONE

Water Signs

"Do you think the undead follow the living?" Pamela asked her two seated traveling companions, Bram Stoker and Ahmed Kamal.

Nestled in a first-class train compartment, twenty-two-year-old Pamela Colman Smith could pass for a fifteen-year-old girl or a woman of thirty. Her copper-hued coat revealed glimpses of a lilac dress, a red Jamaican coral necklace, and a purple sea-glass bracelet. If her mother were still alive, she would disapprove of Pamela's fashion sense, aided by the Lyceum Theatre's costume shop. But the costumers had sewed special earflaps in her lilac hat, which hid sporadically raised letters on her left earlobe. These were the initials that had materialized on her tarot muses, and now Pamela could enjoy the warm gaze of her friends without worrying about the possible appearance of her own earmarks.

"Pixie," Bram said, using her nickname, "you know better than to bring up the undead unless you're asking for one of my Irish yarns." The six-foot-tall, broad-shouldered Bram crossed his legs, taking up even more room in the two seats across from Pamela and Ahmed. Bram's close-set blue eyes sparkled at them.

Pamela glanced at Ahmed Kamal sitting next to her, who shifted his gaze across her and out the window. Stern and slight, Ahmed was barely taller than Pamela, and the effect of his fez and old-fashioned traveling clothes also earned sideline looks on the train platform before they had boarded. Only Bram was more modern, mimicking the Prince of Wales with his casual country-house Norfolk jackets and fur-felt homburg hat. Ahmed's formal jacket and wire-framed glasses bestowed the appearance of a cleric or a judge, and although in his early fifties and younger than Bram he seemed the older of the two.

"Ah, the undead," Ahmed said, stroking his close-cropped beard. "There seems to be a whole industry based on the antics of the undead."

As Bram sat back, Pamela could see him studying Ahmed. This was the first time Bram and Ahmed had spent close time together.

Last year, Bram hired her at the Lyceum Theatre, where her job entailed designing posters and occasionally walking on as an extra in the productions, and he had also recommended her to the newly formed cult, the Golden Dawn, to create a tarot deck. Even now, the final versions of her first four cards, the Magician, Fool, High Priestess, and Empress, were locked up in her desk at the British Museum. Ahmed was her contact at the museum, handling her requests to view mummies and Egyptian artifacts as well as research for the cards. He was also temporarily in charge of the Egyptian Antiquities Acquisition and Evaluation department. The last two months, Pamela had his help putting in requests to view artifacts from the Special Collections room, requests not usually granted to non-staff or women researchers. It was a fluke that Ahmed's schedule allowed him to travel up to Manchester with them, as he was usually traveling to country houses in the south to scout for antiques.

"I hope the undead are popular," Bram said. "My book is centered on their activities."

"And your book is . . . ?" Ahmed asked.

"*The Un-Dead: The Story of a Vampire*," Bram replied.

"Should be *Dracula*," Pamela said under her breath.

"Ah," Ahmed said as he glanced from Pamela to Bram. "Are there spirits protecting this Dracula, or is he a solitary force?" Ahmed asked.

"Oh, he has many little spirits protecting him in their own winged way," Bram replied, shifting his large frame so that his elbows and ankles spilled out into the aisle.

"You should title your book after your main character, Dracula," Pamela said. She knew Uncle Brammie would be sensitive to discuss this in front of Ahmed, but she so wanted Ahmed to know that Bram was more than a general manager of the Lyceum Theatre Tour.

"We've discussed this. No one would know what that means," Bram replied, brushing his hands together as if to shoo her away. "The title will remain *The Un-Dead*."

"So, your 'undead,'" Ahmed said, "has spirits protecting him, much like an afrit. Intriguing."

There it was, Ahmed's "intriguing"— a rare sign that he was in a mood to talk. This train ride was looking promising—perhaps they would all be friends by the time she and Bram got off in Manchester.

"Ahmed," Pamela said, "please tell us the story about the afrit guarding Queen Hatshepsut's tomb and the mummy. You've promised to tell it ever since that sarcophagus arrived at the museum, supposedly with an afrit's curse on it."

Ahmed had told Pamela that afrits were the Islamic version of demons but would not elaborate. Bram drummed his fingers on his armrest and sighed. Pamela knew he did not like to be thwarted from telling one of his own stories about the undead.

Pamela leaned forward and said softly, "Bram, I've been waiting for this story for months."

Though she was allowed to call him "Uncle Brammie" at the start of their relationship, she was told before the London trip that informality was no longer suitable. It was to be "Mr. Stoker" in public or, privately, "Bram." Ahmed had insisted on being called "Ahmed" after she first mispronounced his surname, calling him "Mr. Camel." He only laughed and said as punishment he would make her call him "Ahmed," but only the proper way, with an "ach."

Ahmed leaned forward, his brown eyes wide. "Very well," he said, "I will start with my own experience with the afrit. And I will share my tea with you, yes?" Ahmed stood to retrieve his hamper.

Slanting rain started racing down the outside of the train's window, and Pamela noticed that it gushed toward her, forming a claw shape. *Is this a sign that other forces are listening or merely water racing across glass?* She traced lines of condensation on her side of the window into a circle. She added spikes through it. This shield should protect them if there were bad spirits following them. Pamela was relieved to see that both men were too distracted by the pouring of tea to notice the claw shape or her drawing.

"Yes, teatime is story time," Pamela said, picking up the lunch basket at her feet and opening it. She unwrapped the sandwiches she'd bought for herself and Bram as Ahmed took out a lunch tin. Inside was a corn dish made with raisins and almonds he had once tried to get Pamela to eat at the museum. He motioned the opened tin to her.

"Miss Smith, Mr. Stoker," Ahmed said, "would you like to try my Egyptian dish that will accompany my Egyptian story? My wife, Fatima, taught me back home before I came here how to make this, but this is not as good as hers."

This was the first time that Ahmed had willingly mentioned his wife to Pamela. Months ago, he had left to go back to Cairo to meet his latest child, a second son, in addition to the eldest daughter. Only recently did Ahmed mention now and then that Pamela resembled his wife in her ability to disturb his concentration. She knew she should be polite and accept a portion of the dish, but the scent, reminiscent of unshod feet, overpowered her.

"No, thank you," she said, trying not to choke.

"Goat cheese is not a favorite?" Ahmed asked, his lips starting to smile. "Mr. Stoker?" he added, offering Bram some.

Bram eyed the waxed papers lining the tin of cheese and corn and took a small portion. His eyes widened as he tasted it, but Pamela noticed he chewed very quickly. Pamela's heart felt heavy. Perhaps he and Ahmed were not going to hit it off after all.

After swallowing, Bram asked, "Now what is the story of your Egyptian demon? And where did you study?"

"I was born in Cairo to Turkish parents," Ahmed said. "I studied antiquities in Cairo under the French archeologist Auguste Mariette. As an expert in royal artifacts, during one of my many digs near Queen Hatshepsut's temple, a Turkish dealer contacted me. This man, Ayant, offered to sell me a royal ushabti."

"What is that?" Pamela asked, taking a large bite of her roast beef sandwich.

"A ushabti is a blue statue of the pharaoh, a doll-sized artifact, under a foot in length. Easy to loot from graves," Ahmed answered.

Bram threw his head back and laughed, "Looted graves! One of my favorite subjects."

Seeing him reach into the lunch basket for another of their sandwiches, Pamela felt her chest lighten. Uncle Brammie and Ahmed would get along.

"Ah, but Mr. Stoker, this is more than looted graves; this is a case of defiled royal tombs," Ahmed said.

"Your afrit spirit sounds a lot like our Irish fairies from the other world. They also stand guard in the other—"

"Uncle Brammie," Pamela said, "Excuse me—Bram, let Ahmed continue?"

The Irishman colored. "Oh, yes, of course. Sorry, Pixie." He smiled crookedly. "Rather, Miss Smith. Mr. Kamal, please continue." He gave his beef sandwich a decisive bite.

"After Ayant tried to sell me this ushabti, he put me in touch with two brothers," Ahmed said. "Rasul and his brother, Mohammed, were experienced grave robbers. With another Egyptian, they were scouring the cliffs above the temple of Queen Hatshepsut when they discovered the signs of a hidden airshaft. Tossing a stone down to determine the extent of the shaft, they realized it was enormous. They returned at night with a local boy, ropes, and a donkey and worked to enlarge the opening. The local boy and Mohammed lowered Rasul with a torch down into the hole, and, after waiting a period of time, they put their heads down into the shaft to see if they could hear him. Do you know what they saw?"

"What?" Pamela asked, her heart beginning to beat faster.

"At the bottom of the tomb, Rasul was climbing the rope as fast as he could, batting something away. 'Hurry!' He yelled. 'It almost has me!' Mohammed and the other man tried to pull up the boy as fast as they could. But then . . . ."

Ahmed shook his head and looked away, looking at something outside in the dimming light of the countryside.

Pamela turned to him. "What? What happened?"

Ahmed whispered, "They heard . . . they heard . . . ."

Pamela leaned in closer to him. A piercing screech, sounding like a woman's scream, rang out, sending Pamela sprawling against the window. There was a *whoosh*—darkness enveloped the train.

In the pitch black there was only the rhythmic clacking of the rails, the dank smell of the compartment, and the feel of the textured seat that she clutched. Another *whoosh* and they were thrust out of the tunnel into the flat light of the British countryside. The train whistle roared again.

Pamela leaned against Ahmed and laughed in relief. "Excellent timing!" she said.

Bram chuckled as he slowly clapped, the theatre company's trademark response to successful stage "bits."

"Well played, Mr. Kamal, well played," Bram said. "I might think you were a Lyceum Theatre tragedian, the way you timed that. How did you know when the train was to whistle?"

"I know the tunnel entrances, and most specifically that tunnel, and the darkness that follows. You see, I have made this trip to Liverpool several times before."

"Chasing looted goods?" Bram asked.

"In a manner of speaking, yes," Ahmed answered.

"Now, Ahmed, you must finish the afrit story," Pamela said. "There must be more to the story than that."

"Indeed," Ahmed said. "To continue: Mohammed and the other robber heard Rasul's screams echoing in the air shaft. The donkey anchoring them almost bolted as the rope began to fray. Rasul kept shrieking that something was attacking him. With much difficulty, they finally lifted him out. Once he was on the ground, Rasul claimed that an afrit, an evil demon, had attacked him. It was angry that they had disturbed the queen's temple. The trio went back into town and told everyone an afrit had chased them out and that it would do the same to anyone else. When the brothers and the local boy went back to loot the next day, a terrible, noxious smell escaped from the temple's airshaft. This was a sign for everyone to stay away. But despite the smell, the looters kept stealing everything they could get their hands on."

"Wait. Do afrits smell bad? And are they invisible?" Pamela asked.

"Afrits can threaten people with bad smells," Ahmed said. "The afrit itself is not the smell. And they are invisible, when they want to be."

Bram grimaced. "If they smelled, being undetected would be difficult, even if they are invisible."

"When it suits the afrit, the afrit is invisible," Ahmed said. "The two brothers looted the temple of the queen and continued to loot for many years. They used caution not to sell too many items at a time, to avoid suspicion. This Turkish art dealer, Mustapha Aga Ayant, procured many of these Egyptian artifacts. Most prized among them were the ushabti, these blue statuettes of a pharaoh. Collectors from Russia, Belgium, and even here in England hunt them. The art dealer had diplomatic immunity since he was a 'consular agent.' He could sell these antiquities without being arrested. But many people in Egypt began to realize how many treasures were being stolen and taken out of the country."

"I don't think our British Museum archeologists would consider themselves tomb robbers," Pamela said. "Don't they come back from digs claiming they've saved countless relics from demolition?"

"I have my own thoughts about that, Miss Smith," Ahmed said, looking out the window past Pamela. "But in my story, a new official laid a trap to discover where this Ayat, the art dealer, got this blue statuette and tricked him into revealing the names of the two brothers, Mohammed and Rasul. Arrested, questioned, and beaten, they refused to give up the location of the queen's temple's airshaft. But Mohammed betrayed his brother. He told the official that it was Rasul who had found the queen's temple entryway—that Rasul killed their donkey and threw it down the airshaft to create the scent of rotting bodies. Rumors spread about the afrit to keep the locals away, but the looting continued."

"So there was no afrit in the temple after all," Pamela said.

"No afrit there—*at the time*," Ahmed said. "But officials discovered later the royal remains of over forty great pharaohs. These pharaohs waited centuries to be restored to the other life on the other side of the river. When the main official found all these pharaohs, he hired three hundred men to clear the temple, so that they could take the great ones to a museum in Cairo. But as the workers cleared the temple, they also pilfered and destroyed treasures. Rather than make the trek out of the temple for lamps, some took mummified bodies of royal children and used them as torches to light the pitch-black tunnels."

Pamela shuddered. "They used the bodies of children as torches?"

"Yes," Ahmed replied. "The afrits saw this and remembered."

The wind howled outside and the train car hurled on as dark clouds closed in. The rain streaked by with new intensity. The shield that Pamela had drawn on Ahmed's side of the window deflected rows of dripping water. The dark water pooled and trickled down the glass like beads of blood.

"Some of the findings from the temple you might have heard of," Ahmed continued. "Ramses I, II, III, XI, the Tuthmosis I, II, and III, and Ahmose. During this move, the mummies were set out in the blistering sun, waiting to be loaded onto the barges."

"Such a desecration of the dead. Did you see this?" Pamela asked.

"Yes," Ahmed answered. "I was there. I saw it. Ramses I, partially unwrapped, was lying out on the ground, and his arm slowly rose in the air. His bandaged hand pointed to the workmen who had burned the bodies of the royal children. The guilty parties he pointed to were cursed because the smell appeared whenever those workmen were on any future site, marking those who were robbers that were living corpses. Most of the robbers went mad; the rest were shunned. Others can make excuses, but I believe the afrit marked them with a bad smell."

"What happened to the mummies?" Bram asked.

"The mummies were put on boats and floated down the Nile to the museum in Cairo. All along the banks of the Nile, thousands turned out to honor their ancestors, each of their faces turned toward Mecca."

"Did you see the procession, Mr. Kamal?"

"I not only saw the procession; I was one of the first honored historians in the men's line due to my presence in the tomb when Ramses was unwrapped . . . ."

"Men's line?" Pamela asked.

"Yes, Miss Smith, in my country, we have separate sections for the men, women, and children. The imam recited the prayers for all. The silence among the crowd afterward was very moving."

Bram sat up and leaned forward. "Who else was an honored historian in this procession of boats?"

Ahmed smiled. "I stood next to Émile Brugsch, at that time only a German digger, and Auguste Mariette, my former employer in Cairo. Bergsch is my current employer with the Cairo Antiquities Department."

"Just like my tarot cards, you have worlds within worlds, Mr. Kamal," Pamela said. "Your family is Turkish, yet you worked for a Frenchman in Egypt alongside a German digger. You are truly universal."

"I think the word you are looking for, Miss Smith, is 'international,'" Ahmed said. "'Universal' denotes acceptance, and for me that is truly not the case. Not yet, at least."

There was silence while the three of them squinted out at the inclement weather.

"Ahmed, what does a real mummy look like?" Pamela asked, putting away her lunch box. "An actual mummy—not the bandages, not the outer cases, like those you've shown me at the museum."

"Ha, well," Ahmed said, "the most curious thing that struck me, in addition to a mummy's dehydrated skeleton, was the length of its earlobes."

Pamela shifted in her seat. How much did Ahmed know about the tattoo markings that had appeared on herself and her muses? In recent months, each of Pamela's muses—William Terriss, Henry Irving, Florence Farr, and Ellen Terry—all had noticed a mysterious white tattoo appearing on their earlobes. It was a symbol of three letters—a monogram: "PCS." Pamela's initials. Bram and Ahmed might have noticed the markings but didn't realize they marked her tarot muses.

"Yes, the earlobes were all very much stretched out on all the royal ones," Ahmed said, his half-moon eyebrow arching. "Only priests had piercings or tattoos."

"I thought most religions forbade markings," Pamela said.

"In Egyptian culture, ear markings signify three things: prayer, meditation, and protection from demons," Ahmed said. "I hope your theatrical production in Manchester will be free of demons. If I did not have to travel on to Liverpool to investigate a stolen statue, I would stay . . . ."

Ahmed's words trailed off and he pointed to a dewy symbol on the window. In the condensation, three intertwined letters appeared: "PCS." Pamela wondered if Ahmed had ever glimpsed Florence's markings when she came to the museum; she would be the only one that he knew. If Bram had spotted the magical tattoos of both Ellen and Henry, he had never said anything to her. But now, only three of her muses were still alive. Her Fool, William Terriss, lay interred in a grave, a murder victim.

The three watery letters dripped, their dense weight dragging their shapes downward. As the letters sagged, "666" formed in their place.

Her left ear burned, and her hand immediately went to massage the raised bumps on her earlobe, feeling the edges of each one of her initials.

"Miss Smith, something has been conjured," Ahmed said softly. "Perhaps an afrit is following you."

Pamela swallowed and looked away from her companions. *It's not an afrit following me, but Aleister Crowley, the Golden Dawn Magician determined to own my tarot cards' power.*

CHAPTER TWO

Manchester Childhood

On the Manchester Victoria train platform, Pamela waved up to Ahmed, sitting in her former seat next to the window. His face peered out the window from the same spot that the afrit symbol had appeared, now dotted with harmless water droplets. Midwave, Ahmed grimaced at her; Pamela could make out other passengers entering the compartment and he stood to help them. *At least he will have company the rest of his rainy way to Liverpool.* She made her way to a luggage cart next to Bram.

The rain sputtered to a stop by the time Pamela and Bram collected their bags. A rough-looking man with bruised knuckles and bushy eyebrows approached them as they set their suitcases on the platform.

"'ello, Samuel, from Manchester Royal Theatre. You must be the Londoners. Car out curby, theatre ten digit away," he said. Pamela could see from Bram's wrinkled brow that he was having difficulty making out what Samuel had said.

Pamela stood closer to Bram and whispered, "Car is out front, theatre is ten minutes away." A smile tweaked Samuel's mouth and he loaded their valises onto a cart.

Bram's eyes widened as he looked at her. "Of course you speak Mancunian, you lived here."

"Only until I was ten," Pamela answered. "But I'd love to walk to the theatre." Samuel stopped loading bags and turned to her. "The theatre is on Peter Street across from the Free Trade Hall. Isn't that right, sir?" Pamela asked.

"Beware the Scuttlers," Samuel said, adding, "they're street scum." He hoisted up the handles of the cart and started off.

"Be careful," Bram said, giving her their two-fingered salute before heading to the theatre with Samuel.

Pamela had no idea who the Scuttlers were, and she had no intention of finding out. Would any of Manchester be familiar? Making sure the travel bag under her arm was secure, she found her way out to Victoria Street and walked along the River Irwell. It was just past four o'clock, and, after the shrill whistle etched her ears, workers poured out of the cotton mills lining the waterway. She was aware of coveted glances at her coat, which now seemed garish and more fitted to a slim actress than to her generous size. Some longing looks came from children with frayed coats and no mittens, walking by her listlessly. She didn't remember this Manchester. She gulped and kept going. *But wait—wasn't there a hidden river here? The River Tib?* She walked faster.

She finally recognized the massive and ornate Free Trade Hall, and there it was across the street—the Theatre Royal Manchester. She stopped midstride. No wonder Mr. Irving wanted to tour Manchester. This was where he'd started out his acting career, and Theatre Royal Manchester was a smaller version of Mr. Irving's celebrated Lyceum Theatre in London. Looking at the front of the theatre, a childhood memory bubbled up. She was in a carriage on her way to church, the Swedenborgian one, with her parents, and they had pointed out the theatre to her. The bubble burst when shouts from the crew drew her back.

At the backstage door of the theatre, the load-in for *The Merchant of Venice* was in full swing. Wagons and carts filled with flats, scrims, and canvases queued up as stagehands swarmed around them.

Lovejoy, the production stage manager, shouted directions to local workers as baskets of hardware made their way backstage. Harvey, the London main carpenter, gave Pamela a sympathetic nod as Lovejoy screeched obscenities over the rough treatment of scenery lifted out of the main wagon. Two scrims, tattered canvases of painted scenery, were gingerly handed over to Lovejoy, who carried them into the theatre. Local carpenters vied with hired day workers who dashed across the street, carting costumes and props to the enormous Free Trade Hall

Harvey shouted, "Hey ya local yokels, don't think our props are free because they're stored in your Free Trade Hall."

Howls of scorn and derision erupted from the Manchester crew as they continued to unload the wagon. "The thee-ate-tre! Ooh, we are in Manchester-ah, now, ain't we, children?" the London crewman asked.

A cold wind blew through Pamela's copper coat, its thinness reminding her it was an unlined stage costume and not practical for October much less winter. She shivered. The wind was a bad harbinger for this last leg of the three-week, eight-city tour. In three months, Pamela would return to London with no employment in January, except for the Golden Dawn's poor-paying tarot-deck-illustration job. Just last month, she had word from Alfred Stieglitz in New York City that her unsold paintings from her last art gallery show had "disappeared." The year 1900 was beginning to look grim.

"Lovejoy, we found it!" Harvey shouted from the wagon.

Lovejoy ran out from backstage of the theatre and climbed up next to Harvey.

"Guv'nor," Lovejoy shouted. "It's here!"

The Guv'nor, celebrity actor-producer Henry Irving, came out with his shirt sleeves rolled up and hair disheveled. He strode next to the wagon. Even in late middle age, the star made a striking impression—tall and lithe, wearing deacon's glasses and a long red scarf. Pamela was stunned to see Sir Henry Irving assist on a load-in. The finances for the Lyceum Theatre must be in very bad shape.

Lovejoy unfurled an old tattered canvas, and Henry held one edge. It was the *King Arthur* canvas Pamela had painted as a child while visiting the Lyceum scene shop. Hidden in the castle wall of Camelot, there were the symbols of Merlin—the magical icons of swords, wands, stars, and cups—and King Arthur stood in front, lifting a sword up to the sky. Bram stood next to her as she stepped closer to the canvas.

"I'll never forget that day you came to the scene shop," Bram said softly. "How you told the scenic artists what needed to be on King Arthur's banner. As if you would know at that age."

"I may have been ten years old," Pamela answered. "But I knew what needed to be there—the tools of the Magician."

"You were right, Miss Smith," Bram answered.

Miss Smith. This would take some getting used to.

Bram mimicked King Arthur on Pamela's canvas, an upright sword in one hand and the other hand pointing downward. This was the pose Pamela used in her Magician tarot card.

"Sir Henry the Magician!" Pamela said, as Bram flinched. Henry glanced over to her with his infamous sneer and looked away.

She had said the forbidden title, not "Magician" but "sir." Henry Irving had been knighted four years ago, the first actor to receive such an honor, but he refused to let anyone in the company call him "sir." He was Guv'nor or Mr. Irving.

Lovejoy folded the canvas and handed it over to Henry, who received it as though it were a sacred relic. With an abrupt nod, he turned and walked back into the theatre, with some workers applauding him. But not a nod to Pamela. Pamela's heart seized midbeat.

Henry's coldness toward Pamela started after the death of William Terriss, the only other major actor at the Lyceum Theatre. It was whispered among Golden Dawn Magicians that Aleister Crowley was behind Terriss's assassination. Her Fool was dead. The lessons from Terriss, his derring-do, risk-taking, spontaneous job of life—all these lessons felt as though they had left her. Aleister had failed to become a Golden Dawn chief and was jealous of Pamela's tarot commission. Now, he would kill her tarot muses, one by one, unless she stopped creating her deck. Her second muse, Sir Henry the Magician, was next. Was this why the Lyceum Theatre was failing?

Bram passed her a *Merchant of Venice* handbill she had drawn. Shylock stood out as a defiant figure standing in three-quarters profile. But she gasped when she saw the additions to her illustration. Two locks of his hair stood out as devil horns; the flier's background was now a deep red instead of the yellow she'd designed. The message of this production was clear: the Jewish merchant was Satan.

"Uncle Brammie! No! They can't mean to use this! The audience will think Henry's Shylock is the devil."

"I'm afraid that's their intent," Bram said. "They are billing *The Merchant of Venice* as a melodrama, with Portia, the heroine, taking on the Jewish infidel. If it is of any consolation, the souvenir program cover has your original artwork of Shylock."

"The one where he is wearing the turban?" Pamela asked.

"Yes. I was told that Shylock can hide his horns in there."

"I don't remember Manchurians hating Jewish people here growing up," Pamela said.

Bram patted her shoulder. "That was a long time ago, and things change. Or they come to light."

Pamela saw Bram's lips purse. Bram had his own demons to

fight. Just before the tour launched, Bram had been demoted; he was no longer Sir Henry's right-hand man but a mere secretary.

Pamela held Bram's hand. She felt the raised initials on her left earlobe twitch.

"Bram, do you think Ahmed was right? That a demon followed us on the train?"

Bram stared straight ahead. "I don't know, lass."

The next day, Pamela had her first trip in a motor car. The driver reassured her that, in addition to three speeds, it also had two brakes. After they lurched from the curb, she eventually found it was more comfortable than being on a carriage ride, despite the scent of petrol.

She leaned against the velvet upholstery and gazed at the packed rows of factory houses lining the streets. Children in rags played in the cold mud ditches in front of two-story brick homes, most with one window. She had only recently learned of Manchester's 250 factories processing cotton from America, mostly staffed by child workers. Guilt hung in her stomach like a stone.

Gangs of young boys loitered on street corners. All were dressed in the same outfit: bell-bottom pants, bright scarves around their necks, and shoes with metal toes. Each boy wore the same haircut, very short on the sides with a lock of hair curled in front, anchored by a wool cap. But it was their belts, studded with brass nails and copper rivets, that impressed her the most. They glimmered like metal snakes around their slim waists. A group stepped into the middle of the street, directly in front of their car. The driver throttled the engine and sped around them.

"Are they the Scuttlers?" Pamela asked.

"Yes, and avoid them at all costs," the driver replied.

As the car jostled down the cobblestones of Princess Street, Pamela caught sight of a beautiful church ahead. It was only two stories high with no bell tower, but it had been built exactly to a Gothic standard. *Yes, that is definitely golden Warwick Bridge stone.* Her friend the reverend would be pleased to know that she recognized the stone from her Southwark Cathedral in London.

"Can we stop so I can have a look at that church?"

"Not on your life," the driver answered. "Not only is it Samhain today, full of foolishness and pranks, but that church is dead in the middle of the gang's territory."

Samhain. *How could I forget that it is All Hallows Eve?* This was the day she first experienced magic, floating in her bedroom here in Manchester. Childhood friend Maud was telling stories when they seemed to have opened the door to the *sid*, the hidden fairy world. And so began her obsession with fools, whether in tarot or folktales. And the biggest Irish fool was Nera, the mortal who loved a fairy queen. Churches were known to have doors that opened up to the other side. Perhaps she'd find a church here in her childhood city that would open up to the *sid*. And Nera would be there to help protect her from Aleister.

"What is the name of the church?" she asked, turning around in her seat to watch it disappear from view.

"Holy Name," the driver answered. "You'll need one to survive in these parts, miss."

Before she left the theatre, Bram protested when he heard that she wanted to travel to Didsbury, a half-hour car ride away. Pamela had yet to show him her revised poster for *The Merchant of Venice*; Ellen's train was due to arrive within that hour, and the streets of Manchester were dangerous. Did she want more hardships to visit the Lyceum company?

Last month at the Ludgate Hill Station in London where uninsured flats were stored, an inferno exploded. Thousands of pieces of the Lyceum's scenic canvases—the backbone for sets—were incinerated. Pamela knew in her bones that it was Aleister who had something to do with the terrible fire. The blaze destroyed the company's financial stability: over 350 people lost their jobs. The repertoire was reduced from forty-four state-of-the-art productions to only two: *The Merchant of Venice* and the melodrama *The Bells*. Gone were the witches' lair in *Faust*, the court ballroom from *Much Ado About Nothing*, the castle garden in *The Corsican Brothers*, and the stately palace from *Louis XI*. Pamela heard whispers backstage that these catastrophes, Terriss's death and the fire, only started when Pamela joined the company.

As the cab wove around horses being shod at the side of the road, hedges, not laundry lines, were sighted between houses. Soon, the streets of her childhood neighborhood, Didsbury, appeared.

Didsbury wasn't leafy this time of year, but the wide oak-lined streets were set off by red brick homes. White framed windows and glass doors shone. Even the fourth floors, reserved for maids, nurses, and shunned relatives, were inset with tiny windows. But it was the big window seats on the second floors that evoked Pamela's childhood. The parlor seats overlooked the yards' studied plots, a combination of manicured grass and matured wilderness.

She spotted Fielden Park to her left.

"Stop! This is it!" Pamela called out.

The car stopped. Her childhood home, Oakhurst, still looked like a forested fortress, trees pressing in on all sides. In the chilly car, Pamela could barely see the side garden, glimpsing only a half-dead flower garden tucked under the desolate trees.

The driver got out and opened Pamela's door. She stood on the sidewalk and smoothed stray locks of hair from her face. As she gazed up at the three-story brick building, her mother's words came back to her: *No shared walls for my family*. There were no shared walls, but there were two maids and a nurse for

Pamela. The front door, once robin's-egg blue, was now gray. As grand as the house had been, it seemed to have shrunk.

Reaching into her purse, Pamela pulled out a crumpled letter. It was from her grandmother from Brooklyn, one of the few family mementos left by her mother.

Our Corinne now insists on being called Pamela. Precocious and inventive, she exhibits the gifts of all Colman Women. I had hoped she would publish her artistic work, as you yourself did, Mother, but Pamela is preoccupied with fairies, monsters, and bats.

Every time Pamela read this, she hungered to have her mother explain "the gifts of the Colman Women." Pamela had not been particularly cherished; her mother's hand was never warm or maternal. But she had been trained to believe that she descended from a line of remarkable Colmans.

Pamela folded the letter and put it in her pocket. Leaning against the side of the taxi, the driver smoked a pipe, looking at the park. In the autumn air, its intoxicating scent mixed with wood smoke. Pamela inhaled the musky sweet smell of wood smoke, leaves, and the pipe tobacco, filling her lungs with its deliciousness.

Pamela walked up to the front of her house. Glancing at the second-story window, she recognized her mother and father's bedroom. Three panes of windows let in the afternoon light, the best room in the house.

There was her small window on the third story, where Maud Gonne had told her stories. Beautiful, tall, fanciful Maude. *It's Samhain Eve; could you still fly from bed to window tonight?* Pamela had never told the Golden Dawn magicians that she had floated as a child. They would probably ask her to take a class in astral travel to prove it.

She took a deep breath as she stood before the house. *You've waited years—go! March up to the door, ring the bell, go to the old bedroom, see if you can fly.* A movement in the front window caught her eye. The curtains were held back and then closed tight. Footsteps. The gray front door opened.

Polly the housemaid stood there, with more than twenty additional pounds on her frame and twelve additional years etched in her face. They stared at one another.

"Polly?" Pamela asked.

"Yes, and who might you be?" Polly asked.

"It's me, Pamela, daughter of Corinne Smith. We lived here."

"Oh, for the love of Mary it is!" Polly replied, stepping down to take Pamela's hand. Pamela didn't remember Polly's accent sounding like an East Londoner with a nasal twang.

"Who is it?" an ancient female voice rang out from inside.

"Someone from the neighborhood," Polly answered. Tucking Pamela's arm under hers, Polly led her inside.

"Send her away," the creaky voice called as they reached the foyer.

Polly whispered to Pamela, "You can have a quick look around at your old room before the missus gets too worked up. You'll have to be quick."

They raced to the servant's staircase on the other side of the informal parlor, and they made their way up the three flights of stairs.

Polly deposited Pamela at the door of her old room and opened it. Pamela didn't recognize it. Polly lifted a finger to her lips and hurried down the stairs. Inside the room, Pamela walked over to an empty bassinet, then took in an enormous wardrobe and settee. In the corner where her toy theatre had the place of honor stood a play carriage. Odors of breast milk, talc, and soiled diapers eked out from the corners. Everything was turned inside out. Any link to her childhood's magic was gone; flying was no longer possible here. She sighed and left the room.

Meeting Polly at the bottom of the stairs, she quietly thanked her and stepped outside, where dark clouds had gathered. The driver opened the door to the front seat, but she waved to him and then pointed to the park across the street.

Fielden Park's grove of trees had grown taller. They surrounded a paved stone circle; in the center was a fountain with an angel statue with an outstretched hand. Was this fountain here when she was little? Why was the angel so familiar?

Her cheek stung. A pinpoint of sleet slapped her with dart-like precision. The dream she'd had for the past month came roaring back.

It was snowing, and she was being thrown down in the park by an angry mob to cries of "*Witch!*" and "*Burn her!*" The crowd lassoed the statue with a rope to hang her but stopped when the statue shuddered to life. Her big, beautiful stone arms threw off the rope around her neck, her enormous wings unfurling like an eclipse. The angel scooped Pamela up, and she clung to the granite robe. Pamela craned her neck around to see the face of the angel. It was Mother.

Shaking of the vision, Pamela ran to the taxi and climbed in back. Her hat fell off, and she rested her head on the back seat. The sounds of her ragged breathing filled the cab.

The driver opened her car door. "You all right, Miss Smith?"

"Yes. Yes. Just overcome. Could we go back to the theatre, please?"

After giving her a hard look, he closed the door and cranked the front of the engine to start it. Once back in the car, one wiper smearing rain over the window, the driver looked back at her. "You have to be careful on Samhain. All sorts of shenanigans happen with the hooligans about. And the veil between the two worlds is very thin tonight. But you probably know that, don't you, miss?"

As they chugged down the street, Pamela's hand went to the crumpled letter in her pocket. Holding it up to read, she saw that sleet had dissolved some of the writing. The return address of 'Oakhurst, Didsbury, Manchester' melted into blurry droplets, the same shape as the water droplets on the train window. A blob ran down the paper and settled into a series of veins, curling and snaking into position. Pamela held the paper flat. It was an Emperor wearing a suit of armor. He looked like Bram. Was this magic instructing her to draw the Emperor as Bram? Or a warning from Ahmed's afrit that she needed to put on armor?

CHAPTER THREE

Bram's Blood and Contagion

"Ho!"

"God's blood!"

"Bloody hell!"

As the stage crew cursed, Bram raced down the aisle from the back of the house to the Manchester Royal stage. One of the judges in *The Merchant of Venice* fell to the floor and sat cross-legged, holding his wigged head, background cast members around him.

Bram bolted onstage and crouched next to the moaning actor. A trickle of blood seeped down the man's face, dyeing the front strands of his white wig. Bram tore the wig off and saw a cut above his temple, not deep, but the wound still flowed crimson. Bram looked into the man's eyes, not dilated, and asked him to squeeze his hands, which he did with full strength. Thank God this role of the judge called for an enormous padded wig or he would have been dead. Bram took out a handkerchief and gently held it to the man's wound.

Near the wounded actor lay a fallen section of pipe and crumpled canvas. The flyman must have tilted the hung canvas as it was flown to the floor and the pipe sewn in at the bottom burst through the hem. Bram looked up into the flies to the flymen standing on the rail.

"Lovejoy," Bram shouted, "man down! Pipe down!"

Lovejoy ran out from backstage and sat before the injured man as he groaned. "Bloody hell," Lovejoy said, seeing the wound seep through the handkerchief.

Bram gently lifted the man and positioned him on one of the judge's chairs. It was moments like these where Bram's strength as a former boxer at university was to his advantage.

The wounded actor was a local merchant, hired by virtue of his large donation for the theatre's opening night. He was smaller than average, in his midthirties, just the type to fit into the judge's costume.

Remembering his brother, the doctor, and his protocols, Bram held up one finger. "How many fingers do you see here, sir?"

"One, and I think I'm fine, Mr. Stoker. My family will be coming to the opening night on Thursday, and they'll will be wanting to see me in the show."

"Lovejoy," Bram said, "fetch a local doctor to ensure our actor is up to performing, and then we'll restore for the technical rehearsal."

The head costumer stomped onstage, none too pleased to see the white wig now reddish. He helped the actor offstage as a red circle pooled on the floor and the background cast crept onstage to gawk. A stage crew member kneeled down and swirled a cloth over the considerable circle of blood.

"Lovejoy," Bram said, "can the extras and children be kept offstage until the crew cleans up this blood?" Lovejoy glared at him although Bram's focus was on the rag swirling on the floor turning scarlet.

Blood and its contamination obsessed him. He was raised by a mother who fed him stories of contagious diseases that flourished during the Irish cholera epidemic. Bram himself was a sickly child. Not able to even stand until he was seven years old, he'd sit and gaze out of the third-story window in his family's house, looking to the sea, dreaming. Bram's father provided a decent middle-class existence for his family working as a clerk at Dublin Castle. But it was his mother's tales of being buried alive, grave robbers, and strange diseases that shaped his inner life.

"All right, you lookie-loos," Lovejoy shouted, "get the fuck offstage unless you're part of the inept crew who didn't check the safety list, or the bloody crew who didn't fly the pipe right. And once you fix this, crew—meet me in my office."

As Bram trudged back to his seat, one thought kept playing in his head: *It would have been my office the crew went to.* As he settled in to watch the set restored, he raised his hands helplessly. The floorboards still glistened with blood as flymen and stage crew shouted insults at one another, creating a raucous din.

Sir Henry Irving strode out from the wings in his Shylock costume, an Arabic-style tunic with a large headwrap, carrying a staff. Center stage, Irving slipped on patch of blood but the staff caught him from falling. He turned to the front of the house and roared, "Stoker, what the hell is going on?" Bram stood up.

"Guv'nor, it seems wet weather from the train station soaked the old canvas," Bram said, making up an excuse on the spot. "Pipe must have ripped through the wet hem." Bram knew that unless there was an immediate excuse, the new management could fire the flyman on the spot.

"What incompetence," Irving said. "It's no wonder you were demoted." He stormed offstage. The stagehands on the set went quiet. *Well, that's one way to tell the company the news I'm no longer in charge.*

Bram's heart struggled to beat regularly. It was that morning that he'd been called into the office upstairs, the one Lovejoy now commanded. Three similarly dressed accountants and Mr. Comlyn, the wealthy composer who wrote the music for *King*

Arthur, stood around Bram as Sir Henry sat behind the desk, not looking at Bram once. Comlyn blandly relieved him of his job, "all due to this reincarnation of the Lyceum Theatre." Bram was glad that Pamela took the morning off to work on her tarot cards before she picked up the theatre's fliers at the printer, and that Ellen Terry was speaking at a local school as the theatre's leading lady. His friends were spared the sight of blood, swearing, and the official announcement that Bram had been demoted.

Being second-in-command as company manager at the Lyceum Theatre had been prestigious. Bram's tasks included transcribing fifty letters a day dictated by Sir Henry, dispatching box office totals to banks, screening countless invitations, reading hundreds of plays, casting shows, writing contracts, and sending invitations to the first-nighters. But things had deteriorated since the fire. Gone were the days of Oscar Wilde and Lillie Langtry draping themselves over the box seats, causing a stir in the auditorium. Oscar was now in jail and Lillie had retired from theatrical life and was living in Monaco.

And now, after almost twenty-seven years of working with Sir Henry, their partnership had been wiped out with the signing of a redundancy document. Henry's signature proved that Bram had always been a hired lackey, not a partner in Henry's eyes. It was enough to reawaken Bram's urge for a nighttime narcotic. Tonight, he would need it to keep all the demons in his head at bay.

Three years ago, Ellen tried to talk Bram out of using blood during a read-through of his play, *The Un-Dead*, taken from his published novel. When the vampire bit Miss Lucy, Bram championed for two wound holes on the actress's neck to discharge blood, so the audience could understand the vampire was consuming her blood, not necking with her. But Sir Henry found that idea gruesome and tawdry. And would the Great Man, the actor-producer of the day, take on the role of Dracula himself? The night before the presentation, Irving skimmed through the script, pronouncing it "dreadful." He didn't even bother to attend the in-house reading open to the public, where a third-string company member read the role of Dracula, badly.

After the poorly attended reading, Bram confided in Ellen what Henry had said about the script. "Perhaps Mr. Irving's 'dreadful' means that he thinks *The Un-Dead* is so good a ghost story that it inspires one to dread."

Ellen patted his arm, saying, "My poor lion, still chewing on imaginary meat."

As of yet, Bram had yet to earn a farthing from *The Un-Dead.* One review had said, "Stoker's book isn't 'undead' but it doesn't read as particularly alive either." Bram writhed in his seat remembering the scathing reviews. *If I were ruler, I'd rise above these petty bureaucrats and reviewers and publish my book as* Dracula, *to great success.*

One of the accountants who fired Bram that morning stepped out from the wings. He slipped on the still-bloody wet floor and fell on his bum. Bram put his head between his hands so no one could see him laugh. These bean counters couldn't even tread the boards.

How much longer should he wait for Pamela to come back? He could wait in the lobby, but a masochistic part of himself wanted to see the rehearsal, to see how all the company took in the news that he was no longer in charge. Cast and crew dribbled onstage, glancing Bram's way with baleful looks. Stoker, the company sheepdog, came out and plopped itself downstage center, and kept a mournful eye to Bram, for once not begging for treats. Obviously, the dog had heard the news. This wasn't a technical rehearsal, or "tech"; it was a wake.

Bram felt a chill sweep from the stage to the audience. Did someone leave a backstage door open? Another pipe dropped far upstage. A scream rang out, followed by whistles and shouts. Bram stood as Lovejoy ran onstage. No one was hit, but this had never happened under Bram's watch before, two pipes falling during a put-in. But this was no longer Bram's watch. As the swirl of cast and crew grew onstage and squabbling broke out, Bram knew he had to leave or he would be onstage, taking over.

Bram got up and went to the lobby box office. He knocked on the door, and a young man threw it open and stood there.

"Yes?" the young man said, his hand on his hip.

Looking down at the shorter man, Bram said, "I'm the company manager. May I sit in here? There's no light to read by in the theatre."

The ticket-taker tugged on his waistcoat and looked at his pocket watch. "It's time for me to leave anyway, so you may stay here as long as you don't touch anything, and make sure someone in charge locks up when you leave."

Bram was shown in, and the door slammed shut behind him as the box office worker left. Bram sat in a big leather chair and sighed. *Where is it, the balm that nurses almost every hurt?* From his coat pocket, he took out a small book. He opened *Leaves of Grass* to a dog-eared page:

From wounds made to free you whence you were prison'd
From my face, from my forehead and lips,
From my breast, from within where I was conceal'd, press forth red
Drops, confession drops,
Stain every page, stain every song I sing, every word I say, bloody drops

Bram thought back to meeting Walt Whitman. The poet died almost eight years ago, but meeting him was a life dream. Of course, Sir Irving had invited himself along. This was on the last American tour, and Whitman was quite on in years. His white beard and mustache made him look like an elder fairy king. All Sir Henry could add to the conversation was that Whitman reminded him of Tennyson. Irving left early, and then Bram had time with his idol from his Trinity College days. He still had some of their correspondence at home. Unless Florence threw it out while he was on tour.

Florrie, his beauty of a wife, once courted by Oscar Wilde, was now disenchanted with Bram, or Bram's lack of success.

"You're an afterthought to the Great Man's plans," Florrie had said at their last at-home meal.

His son, Noel, had witnessed this exchange and told Bram that he would never study anything remotely related to the theatre arts. In fact, he was studying to be in the profession Bram loathed most—an accountant. A bean counter.

A rap on the curtained box office window startled him. An outline of a large man loomed on the pulled-down shade.

Bram shouted, "Can't you see we're closed, man?"

The rapping continued. Peeved, Bram hoisted himself out of the chair. His face almost matched his red hair as he yanked up the window shade. On the other side of the glass, the imposing silhouette of a man, wearing a purple coat and black hat, leaned against the window in a louche pose, looking away.

The arrogance of this man; can't he hear? The ticket office was closed.

The man turned back to the window; he was a dark-complexioned Black man. He looked Bram dead in the eye and executed a classic, low-comedy double-take, ending with both palms on the glass.

Bram burst out laughing. He grabbed the keys to the box office door and flew out of the box office into the lobby, then threw open the doors to the street and embraced Satish Monroe.

Satish Monroe. Former Lyceum Theatre actor and bon vivant, one of the most delightful men he'd ever spent time with. Almost two decades ago, Bram had hired Satish Monroe at the last minute to replace Edwin Booth. Now, Satish had struck out on his own.

After a pretend round of boxing, both men laughed and embraced each other again.

"Mr. Monroe, by the devil, what are you doing in Manchester?" Bram asked.

"Ah, Mr. Stoker, Duse Mohammed Ali set up a tour for me," Satish answered. "Duse's a big publisher now and didn't wish to leave London to exhibit himself in a one-man show. I'm touring manor houses between here and Liverpool the next few weeks."

"What's your lodging? What hotel here?" Bram asked.

"Ah, dream on, Irish!" Satish said. "You think they'd let a Black man stay at a hotel here? I'm lodging with Ted Pablo. Come get a drink and then to supper. Let's bend an elbow over a pint first and then pick up Pixie on the way. She'll enjoy Ted Pablo and his horse."

Bram went back into the office and locked up. As he came back out, he saw Satish reading the tour's poster on the streetlamp.

Satish turned to him as he approached. "Irish, there are some very old nags in this horse race."

Bram felt his shoulders relax. "You haven't heard the worst of it," he replied.

CHAPTER FOUR

Lightermen and Mudlarks

This better lead to unlocked pools. Aleister leaned over the side of the barge, holding himself far over the churning water. Beneath the surface reflecting the bright afternoon sun, swirls and eddies held the secrets of drowned men and lost treasure. The flat-bottomed barge chugged past the Southwark dock en route to their rendezvous. A half-submerged beer barrel with a painted crow drifted by. *How apt that Crowley Ale, the source of my fortune, would make an appearance.*

Waterfront taverns lining the shore slid by as a bracing spray slapped him across the face. He laughed and dried his face off with his scarf, shaking his mane of thick hair. *Serves me right. Water is not my element. Give me mountains and forests any day, not this muck.* Settling down onto the main bench, he watched the lighterman steer around the other barges.

Aleister cupped his pipe with one hand as his traveling companion, Alfred Duggins, reached over and lit it. The wind ripped the matchbox out of Duggan's hand and it flew into the river. Aleister watched the young man reach down for it, but the smell of sewage overpowered him and and Duggan gagged. *It would be a pity if the dilettante got sick all over his chesterfield overcoat.* Looking away, Aleister watched the matchbox drown in the current. He wished it was as easy to toss Pamela Colman Smith into the drink.

What a common name, Smith, for such a strange young woman. It was outrageous. Here he was: young, from an elite family, accomplished, and if not a graduate from Trinity at Cambridge he was at least a published poet, chess master, and in possession of a brilliant mind. What a pity that Florence insisted that the Golden Dawn magic school exile him. Idiots, to award the Smith girl the position of the tarot deck creator.

It all started when Florence Farr objected to his Sex Magik rituals with the level-one girls. Farr was a frustrated, divorced hag who was offended by Aleister's idea that sex should be freely shared among both sexes. If the prudes in the group were so concerned, they should have knocked on the magic Vault if they didn't want to see him in action with the latest recruit.

But the loss of the tarot deck project! Those tarot cards' design and power should emanate from him. From his preacher father, he knew how to galvanize a following. A group. A society. A cult. The process would follow the progression of the seventy-eight cards. But Smith was depleting the pools of magic he needed to conjure the cards' power. She mindlessly dipped into the sacred sources, assigning muses for each card. Miss Smith had no right to dip into a magical source.

"What is the purpose of this excursion?" Duggins shouted as the barge's engine shifted to louder thumping.

"A mudlark has found the most fascinating artifact along the banks here."

Duggins wrinkled his nose. "How revolting. You brought me out here to look at low tide garbage?"

Aleister cocked his head. "I'll need your opinion, oh leading archeology expert from Oxford, as to the origins of the mudlark's find."

"So, the Crowley Ale and mutton supper wasn't a lure for my company?" Duggins asked.

"In a way," Aleister replied. "A rustic supper in exchange for a rustic's opinion."

"Yes, that's your merchant class idea of commerce: a barrel of ale for a barrel of education," Duggins said.

Aleister felt his face get hot. He knew Duggins's family ran in the same circles as Lord Curzon but were untitled landed gentry. He remembered the slur from school: *family fortune made from trade, means a name that's never made.*

Ten years old, and he was sitting in the back of the wagon. Traveling the backroads with his father, who was content to navigate every bump in the road as a Christian challenge. When preaching from the back of their caravan, Reverend Crowley propped up both Aleister and a King James Bible on a beer barrel, before a slavish crowd standing in mud, adoring the oratory. Frothing over descriptions of lashings for punishment and discipline, the reverend held the crowd as he built to the crescendo of his sermon on the Plymouth Brethren Doctrine.

"Evil must be rooted out and punished."

"Amen!"

"Tell us, brother!"

The open mouths of the crowd, their closed eyes, and their ecstatic swaying fanned out before young Aleister. His brilliant father knew how to build anticipation.

"The wicked beast in all of us must be flayed, struck, made subservient."

The first thrills of sexual longing coursed through him.

"Pain can be a reward, a proof of devotion."

After his father died when he was fourteen, Aleister was caught having sex with the cook. The order to "bodily correct" him came from his mother, who said he was "the Beast 666." Aleister still felt the sting when his mother called him the devil. But not even the years at boarding school, where he was slapped, whipped. and beaten, led to religious ecstasy. With the headmaster's approval, fellow students had permission to crush him into submission.

Aleister's choice for his magical name with the Golden Dawn was Perdurabo, meaning "I shall endure until the end." How apt it was that this phrase, chosen at the age of twenty-five, was also recited by the schoolboy Aleister between gritted teeth during beatings.

The lighterman throttled down the engine just as the sign for the Pelican Stairs appeared alongside a battered wharf. Once off the barge, Aleister climbed the steep stairs to the Wapping Wall street level—he knew if he stepped lively enough he would be free from paying for the barge trip. Looking down, Duggins was counting out coins out for the lighterman. *Family fortune made from land, forced to pay with open hand.*

Soon, both young men were standing outside the old pub, The Prospect of Whitby.

"How on earth did you ever find this place?" Duggins asked, panting.

"A hack novelist from the Golden Dawn, Bram Stoker, told me about it," Aleister said. "This is his old haunt, where he would go to drink after grave robbing with his doctor brother."

They entered the pub, and its large flagstone floor, rich hewed beams, and gas-lit sconces fed Aleister as much as the grub and ale. Tables full of tradesmen fell silent at their entry until the bartender motioned to sit. He barked out, "Mairead!" and pulled more drafts. They settled in next to the glass-paned window overlooking the river and pulled out their pipes and began to smoke.

An attractive young barmaid came out of the kitchen, gathering up weeping glasses of freshly poured ale. Holding three pints in each hand, she advanced to the tables and placed a foaming drink in front of each customer. She came up to Aleister's and Duggan's table and hung back a good foot. Mairead was exceptionally pretty, with long brown hair swept up on top of her head, green eyes, and a snowy complexion. She tapped her foot, a hand on her hip.

"Mairead, is it necessary for you to stand so far away from us?" Aleister asked.

"I don't cross grabbers' reach until I know your friend. What can I get you for?" Mairead asked.

"Two Crowley Ales, a mutton dinner, and the dumplings," Aleister answered.

"Coming up," she replied, but before she could go, Aleister motioned her closer. With a furrowed brow, she leaned in, still a foot from the table.

"Oh," Aleister said in a low voice, "I would also like to have a look at the latest treasure my mudlark has brought in."

Mairead hissed, "No mention of that in here. Me Da will have a word with you about it out on the deck after your meal. You should know better."

She pivoted away, and Duggins laughed.

"I don't believe you've been put in your place quite like that before, Mr. Crowley."

Aleister smiled back. "Check but not checkmate."

Later, as Aleister creaked open the door to the deck, Davy Jones turned around, smoking his cigar. His wool cap barely contained his mop of curly red hair. On his wool coat, the dew of dusk's encroaching fog settled in a jeweled varnish. Where his daughter was slight and delicate, Davy was sturdy and bullish.

"How do you, Mr. Crowley?"

Aleister nodded and motioned to his friend. "This is Mr. Duggins. He's a fan of mudlarks and their catch. I received word you might have something for me?"

Davy dug into his pocket and pulled out a frayed handkerchief, holding it in his hand. Aleister grinned as Davy's dirt-encrusted fingernails unwrapped the hanky. In his palm lay a small ring with a symbol on the front.

"Oh, I say," Duggins said under his breath, "that looks for all the world like an amulet-ring."

Aleister kicked him in the shins.

"I say," Duggins said, "you said you wanted an appraisal before you bought it."

"Exactly!" exclaimed Davy. "That were just what I was thinkin' it was, an amulet-ring. And the going rate for amulet-rings be about . . . ."

Aleister sighed and opened his billfold. "About the same as the pilgrim's badge."

"Oh, no, Mr. Crowley," Davy replied. "Your friend here just pointed out, it's two things, an amulet and a ring, so I figure twice the price for it."

"Yes, thank you, Duggins, you've just cost me twice the price." He handed over two notes.

"Do you have any spearheads?" Duggins asked, as the handkerchief passed to Aleister. "Or better yet, do you have a collection I could look at?"

Davy snorted, his laughter turning into a cough. Holding out his hand for Duggins, coughing all the while, he choked out, "Fag?" Duggins' cigarette case opened, a match strike following. The hacking stopped as Davy greedily inhaled the tobacco's fumes.

"Now, a collection, Mr. Jones?" Duggins asked. "You have such a thing?"

"Oh, sure. I'll just lead you to my collection and have you call the police or detectives, or whatever they're called now," Davy said. "This is how this works: you suggest to me what you might be looking for, and I'll have me mudlarks look. Eventually."

Duggins weakly said, "Oh, yes. I see now."

"Whatchya lookin' for exactly?" Davy asked.

"Shields, statues, swords," Duggins replied.

Davy burst out into a spasm of coughing, hanging on to the banister but coming up grim and determined. "If we were to find any of those, we'll be going through lawyers for museums. I'll tell you what's on the menu for the likes of you—beads, mace-heads, and axes."

"Really?" Duggins sneered.

Turning to Aleister, he said, "I don't want to be meetin' any more of your friends, Mr. Crowley."

With a wink, Davy turned to Duggins and whapped him between his shoulder blades. Duggins gasped at the sheer force of the blow and tumbled over, landing in a heap. "If I find a rapier, I'll be sure to get it to you."

Davy made his way to the door, slamming it on his way out. Aleister held out the amulet-ring to Duggins, who clung to the deck's railing to right himself. The whole trip was worth it to see him crawl up to latch on to his hand. He shook Duggins off, who discovered the knees in his trousers were now torn.

"What the devil," Duggins said, pouting like a child. "I didn't sign up to be roughhoused tonight."

"Let's head over to my flat for a proper drink and examine this ring in private," Aleister said. "We don't want to show off in public."

Back at his flat, Aleister gave him his drink, lit the fire, and positioned Duggins in a chair by the hearth. Duggins finally stopped moaning about his sore back and his torn trousers and took out a jeweler's loop. Aleister handed over the amulet-ring and sat in the other chair.

"Bronze. Fifteenth century," Duggins said. "Possibly Viking in origin. And talismanic. The inscription on the inside is in a language I don't know. At one time, there were three stones or gems set in it. Probably at the bottom of the Thames by now."

"Bottoms up, Duggins," Aleister said.

"Bottoms up, Crowley." After downing his drink, Duggins inspected Aleister's family inscription on the glass. "'Water is best,' apt hypocrisy for an heir to the ale business. But think what you would have learned if you had been admitted to the Hypocrites Club at Oxford."

"Oh, I don't think I needed to go to Oxford to learn how to be a hypocrite," Aleister answered. He took the ring out of Duggins's hands, pocketing it.

"I'm not sure I was done looking at that," Duggins said.

"Well, you've answered the question I had about it."

"What was that?"

"Determining its origin," Aleister said. "I thought it might be Egyptian. Obviously it's not."

"I never said that, Crowley," Duggins said. "I said I didn't recognize the language. But I do know Viking symbols, and these are possibly Viking."

Duggins left an hour later, properly soused, and Aleister sat in the white temple in the bedroom. He concentrated on the ring.

"Give me a sign." Nothing. *Try to be more specific.* "Show me automatic writing to draw Pamela's tarot cards." Still nothing. "May the gods give me the power of skrying so that I might watch over her." Stillness. "Give me visions to enlist a devoted following."

The wind howled outside his bedroom window as he raged inside.

He could see the mindless multitudes signing up for the Golden Dawn's amateur magic lessons, draining the pools of enchantment, which were supposed to be accessed by only the highest tiers of magicians. Not only were pools not being unlocked for him, but others were using them. Time for some assistance.

He stood up and raised his arms to the heavens. “In the name of Din and Doni: I invoke thee: Appear! Appear! Taphthartharath! In the Name of Taphthartharath: I invoke thee! Wherein now Mercury takes refuge, send thou unto me the powerful but blind force!”

The image of Pamela appeared. Plain as a pikestaff, sitting at a desk, surrounded by ancient icons: falling towers, a skeleton, angels, devils, kings, and queens. He shook his head in disbelief.

“A children’s book illustrator, obsessed with fairies and music making colors. She must be bound!”

He took up the amulet-ring and tried it on. The bronze bent with ease.

“Bring me the spirits of Mercury!”

The ring remained uninspiring and dull.

Aleister whispered, “Taphthartharath, appear to divide the Magician!”

The ring vibrated on his hand.

“Curse her hand,” he whispered.

CHAPTER FIVE

Ahmed at Thorton Hall

Ahmed continued on to Liverpool after the train dropped off Miss Smith and Mr. Stoker in Manchester. During the last part of the journey, he had been aware of Miss Smith discretely drawing the circle on the train window. Now, Ahmed watched the numbers "666" dribble down the glass, little snakes of moisture seeking other forms. From his pocket, he took out his black handkerchief and wiped away the rest of the numbers. A slight trace remained in the shape of a shield. Not a good sign: it meant the afrit was leaving earthly footprints for someone or something to follow him. He returned the damp cloth back to his breast pocket.

The first time Pamela saw Ahmed's black handkerchief, she asked if she might have it as a study item for her cards, and he snapped at her, "Absolutely not." Later, he apologized, saying it was a special token from a friend. He didn't tell her it was dyed in mummy, the black essence exuded after embalming. Like Bram, Pamela believed a mummy was the wrapped body, when in fact is was the fluid oozing from Egyptian corpses.

Ahmed's handkerchief was infused with the powerful magic of mummy, and he needed it to track down the Egyptian art stolen from tomb sites and transported to this country.

He watched the blur of the English countryside race past outside the train and hoped that his warning about Egyptian earlobes would give Pamela pause when she picked her next tarot muse. It could not be an accident that all her muses were marked with earlobe tattoos.

When Ahmed arrived in Liverpool, he was pleased to meet a young man near the luggage stack.

"Hello, Mr. Kamal, I'm here to take you to Thornton Manor," the young man said.

Before Ahmed could say a word, Ahmed's trunk was picked up and carried to the street. There, a red motor car with two open-air double burgundy seats awaited them.

The car started and rolled out on the cobblestone streets, and after few minutes in the cold late-October air, Ahmed draped the fur on the seat next to him around his head. After almost an hour, the car puttered into a circled drive before a stately house. The manor house had lit candles in every oversize window, with a maid and butler waiting at the door. Even in the dark, Ahmed could tell it was a magnificent pile, as his cohorts at the museum had called it, as the entryway was enormous and grand. There was an ornate rounded ceiling, stone floors, and an enormous fireplace with a blazing fire. How he wished Fatima were here to see this with him instead of nursing their newest child at home. How was their eldest, Mona, handling three younger brothers now? He would make many notes of this grand house in his next letter to his wife to share with them.

Shown to his room to bathe, Ahmed was astounded at the amount of soot in his hair, on his glasses, and on his coat. The valet assigned to him offered to take all his clothes and have them laundered for the next day and informed him that dinner was in two hours, at nine o'clock. Ahmed gave thanks with his prayers and enjoyed the hot water bath prepared for him. His engraved invitation for this weekend read "full evening dress optional" but with a handwritten note added below: "native dress allowed, if that is more to your comfort." Native dress complete with fez it would be.

When he entered the music room at Thornton Manor, he, who had seen Egyptian palaces and tombs, still gasped at the chamber's sheer size. The arched dome of this room's ceiling created a huge, womb-like enclosure, with the struts leading to a focus of the plaster barrel-vault ceiling circles dotted with painted panels. He arched his neck to take in the artwork.

Yes, nothing announced English taste learned from a Grand Tour more than Baroque scenarios: putti, floating ribbons, and pastel Europeans lounging against pillows. He glanced at the footmen in white powdered wigs stationed at the doorway, their silent half-closed eyes unnerving him. Ten lit candelabras lined a long table against a frescoed wall below the minstrel's gallery. Cello music wafted down as Ahmed walked along a wall of large portraits, all of one man, William Lever, the host. They depicted Lever over several decades but always with the same shock of hair standing straight up from his forehead. Another doorway with more footmen and, beyond that, a milling crowd. *This must be the reception area.*

He stepped into the great room and saw the formal evening wear of the men with their white shirts, vests, and dark tuxedos. His fez and formal jacket marked him here as a foreigner. If they could see his mummy-dyed handkerchief hidden in his pocket, they would consider him unworldly. He was more out of place than the knee breeches of the seventeenth-century-adorned footmen.

Mrs. Lever, the hostess, sprang forward from a tight clique of well-dressed men and extended her gloved hand. Should he shake the hostess's hand or to hold it and bow to her? Surely, he would not be expected to kiss it in the French fashion? She put him out of his misery, clasped his hand with hers, threading his arm in her grip, and escorted him back to her group. Mrs. Elizabeth Lever was a very short woman with an elaborate hairstyle. Tightly wound and coiled upon itself, her hairpiece perched on top of her head like a small melon. She had kind eyes with heavy lids and a delicate, clean air.

"Mr. Kamal, let me introduce you," Mrs. Lever said.

Her son, a gangly adolescent, was in the center of the group. He wore his freckles and formal wear with a slouch, his blue eyes open wide.

Before he could introduce himself, she announced a barrage of titles in such quick succession that Ahmed had no idea who was what. He looked back at the expectant faces.

The young boy nudged his mother with his elbow. Mrs. Lever added, "And this is my son, Mr. William Lever, who is also truly pleased to have the pleasure of your company."

"The pleasure is mine also, Mrs. Lever," Ahmed replied. "I see your resemblance shining in this young face."

"William Sr. will dispute that," Mrs. Lever replied, looking around. "He should be here shortly."

William's small hand reached out to him.

"How do you do?" Ahmed asked, shaking hands. William Lever II's clap was firm.

"I am well. I have been looking forward to meeting you," William answered.

"And why is that, my young friend?" Ahmed asked.

"Because I have never met an Arab before," William said. "I have heard about them, but I have never met one."

Ahmed stilled his breath. The question of "who his people were" was to have come from the adults, not the child. "I am considered a Turkish Egyptian, Mr. Lever."

"But you are wearing the little hat of an Arab," William said, pointing to his fez. "You are a Muslim then?"

"Yes, I adhere to the faith of Islam."

William, Mrs. Lever, and Ahmed broke off into their own huddle.

"You see, William," Mrs. Lever said. "You don't have to be Egyptian to be an Egyptologist. You could be an English Egyptologist, like all the famous ones. Is there such a thing as a Turkologist, Mr. Kamal?"

Ahmed tried not to laugh. "Not that I know of, Mrs. Lever. My family has lived in Cairo for many years, my wife is from Alexandria, and I have been fortunate to study the historical artifacts of both Egypt and Turkey."

William asked, "But wouldn't England be your adopted homeland now, Mr. Kamal? Aren't we the homeland of world antiquity?"

"You must excuse my son's enthusiasm, Mr. Kamal," Mrs. Lever said. "He has studied Egyptian art and has been quite determined to meet you."

"You studied Egyptian art?" Ahmed asked. The son's interest in Egyptian art was probably due to the family owning stolen artifacts. Did they know he was here to try to reclaim the Sekhemka statue?

"Well, Mother is an art collector, and we talk about the pyramids and mummies," William answered. "My main question is, have you ever seen a mummy?"

William Lever Sr. came into the room with two men in turbans and bounded over to them. He was an elongated version of his son: blue eyes, slack mouth, jerky movements.

"William Hesketh Lever here," Mr. Lever said. "Glad you could make it, Mr. Kamal."

"Thank you for inviting me," Ahmed replied, keeping his composure as the ensuing handshake jarred every bone in his hand.

Turning to the two men flanking him, Mr. Lever said, "This is Mancherjee Merwanjee Bhownagree, who just won his seat in reelection to Parliament. Second Indian ever to do so."

Ah, so this was how young William learned to define people by their country's background. He could see by the twinkle in Bhownagree's eye that the mispronunciation of his name was a common event and was not to be addressed. They bowed to one another dutifully.

"This is Dhunjibhoy Bomanji," Mr. Lever continued. "And if these two names aren't a mouthful, I don't know what is."

Bomanji was the host from last year's retreat he had taken with Pamela. One of the guests sitting in the center cluster of chairs rose and made her way to Ahmed.

It was Florence.

Ahmed inhaled. She was even more beautiful than at their last meeting.

Bomanji waved his hand to bring Florence into the center of the group, saying, "This is Miss Florence Farr. She and Mr. Kamal were guests at my estate, Pineheath House, last fall."

Florence smiled as she sidled up to Bomanji's side and said, "Yes, thank you for your hospitality, Lord Bomanji. It was most enjoyable."

Florence motioned for a footman to light her cigarette. Mrs. Lever winced as her husband smirked. Even Ahmed knew that smoking was only for men, after supper. *Miss Farr understands that she is the entertainment for tonight, and she is living up to the task.*

"Where is your home, Lord Bomanji?" Mrs. Lever asked.

"Yorkshire," Bomanji replied. "If I remember correctly that weekend, Miss Farr chanted poetry for us. And in London, I believe, she sings to a mummy?"

William turned to Florence, almost knocking the cigarette holder out of her hand. "You sing to mummies?"

Florence laughed loudly, putting one hand on Ahmed's shoulder. "Yes, in addition to reciting poetry, I am a mummy conduit."

"Which mummy do you channel, Miss Farr?" Mrs. Lever asked, tilting her head at her.

"Why, the mummy Mr. Kamal safeguards at the British Museum," Florence answered, "Mutemmenu."

All eyes turned to Ahmed. The black-dyed handkerchief in his vest pocket thumped and then stilled. The mummy tracker spirit with him was not pleased, and the hope to track down the statue discretely was now dashed.

"You're a mummy hunter!" William Jr. cried out. "I knew it!"

The Lever supper that evening was a smaller affair, men and women seated next to one another, the host and hostess anchoring the ends of a long table. The Levers were teetotalers, although several men had engraved silver flasks next to their place settings, which they discreetly guzzled from time to time.

Ahmed was next to the hostess, Mrs. Lever, and the younger Lever. At the other end of the table, William Sr. shouted responses to a question about Lever Soap, the source of the family's fortune.

Florence's bright blue eyes met his as she slid into her seat across from him. "Ah, Mr. Kamal, from Yorkshire to Cheshire, we meet again."

Smallhythe, Ellen Terry's country home, had been where they had last socialized. He had initially declined to go, but Pamela wore his resistance down by insisting he mingle with her artistic friends, knowing he socialized very little outside the museum. All sorts of people from her theatrical world were there: women dressed in pants, former recruits from the Golden Dawn cult, sullen writers, circus performers, Gaiety Girls. At one point during a ceremony, Ellen Terry recovered her memory, incantations manifesting the appearance of beetles and bats. A midsummer night's eve of celebrations followed, and Florence had played her hand harp for him as though he were the only audience. After it was over, she'd resumed socializing with the other guests as though nothing had happened. *This must be what actresses do*, Ahmed thought later on. In his letter to Fatima, he didn't mention Florence's special focus on him. Or how uncomfortable she made him feel.

Another opportunity to be together had never presented itself, and it would be unseemly for Ahmed to be in the company of a divorced English actress/mummy channeler. His job was to solicit artifacts from the cream of English society, not to associate with stage performers who dangled inappropriate meanings into conversations.

In a way, it was a relief for Ahmed not to take on the sin and guilt associated with sexual relations outside his marriage. In his family, moderation was the most important moral code, and Fatima was a devoted wife and mother. The Prophet drank wine, but that did not mean that Ahmed was free to drink to excess. The liberties of this English culture could be intoxicating, but at present he wished Fatima were sitting across the table from him, taking in the many pieces of silver tableware and the profusion of drinking glasses. How her eyes would widen at the many dishes served.

Catching his eye, Florence smiled at him. In a half whisper she said, "This is certainly a different environment than when we last met at Smallhythe, isn't it?"

"Yes, Miss Farr, I did not think you would be in this area of England. You do not have acting engagements at present?"

"Miss Farr is quite the actress," Mrs. Lever said, loudly. "We were first acquainted with her talent in a George Bernard play," Mrs. Lever said. "She smoked a cigarette and dressed up as a Gypsy. What are you dressing up as next?"

"I do like wearing the odd tunic now and then," Florence replied. "Cigarettes have been the devil to give up, but, no, there is no play for me on the horizon. I have taken a leadership position with the Golden Dawn."

"I don't like getting up at dawn," William Jr. said. "Even if it is golden."

"Golden Dawn, that's a woman's suffragette group, isn't it?" one of the younger wives next to William Jr. asked Florence.

An elegant older man on the other side of Florence spit out, "The suffragettes! Insufferable, spoiled women who want to be taken care of and yet have a voice in everything."

Mrs. Lever chimed in, "Now, Lord Compton, let us stay on course with the subjects of art and commerce and leave the world of politics off the table."

Lord Compton! Precisely the person Ahmed had come to see about the statue. Compton's father had stolen artifacts out of Egypt several decades ago. He turned to look at his lordship. He was the epitome of the age: handlebar mustache, shiny, smooth hair, half-closed eyes, and a look of perpetual irritation.

"Thank you, Mrs. Lever," Lord Compton answered. "Women should stay out of politics entirely."

Florence leaned back. "I agree we should not spoil an excellent supper by talking about politics. Let us talk about art! Mr. Kamal here is an expert on Egyptian art. You know something about that, don't you, Lord Compton? Your family owns a famous Egyptian statue, don't they?"

Lord Compton bristled and sat up straight in his seat. "My family found a statue, the Sekhemka, if that's what you mean."

Ahmed's heart pounded. He steadied his hands in his lap. In a measured tone he asked, "Your family found the statue Sekhemka? It was not attached to any ownership at the time?"

"None that was applicable," Lord Compton replied.

"Where is the statue now?" Ahmed asked. Mr. Lever stopped talking and turned his attention to them.

"Oh, it was too big for our place," Lord Compton said. "We gave it to a museum thirty years ago."

"Which museum?" Florence asked.

"Liverpool, of course, Miss Farr," Lord Compton answered. "Perhaps they have a mummy there I could show you? They unwrap wonderfully well."

Florence looked at him with a bemused smile. "Ah, Lord Compton, could you? I know so little about actually unwrapping a mummy. Where did you say it was?"

Mrs. Lever bit her lip as Mr. Lever looked up from his plate and grunted, "Liverpool Museum. But it wasn't always called that."

Mrs. Lever sat straight up. "I believe it was called the Derby Museum after the 13th Earl of Derby," she said. "But this must have been forty years ago. He donated his collection of Egyptian findings there."

Ahmed fought the bile rising in his throat.

Findings. Yes, he simply kicked a rock and found priceless antiquities.

"Well, whatever it is now called," Bomanji said between bites, "My daughter wants me to be on the museum board."

"No, no, Mr. Bomanji, you must not be on the board at the Liverpool Museum," Lord Compton said. "I want to start our own art museum here at Sunlight Village. You could donate many items for it."

"When are we all to see this famous Sunlight Village?" Florence asked.

Mr. Lever yelled from down at his end of the table, "Tomorrow morning! Sunlight Village. All of us! We will travel the four miles together. You will be astounded at what I have created for my workers! Nothing less than Utopia!"

Mr. Lever's volume led to more than a few people turning their heads away from him. Ahmed noticed Mrs. Lever's pained expressions.

"So sorry. He's going deaf," Mrs. Lever said quietly.

As the guests oohed and ahhed over their upcoming trip, Ahmed leaned over the table to Florence, whispering, "Are you going tomorrow morning?"

"I must," Florence answered. "I will be giving harp lessons to the children of the Sunlight Villagers. I may get a bar of Lever soap at the end of the day."

"I'm not sure that's a fair trade," Ahmed said.

"True," she answered. "But as for your trade, you will be traveling to Liverpool to visit your Sekhemka."

CHAPTER SIX

Ted Pablo's Circus

Pamela hadn't been able to make any new sketches for the Emperor or Hierophant, as the new poster for *The Merchant of Venice* was her first priority for the theatre. But now that it had been dropped off at the local printing press and was almost ready to be picked up, she sat down at her hotel desk. Rumpled sketches surrounded her chair as she tried one more time.

The spasm hit all at once. Her drawing hand flew up, crumpling in midair. Unseen barbed wire threaded itself throughout her digits and jerked her palm inward. Quickly, she soaked a handkerchief with hot water and wrapped it around her throbbing palm.

Mr. Crowley, you are going to have to do better than sending me a muscle cramp to detour my tarot deck.

Pamela was now aware that Aleister's magic could reach her without his being there. She would need to tap into the Emperor's gifts. According to Arthur Waite, one of the Golden Dawn chiefs who was supposed to be helping her with the tarot deck's meanings, "the Emperor is to be depicted as the power of this world." What did that even mean? And the Hierophant? "Not a pope, but interpreting mysteries." How she disliked having to consider these directives from Waite.

Pamela tried two or three rough images, but the handkerchief's embroidered strawberries distracted her. This was the handkerchief Ellen Terry had given her; it was the prop when she played Desdemona in *Othello*. Ellen as her Empress was as maternal and loving as one could wish. Whereas Sir Henry as the Magician was not about to share any of his magic, even if it imperiled the future of the Lyceum Theatre. When she created the Magician tarot card, she made sure that on the table before him were all the minor arcana symbols, wands, pentacles, cups, and swords. But he only wanted to use it for his own purposes.

Pamela picked up her pendant watch on the desk; it sat at three o'clock position, and Pamela remembered the posters ready for pickup. She threw on her warmer coat and locked up her room to run to the printing press.

Just outside the hotel, she heard a familiar voice.

"Well, if it isn't our Pixie from the Lyceum Stage."

She turned, and her stomach dropped. People passing her twisted their heads to gawk back at the person who had spoken. A tall Black man in a burgundy wool coat ambled over to her. The green parrot feather in his fedora's brim and a red pocket square near his heart blossomed on the gray sidewalk. Her heart picked up a trilling beat, and the star necklace he had given her grew warm around her neck. Satish Monroe.

"Mr. Monroe," she replied, "you're in Manchester?"

He had been a replacement in *Macbeth* for only one night when she first joined the Lyceum company, but he had proved himself to be the highlight of her time with the Lyceum Theatre.

"In Manchester, and I'll be in need of your company at a friend's family supper tonight," Satish said. "Come with me?"

She hesitated for a moment. Was he courting her?

"I'll pick up Mr. Stoker on the way, and we'll meet you back here at seven."

He was not courting her. But this was Satish, the first actor to talk to her, who encouraged her, gave her the star necklace. Even while she had been a lowly extra, costumed head to foot in armor, he still made her feel special.

It was decided the three of them would leave together at dusk. Pamela raced to the printers around the corner, picked up the bundled of posters bound in brown paper and left them at the front desk to bring the theatre the next day. In her hotel room, she spent extra time with her dress before they came, weaving her hair in a complicated braid, one she practiced in Jamaica on her pony's mane many years ago.

Teased relentlessly by Edy and the backstage crew during the *Macbeth* performance, Pamela remembered the company's whispers : *He's sweet on you.* Of course they would say that. Pamela looked foreign to them, and Satish was the only Black actor in the company. She first noticed him when he watched her telling an Annancy story to the children in the company. She was in charge of them during breaks. Between scenes, she and Satish talked about Jamaica and Jamaican food that they missed—the salted cod and goat-meat dishes, the flatbread bammie. But Pamela found his interest in her was only from a homesick islander who wanted to talk about food. Or so she thought, until he made his entrance standing next to her. He lifted the visor of her helmet.

"This is of the air, little one. It will protect you." He handed her a small drawstring bag just as she readied herself to charge the battlefield.

He chucked her under the chin and patted her cheek. Like a pet.

She shoved the bag in her boot and charged into the onstage battle scene. In her dressing room, she discovered a fine chain with a five-pointed gold star chiseled into a Mali garnet. A

Mali garnet, second in power only to a topaz for second-sight channeling.

Satish was gone before the company curtain call.

Tonight, she wore the necklace outside her blouse, instead of under her clothes.

Bram and Satish escorted Pamela to the circus performer's house, only ten minutes away from her hotel. Bram and Satish talked the entire time about Ted Pablo's amazing circus act, both their arms looped through hers, talking over her head. It was odd that they should be so taken with a bareback rider; they typically disparaged any animal act.

When they arrived, Ted Pablo opened the front door to a white-washed, two-story house. Satish offered Ted a bottle of wine and Bram handed over a loaf of bread as Satish introduced Bram and Pamela to a short, compact man with a broad nose and a dark complexion. Was he related to Satish's family in the Caribbean?

Ted's calloused hands covered Pamela's.

"Ah, I think I sense a horse wrangler here, is that right, Miss Smith? I recognize that plait in your hair as one in my horse's braid."

Pamela blushed, replying, "Well, I know a thing or two about horses."

"Well," he answered, "first things first, you must meet our star! I was just taking her saddle off from her workout."

He offered his arm to Pamela and she took it, her cheeks burning with pleasure. They navigated the uneven cobblestones down a narrow alleyway next to the house. Bram and Satish followed them, and they entered a courtyard with a big dirt circle in the middle. Ted took down a lantern from a hook, and as he lit it, Pamela made out a corridor of paddocks. Inside the stables, resting horses shook their heads, accompanied by snorts, one-footed stampings, and whinnies. At the first stall, Ted unlatched the top window, and a beautiful black horse stuck its head out.

"Ah, Little Beda, my girl, you enjoyed our dance, didn't you?" Ted cooed to the glistening steed. He held the light high and stroked her glossy head in the cold air. Steam came out her nostrils like a fog.

Pamela came closer to the animal's stall. She couldn't keep her eyes off the horse. Slowly, she placed two hands on the railing, her head just coming up to the level of the open half window. "May I touch her? I had a horse once; I loved her dearly."

Bram smiled. "You had a horse once? When was that?"

She inhaled the aroma of straw and manure, and her eyes smarted. "When I lived in Jamaica. I was ten. Pegasus and I took my cart everywhere on the island."

Satish patted her shoulder. "Of course an island girl knows how to ride."

She shrugged his hand away. She was more than an island girl; she was a published author, a designer, a performer, and artist. She felt her infatuation with Satish deflate.

Ted stepped away from the horse. "Well, if you know horses, you'll know how to introduce yourself," he said.

She reached up and stroked Little Beda's neck. The horse swung her massive head closer to Pamela. She lightly blew into the horse's nostrils. Warm air blew out through the horse's lips, and the horse rested her giant head right on top of Pamela's.

Bram, Satish, and Ted burst out laughing.

Pamela stood still. The horse's long tongue began to curl down around Pamela's head. It was pulling and tugging her braid apart, finally licking a strand that came free.

Ted laughed louder than the rest. "Little Beda's mother was my father's favorite horse, and she always did this to him. How did you know this, miss?"

Pamela lifted her shoulders and looked into Little Beda's eyes, and she kissed the salty bridge of her nose. "We understand our first hello is to taste one another."

"Would you like to ride Miss Beda, Miss Smith?" Ted asked, his face creasing into a smile.

Pamela nodded, and he unlocked the gate and led her out into the courtyard. In the middle of the dirt work area, a chalked circle was drawn, like the face of a clock with the hours marked. Little Beda trotted over to number twelve. Rearing up, she pawed the air with her front legs. She shook herself and settled into an "at attention" stance. Ted stood next to her, holding her bridle in one hand and a slender wand in the other, humming a familiar tune. Leaning near her twitching ear, he crooned the waltz until Little Beda started pawing the ground in time to the music.

"Do you know this tune, 'The Argyle Waltz'?" Ted asked.

Bram and Satish laughed, and Bram answered, "That was the pre-show music for *Olivia*. We know it well. Miss Smith, you know it."

Now that she remembered it, Pamela hummed it. Little Beda huffed in response. The horse's head bobbed near Pamela's ear, her warm, raspy tongue making its way over her ears, nickering her.

"Little Beda is the most responsive and alert of horses," Ted replied. "I can tell at a glance if she will work with someone. She seems fond of you. Shall we give this a go?"

Pamela kicked off her shoes and tucked her hem into the waist of her skirt, creating "riders' bloomers." Being barely five feet tall, getting up into any saddle was difficult. She had always been described as "round" or "soft," but Ted helped her up into the saddle with ease.

Ted hummed as he walked alongside them. The trio followed the clock's circular outline; every muscle tensed, a test between rider and horse. The waltz soon picked up its pace, and Ted ran at an easy stride, Little Beda and Pamela trotting along. She was steady and controlled in the saddle. The reins lay easy but firm in her hands. The tune began to speed up and so did the run, the horse picking up its heels and nodding, her ebony mane dancing in rhythm. Soon, Bram and Satish clapped in time. Pamela found herself smiling, the first time in weeks.

"Stand, Miss! Can you stand?" Ted asked as he kept up his pace.

Ted was now running alongside, his hand raised straight up. She took a deep breath. He motioned Pamela to grab his hand. *Clear your head.* The spinning stopped. She centered herself, keeping the reins clear, and grasped him by the sleeve. Hoisting herself up, she kept one foot in the stirrups and placed one foot on the saddle. Another hop and she was standing on Little Beda's back. Arching her feet, she anchored herself in the center of the saddle.

The smell of fresh hay, the sounds of laughter wrapped around her., The heaviness anchored inside of her was lifting up and away. Cheers from her Miss Jones in Jamaica? Her body pitched forward. Her feet had no feeling. She was aloft. She was the waltz and the air, and they together streamed out into the cold air as though they themselves were a breeze. A wind. A ribbon of blue encircled her, keeping her warm. Inside, she sloshed with tenderness, with care. With hope. She was flying.

With a breath, she dropped down. As had happened before when she tapped into her magic, Pamela's flying was not seen by Ted, Bram, or Satish. She could tell by their nonchalant chatting as she settled into Little Beda's saddle that nothing unusual had happened just in front of them. She put feet in the stirrups and coaxed the horse into a jog and then a stop. Pamela dismounted.

"Well done, Miss," Ted said, clasping her by the shoulder. "Little Beda found a soul mate. I'll brush her down. Why don't you all head inside for Bess's supper?"

Once inside the house, Pablo's wife, Bess, served them ale with speed and a resentful set to her chin. The fire in the hearth cast a golden sheen on the walls and the two lamps provided the only other light. The four children carried aspects of both their parents; two had the coarse hair and broad nose of Ted, though one of them had a much ruddier complexion, and the youngest had all the features of the Manchester mother. It was hard to tell if the children's features resembled those from India or the Caribbean; they certainly didn't look like the actors' children in the Lyceum casts nor her far-spread cousins in Brooklyn and Philadelphia. Pamela wondered if they, too, had to answer questions such as, "Where are your people from?" Pamela could usually predict the question the minute an observer started staring at her hair. Offering her lineage as that of American parents moving to London, and that she was born in the suburb of Pimlico, rarely satisfied their curiosity. She knew she looked odd and was tired of defending it, but tonight she felt that she fit right in.

After introductions and a few awkward moments before Ted came in, they seated themselves at a long wooden table.

Bram inspect the bowl of peppers a child brought to the table. "Ah, that looks very . . . flavorful."

Pamela laughed. Bram's diet of unseasoned meat and potatoes on the tour was well-known.

"Bess," Ted said to his wife, "you see why I told you not to flavor the food too strongly."

Bess, a tiny woman with a messy pile of brown hair, set down the main dish next to Pamela. "You were most particular about it, but I stewed the peppers separately." She had a strong Manchester accent, similar to actors from Bethnal Green, with rolling *r*'s and raw vowels.

Pamela watched as she carefully spooned stew onto her plate.

Bess held the ladle up. "You good here, yes?" she asked.

Bess's mouth was pulled down and she squinted her green eyes. Pamela noticed the rest of the empty plates on the table. How thoughtful of Satish and Bram to bring wine and bread. She shouldn't have arrived empty-handed.

"Thank you, that's lovely," Pamela answered. The child next to her offered the bowl of peppers. "I love spicy food, so I'll take a pepper."

"We have to share them?" Satish asked. He made an elaborate mime of reaching to pile hot peppers onto his plate. Howls of laughter erupted from the children.

As the rest of the guests waited to fill their plates, a strangled noise, like the falling whimper of a dog, rose up from the corner of the room. Pamela snapped her head to see where it was coming from. The children's giggles died down.

There it was, high up, a flicker. A shadow crawled down the golden wall. At first, it seemed a large shape, like the shade of a man, descended from the ceiling. It picked up speed and twisted like a cyclone crossing the wall. The mottled specter writhed once it landed on the stairs. Pamela stood and, instinctively, took the strawberry handkerchief out of her skirt pocket and held it out in her palm to stop it. It approached her hand; then it recoiled to the back door and vanished. The children whimpered and the dogs in the courtyard bayed. The neighing of horses echoed until they faded away.

"What was that?" the children cried. "Mother?"

"By the gods, what on earth?" Satish asked.

"Theodore," the wife cried as she stood. "There's never been such a thing in this house! What brought it in?"

Bess made the sign of the cross and swatted her eldest son next to her to do the same. This sent the next child on the bench to smack the next one until all the children crossed themselves. Pamela did the same.

The youngest child turned to Pamela and said, "Thank you for using your hanky to make it go."

A pit twinged in Pamela's stomach. Did she put it outside? Could this be the thing from the train? Bram was at the door; he shook his head and slid back on the bench.

"It's gone," Bram said, eyeing Pamela as she put her handkerchief back in her pocket.

"Now, Mother, I'm sure there's an explanation for it," Ted replied. "It was the shadow moth crossing the light of the fireplace or some such thing. Please sit. Let's have our guests enjoy their meal."

No one lifted their fork. Pamela's throat clenched at the thought of eating.

Bram leaned across the table to Satish. "What was your line from *Macbeth* about spirits?"

Satish shook his head. "I'm not sure that would be comforting to our hostess right now."

Ted gently rapped the table. "If it's by Shakespeare, it's fine by me. He knows there's more in heaven and earth than we know."

Satish smiled. "Well then, let me think. It's only been two or three years since I performed the Scottish play."

He threw his head back, massaging his temples. Then he nodded and, in a deep, lustrous timbre, began: "The earth hath bubbles, as the water has, / And these are of them. Whither are they vanish'd?"

Pamela applauded. "Excellent, Mr. Monroe," she said as she wrapped an arm around the child sitting next to her. "You see?" she continued. "Bubbles of the earth, that's all it was." Pamela made bubbling sounds with her lips until the children laughed.

"Or of the air, Miss Smith," Satish said.

"This is of the air." That is what Satish had told her when he gave her the star necklace.

"Yes, of the air," Pamela said. "Like a flying bug." She imitated a fly sputtering.

The children tittered and Ted held up his hand. "Bless this food, bless the bed, bless that we are fed. Amen." The children boisterously dug into their supper.

"That bug from the wall needs to stay outside," one of the children said. Pamela felt her throat relax. The spell of the shadow was gone.

"Amen," Satish said loudly, and everyone laughed.

Once everyone began to eat, Pamela turned to the head of the table and waited for moment to address the host. "Mr. Pablo, your father was a circus owner in these parts?"

"Yes," Ted answered. "And, it's 'Ted' to you. He was famous for his ability to come into a town, managing twelve steeds on a single lead. He was a skilled equestrian, ropedancer, acrobat, and showman, the first Black man to own a major business in all of Northern England."

"How did he accomplish that?" Pamela asked.

"My father and his first wife started the circus," Ted said. "A circus building collapsed on her, killing her. He started over with my own mother. Eventually, he became famous for his acrobatic horse shows. And for his acts of kindness toward other performers. One of those daring circus performers is sitting here with us tonight."

Pamela turned to Satish. "Did you perform with the circus, Mr. Monroe?"

Satish laughed, and his hearty, earthy tones shook the gloom from the corners. "No, Miss Smith," Satish said. "I met Ted, here, when he was a bareback rider for his father, Ted Pablo the First. It was in Bolton, wasn't it? But I was not a circus performer."

"Ah, Mr. Monroe, let me tell the whole story," Ted said. He wiped is mouth with a napkin and began in a master of ceremonies voice: "Ladies and gentlemen." The children tittered. In a normal voice, he continued, "My father had an outdoor summer exhibition, and we would arrive in town days before our performance. We posted banners, talked the show up, and handed out pamphlets that promised 'Pablo Fanque's circus and death-defying acts to be enacted in the town square.'"

Pamela caught the nodding heads of the children, familiar with their father's story.

Ted continued, "When we performed in Bolton, our high-stepping rope acrobat, Madame Caroline, stumbled while performing on the tightrope. She hung on with both hands, but she was suspended sixty feet over a hard brick street. Suddenly, this booming voice rang out, 'All the men put your coats in a pile under the rope!' It was this one right here." Ted motioned to Satish. "He and my father cajoled the entire gathering to disrobe and put as many layers of clothes as possible over the bricks. If you can image my father, the Black circus owner, and this one from the tropics telling a town square of English audience members to strip off their coats. Let's just say that they used every stage trick to get them to comply. Then, as Madame Caroline began to lose her hold, Satish encouraged her to let go and fall onto the largest mattress of coats and hay imaginable. She landed unharmed."

Pamela's head spun. A vision of when she flew fluttered in her mind.

Satish caught her eye and smiled. Did he know she flew?

She looked at Bram, still wearing a grave expression. He finally winked at her. He knew about Aleister stalking her, but he didn't know that she could fly. He did just see her work magic on the shadow here with her handkerchief, and he didn't look pleased.

Maud had looked at her with an expression like that, the first time she flew. They were upstairs in her bedroom during the Samhain festival, and, outside, children ran down the street shouting and squealing. Did this event only happen because she and Maud were conjuring magic at a witching hour? Or did Maud only witness Pamela's magic? The color yellow seemed to drip on the wall from the candles' light. Flying only to fall. She thought about falling.

Ted looked at Pamela. "Are you afraid of heights, Miss?"

She looked at the shining faces of the children at the table and softly said, "When I was younger, I thought I could fly. But my heart is heavier now."

One of the children piped up. "Don't you have to have wings to fly?"

Bess tore a piece of bread in half and gave it to the child. "God gives wings to all creatures who are meant to fly—angels, bees, butterflies."

Bram lifted his glass of wine to toast her and added, "And bats."

The boy's eyes widened. "Bats are evil."

"Why is that, my boy?" Satish asked, his eyes twinkling.

"They drink your blood and are the work of the devil."

Satish and Bram laughed as Bess crossed herself once again.

Stretching his long legs in front of the fire, Satish purred in a rumbling voice, "There is a story about the Loogaroo from the Caribbean, the woman who is also a bat. Her magical powers only come about when she collects enough blood for the devil. This Loogaroo can let go of her own skin and become a flame, flying through the air to hunt for victims during the night."

Two of the girls whimpered.

"Ah, now, don't you worry," Satish said. "The Loogaroo must always stop to count things it finds. So, the trick is to leave a pile of rice before your door. The Loogaroo will just stay there, counting every grain until the sun comes up, taking away all its magic."

Bess replied, "Everyone knows you need a crucifix to keep back the evil beasts, not piles of rice."

Bram's eyes lit up. "Why, Bess, are you saying that you've read my book, *The Un-Dead*?"

Bess looked confused for a moment and murmured, "Well, I didn't read it. Ted got it from a bookseller on the road and read it to the older boys."

A boy chirped, "And every time he read us a chapter, after confession in church we'd have to do two rosaries, an Our Father and a Hail Mary. Father Clarence doesn't like us reading about the devil."

"But were you frightened, my boy?" Bram asked.

"Oh, Mr. Stoker," the boy answered. "I'm filled with dread every time I think about it. And I think about it all the time."

Bram and Pamela laughed so hard, the sounds echoed off the walls.

Wiping the water from his eyes, Bram said, "Ah, you see, Pixie? Sir Henry was right. *The Un-Dead* is dreadful."

Pamela leaned across the table and patted Bram's hand as her necklace tingled her skin. Would her tarot cards bring her the same sort of thrilling dread?

CHAPTER SEVEN

Scuttlers

"Opening night is in twenty-four hours," the stage manager Lovejoy barked from the center stage of the Theatre Royal Manchester.

The cast stopped their chatter as they lounged in the house. As leading lady, Ellen Terry sat in the middle of the middle row, surrounded by the cast. In her midforties, she flirted and teased like a coquette, knowing just the right words to bring the shyest member out. Everyone was in love with her.

Lovejoy blasted a shrill whistle. "The days of treating our visiting theatre like a camping site are over. We'll have none of your personal effects anywhere but at your dressing spaces."

Pamela, seated in the second row, jerked her feet off the back of the chair in front of her, petticoats and boots clumsily entangling in the folds of her red skirt. The sketchbook in her lap fell to the floor, and the rest of the cast in the auditorium snickered. As she swung her feet to the floor, Lovejoy glowered at her. This stage manager had never cared for her, not the way Uncle Brammie did. Even Ellen's kiss, blown toward her, didn't cool the heat burning in her cheeks.

Sitting next to Ellen was Edy, her onetime flatmate, former best friend, and Ellen's daughter. She'd arrived on the train yesterday, but she avoided her gaze.

Lovejoy called out, "After mail call, you will all check your props backstage, mend your costumes, and sign out your weapon, if you have one. First up, Miss Terry, a letter for you!"

Ellen held up her hand as Lovejoy neared the lip of the stage, and Sir Henry bolted out from the wings. He snatched the letter out of Lovejoy's hands, glanced at it, and carried it to the edge of the stage.

"Madame, from one Royal Theatre house to another," he said in his loftiest accent. From her second-row seat, Pamela saw Irving's hand tremble as he held out the letter to Ellen.

Pamela craned her neck to try to see the letter. Which other royal theatre was writing Ellen here in Manchester? Theatre Royals were given permission by the Lord Chamberlain to stage dramas; without such a patent it would be illegal to do this tour or plan a season with serious plays. But each theatre had only touring business in common, not personal relationships with actors or actresses.

Ellen stood and plucked the letter from his hand, pocketing it. She curtseyed. "Thank you, Sir Henry, for my delivery from the Royal Theatre." Henry strode offstage. With a toss of her head, Ellen sat further off from the company, her Jack Russell, wolfhound, and Eskimo dog trailing her. Pamela felt a pit in her stomach. This was the first public spat between the two theatre stars.

As Ellen's dogs vied to sit on her lap, Lovejoy continued his mail call. The smaller Jack Russell, Mussie, won the lap contest, leaving Trin, the wolfhound, and Bruin, the white Alaskan, to sulk, each one sitting her feet, whimpering. Pamela felt like sitting at her feet and whimpering as well.

Mail call continued as whispers sprang up in the house. "It's a love note from the prince." "Nah, official termination letter." "How do we even know the letter were from him?"

Was Ellen saying she was delivered of Sir Henry's employment? Why would he make such a spectacle of himself after all these years of hiding any trace of romantic attachment to Ellen in public?

Pamela got up and plopped next to Edy.

"Are we friends or fiends?" Pamela asked.

"Still dear fiends," Edy replied, with a terse smile.

"Why does your mother have royal theatre correspondence? Did one of the royals get involved and ask her to consider Beerbohm's offer?"

"Beerbohm would have to offer mother a lot of money to leave here," Edy replied. "His Haymarket isn't nearly as good, even if Prince Edward did rifle through their chorus girls and now favors them over us."

Queen Victoria had been the Lyceum patron for decades, and she'd helped establish it as the repertory theatre of her age. But she was getting on in years, and Prince Edward, soon to be King Edward, was now the devoted patron of a rival theatre producer, Herbert Beerbohm Tree.

"But Edy," Pamela said, "it's said more theatre artists will be knighted. If Beerbohm gets to be a sir, working for the Lyceum or the Haymarket will be the same."

"Bosh," Edy said.

"It's not bosh to tell you I overheard Henry saying Beerbohm was aping his business and stealing his best actors."

"We're still the Lyceum, the queen's favorite," Edy said, almost hissing.

"But not the prince's favorite, Edy." Behind her hand, Pamela added, "You know Beerbohm's luring actors with the promise of better leading roles. Which you know most actors won't get here as long as Sir Henry is our star."

Lovejoy shouted, "Miss Smith!" and Pamela ran toward the stage. *Since when did she get mail?* After she took her letter from his surly hand, she beelined for the dressing room she shared with Edy.

As she made her way into their tiny, private quarters, melancholy came over Pamela. She knew there would be no confidences and giggles before the makeup mirror during the preshow, as in days past. And sure enough, as soon as Edy came in, she went straight for her cot, piled high with costumes and fan mail for Ellen. Pamela watched as she busied herself, sorting the mail to be answered and inspecting Ellen's elaborate ballroom costume for Madame Sans Gene.

Rather than sitting on her own cot, a messy nest of art supplies and props, Pamela went to her perch, the seat before the big mirror, which they used share. She let out a sigh of relief when she looked at her mail and saw that the return address was Bayswater. At last, a letter from a friend not in the theatre.

> *Dear Odd-Duck, We are planning a "Neglected Artist" series December 8 and thought of you. Will be an "at-home" salon, fifty to sixty art buyers come through, some with cash! Send me word if you have something to show. Rosa, accountant for the show, says we need Pixie's Opal Hush recipe to entice the buyers. She also says: Beware of street gangs and we expect you back here by the end of December to move in, found a fourth flatmate. Your only true friends. Cheers and Cheese! RB & JB*

Thank the gods for new friends Rosa and John Baille. They were not old, resentful friends like sour Edy. But could she get them artwork for an art show next week? Impossible.

Pamela met John and Rosa, brother and sister, at one of the soirees she and Edy threw, and they became instant confidantes. In their company, it seemed as if a fog lifted. Their New Zealand accents, along with their raucous sense of humor and unpretentious artistic bent, were refreshing.

Neither the Lyceum Theatre nor the Golden Dawn impressed either of them. When Pamela had chosen her Golden Dawn motto, *Quod Tibi Id Alliis*—"whatever you have done unto thee, do unto others"—and shared it with them, Rosa had thrown back her head and roared. "Excellent choice, Pixie! That's a preemptive stroke, if ever I heard one."

"It's Christian-like, Rosa," Pamela answered.

"Waite, your coworker on the tarot deck, what's his motto?" Rosa asked.

"*Sacrementum Regis*, 'sacrament of the king.'"

"You need to get away from these impostors and move in with us, Pixie," Rosa said.

But the idea of moving in with Rosa, John, and possibly other flatmates gnawed at her—would she be able to have a place to draw and paint? She had only lived with Edy for six months when it was determined that Pamela was too messy and disorganized to live with all of Edy's house rules. But still, though Pamela had moved to England a year ago, she had always lived near her.

She still needed to draw more rulers, kings, emperors. Pamela looked at her sketchbook with the renderings for her next tarot card, the Emperor. She pulled it out: the seated figure at a throne held a globe and an ankh scepter with ram's heads. Sir Henry had first shown her the Egyptian ankh scepter when she and Edy were studying hieroglyphs. Pamela smiled to think that some of Sir Henry's lessons were making their way into her cards.

Clearing her throat in the small confines of the dressing room, Edy took out her sewing kit and, without looking at Pamela, asked, "Good news in your letter?"

It had been a long time since Edy had cared to ask anything about her. Pamela felt a lump in her throat. "Yes, I have some friends who want to help me."

"Of course you do," Edy replied. "We all need help."

"Edy," Pamela said. "Do you need any help?"

"No, Pixie, we all have our jobs to do here. Speaking of which, the laundress is waiting for your help to iron costumes." With that, Edy gathered up the mended costume and left.

Pamela noticed a postscript in the margin of the letter. "We're reading newspaper accounts of Manchester street gangs and expect you back in London by the end of the year."

How did they hear about Manchester street gangs in London? The strawberry handkerchief in her skirt pocket tumbled about. On top of everything else, could there be a spirit from the train following her?

After a restless night back at the Midland Hotel, Pamela decided to find that church the driver drove by on their way to Didsbury. She would make sure her handkerchief was blessed in case she had to repel more spirits or afrits or whatever Aleister had sent. Then she could concentrate on drawing more tarot cards.

She unpacked the violet linen dress that did nothing for her figure except make it rounder no matter how tightly she belted it. She dressed quickly, but the mirror reflected a round purple lolly. Her coat would cover most of it, but her hand reached into the trunk and she draped the paisley shawl with the fringe over her shoulders. Edy's admonishment that she needed to sort out her job rang in her ears. She wound her watch to ensure she would be on time for the "beginners" call, pinned it under her shawl, and locked her hotel room.

At the bottom of the stairs, she found confusing new signs in the lobby. Should she turn right or left to exit to the street? She ended up going down a corridor and soon found herself on a landing, which seemed to be in the back of the hotel between the main restaurant and the kitchen.

After three years of construction, the Midland Hotel was still a work in progress. Only the lobby and the first three floors were completed, so the majority of the theatre company was lodged on the second floor with tiny rooms, while Henry, Ellen, Bram, and the syndicate's accountants stayed in the corner suites on a higher floor. Was it just a coincidence that the Lyceum's new syndicate owners got them the best rooms? There were company rumors that the theatre's syndicate owned the Midland Railway and the Midland Hotel. Was the world becoming one business owner?

As Pamela wandered down a narrow hallway to the dining hall, a waiter with a tray with plates of uneaten food on his shoulder staggered toward her. Pamela plastered herself against the wall so he could step into the kitchen. As the swinging door pushed open, waiters sprang forward like wild dogs to meet him. In the blink of an eye, they lunged, snatching leftover bread, oysters, slabs of meat, and pastries. Pamela gasped and stood spying as the door swung open and shut, astounded at the savage gobbling. The gorging lasted all of half a minute. The waiter carrying the tray looked up, a slice of bread in one hand and an oyster shell in the other. His black hair flopped over his forehead and his eyes were shining. His pale face became even more ashen. He bolted to the door and held it fast so its flapping would stop. Pamela steadied herself against the wall as she recovered from the scene.

Was it gluttony or starvation she had just witnessed? Pamela shook her head and made her way down to the ground floor.

As she passed the restaurant, Ellen waved to her. There was Sir Henry, taking tea with her.

"Darling!" Ellen called as she neared their table. "They have brought us every pastry conceivable. Please stay and have some tea with us?"

Henry looked away and then said, "Yes, Miss Smith, please sit for a moment."

A moment and not a second past.

The waiter, whom she had just seen filling his face with food in the kitchen, came to the table. His slack jaw and wide-opened eyes pleaded for secrecy.

"Miss," the waiter said. "Compliments of the hotel, would another place setting for tea be agreeable?"

Pamela looked at Ellen's smiling face and turned back to the waiter. "Yes, tea to accompany these fine desserts would be fabulous. I hear the food is fantastic here."

The waiter squirmed. "Yes, we are in the early days for our restaurant but we think the fare here is excellent."

As the waiter bustled away, Ellen patted Pamela's hand. "You seem to have made an impression on that waiter. Had you met earlier?"

"Only in passing."

Henry reached over to his stack of newspapers and correspondence on the chair next to him and picked up a handbill for *The Merchant of Venice*. Her doctored artwork, depicting Henry's Shylock as a devil with horns, was placed delicately on the table.

"Miss Smith," Henry said. "I'm sorry to see your artwork defiled. It has made the use of your posters problematic. Jewish patrons are outraged and have demanded that we use no illustrations in advertising our show. So we will not be using your artwork now or in the future. If there are to be future Lyceum Theatre shows, the syndicate will pick set designers. Your work possibilities are out of my hands. But I do hope you will remain with our tour."

The waiter was back with Pamela's tea. Pamela put her hands over the poster as a place setting was set out for her and cup of tea poured. Only once did the waiter give a curious glance to Pamela's shielding of the paper.

"Oh, Pixie, Sir Henry is so sorry," Ellen said.

Pamela studied Henry's face. He had never hired her to do more than sketches, never to design sets, costumes, or anything substantial, despite her numerous pleas.

She stammered, "Yes, I had always hoped . . . ."

The words stopped there. There were always so many hopes. Hopes that Ellen Terry would take her in. Hopes Edy would be her sister and Bram her uncle. Hopes she wasn't a weed in a garden of heirloom roses.

"Yes, we have great hopes for you, Pamela," Henry interrupted. "It's a shame that it never worked out for us to develop your artistic talents. We're so glad you have your tarot cards to work on."

She took a sip of the hot, strong tea, reached for an éclair, cut a section off, and popped it in her mouth. More tea. The scalding drink burned the roof of her mouth. There was no future for her as a designer here.

"Well, tea soothed the savage beast," Pamela croaked. "I'm off to look at stained glass windows in a church and hope to be inspired for the next card. I'll be back in time for our rehearsal." *Make the tone as light as possible.* She forced herself to smile. The pitying looks from her two adored ones as she stood made her want to bolt from the room.

"Is it safe?" Ellen said.

"Of course," Pamela replied. "The wardrobe lady recommended it. I'll be at the theatre in plenty of time." She tapped her foot against her chair leg. The wardrobe lady had actually told her she was out of her mind to go to that neighborhood, but they didn't need to know that.

"What is the next card, Miss Smith?" Henry asked, using a low tone he usually reserved for Ellen.

"The Emperor."

"Ah, someone who understands rules and retribution," Henry answered. "Who could be your role model for that?"

"Still wool gathering," she said. "Sights to see, so I'll say goodbye."

Pamela practically ran on her way out of the restaurant.

Outside the hotel, Manchester's factories spewed noxious fumes into the air. Dubbed the "Chimney of the World," the city was thriving and destroying its population at the same time. Pamela could barely breathe as she hurried along the street. Crowds of dapper men and harried market vendors discharged from the Central Railway Station, mingling with working-class men as they handled boxes, wheelbarrows, and carts. As she walked by a group of men, she saw dots on detachable shirt collars. She tried not to inhale when she realized what it was—charcoal "snow" from nearby factories. She hurried her pace.

Walking down Oxford Street, even with all the foot traffic and carriages, disapproval of her came from more than a few. Was it her purple paisley shawl or the fact that she was walking alone? An open-mouthed girl had her jaw shut by her mother as they walked by.

"Hussy," the mother hissed.

"Whatchya?" "Muffins for sale?" and whistles from the carriage men came from every direction. Even the bobby on the bicycle gave her a disapproving look as he pedaled past.

This was the first time she had been harassed for walking unescorted. This was broad daylight. She had the right to walk in the open air here. Well, the air was as green as pea soup here in Manchester, but all the same. Where was that famous ditch to the other world? Wasn't it supposed to be right about here? There was just enough time to get to the church for a handkerchief cleansing and to light a candle for protection against the afrit. *Oh no, what is that?* She came to a complete stop.

At the next street corner, ten or maybe twelve young men, fifteen to twenty years of age, were slumped against the bridge railing. Human trolls. They all wore the same strange outfit: flared trousers, floral scarves at their necks, and caps crowning the most unusual haircut she had never seen. All had shaved heads except for one lock of hair twirled on their foreheads, anchored by their woolen caps. On the front edges of the caps, the gleam from the edges of razors shone, metal shards sewn into the bills. Knives in their hats? Their costumes' effect was part prisoner, part monk. Around the waist, each wore an ominous belt with gleaming metal points. Even their shoes had copper points, so the clamor on the cobblestone rang out as they mingled. They saw her and, like a herd of jackals, loped in her direction.

She tried to keep the alarming noise inside her head from overwhelming her as she clutched her purse tighter. What was it Bram always told her—that she reacted emotionally first? *Think straight.* She scanned the bridge. Underneath, the River Medlock was a paltry inlet; maybe she should dive into that? The ooze on the water's surface dissuaded her instantly. She needed to be on the other side of the street. She darted between a cluster of wagons and a bus, crossing the street in three quick leaps. A small roar went up from the group and they started pounding on the bus to hurry in pursuit.

Someone took hold of her elbow. It was the waiter from the Midland Hotel, carrying a canvas bag.

"Miss, Toby Dolan here. When they told me you were headed down Oxford, I knew I had to do an errand this way. And who might you be?" His pale face, framed by thick black hair, was serious, as he hurried her along.

"Pixie . . . no, Pamela. Pamela Colman Smith," Pamela said as her eye caught the gang crossing the street to them. She clutched Toby's elbow.

The shortest and plumpest of the group ran up to them. He was pug-nosed with a patch of red curly hair cut like others, a cartoon version of his scraggly companions. He spit out his words: "Hey, Toby, whatchya got there for us?"

"John-Joseph, fancy meeting you," Toby answered.

"Tobes!" John-Joseph said. "Waiters walk with swells now? Swells with purses?"

Toby, still holding Pamela's arm, positioned himself in front of John-Joseph, who seemed to be the leader of this crew.

He opened the canvas bag and the scent of warm bread drifted out. "My friend here made sure I was able to donate these to the Bengal Tigers today."

A small cheer went up as they gathered around. John-Joseph snatched the bag from Toby and yelped with glee. A glimmer, a shine in the dull sunlight, bobbed as he dove into the pastries. The sparkle of sharp razors embedded in the brims of their caps danced as each boy held out a hand. Pamela glanced at the boys' outfits, each wearing red belt buckles. *Wait, that's not dye but dried blood.* Finally, the last remaining hands grabbed the bag and divided the spoils to triumphant grunts.

Pamela remembered the snapping pet alligators in the pond of the sister of her caretaker, Miss Jones, in St. Andrews. The creatures fiercely lunged at the first signs of offered food, and then a coiled politeness passed between Pamela's hand and their teeth for the second and third helpings. Toby smiled and winked at her. Suddenly, the mob didn't feel like a mob.

"We'll tell the Prussia Street Lads to let you pass on your way back," John-Joseph said, his mouth full of éclair.

"Please do, John-Joseph," Toby said.

John-Joseph licked every finger clean and turned to Pamela. "Thank you, miss."

"You are most welcome," Pamela answered, using extra effort to be firm and confident.

"Thank the nice girl here, you heathens," John-Joseph said.

A weak chorus of "Thanks, ma'am" and "Yeah, thank ya muchly" went around the group.

Toby sized up the distracted mood of the group and put Pamela's arm through his. "All right then, John-Joseph, we'll be heading off now."

"Where is it you going with the miss?" John-Joseph asked.

The eyes of the group turned to Pamela and she gulped. "Holy Name Church to light candles. You're welcome to accompany us."

Hoots and hollers went up, and some of the gang bent over laughing.

John-Joseph squinted his eyes. "Thanks, Miss. Some of us here be Catholic, but we'd need a date with the confessional first."

Another taller member stood closer to Pamela and exhaled the stench of beer. "Ya got a coin you'd be using for the lighting of a candle?" he asked.

Another asked, "How many coins do ya have on ya?"

The crowd pressed in on them.

Pamela took a deep breath and said, "I do have two coins to light candles. One for my dead mother and one for my dead father."

"An orphan!" the leader cried. "Ah, for the love of Michael, we can't take away an orphan's candle money. Off with you. And Toby, see you here again on Friday. With more of the bread."

They marched away down Oxford street, a ragtag group following John-Joseph like krill swept along the path of a whale. The sounds of their metal-tipped shoes clattered, a retreating army of tin and copper.

Sounds of horse-hooves and the cries of vendors swallowed up their noise.

Toby linked Pamela's hand though his. "It's best if we walk like this, miss. We have two more Scuttlers' bridges to get over."

The Scuttlers that Rosa worried about in the letter from John were here after all.

As Toby steered Pamela along yet another bridge, Pamela shivered. Maybe the afrit in her handkerchief was summoning all this chaos. But the thresholds of bridges always summoned memories of chaos: falling off Waterloo Bridge as a child, Aleister turning into a lizard on London Bridge, and now these Scuttlers on the Manchester bridge. Maybe three is the lucky charm and this would be the last hostile encounter on a bridge.

"What's the water below us, Toby?" Pamela asked, peering at the sludge of a river. "I heard from the laundress that there's an underground tunnel to the other world?"

Toby adjusted his red scarf so it showed prominently from his jacket. They picked up their pace. "That's River Tib to us old-timers, River Irwell to the rest. It's too bad we can't fly, miss, and avoid all the riffraff on the street."

Violets. The scent suddenly came over her. Maud. Her first childhood friend and love. Maud was always urging her to fly. Grit stung in her eyes. Bram's voice in her head: *Think straight.* Pamela tripped, and only by hanging on to Toby did she manage to remain upright.

"I need you to walk with me to one place that is guaranteed to be safe," Pamela said. "Holy Names Church."

"What do you need at the church?" Toby asked, linking her arm through his.

"A priest who can bless a cursed handkerchief," Pamela replied as they carefully made their way down the street.

CHAPTER EIGHT

Hierophant and High Priestess

Ahmed's promenade in Thornton Manor's formal gardens after morning prayers proved unsatisfactory. He had been jarred awake by a disturbing image of Pamela falling, and the malaise of impeding harm still hung over him. Pamela had described several accidents backstage to him, but in this dream she was in a temple. He toyed with the idea of sending her a telegram, but what would he say? Beware of falling? His handkerchief, folded neatly in his breast pocket, usually vibrated when a dangerous omen was nearby, but it continued to be mute.

During his walk, a raw spit of morning mist hurried his every step. Coming around the front of the house, though, he stopped in his tracks. In the gravel courtyard was a brightly painted yellow touring bus, with two men tending the steam engine.

Was his transportation to the Liverpool Museum to see the Sekhemka statue finally arranged? For two days, Lord Compton had promised to take him, but he'd ascribed the delay to the delicate nature of arranging a meeting with the museum's antiquity director. Ahmed was aware that an Egyptian authority discussing the retrieval of the Sekhemka statue would seem an odd request. But at least the request was being entertained.

One of the two men wore a brimmed cap and driving gloves—the chauffeur, evidently. He went inside the bus and wiped down the windows as the mechanic adjusted the engine. With a slight pop, the motor chugged to life.

Still weary from his bone-rattling ride from the train station to Thorton Manor, Ahmed was relieved to see this automobile might provide a more comfortable ride.

Crunching sounds of his boots on gravel caused the two men to turn to him as he drew closer. The engine was a whirring boiler inside a metal box strapped to the front fenders. Whips of steam poured over the front of the car. He had seen steam engines in boats on the Nile River but never in an automobile. The polished-wood exterior and large glass windows were similar to those of a horseless carriage. There were three rows of upholstered seats with armrests, the height of luxurious English traveling. On the doors was painted a sunny, bucolic landscape with the caption "Sunlight Village." Sunlight Village, indeed. The sun hadn't been out in the three days they had been there.

The mechanic stood up as Ahmed approached. Ahmed could tell the man was fixated on his fez, but he ignored the man's stare as he peered into the noisy engine. It whirred and belched steam in the frosty air.

"It's a Daimler," the mechanic said, over the clanging motor. Between his Liverpudlian accent and the noise, Ahmed strained to understand him.

Ahmed nodded his head. "How long does it take to ready this Daimler?" he asked the chauffeur, who squinted at him.

"An hour to warm up to a full head of steam."

Like the mechanic, the chauffeur gave Ahmed a once-over look before strolling to the rear of the car and fiddling with the trunk straps.

A full head of steam: that's what he would need to get Sekhemka back.

After an uneventful and somewhat smooth ride, the car sputtered to a stop in front of the Liverpool Museum under a dark sky. Ahmed almost smiled when he saw that this museum looked like a smaller dingy version of his workplace, the British Museum in London. Both had a Grecian-type center building framed by pillars supporting a stone triangle. Granted, the Liverpudlian museum was smaller in scale and lacked a frieze on the front, but otherwise the two museums looked similar.

Entering into the lobby, Ahmed noted the similar number of granite columns. He had done his research to show his contact here he knew the business of museums and their exhibits. Although this museum was only thirty years old, Ahmed could see how the architects imitated the grandeur of the older museum.

At the front desk, Ahmed introduced himself to a young man whose nose was stuck in a book. He asked to be to the director of Egyptian art.

"Which director?" the insolent young clerk asked.

"I wish to meet the director of Egyptian antiquities, please?" Ahmed asked, cursing himself for not asking Lord Compton for a name. His host had excused himself from this trip at the last minute, and Ahmed had forgotten to ask for a written introduction.

"Those meetings are by letter of recommendation only," the young man answered.

"I'm sorry," Ahmed said. "I don't know the name of the man I am to meet. Lord Compton arranged it." Would the lord's name be enough to make an impression?

"I would be glad to be of service when you have a bona fide name and appointment, Mr. Kamal," the clerk said, and he went back to reading his novel, *The Sorrows of Werther*. Sorrows indeed.

A middle-aged man with floppy brown hair appeared next

to Ahmed. "Hello, Mr. Kamal, I am George Lane Fox-Pitt," the man said, extending his hand. "I was on the phone with Lord Compton just now." He shook hands with Ahmed with the lightest of touches. "My father was a major donor of Egyptian artifacts here, and my job is to see to the distribution of his donations. How may I assist you?"

"Pleased to meet you," Ahmed said, relieved to his core. "I am Mr. Ahmed Kamal, British Museum Acquisitions Director. I was under the impression that I would be meeting with the antiquities director here today. I am to arrange the retrieval of a statue from Cairo. It was mistakenly donated here."

"I'm so sorry, Mr. Kamal. Our antiquities director, Mr. Flinders Petrie, left this morning on a business trip back to Egypt. He'll be gone for a month," the man said, his hair falling into his eyes. "Were you hoping to discuss donations to his Egyptian Explorers Fund?"

Ahmed shook his head. He wasn't pleased to hear that Petrie served as antiquities director here. He had dealt with him in London, and he had been rude and dismissive. William Flinders Petrie was the first chair of Egyptian Archeology and Philology at the University College London. He set up and organized the Egyptian Explorers Fund, which in partnership with the Thomas Cook & Son travel agency managed and underwrote steamship tours on the Nile. The tours were geared to Egyptian art collectors, mostly from England. Petrie was well aware that Egypt's historical sites were being pillaged. He once wrote to Ahmed that the store of remains of the Egyptian artifacts "was a house on fire, so rapid was its destruction." Unfortunately, Petrie's own tours encouraged scavengers, looters, and tourists to damage ageless works, by digging out whatever they could transport home.

"Lord Compton arranged for me to meet with the director of antiquities here to discuss the release of the Sekhemka statue," Ahmed said, digging his nails into his palm.

"Sorry, I know nothing about this statue," Fox-Pitt said. "We are all currently busy with organizing our inventory for a shared-works exhibit that Petrie arranged before his trip. However, I'll be glad to show you the Egyptian collection that we have on display now."

Coordinating a shared-works exhibit. Anticipating his visit, they had scuttled Sekhemka to another museum.

"Could you tell me which institution Mr. Petrie has transported artifacts to for this shared-artifacts exhibit?" Ahmed asked.

Fox-Pitt flinched. "I don't believe I said he was transporting anything. I will tell you that we are coordinating this next exhibit with the Northampton Museum. That is all I know. Now, shall I show you our collection?"

After a miserable lecture from Fox-Pitt about second-class artifacts from Turkey, Ahmed was back at Thornton Manor, for tea and lemonade in the French drawing room. As Ahmed sat in an overstuffed chair, he felt closed in: every conceivable space was packed with publications and statues. Why must these collectors acquire so many things from other countries? Firelight flickered from the white marble fireplace mantel where Bomanji and Bhownagree leaned, smoking with the senior Mr. Lever. Ahmed sat on a settee, and Mrs. Lever led the young Lever over to him.

"Mr. Kamal," the tiny Mrs. Lever said, "my boy is anxious to consult with you. I'll be back in a moment." She turned and joined another conversation. The boy, holding a glass case, sat down next to him.

A memory of a different display case came back to him. Ahmed had retrieved a glass display case of Egyptian precious stones for Petrie of the Thomas Cook & Son tours to examine in his office. Pamela asked to be included and was standing next to Ahmed when Petrie grabbed the case out of Ahmed's hands and walked out of the acquisition room. It took an intense exchange for Ahmed to prevail and get the gems back before Petrie walked out with them. Pamela later commended him on his diplomacy and told him that he could be the muse for her Hierophant tarot card.

"Why the Hierophant?" Ahmed had asked. "Why not a judge?"

"You will always be my Hierophant," Pamela responded. "He is the high priest who holds the secrets of the Grecian Eleusinian Mysteries, which represented the myth of Persephone. You are the true keeper of the Eleusinian Mysteries."

But now, Ahmed had to keep from sighing in exasperation as young William arranged his pilfered goods on the table before them. How would he keep his composure tonight?

Irritated by today's failure to find Sekhemka, Ahmed tried not to resent being saddled with the boy. His host, Ahmed realized, had sent him on a fool's errand. Did Lord Compton know that Sekhemka had already been sent to another museum? How frustrating that Fox-Pitt refused to even acknowledge whether the museum ever possessed it. The interminable lecture on Turkish antiquities had tried his patience, and only after that, with only half an hour before closing time, Ahmed was granted a walk-through of the two floors of the Egyptian collection. His statue wasn't there, but there were many other precious artifacts listed as "missing" in the Cairo antiquity office. He documented as many items as he could in his diary. At the end, his stomach was in knots.

From the fireplace, Ahmed overheard Bomanji and Bhownagree argue with Lever over tariffs and palm oil harvesters. At least he wasn't obligated to listen to that conversation.

Florence entered and Ahmed stood. Her pale, oval face contrasted with her dark hair, gathered in several knots in the back. Dressed in a long golden tunic, she was beguiling.

"Miss Farr, you must entertain us with your harp playing," Mrs. Lever announced, jumping up from her seat. She pointed to a large harp with a mermaid on the front curved bow. "We have just the instrument."

As Mrs. Lever swept her away to the corner of the room, Florence turned her head and made a wry face that only Ahmed could see. After arranging her chair for a moment, Florence made a loud run of arpeggios, startling everyone in the room.

"Sorry, these fingers are rusty," Florence said, a sparkle in her eye.

As the harp music abated to a tinkly trill, William opened the display case on the low table in front of them.

"Here are my Egyptian antiquities, Mr. Kamal," the boy said. "Could you appraise them for me, please?" He held out a magnifying glass.

Ahmed squinted. Some of the artifacts were not Egyptian but typical river-sludge findings. There were Celtic Bronze Age axe handles, Roman coins, and Viking rings. There were a few pieces that could possibly be Egyptian in nature, but they had been handled so much that their authenticity could not be verified. Still, it was a noteworthy collection: fragments, possibly maps, a nose piece from a mask, two small flasks, a vase with hieroglyphics on the front lip, and a collar necklace inlaid with lapis lazuli. It was the last container that stood out.

Nestled in a red velvet case was an ancient paper, almost a foot long and half as wide. Immediately, Ahmed could tell by the marking that it was a prized relic. Yes, it was in poor condition, but it definitely looked like papyrus from *The Book of Dead*. It was. Ahmed raised the magnifying glass. Yes, it was possible to make out the images. There was a pharaoh on a throne, surrounded by his *shabti*.

"Ah, there, that is Anubis," Ahmed said, motioning to the papyri. "He has the black jackal head and weighs the heart on the scale, one feather counterbalancing the other."

"What are those things around him?" William asked.

"Why, *shabti*, or ushabti as some say, come to life, waiting for their instructions on how to serve Anubis."

"Is that the god Thoth?" William asked, pointing to a figure on the side. "He writes everything down?"

"Yes, and you see this bird-headed one?" Ahmed asked. "That is Ani Ba, watching over him. Next to him, this combination of lion, crocodile, and hippopotamus? That is Ammit, waiting to snatch up the soul, should the feather be outweighed by the unbalanced heart." He pointed to the image of the scale on the paper.

"He judges like the devil on judgment day," William said.

"Quite!" Ahmed said. "Good comparison, Mr. Lever."

Florence stopped playing the harp and placed her hands on her back as she stretched.

"That's enough for now," she said, strolling over to the couch where William sat. She reached for a cigarette from a glass bowl and lit it with a steady hand. Bomanji and Bhownagree sprang from the fireplace mantel and joined her as she looked at Ahmed.

"Now what is this, Mr. Kamal?" Florence asked, exhaling smoke away from him. "Can you tell?"

"It is possible that this is a written spell from I *Book of the Dead*," Ahmed said, seeing that the two men surrounding Florence were only looking at her. "You can see, despite its age, this artifact is in better shape than most papyri."

The ruler Mohammed Ali had outlawed the sale of such in 1835, but sellers, such as the notorious L. Philip in Cairo, made a fortune by selling to English tourists. In fact, Philip was arrested for selling pages from this very book several years ago. He was sentenced to hard labor for a year with a fine that bankrupted his business. It was also rumored his thumbs were cut off.

Trying not to give too much away, Ahmed cleared his throat and patted his pocket to let his spirit handkerchief know it was now time to work. A slight shudder from his magical conduit let him know the order had been received.

"If I am to continue with this appraisal, I really need my artifact gloves," he said.

William motioned over the footman and asked him to remove his gloves. As the boy put them on his hands, Ahmed stood.

"I'm sorry, Mr. Lever, but those are not an acceptable substitute," Ahmed said, taking out his gloves from his jacket. "You must allow me." The boy waved the footman away and motioned to the box. Ahmed lifted up the cotton-lined container housing the papyrus. William took it out of his hands. Just like Petrie.

"It is not advisable to handle these ancient pieces," Ahmed said, trying not to panic that the case was in the young boy's hands.

"That's all right, I'll leave it in inside," William replied. "I just want to show Miss Farr."

William lifted up the box to show her, and Florence's hand flew up. A brilliant flash of light stabbed the air, and the papyri disappeared. Shreds of smoke dissolved into spider-like cinders, floating on invisible currents.

"No!" Ahmed shouted.

It was one of his worst nightmares come true, an ancient artifact ruined by exposure to air and movement. Why didn't his mummy cloth prevent this?

Ahmed took a deep breath and closed his eyes. It took everything he had to keep from shouting the most extreme damnations he could think of. When he lifted his head up, Elizabeth and Lord Compton were standing over them, William sobbing over the motes of papyrus floating in the air. Ahmed put his cloth back in his pocket and bit his lips.

Tears stung in his eyes. Another prize lost to this family's looted treasure chest. What are such artifacts but toys to spoiled children?

The wails of his son brought William Sr. over. Reaching his son, he led him to the nearest couch, quietly asking questions.

A gentle touch on his shoulder startled Ahmed. Florence stood before him with tears in her eyes.

"Mr. Kamal, we feel the loss of your country's treasures acutely. Not as severely as you feel it, of course."

William Sr. sauntered over to examine the nearly emptied box, now containing only smudged shreds of papyrus. He tutted sympathetically while Lord Compton turned to the hostess and shook his finger at her. "Really, Mrs. Lever, if you are to entrust these items to your son, he must learn the first lessons of conservation. Proper care of artifacts must be of the utmost concern, especially when one is archiving the most fragile of items. The whole point of conservation is to preserve these objects for future generations."

Mrs. Lever called for the footman to come and take away the display cases. William Lever Sr., wife, and son accompanied the cases out of the drawing room. Once they left, Florence and Lord Compton sat next to Ahmed.

"I've been talking to Lord Compton about the statue," Florence said in a low voice to Ahmed. "Sekhemka is now housed at the Northampton Museum."

Ahmed looked over at Lord Compton, who gave no suggestion as to how he really felt about Sekhemka's ownership.

Florence went on. "I suggest you go to the Northampton Museum and authenticate its origin markers."

"And then?" Ahmed asked, wondering where Florence learned about authenticity markers.

Lord Compton cleared his throat. "And then, we will begin a conversation as to the rights and manner of conservancy best suited to keep Sekhemka intact."

Ahmed took a breath and forced his heart to beat at a slower rate. He exhaled and picked up his teacup. "I agree, Lord Compton," Ahmed said. "The first step of any dig or reclamation is to identify provenance."

"Agreed," Lord Compton said. "Now that we have addressed the matter, enough of this artifact business, eh?"

He winked at Ahmed and stood. Addressing Bomanji and Bhownagree as they started to sit beside Florence, he boomed, "Sirs, can I pull you away from your business?"

Bomanji and Bhownagree grunted, neither of them happy to leave the charming Miss Farr.

Lord Compton opened his evening jacket, showing the several cigars bulging inside his pocket.

In response, Bhownagree opened his tunic to reveal a flask, while Bomanji opened his own jacket, holding yet an even larger flask. The men looked at Ahmed quizzically, to see if he had any interest, but he shook his head. He knew that the pair probably wouldn't even partake of the drink but considered it important to demonstrate to their English acquaintances that they prized the same things. The three men excused themselves and headed out the French doors to the garden.

The moment they were gone, Florence sprang up from her seat and went to a large book on a table near the fireplace. She opened the cover and lifted out a papier-mâché set of pages. Ahmed drew closer; it was a false-bottomed box, and Florence took out a gauzed-covered insert. From his pocket, Ahmed's handkerchief vibrated violently. Was it because of Florence's book? If not, what was she doing with the Levers' private property?

Florence motioned Ahmed over, and he reached for the magnifying glass and hurried to her side. He unwrapped the gauze and opened the box. Another piece of papyrus lay nestled between layers of muslin. There it was: the drawing of a pharaoh sitting on a throne, surrounded by his *shabti*, Ani Ba and Ammit watching the weighting of the heart on a scale. Ahmed leaned down and studied the papyrus with the glass. It was the original artifact. He stood dumbfounded.

"What magic trick is this?" Ahmed whispered. "I thought it was just destroyed."

"This is the original," Florence answered.

Without touching the contents, she replaced the lid over

the papyrus, making sure that it was firmly attached, and placed the box back in the bottom of the book, restoring the fake pages. The mummy handkerchief shook at Ahmed's breast.

Suddenly, Mrs. Lever appeared at their side along with the butler holding a metal box. "Mr. Kamal, here is a travel safe for you to store the real papyrus," said the butler.

"Yes, I concocted a fake paper ahead of time with the help of Miss Farr," Mrs. Lever said, her eyes sparkling. "I knew it was only a matter of time before my son ruined the original papyrus."

"You . . . you made a copy?" Ahmed asked.

"Yes," Mrs. Lever said. "I wanted my boy to think that he destroyed the original, so I recruited Miss Farr to help me stage this. She is a master of calligraphy and stage magic."

Mrs. Lever smiled at him. Florence sipped tea like a cat who had stolen cream.

"And you burned the fake?" Ahmed asked, sitting down.

"It's just an old theatre trick, Mr. Kamal," Florence said. "A sleight of hand using flash paper, charcoal, and a cigarette." She crushed her cigarette out in the crystal dish before them.

"Mrs. Lever, I appreciate the offer, but are you asking me for payment for having pulled this trick?" Ahmed asked.

"This is a gift to you and your country, Mr. Kamal," Mrs. Lever said, almost pouting. "Our family has been fastidious collectors of Egyptian art for almost forty years. We want to see your country's antiquities restored as well. And I have felt, well, a sense of malevolence ever since that paper arrived here."

"Thank you, Mrs. Lever," Ahmed said. "I do appreciate the gift of this papyrus." Mrs. Lever and Florence beamed at one another. "However, it is the statue Sekhemka I am most intent on recovering."

Florence trained her eyes on him with such kindness that he considered telling her about Sekhemka. "Why is that?" she asked, briefly touching his hand. As shocked as he was at her familiarity, her touched persuaded him instantly.

"Within any statue of Egyptian origin, there is a place to be occupied by a god," Ahmed said. "If you can imagine it, the statue itself is a meeting place between the supernatural and the earth. But the statue is also a physical body, enabling the supernatural powers to act here in our material world. Without this whole physical shell, the supernatural forces cannot intercede here. So many statues are maimed when they are looted. By removing their whole appearance, the pillagers destroy the gods' ability to act or avenge themselves."

Florence gasped. "The broken noses! I've always wondered why so many of the Egyptian statues are mangled. Looters are breaking the gods' conduit to act here in our physical world?"

"Not looters," Ahmed said. "That would destroy the value of what they are hoping to sell. The vandalism is done by the enemies of the gods. This would deliberately maim their ability to act."

"The enemies would break the noses of the statues of their enemies?" Mrs. Lever asked.

"More precisely, the enemies are destroying a god's ability to breathe when they break the nose," Ahmed said. "When they break the arms of the statue of a god, it is to keep the god from fighting back."

Mrs. Lever shook her head. "Oh my. It never occurred to me that a god could intercede in events on earth."

"They are not passive ghosts," Ahmed answered.

"That idea isn't in keeping with my Christian faith, but it's very interesting! Well, I'm off to console my son over this supposed destruction of one of his artifacts," Mrs. Lever said. "Here's hoping we can keep the real ones safe for you. We will continue to encourage Lord Compton to negotiate the return of your Sekhemka."

Ahmed watched Florence amble toward the fire. Her robe hung low in the back, revealing her long neck. Her dress was more familiar to Ahmed than Mrs. Lever's corseted costume.

Cousins and aunts wore similar tunics to Florence's but with far less skin revealed.

Florence caught Ahmed admiring her. "How do you like my Grecian-inspired dress?" she asked.

Ahmed exhaled to keep his face from reddening. "I was thinking it is very Turkish in inspiration," he replied.

"Ah, Mr. Kamal, I see you may know a great deal about Egyptian dress in antiquity but little about the statues of Persephone," Florence laughed.

Persephone again.

"She was a Greek princess . . . ," Ahmed faltered. The myth he was somewhat familiar with escaped him.

Florence warmed her hands in front of the fireplace, and a different wavering of light floated over her head.

"She descends into the underworld, abducted from her mother by Hades," Florence said, her hand flying to her earlobe as she winced.

He moved closer to her. "What is it, Miss Farr?

"I'm not sure. I think I was just bitten by something."

"Let me see."

"No, no, don't bother." She turned away from him, brushing strands of her hair to cover her ear. "Well, Mr. Kamal, it has been a long day. We'll discuss your access to the Northampton Museum tomorrow. Good night."

He held out his hand.

She took it, turned it over, and kissed his wrist. He was disorientated. She was kissing his hand? Anyone could come back into the room. How could she be so bold? Her hair swung back, revealing her shoulder and her long, lean neck. Ahmed stilled himself and looked at her with what he hoped was the blank, uninterested look of a married man. He shook his head, and she turned and quit the room with accelerating steps.

But there was no doubt on what he had seen on her earlobe—the glowing initials "PCS." Pamela's initials.

CHAPTER NINE

Holy Names Portal

As Toby slowly extracted the last bribe from his coat pocket to offer to the street gang, Pamela stopped tapping her feet together to keep warm. It wouldn't do for them to think she was nervous. She had peeked at her pocket watch on her blouse before they came upon this last group; she now had only two hours before she had to return to the theatre. Toby held out the small cloth bag. The leader of the Grey Mare Boys snatched the bag out of Toby's hands. The boys settled down and, like communicants queuing for the sacramental host, dutifully fell in line to feed from the wad of smashed rolls. This gang didn't wear hats with razors in the brims or metal shoes. Their uniform was a simple red scarf around the neck, which Toby was now sporting.

As she stood amid the swirl of ravenous boys devouring the last crumbs, the leader turned away from the crowd and bumped into Pamela. The handkerchief in her inner skirt pocket immediately heated up. Was this a warning from the afrit? A hand hovered near her, and she clamped down on her purse with one hand and shielded her skirt pocket with the other.

The pickpocket's prying hand was still poised over her, so she kicked his ankle. His attempt was a tried-and-true move: jostle one side, steal from the other.

Thwarted, the boy spun on Toby. "Don't you be bringing any grief tourists to us!"

Toby made his way over from the boys still jostling for scraps. "Yeah, she's not one of those church ladies; she's just a regular tourist."

"Off with you then, cousin, until later," the boy said, jostling with the lads over the scraps in his hand.

Toby and Pamela pushed through the group and continued down the street. "He's your cousin?" Pamela asked.

Toby nodded, tucking his red scarf back underneath his coat. So, he was a part-time Scuttler. They picked up the pace. *What else is hidden in there, a knife, a rope?*

"Do you have to feed them every time you see them?" Pamela asked.

"Yes. I need their protection as I walk the same path every day to work," Toby said. "We all have family working the restaurants and hotels, and whether it's the Bengal Tigers or the Prussia Street Lads, we all have to tithe for safe passage. The gangs here be Germans, mostly, except for us Irish Grey Mares."

The Irish twang in his voice twisted hard when he said "mares." He could have been sent by the Seelie fairies from her youth, the ones who safeguard children. Pamela was convinced that the reason there were so many Irish in her life was because they were sent by the Seelies.

"I don't recall Manchester being so full of beggars when we lived here," Pamela said as they trotted along.

Toby stopped. "Beggars? They're fighting for their lives. Where did you live?"

"Didsbury," she replied.

"No poor there," Toby said, his mouth tightening.

"The poor area is in Salford," Pamela said, remembering snatches of conversations from her parents.

"No, miss, that was over ten years ago. The bad part of town is now in Angel Meadow, on the other side of town," Toby said. He pointed down to the next block. "You see, there's your Holy Name Church. I hope you find your priest to do the blessing on your cloth."

Pamela felt the handkerchief move in her pocket. *Bless it or exorcise it.*

He pointed down the street to a plain, squat chapel, two stories tall. No bell tower. Pamela's heart sank. This was no gothic fairy tale. What sort of miracle could happen here?

"Now," Toby said, "When it's time for your return, ask Father Vaughan to get you to the trolley."

She took another look. At one time, Holy Name could have been a fourteenth-century ideal, but now it was a grime-covered, ominous building, something out of Bram's *The Un-Dead*. Maybe she was just spoiled by the sumptuous, clean lines of Southwark Cathedral.

"Thank you for being my escort, Toby," Pamela said.

Toby nodded his head. "I'll be heading back. Remember, Miss Smith, don't be out on the streets here without a guide."

She only had enough money for the candles at the church and the trolley. Should she tip him?

He shook his head as she took out her purse. "A return payment for me would be keeping mum about the leftovers. And get back before dark." He turned on his heels and sprinted away.

She almost called out that she had to be back at rehearsal before four, but he was already halfway down the street. The unimpressive Holy Name's front doors stood before her. There were waterspouts but no gargoyles. More disappointments. *What's a church without gargoyles?*

She dug into her inner pocket and took out the handkerchief. It was still warm from the earlier confrontation. A blue, dusty tint covered everything but the embroidered strawberries in the corners. *So, little afrit, are you in my handkerchief to warn me about the pickpocket? Are you a friend or foe?*

Certainly, when it expelled the spirit at Ted Pablo's house, it felt friendly. She rubbed the cloth between her hands to see if she could sense the spirit living in the threads. There was a slight pulse, but it was hard to tell if it was a spirit or the color blue sending out the throbs of life that only she could sense. Well, the priest would be able to tell if it was evil and could have it banished. She stashed it in her outside coat pocket and made sure she had her coin purse. It was her turn to bribe someone.

She opened the church doors and went into the apse. Her mouth dropped open. The interior could have been plucked out of Renaissance France. Polished wooden planks paved the aisles, and silver candlesticks decorated a high altar backed by four curved stained glass windows. Vaulted arches and ribbed struts curved overhead as though woven by a gigantic spider. Windows, forty feet up in the air, cast shafts of light sprinkled with dust. And the pulpit, just a little tree house of a stand with a floating ceiling of its own, jutted into the pews. On the pulpit were ten English Catholic martyrs painted with gilt backgrounds. The bas-relief at the front of the altar was a re-creation of Leonardo's *Last Supper*! Against the sides of the church, Derbyshire alabaster decorated the confessional booths, each with its own fireplace. In between the booths an elaborate plaster rendition of the Stations of the Cross filled the wall. And there were statues of the saints everywhere. Saint Joseph. Saint Thomas. Saints floating on clouds to heaven above her. Saints stationed in front of the gates to hell. Pamela started to laugh and she felt her hands clutched at her heart. How could this dowdy little church hold all this artwork?

Her eyes were arrested by the statue of the Virgin Mother on a pedestal to the side of the main altar. Pamela kneeled before her, drawn to her beatific, calm expression. The flowing marble robes, the immense crown perched on her head, the kind gaze—this Virgin Mary was a combination of her High Priestess and Empress tarot cards. She reached for the Virgin's open palm. It was cool to the touch.

Time to find the priest. She hurried past the statue and noticed the two stained glass windows at the back were infused with sunlight, streaming colored rays into the airy vault. Pamela had to make herself keep looking, but the feeling of the room infused her with wonder. This feeling of awe was what she wanted all her tarot cards to be like. She cast one look back at the main stained glass window with the Christ in the middle, perfectly scaled and colored in brilliant shades of reds, blues, and yellows. For a moment, Christ held Pamela in a direct gaze. In one glass frame, he cradled a shepherd's crook in one hand and a lamb in the other; in another window he wore a bronze robe and held a text and a lamp. The lettering at the bottom was in the same style as her tarot cards. One read "Pastor Bonus," the other "Lux Mundi." The sun brightened through the colored panes, infusing the glass with a surge of intensity. Bronze and red rays fell on the stone floor in front of Pamela, visiting orbs from another world. Her handkerchief shifted in her coat pocket. Perhaps the spirit that followed her knew she was getting ready to evict it.

Organ music started, startling Pamela, and the familiar tune of "Dies irae" drifted down, the music of her Southwark Church in London. She whirled around and looked up.

High above in the organ loft above the entrance, the back of an organist writhed and swayed as his feet reached for the pedals near the floor. The pipes reached all the way to the vaulted ceiling, their gold tips reflecting the sunlight of the back windows with a flame-like glare. A wheezing vibration shook the tiles of the floor, and Pamela's feet shook.

"Ah! I see you are taken with the window of 'The Good Shepherd,'" a voice said. "Or is it Christ in 'Light of the World' that you prefer?"

As she turned, a priest in a simple robe stood before her, his kind eyes sparkling as he grinned. His weak chin, bushy eyebrows, and receding hairline made him look like a jolly scholar. The organ music ended with a flourish, the echo of the last chord falling like an invisible, dwindling waterfall.

The priest called out to the organ player. "Thank you, Brother Timothy. That was ferociously grand. Can we have a wee break?"

Brother Timothy made a huffy snort. It took everything for Pamela not to laugh. The sounds of footsteps on a staircase followed.

"How do you do?" Pamela said. "I'm Pamela Colman Smith."

"Father Vaughan," the man answered. "Delighted to show you around, if that's what you are here for."

"I've come here to ask you to exorcise a handkerchief," Pamela said, feeling her body heat up in a nervous tremor. "Or maybe it just needs purification. Perhaps you could help?"

"Exorcism? For what?" Father Vaughn asked, his eyes no longer sparkling.

As she reached for the handkerchief, it moved in her hand as though it were shirking from her touch. She held out the cloth to him.

"I think I trapped a spirit that was following me in here."

It was his turn to try to hide a smile.

"Purification for a handkerchief?" Father Vaughan asked. "As Catholics, we don't believe in prayer cloths, per se, but as James in the Bible recommends, we sometimes anoint cloth with oil for those praying for an ill Christian."

Pamela gulped. "Whatever you could perform to help me, I would be most appreciative, Father."

He eyed her and motioned her to walk. "If you felt moved to make an offering at the Lady Altar for bothersome household items, I'm sure it would be fine."

"The Lady Altar purifies things?"

"Oh yes, you'll see," Father Vaughn said, motioning for Pamela to follow him across the aisle. "It's a small-scale reproduction of an altar of Notre Dame des Victoires. Perfect for prayers for small pets, household objects, and broken hearts."

"I see," Pamela said, trying to keep up with him, and trying to keep her heart from sinking. He wasn't taking her seriously at all. Her feet still vibrated from the organ music. She shook one foot as she walked to get the feeling back. Father Vaughan motioned to the windows lining the stone walls as they passed.

"The four Evangelists, created by Hardman, Woodruffe, and Lavers of Birmingham. Not bad, are they?" he asked, as he hurried ahead of her.

Pamela finally caught up with him. "Father, but how did all this artwork come to be here?"

Father Vaughan stopped and looked at her with a wry smile. "You know those hansom cabs everyone takes to get around? Holy Name Church was fortunate with its first investor, founder of the cab, Mr. Joseph Aloysius Hansom. So, remember that the next time you take a hansom cab somewhere."

Father Vaughan continued ahead of Pamela, pointing out more statues and altars. The buzzing in her feet became stronger. Did her toes become numb from the organist playing "Dies irae"? She put a hand on the floor—no, it was the stones themselves—they were chattering away. She sometimes had these sensations when she consulted with Waite while they were working on the design for a tarot card. But with him, she felt a clicking in her head. Around Uncle Brammie, at times she felt a whirr around her, like the wings of a hummingbird, braising her cheeks. But this vibration from the floor was definitely agitation from the stones.

She almost called out to the priest as he scurried down the aisle to ask if he felt the tremor, but perhaps he was just accustomed to organ music disturbing the foundation here. Midstride, she was immersed in the red and blue rays from stained glass windows above her. She squinted upward to follow the midair path, and a painted path appeared before her. The rays undulated like errant fairies on the floor revealing a treasure map. She passed a small side altar featuring a saint's relic, a fingernail, from what she could tell. But she circled back. On the wall above the glass case hung a display—an axe, a ring, and a sword. They definitely weren't Christian. Not Celtic or Druid. Viking.

Pamela pointed to them and called out. "Father Vaughn, wait! Aren't these from the Vikings? Is this church built on Vikings' ground?"

"Viking burial grounds are six blocks from us," Father Vaughan said, coming back and planting himself before her. "On Grosvenor Street, there lies the supposed home of the spirits of the Vikings. It's called Nico Ditch, from AD 870."

"Nico Ditch!" Pamela exclaimed. "At the theatre, the wardrobe mistress told me about the slaves, the thralls that still live in the ditch. She said the spirits from the ditch have appeared in churches here."

Father Vaughan's eyes grew solemn. "It has happened that some rituals have been required to sanctify environments where the spirits have tried to settle. We pray for the souls of those who believe in the spirits of Nico Ditch." He stopped in front of the small altar tucked away into a recess, where a small coin box stood before a stand filled with sand anchoring votive candles. The altar's white marble sparkled with veins of dappled silver, picking up the silver in the candelabra set on its surface. Pamela's fingers traced the river of undulating glimmers in the marble. From above, a portrait of the Virgin dressed in a blue robe gazed down at her.

Pamela felt for the handkerchief. It quivered in her hand. Now was the time to banish the afrit.

Father Vaughn reached behind the candelabra and brought out a small bottle of oil. He uncorked it and let three small drops pour into his palm, then rubbed his hands together. He signaled to Pamela for the handkerchief, and she handed it to him. He turned back to the Virgin's portrait, lifted the cloth up, and recited a brief Latin prayer. When he was finished, he kissed it three times and gave it back to her.

A man in a brown robe appeared at the door leading up to the organ loft and beckoned Father Vaughan.

He turned to her and whispered, "Just a moment, my dear. Brother Timothy needs a consultation." He hurried off to the brother, and the two of them began a lengthy, whispered conversation.

The handkerchief in her hand felt limp and lifeless. This Lady Altar was the perfect spot to evict the afrit. Now was the time to pay for the ritual. Lighting candles in churches was one of her favorite rites. She removed some coins from her change purse and plunked them into the metal collection box before the altar. The glass votives holding the unlit candles waited. She took one of the long matches and struck it against the slate board next to the altar. The intoxicating smell of sulfur filled her nose. The sputtering flame lit the wick, which, once ablaze, swayed with rays of amber. When she performed a Golden Dawn ritual, it was the same. You light a candle and chant a spell. Prayers, chants, spells—they all help make amends with whatever was bothering you. What chant should she use?

She fumbled to put her handkerchief back in her purse for safekeeping. Out of the corner of her eye, she caught a movement scuttling across the wall. The painting—there was something in it thrashing. She drew nearer. It was a violent scene—souls trying to escape a terrible place. The blur of a single hand reached out before Pamela's face, and she yelped. The hand waved desperately about trying to save figures from the monsters and flying creatures that tormented them.

She leaned near the canvas, but as she came closer, the vibration from the floor started up again. The shaking underneath her feet became so violent that it knocked her off balance. She reached out for a nearby marble pillar to steady herself. When she righted herself, she saw it: the distressed souls in the painting had come alive. The tortured figures were trying to escape the demons by fleeing the canvas, but as they crawled onto the stone walls, the grotesque mob of torturers followed them. Pamela clung to the pillar as monsters and demons devoured the writhing souls trying to escape. The sounds of the tormented souls screaming in pain and agony escalated as they fended off the horrible creatures as best they could.

"Father Vaughn!" she cried out, holding on to the nearest pillar.

The monsters began to grow, until they were at least forty feet tall, crowding out one another. The vibration under her feet grew so intense that she wrapped both arms around the pillar to anchor herself. The top of the pillar began peeling away from the vaulted ceiling and splitting in two. The two halves darkened, and as the ends sped down toward her they turned into dragons. Each one flipped and dove in swooping arcs, coiling around Pamela as they descended.

"Help!" she cried out. "Help! It's alive and—"

Pamela's coin purse fell out of her coat onto the floor as dragon heads darted around her. Their fiery exhalations crystalized into stone, creating a tomb above and over her. Darkness. She felt her way along the walls. She was encased in a tunnellike passageway.

Breathe. Breathe. This is just a bad dream. Creep. Crawl. Stand. Walk. Stumbling along in the dark, she no longer felt her legs. One foot stepped out into a void of blackness. She pitched forward and fell headfirst into darkness.

PART II

Missing

CHAPTER TEN

The Emperor Recruits

"No Foolin', We're Not Deep Enough!"

Bram chuckled at the headline as he snapped open the pages of the *Dublin Evening Mail* and settled into his chair, enjoying the luxury of breakfasting at the Midland Hotel. A born Dubliner, he wasn't surprised to read about a current scandal over missing funds invested in Dublin Bay, but the fact that this article was front-page news here in Manchester surprised him. English investors were enraged to learn that the money they invested in the dredging of Dublin Bay to accommodate Queen Victoria's oversize royal yacht had somehow vanished. Political graft and corruption, Bram observed, hadn't changed in the twenty years since he'd left Ireland. He skipped to the theatre section to see which moonlighting student had taken over his old job as reviewer.

"More coffee, sir?" The black-haired waiter was at his table, holding a fresh pot. The young man's hard *r* in "sir" gave him away: he was hardly a "Jackeen," a self-assertive blowhard, according the English. There was something more conciliatory in the young man's bearing.

"Your people from Dublin?" Bram asked, letting his own accent become more pronounced. Even Bram's illustrious Irish friends, Oscar Wilde and Bernard Shaw, had tried to hide their own Dublin accents, but he could always spot one.

"Kilbarrack, right outside Dublin Bay," the young man answered.

He looked the boy over, noting the red scarf peeking out of his vest. Was he one of the gang members he had heard about at the theatre? The head of wardrobe had warned cast members not to walk alone on the streets because of thieving gangs, who were more stickup hoodlums more than pickpocket artists. When he had gone up into the bowels of the theatre to ask her what they should look for, she was belligerent.

"Typical gang look," she had snapped at him as she sewed. "Double-cut hair, with sides all bare and the top a mop, wearing metal shoes, caps with razors, red scarves. The usual look, you know. Unless they don't have gangs in London."

Bram didn't know how to answer her. He hadn't noticed how gangs in London dressed. This waiter, with his oval face, dark eyelashes, and slim build, didn't look like a gang member.

"Your family at home work the docks?" Bram asked.

"They work the docks, sir, when they can," the boy answered.

Bram put down his paper and motioned for him to pour more coffee. Now that he had been temporarily hired back to his old position as tour manager by Henry last night, he felt at leisure to breakfast a little longer, as he wasn't due at the theatre for another hour. "I know the harbor well. My father worked all his life as a clerk at Dublin Castle."

"My da thought he'd be digging out the wharf for the queen, but that job dried up," the waiter said, shifting from one foot to another with nervous energy.

"Sorry to hear that," Bram said. "What's your name?"

"Toby Dolan, sir," the boy said, stilling himself.

"Short for Tobin?" Bram asked. Toby nodded. "I'm Mr.

Stoker, and I'm thinking your parents went about naming their children in some sort of alphabetical order. You have older siblings, am I right?"

"Eleven boys and two girls, sir," Toby answered.

Bram nodded his head. Catholics. How lucky he and his four brothers were to have parents who had made sure they didn't have to dig ditches nor subscribe to the Catholic ideology of procreation. He reached into his pocket and took out a crown and placed it on the table. Toby froze in place. Bram nudged it closer to him. It was the recently minted "Widow Head," featuring the elderly Queen Victoria decked out in her mourning tiara, necklace, and earrings. It was more than a week's salary for someone like Toby.

"Take it," Bram said. "It will be a down payment for future coffee service and your company."

Toby swiftly pocketed the coin and, standing closer to Bram, used the serviette draped over his arm to brush away imaginary crumbs off the table.

"Thank you, sir," Toby said quietly. "I can tell you that this will help my family."

"Are all eleven of your brothers currently at home?" Bram asked.

"Yes, my ma is desperate to keep them from signing up to fight in the Boer War."

"What's this red scarf all about?" Bram asked quietly, motioning to the red scarf now spilling out of the boy's vest.

"It's a token from a friend," he said, quickly stuffing it out of sight.

Bram remembered a chant his own brothers had taught him: "Queen, return to your own land; you will find no more Irishmen ready to wear the red shame of your livery."

"And these sorts of tokens help to negotiate your way around the streets here, I would venture," Bram said.

Toby's eyes darted around the room. Bram noticed the head waiter glaring at them.

"I might need to hire some rough types to fill out the Royal Manchester Theatre stage," Bram said. "They would work as extras during a fight scene. It's decent pay. Maybe as ringleader, you might know some people?"

Toby choked back a laugh. Softly he said, "Mr. Stoker, I'm more of a ring wrangler than leader, if truth be told."

"Even better that you try to keep your group from fighting than fighting for them," Bram said. "Which group is this?"

The boy leaned over Bram's shoulder and poured another dribble of coffee, mouthing, "Grey Mares Gang."

As the head waiter neared their table, Bram said loudly, "Well, thank you, Mr. Dolan, for your directions. I'll be bringing more guests to the hotel, and we'll be sure to ask for you if we have any more questions."

After the head waiter and his fish eye had passed, Toby made a short bow.

"Thank you, Mr. Stoker," he said.

"Until we meet again, Toby," Bram said, returning to his paper.

He perused the pages, looking for the article about the Lyceum Theatre tour's opening night. *Ah, there it is. Good, now the great man will have the press he needs to show the syndicate that he can still sell tickets.* Just below the piece on the Lyceum was a yearly roundup of Ireland's best theatre productions—one of the best being a *Robinson Crusoe* staged as a comedy pantomime. *God save me from having to review something like that again.*

Bram always tried to find copies of the *Dublin Evening Mail*, no matter where he was, whether on tour in America or managing the Lyceum in London. In the States, he was lucky enough to get this newspaper weekly. Writing theatre reviews for the paper all those years ago served as his passport out of Ireland and spared him from clerking at Dublin Castle, like his father before him.

Twenty years ago, he had taken on the volunteer post as theatre reviewer and raved about Henry Irving in a touring production of *Hamlet*. This led to a private dinner with the actor and an offer to come and work for the Lyceum. Bram quit his job, married Florence, and moved to London, all within two weeks. But even now, despite all the time that had passed, he still liked to see how the city of his birth was faring. Thanks to Manchester's large Dubliner population, he'd been able to get his hands on a paper every morning this week.

Beneath the paper's Lyceum Tour article was a bigger half-page ad for a touring circus act.

Little Beda, The Thinking Horse, and her trainer, Pablo. This upcoming attraction is said to be the best horse show of 1899 in all of the British Empire.

If only he, Pamela, and Satish Monroe could go to Dublin to see this show! The night he'd spent at Pablo's was one of the most enjoyable evenings he'd had in years. No worries about being asked if so-and-so could be interviewed for a possible Lyceum job, no whispers of a newspaper man needing a payout because of the offstage relationship between Ellen and Henry, no interruptions because Henry Irving just happened to walk in. In London, Bram still had his men's clubs for amusement, but his wife was demanding more often that they appear in society together, which usually meant late hours socializing after the Lyceum Theatre's curtain rang down. And then there were Bram's recent attempts to win his adolescent son's approval, which had been dismissed with disdain.

Bram drank the last of the coffee, now lukewarm. The dregs clung to his mustache. He wiped them off. "The dregs"—that would be one way to describe this tour to Manchester. From the very first day of their trip here, when "666" appeared on the train window, Bram knew that this tour would be difficult. That apparition—or afrit, as Ahmed called it—was more childish prank than magical spell. But it was impressive. If Aleister conjured it to scare Pamela from creating her tarot deck, it worked.

She hadn't shown Bram any new designs for tarot cards lately. Would her cards eventually be popular? Lucrative? Would they have the sort of renown he wanted for his book? She had read his unpublished novel, *The Un-Dead*, and proclaimed that someday he would be "Emperor of the Undead." But what were the chances of success for an unpublished tarot deck and a horror novel? If there were publishers outside of the Golden Dawn for Pamela's tarot cards, perhaps his novel would sell as well.

Even now, the only successful commodity he had ever worked with—Sir Henry's love child, the Lyceum Theatre—was at the mercy of the syndicate, a new consortium of greedy investors who were trying to suck every last bit of profit from the Lyceum's business. It was likely Aleister would try to do the same with Pamela's cards.

He walked out of the hotel restaurant to Peter Street—a good thing that the theatre was conveniently down the block. Seeing the Theatre Royal Manchester come into view, Bram picked up his step. Behind the backs of the syndicate, he and Henry were to meet to discuss Pamela's new poster for *The Merchant of Venice*. Henry said he would reinstate him as full-time general director and would pay for Bram's salary out of his own pocket. Syndicate be damned! How pleasant it would be to approve Pamela's poster, as first piece of business as the newly reinstalled general director of the Lyceum Theatre.

As Bram threw open the stage door, a loud sequence of drums deafened him. Perusing the sign-in sheet near the door, he saw that the majority of the cast and crew had checked in, but Pamela's name had no mark next to it.

"Lovejoy! Where are you at, man?" he bellowed.

The drums ceased. Bram hurried to the stage and saw Lovejoy's silver-haired head pop up from the orchestra pit, baton in hand. He was at it again, sneaking in a rehearsal with the musicians, even though he was only the stage manager. Tonight's performance of *The Bells* had a dramatic score and proliferation of drums. The play should have been called *The Drums* instead of *The Bells*.

"Mr. Stoker," Lovejoy said. "Getting the drums right until the conductor arrives."

"Where's Miss Smith? Have you seen her today?"

"No, sir. She hasn't come in yet."

Not a good sign. Pamela was late for all sorts of appointments but never for meetings involving her artwork.

"Find me the moment you see her or hear from her."

In the old days, she would have stalked him from the moment he entered the building if there was a chance a piece of her artwork would be used. Something was wrong.

Bram bolted for the stairs, racing up to her shared dressing room on the fourth floor. He swung open the door to a room full of women. The heavyset head of wardrobe, the one who warned the cast about the gangs, looked up at him from her list. Damnation! What was her name? Five other local women stopped sorting out piles of freshly laundered costumes and stared at him.

"Ah, madame," Bram addressed the leader, "so sorry—your name again?"

"Of course the front-of-house don't remember my name," the woman said, crossing her arms.

Bram went up to her and offered his hand. She begrudgingly gave him hers, and he kissed it. "My apologies. May I introduce myself," Bram said. "I'm Mr. Stoker. May I ask your name?"

The other laundresses tittered. She silenced them with a look that would have etched glass. "It's Mrs. Sarah Corely," she answered, keeping her steely gray eyes trained on Bram.

"Well, Mrs. Corely, I want to thank you for advising the cast on watching themselves. Speaking of that, I was wondering if you knew the whereabouts of one of our members, a Miss Smith? Do you know if she has come in yet? She's not on the sign-in list."

The formidably sized woman stood and patted his arm. "Not seen here yet, but there's plenty of time left till half hour, Mr. Stoker. She's probably still visiting the church."

"How do you know that?" Bram asked.

"She asked my husband to take her there in his motorcar, but he had a booking this morning. Last week, he drove her out to Didsbury."

On the vanity table were Pamela's artist supplies. An open sketchbook revealed a drawing of himself as an emperor, a scepter in his right hand, a globe in his left. Bram's heart tugged. Yes, she would see him as an emperor who represented rules and regulations, not a richly dressed monarch. Ever since he had hired her to work at the Lyceum, he had been her taskmaster, not her mentor.

As he gazed at the drawing of the emperor, the globe on the page turned into the snow globe. It was exactly like the one he had given her one Christmas. Bram blinked. The snow swirled inside it and then the globe fell from the emperor's hand. He glanced at the laundresses, who'd gone back to sewing and gossiping, not seeing the magic on the page. Staring at the sketch, he watched the globe moving across the page. The orb rolled off the page, onto the floor, and out the door. A chill went through him. Pamela trusted him enough to send him magical sign that the world had gone sideways.

"How far away is this church that Miss Smith went to?" Bram asked, his heart beating faster.

"Holy Name. It's about a mile away," Mrs. Corely replied.

What on earth was she doing that far away right before the show?

"Is your husband here at the theatre with his car now?" Bram asked.

"Yes."

"Get him to bring it around to the front right away," Bram said, moving quickly to the door.

He could hear the laundress lumber down the back stairs to the garage entrance while he ran to the lobby. He opened the door and saw Ellen and Sir Henry talking to each other, the dogs next to them. As he approached them, the phone inside the box office rang. The gangly ticket taker opened the door and yelled, "Excuse, Mr. Irving, there's a phone call for you. Says it's urgent."

Henry went inside the office and picked up the phone. Bram went up to Ellen and took her hand.

"Pa," Bram said to Ellen, seeing her eyes crinkle at his nickname for her. "You haven't seen Pamela today, have you?"

"No! What's wrong?" Ellen cried. "What's happened to her?"

Henry quickly came out to join them, shaking his head. "That was Miss Florence Farr. She's in Liverpool but will be on her way here. She says she had some sort of psychic message this morning indicating that Pamela was in danger but that she was in no position to explain more until she arrives."

"I knew it!" Bram said.

"You knew Miss Farr had received a psychic message?" Henry growled, his voice lowering as it did when he was peeved.

"I only now realized when Pamela hadn't signed in today that something was wrong," Bram answered. Was Henry upset over Pamela's disappearance or her being late for the show? He almost brought up the snow globe drawing coming to life, but he checked himself. He didn't need to be seen as a loon.

A man in a chauffeur's uniform opened the front door and shouted through to the lobby, "Car here for Mr. Stoker." He dashed back out to the car idling on the street.

Bram put on his hat, and Ellen clung to his arm.

"There, there," Bram said to her, "I'm sure we got the message in time."

Henry gave Bram "the look," his head tilted to one side, his eyes boring into Bram's as though he were the most dimwitted person alive. "Get back here before the six thirty 'beginners' call."

Mrs. Corely came in from the street, still shouting toward the automobile idling in front of the theatre. "You bring 'em all here quick, you hear me, Nick?"

Henry patted a sniffling Ellen on the back. "Pamela's simply looking at the stained glass. Remember all the times on tour when we lost her to statues, windows, and altars?"

"Oh, my husband said she didn't want to look at art," Mrs. Corely said as she came up behind them, nearly making Bram jump out of his skin.

The other laundresses from upstairs poured into the lobby and joined them, noisily clucking like hens.

"Oh, that Miss Smith, we love her so," one said. "What a pity if she's gone missing to the gangs."

"Oh, now, she came from Manchester as a child," another said. "She knows how to handle herself on the streets."

"Told me she wanted to go and find that ancient route," a third said.

"Excuse me, madame, what ancient route?" Henry asked.

"Oh, sir," Mrs. Corely interrupted, "she was just asking us about Nico Ditch. Wanted to know if there were any churches here connected to the ditch."

"Good woman, what and where is Nico Ditch?" Bram asked Mrs. Corely.

"Ditch built by the long-ago people in Manchester to keep the thralls out," she answered, almost humming with delight at being the center of attention.

Bram's heart sank. If Aleister was tracking her with an afrit, this was not a good sign. Pamela could be trying to find a church to to expel the tagalong spirit. From his studies with the Golden Dawn, he knew ditches were notorious thresholds for demon activity. Perhaps she was trying to reroute it through a church to a ditch.

"Thralls?" Ellen asked.

"The slaves the Vikings took," the laundress said, her chin jutting out. "I though you theatre people would know the history here at least. The thrall slaves—the ones who, once freed, came back here to kidnap locals and hold them for ransom for the Vikings. They especially dislike theatre people poking about."

"Poking about where?" Bram asked, trying to breathe evenly.

"The magical underground pathways from churches to Nico Ditch," Mrs. Corely answered, and the other laundry women nodded their heads. "She must be at Holy Name; it's the largest church here."

"What sort of ransom do the thralls demand?" Henry asked.

"Magic for magic," Mrs. Corely replied.

Bram ran up the center aisle of Holy Name Church, calling, "Pamela! Pixie? Where are you?"

Two men, one wearing a brown robe, emerged from a room to the side of the pulpit.

The man in the robe hurried forward. He almost tripped on the gray flagstone in front of a small altar, clutching the handrail at the last second.

Bram held out a hand to steady him and draw him up. That's when he saw it. The man was holding Pamela's purse, a one-of-a-kind cloth bag with an embroidered replica of the Lyceum Theatre stitched near the top.

"Where is she?" Bram cried. "What's happened to her?"

CHAPTER ELEVEN

Turret Visitations

Pamela opened her eyes, her back cold and stiff from lying on a stone floor. At her back, the cold bricks' icy reach pierced through the shawl around her. She clenched her hands to warm them, then stood, but there was nothing to guard against the freezing floor numbing her feet through the soles of her shoes. She pounded against the wall of dank bricks. Perhaps one of them would break free.

Disoriented, she looked around. Her eyes fell on the curved walls of her cell. There it was: she was in a tower, an ancient turret, not a typical prison, like the one she was kept in overnight with the suffragettes in London. The room was the size of a linen closet, the only escape a large wooden door with a metal slot at its base. Thin slices of light pierced through the one cross-shaped window open to the outdoors. Slivers of light peeped in through breaks in the mortar between the silver stones as a frigid breeze moaned. Her breathing came to her in gasps, followed by a coughing spell.

The slightest ticking pulsed on her heart. Her pocket watch! Twisting it, she read the clock dial: six thirty. *I should be signing the call sheet now*. Where did the time go from when she fell down the vault in the church? She rewound her watch and then reached into her skirt pocket for a handkerchief.

The handkerchief was soft and warm. A memory of Ahmed tenderly holding up his handkerchief flooded her.

"Are you picking up messages from your hanky?" Pamela had teased.

"When you have a handkerchief blessed with magic, you'll know," Ahmed had answered.

She cringed at the thought of teasing him about his hanky. Lightheaded, she brought the cloth up to her face to fight off dizziness. Scents of frankincense, beeswax, and lilies comforted her. Church smells from Holy Name Church. She braced herself against the window to look outside; a close stone wall was all she could see. She took in the round stone room, half the size of her Midland Hotel room. But it was nothing like a hotel room, more like a stone prison. Waves of panic engorged her throat. Blurry yellow shapes drifted down the hazy rays.

Outside the window, the last slanting lines of sunshine shifted. December at six thirty—it should have been dark. Fuzzy shapes clung to the beams of weak light. At very top of one beam, there seemed to be a sea creature floating, clinging to the highest reach of the thread of light. Was it clinging to sunlight or another sort of light? How could there be a sea creature floating in the air? Was there something wrong with her eyes?

She had once asked her guardian in Jamaica, Miss Jones, to check for monsters in her eyes, as sometimes, looking out to sea or across the horizon at a ship, she thought she saw one. Miss Jones had told her there are monsters in and around everyone, but they only stay if you feed them.

Pamela crouched to get a better look at the monster, but the light disappeared. Was it a sign? Her last memory was the image of the gray flagstone on Holy Names' floor. Was she feeding a monster there unknowingly? Had she fallen in the church? Was she unconscious and in a coma?

She bent and yelled through the flap in the door. "Help!" An excruciating pain barreled down her throat, cutting her words off.

She gulped as a sweet scent of violet wafted over her, the scent of her childhood friend, Maud. The pain down her windpipe lessened as she breathed in its delicate aroma.

Bram, Ellen, Ahmed? Where were they?

"Fly!"

It was Maud's voice!

The light from outside streamed in the window, almost blinding her. She turned away from it as a small black form in the center of the cell splayed out. Squiggles of eye-monsters swooped before her. Swirling lines with little serifs turned black. Letters too disorganized to read. The letters transformed into little ghostly hands all around her, holding her as though she were a balloon about to drift up and away. The hands belonged to a motley crew of spirits who came into view, jabbing and poking one another. Their tunics were ragged, their long hair matted, and their faces dirty. The language they spoke to one another was harsh and unintelligible.

"A prisoner of your dreams, are you?" It was the voice of Aleister: part university, part Bohemian affectation, all slurry vowels and clipped consonants.

Pamela tried to shake off the elfish ghouls, who pinched and twisted her arms and legs.

"Magic man!" one with a bulbous nose shouted. "She's here. She's enthralled. Come and get her and give us our reward!"

"She's worth very little magic," Aleister's voice purred.

"She's worth what you promised, or she'll be back at that church in a heartbeat," the ghoul said.

Her captors tittered and sniggered, their echoes swirling around Pamela's head.

"Aleister, is that you? You let me out of here!" Pamela shouted.

"All right, thralls, here's your payment," Aleister said.

A tinkling sound rang out. The creatures stood and lifted up their faces and hands as though being bathed in a beatific rain of sparkling coins. They evaporated all together.

The sound of someone puffing on a pipe filled the air.

"Here's our deal, Miss Smith," Aleister said. "Give up the tarot-deck drawings. I'll let you keep your first four cards for party tricks, since you've already drawn them, but enough is enough."

Pamela felt a kick in her stomach. He must have wanted the power of the deck very badly if he was willing to transport her here and hold her captive.

"Why do you want my tarot cards?" Pamela demanded.

"You're corrupting the source," Aleister snapped. "That energy belongs only to more experienced magicians."

The blood in her veins pounded. More experienced magicians be damned!

"I'm not going to give up my magic," she shouted. "You have another thing coming if you imagine you can take it from me."

The handkerchief in her palm heated up, and she was able to wrap her fingers around it. She clenched it in her fist and shook it with a fury she hadn't realized she possessed.

"Oh, really, Miss Smith, it's you who have another thing coming."

Whirls of dust encircled Pamela as the cell's only light sputtered and went out.

"Things will only get worse for you and your friends if you insist on owning magic that isn't yours."

Pamela was about to protest about owning her own magic when a vise tightened around her neck. She cried out. The handkerchief went cold, and the hold around her throat disappeared as she was left choking in the dark confines of her prison cell.

In the still air of her cell, she could smell dust, incense, and iron-tinged water. A muffled voice echoed and was followed by the sounds of a clanging door off in the distance.

"Help, help! I'm here!" she shouted.

Hunger and thirst clawed at her in the darkness. She gave a little hop, lifting her arms, and flapped as fast as she could, only to fall in a heap on the dirt floor. She had flown three times: once as a child, once when confronting Aleister on a bridge, and once on Little Beda. Whatever had enabled her in the past appeared lost.

She stood and then sat. Every position was uncomfortable, but trying to sleep had been tortuous. With no blanket or cloth to cushion her, her jacket became her mattress and her skirt, her blanket. She did sleep once, a blessed relief. How long did she sleep? She checked her watch: eleven o'clock. Eleven o'clock at night, when the show came down? Or eleven o'clock the next morning with no light outside?

To keep the panic from rising in her throat, she exhaled. *Draw something*, she advised herself.

She licked her index finger, and, on the dusty wall, she drew. Tracing the lines of the lemniscate—the symbol of eternity worn by the Magician—over and over always calmed her.

When Waite had first recruited her to create the tarot cards, she'd been so excited. The chance to take on all seventy-eight cards was just the challenge she wanted: a new tarot deck. She was given an ancient sketchbook of cards from Milan, the beautiful Sola Busca deck, and would use them for inspiration for some images. Otherwise, she went to sketch at the museum with Ahmed. But first there were the required studies with the Golden Dawn she had to complete: science, math for astrology, memorization of the Tree of Life, a tedious curriculum. She might as well be back at the Pratt Institute of Art in Brooklyn.

As she continued to draw in the dust, the interlocking circles of the lemniscate became tighter and tighter.

Here she was, experiencing one of her worst fears: being shut up and enclosed. No, wait: she also had the fear of falling. Her ride on Little Beda's back had seemed to cure that, though. How many more fears were there?

The Fool card always cheered her up. Leaving the lemniscate, she began to sketch the Fool tarot card.

At the bottom right-hand side, a little white dog pranced next to a traveler, who looked up at the sky, a bundle over his shoulder. Even though this figure was the Sola Busca's Five of Cups tarot card, to Pamela is was her idea of what the Fool should look like. Waite once told her that the Fool summed her up perfectly: light-footed and extravagant, lacking discipline but full of enthusiasm.

Her Fool's muse was William Terriss, handsome "Breezy Bill," a star of the London stage. This "darling of the gallery girls" was Pamela's idea of perfection. Men wanted to be like him, and women wanted to be with him. "Breezy Bill"—the one who had saved her when she fell off the bridge, trying to reach her hat that had fallen off. He was the one who had jumped in to rescue her. Recovering on the rocks, she had asked him, "Are we alive?" and he had answered, "So alive."

But it was rumored, a week before he'd died, Terriss had confided to his men's club, the Green Room Club, "What do you think? I've had my fortune told and the woman says I will die a violent death."

And now he was dead, stabbed to death at the backstage door of Adelphi Theatre by a crazed man, the deranged Archer Prince, a thwarted actor. The murderer was now in Broadmoor Criminal Lunatic Asylum rather than prison because it was only an actor who was murdered, by another actor. It was said that he was even allowed weekend privileges of being released into the care of his brother, so he wasn't even shut up the way that Pamela was now.

Ellen said William Terriss had the most beautiful of everything, except common sense. He dove off bridges and jumped down from trees like Robin Hood. He was a fool, with all of a fool's hidden talents, who now had leapt into the unknown.

Just then, Pamela felt it: blood running through her veins. The tips of her fingers throbbed. A clicking sound came from behind her. Then she heard a voice, William's, and he commanded, "Fly!"

Light! A circle of light was glowing right in front of her. A gorgeous, golden-yellow wash began to undulate and float as a ghostly mist. Her head snapped back, and a rush of dank air brushed across her face. Now she was up in the air—no longer imprisoned in a crypt but outside, several stories up.

For a few moments she couldn't get her bearings. A form began to take shape in front of her. It was a spire of a church, with four heads at the base of the buttressed pinnacle. She was floating in front of the stone face of a beautiful young man, with long, streaming hair. Below, his trunk was adorned in a floral tunic. The face was so familiar.

The granite face moved. The eyebrows creased, creating a quizzical, almost comical expression. He cocked his head sideways and laughed, revealing his identity.

"William! My Fool!"

Blinking his stone eyes, he replied, "You've troubled the pools of magic, girl, haven't you?"

She reached out to embrace his torso, which anchored him to the roof, but as she tried to go toward him, the wind pushed her away. She had managed to maintain a wobbly position almost within reach of William.

"What pools?" Pamela asked.

"Do you not think magic has a source?" William asked, his eyebrows still knitted together.

"Aleister's done this, hasn't he?" Pamela asked. "Kidnapped me and poisoned my mind?"

"Why would he feed you if he wanted you dead?" William asked.

Pamela stopped treading air. “For ransom?”

William’s head tilted. “Don’t you see? You have magic in your cards that will summon many people. His heart doesn’t know how to do that.”

She tried one last time to reach the spire where William docked. “I don’t know how to summon anyone!”

With a shift in the air, she fell in the vortex of wind that had been supporting her. Over and over she tumbled. Then blackness.

CHAPTER TWELVE

A Mummy's Three Sexes

Descending Thorton Manor's main staircase, Ahmed was startled by the sight of Florence in the front hall. She was swaddled from head to foot with a gauzy fabric; a maid was trying to arrange material away from her mouth. It was uncanny how much Florence looked like his wife and cousins in Cairo when they wore their traveling clothes.

"Good morning, Mr. Kamal," Florence said as he neared.

"Miss Farr," Ahmed said, trying to remember if she was scheduled to give harp lessons at Sunlight Village today. "I see you are dressed for travel."

"Dressed more as beekeeper than intrepid explorer, but the dust on the roads ruined my other clothes."

The scent of her rosewater perfume wafted over him. "Even though bees would enjoy your keeping, exploring is much more your cup of tea, I think."

The maid scuttled away, and Florence whispered, "Speaking of exploring, Mr. Kamal, the maid overheard your call to prayer and wanted to know if there was a flying carpet in your room, which she heard about from the Arabian Nights stories."

"In a way, there was," Ahmed answered.

She nodded her head, and when she didn't smirk or raise her eyebrows, he felt relief.

He rarely felt comfortable acknowledging his faith with his English acquaintances, much less joking about it. Trying to find places to pray five times a day was always a delicate task, whether he was at work or a guest in someone's home.

He was about to ask if she thought his prayers had bothered the Levers when Florence rustled about in her coat pocket. She handed him a packet of letters.

"Here are several letters of introduction for you," she said. "Lord Compton and Mr. Lever have asked the donors of the Northampton Museum to help you retrieve Sekhemka. Mr. Dhunjibhoy Bomanji will be a reference, and his daughter, Mehroo, will also vouch for you. These other letters are from Mrs. Lever's friends, who understand your desire to get your statue back. I've been called back to London by Miss Horniman, and Mr. Lever needs his car in London, so I have first-class transport."

"I am sorry you are leaving our company so soon," Ahmed said, taking the missives. "All is well in London?"

"Miss Horniman has some Golden Dawn business that needs my immediate attention. And it will be good to get back to the museum and my communion with Mutemmenu."

Ahmed stared down at the floor and sighed. Ah, these deluded English with their obsession with mummies.

"What? You doubt my connection with her? I have had direct communication with her. We sing court songs together!"

"Miss Farr, I have no doubt you feel you have a connection with that coffin—"

"Mr. Kamal, I have more than a connection with Mutemmenu. She is my Ka."

His blood heated up and his heart beat faster. It would do no good to lose his temper.

"Miss Farr, there is no proof that the mummy casket holds the remains of a court musician."

"There certainly is! I had communion with her!" Florence insisted, batting away the netting falling over her eyes.

"Well, if you did have communion with someone, it was not with Mutemmenu," Ahmed said as gently as his temper allowed. "There is no proof of that, and had you truly studied Egyptian history you would know it's very unlikely."

"How dare you, Mr. Kamal! I am an expert Egyptologist and leader of the London Chapter of the Golden Dawn," Florence said, swatting away the netting on her hat from her face.

A different scent stung his nostrils, an acrid waft of incense. Ahmed glanced around the entryway to see if anything might be lit nearby, a cigar, a cigarette, but there was nothing. The last thing he needed here was a warning sign from a spirit back home.

"I give lectures on this very subject and know what I have experienced sitting next to this mummy," Florence said, struggling comically to keep the netting from getting in her mouth. "As an authority in the only organized English group that studies magic and spirits, I expect a little more respect from you. I am the Praemonstratrix of the Golden Dawn, the educator in tarot education, spells, and Enochian magic."

"Miss Farr, you may have sat next to this mummy and sung to it, and it may have sung back to you, but no one in the Old Kingdom had a Ka, except for the pharaoh. The pharaohs alone are the chosen ones to manifest a person's vital energy. It just does not happen with ordinary people."

She flinched at his final words. "Mr. Kamal, good-bye. I doubt our paths will cross again."

Turning, she swept down the hallway and out the door, without a glance backward.

Ahmed instantly regretted talking to her about the dead in this public area. Her practice was a source of great pride to her, no matter how misguided.

The household staff, which seemed to spring out from under the staircase, made their way out to the car bearing Florence's bags. With a heavy heart, Ahmed made his way back up the staircase. A whoosh of satin skirts revealed the diminutive Mrs. Lever descending with a spritely step.

When she landed on the foyer, she came to him, her head barely even with his shoulder. She cocked her head. "Oh, Mr. Kamal, how disappointing for Miss Farr! All that singing and chanting for something that wasn't even a Ka. What is a Ka, exactly?" she asked, slipping her arm through his and leading him down the stairs.

Through the open front doorway, they heard the departing touring motor car spray gravel. For a split second, Ahmed was seized with an impulse to chase after the car like a dog and ask to accompany Miss Farr back to London.

He took a breath. That would be ridiculous. This was a woman, after all, who believed that her Golden Dawn magic enabled her to skry with others, invisibly connecting with them on an astral plane. Ahmed knew spirits only came when they received warnings or biddings from the gods. Like the afrit that threatened Pamela on the train to Manchester, they were in service to a higher power. Like the creature that lived in his handkerchief.

"Mr. Kamal?" Mrs. Lever said, interrupting his thoughts as they turned back from the departing car. "You will miss our guest?"

"Mrs. Lever," he replied. "I would be glad to talk to you about Ka."

"Over breakfast, then?" she answered, pulling him along. "I asked Cook to make more of that green dish you liked. And of course, excellent Turkish coffee is on the menu."

As Ahmed followed his hostess, the sharp scent returned. Looking down, he saw a hazy strand of smoke snaking alongside him; it streamed from his vest. He passed his hand through it, and it dissipated. By the time they reached the dining room, there was no sign of it. Did it return to his mummy handkerchief?

Whatever was living in there didn't feel ominous—more like an annoying cat who is stalking your steps.

Mrs. Lever explained that her husband was absent: he had obligations at the village with the two Indian houseguests. But soon her son and Lord Compton appeared, and after they had helped themselves to the buffet, all sat down at the enormous table. A timorous maid set small cups of coffee at each place. Mrs. Lever's promise of excellent Turkish coffee was an overreach. The beans were decently prepared, but coffee grounds floated to the top of the cup, and a coarse sugar film coated the bottom.

"Now, Mr. Kamal," Lord Compton began, "let me tell you of my time saving antiquities during our excavations in Egypt. Thanks to the Continental Tour tradition, when most young men return to England with enough artifacts to fill a curiosity cabinet, I learned to pick only the choice morsels to rescue."

Most of these tours were acts of downright pillaging; the tourists were stealing treasured artifacts from poverty-stricken locals. Ahmed had an impulse to ask, "What morsels did you pick up?" but he remembered the strict orders from his Egyptian boss not to ruffle the feathers of any potential English sponsors who might underwrite future Cairo museum excavations.

William Jr. ducked his head as he asked, "Why don't you believe Miss Farr can channel the lady mummy in the museum?"

Had everyone in the household heard the conversation with Florence in the foyer?

Lord Compton smiled. "I would be interested in your point of view on that topic, Mr. Kamal." He heartily sipped from his cup then, smacking his lips, and said, "Now, there's a cup of coffee!"

It took everything for Ahmed not to answer, *It certainly is here in England, not so much in my country*.

Lord Compton and Mrs. Lever were trying to make him feel at home, even if they had no idea what his home life was like. For one moment he was homesick for the clamor of his children.

At most meals, they would climb or totter over to him, his wife halfheartedly admonishing them to leave him in peace. He took a deep breath and looked at William.

"From the signs on Mutemmenu's coffin, we were able to establish that she was a lady who lived in Thebes, attending the college of the God Amen-Ra," Ahmed said. "I determined that she was a musician, a chantress of Amun, from the ninth or tenth dynasty."

Lord Compton half closed his dark eyes and asked, "And you deduced this from what studies?"

Because I read and write five languages you have never heard of—this almost rolled off Ahmed's tongue. So much for making him feel at home.

"As a senior staff member of the Supreme Council of Antiquities for the Egyptian Museum in Cairo, I know all the true symbols of Egyptian writing," Ahmed said, trying to slow his pulse. "It is my life's business to understand the symbols on coffins and artifacts. And for that, I must know the Arabic, Egyptian, Coptic, Berber, and Tarifit languages. Our team here and in Cairo has been conserving and interpreting the mummies from the Valley of the Kings for many years now. The tombs found in the temple at Deir el Bahri were identified using many languages and translations."

William Jr. asked, "What is Deir el Bahri?" leaning near Ahmed with the coordination of a drunken puppy, almost knocking his plate off the table. Yes, best not to let him handle any future artifacts.

"It is a tomb originally built for an eighteenth-dynasty queen but abandoned," Ahmed said. "Three thousand years ago, after flooding and looting, the devoted priests and officials decided to take all the royal mummies they could and put them in Deir el Bahri or the tomb of Amenhotep II."

William looked at his mother. "May I show Mr. Kamal my treasure, Mother?"

Ahmed leaned back in his chair. Of course, that was why he had been asked to breakfast: more antiquity evaluations in exchange for a meal. A kindly blink from his mother cued the young boy to jump up from his chair, and he dashed up the hallway stairs.

In the corner of the room, there was the spirit again, a wavering column of fumes, twisting around a large potted palm. It must have escaped his pocket when he was distracted.

Ahmed glanced at his hostess and Lord Compton. They appeared to be preoccupied with their food. The distant shriek that echoed in the hall didn't register with them at first. That tone . . . it was far away and yet familiar. Yes, from his triumphant dig at Deir el Bahri. It was the donkey at the bottom of the pit, braying. The hapless creature had fallen through one of the vents leading to the temple room and revealed the location of the temple. But it had also released the afrits guarding the tomb, one of whom had dogged Ahmed's travels ever since. His penance for identifying and bringing the mummies to light were the constant warnings, whenever he risked betraying|his country's riches. *Keep your ancestors safe*, they seemed to be saying.

When William reappeared at Ahmed's side, the afrit shriveled to a small, undulating river of smoke hovering around the potted plant.

William presented a muslin bundle. He unwrapped it to reveal a sculpture, about two inches in height, nestled in his hand. He placed it on the table in front of them. The afrit exhaled and swirled into dust motes hanging in the air like an annoying toddler. The statue was just a common find, nothing for the spirit to become enraged over.

In a half whisper the boy said, "I think it is a king because he is holding a crook and flail—royal scepters."

Trying not to grimace at the boy's declaration, Ahmed took out his black handkerchief and picked up the statue, about the size of a large hen's egg, and turned it over. The blue figure was a mummiform of a man carved with crossed arms which held scepters, his beard and wig tightly braided. Ahmed took out his monocle and examined the artifact. He sniffed the surface to see if the patina had been recently painted. The black material of his cloth vibrated slightly, indicating it was not a spectacular find but at least an authentic one.

"You have a *shabti*, a carved stone that serves as an incarnate of a high priest from the fifth Dynasty of the Late Period," Ahmed said. "*Shabti* were made to be placed in the tomb, to be reincarnated as workers in the next life. These *shabti*, or ushabti as my children call them, were images of high priests. But you see, in this case, this is a priest holding a spindle and a hoe. This is not a king holding scepters. This is a good servant for the king."

Ahmed handed the piece back to William, whose lower lip quivered.

"So, this *shabti* is not a king but a field hand?" Mrs. Lever asked.

A snicker emanated from the last wisps of smoke in the corner. Ahmed subtly tried to wave the spirit off, but it only flattened itself against the wall. He folded his handkerchief, putting it back in his vest pocket. Once in place, he tapped it, calling the sulky smoke to dance across the room and make its way into Ahmed's pocket. Once it settled down, Ahmed took note that everyone in the room seem oblivious to the smoke that paraded by them all.

"This *shabti* could have been a priest willing to work as a field hand for the pharaoh, Mr. Lever," Ahmed said. "But Mrs. Lever, I must ask, how did your family come into possession of such a piece?"

William chimed in: "Lord Compton gave it to me." The boy awkwardly went back to his chair and sat with the *shabti* in his lap.

Lord Compton looked off, adding, "Oh, a Frenchman who owed me a great debt repaid me with this. You know how the French are. They'll sell anything."

"My first teacher and greatest advocate was a Frenchman," Ahmed said. "He had great respect for the treasures in our tombs and temples. It is because of this respect that the French and German continue to be granted licenses from the khedive to dig for antiquities."

Unlike the English, he almost added.

Lord Compton cleared his throat. "And yet, it's thanks to the resourcefulness and technology of the English teams that some of the greatest treasures have been recovered."

Ahmed felt his shirt collar tighten. Wearing English clothes instead of his tunics was always an ordeal. "'Recovered treasures,' Lord Compton?" Ahmed asked. "Stolen, it may be argued. Hence the current ban on new English digs along the Nile."

There was an awkward pause as the maid brought in fresh coffee. What he would give for a decent serving of mint tea!

Young Lever spoke up again. "But why don't you believe Miss Farr, that the lady mummy is inside the coffin?"

He was persistent, this young boy.

"I evaluated what was inside the coffin," Ahmed said. "And the hipbone of the body was identified as a man's hip."

"Why does Miss Farr think it is a woman?" William asked.

"Well, it was dressed up to look like a woman. There is swaddling and padding over the breasts and thighs."

The silence at the table was abrupt: no eating or fidgeting.

"Well, how about that!" Mrs. Lever chirped lightly.

"The mummy was a man trying to be a woman?" William asked.

Lord Compton harrumphed.

"It was probably a eunuch," Ahmed slowly said. "In ancient Thebes, there were three sexes, male, female, and eunuch."

William piped up, "It's like the Christmas pantomime! The man plays the woman's part."

"Such nonsense!" Lord Compton barked. "A mummy

eunuch? There would be no such thing. You are male or female, as God created. A eunuch is a thing, not a person."

The blue smoke from Ahmed's vest pocket rose up and swirled around his face. Blue grit engulfed his eyes. He blinked, trying to see. More braying from the donkey. A quick vision blasted through his brain. The poor creature, the donkey, was stuck within the confines of the ruins. A human voice brayed. A girl. In another ruined cell, Pamela pounded her hands against a stone wall, crying for help.

"Are you all right, Mr. Kamal?" William asked.

"Fine," Ahmed said, looking up as the airstream of blue motes mixing with black flew into his handkerchief.

Ahmed had his suitcase packed within the hour and was on the late-afternoon train. He had every intention of taking the train back to London, but when the curved ceiling of the Central Station in Manchester splayed out above him, he found himself asking the porter for his suitcase. His well-insulated valise contained a papyrus and a small statue, given to him at the last minute by William. As Ahmed checked to make sure both pieces were well wrapped, he discovered a note written in a childish hand around the *shabti*.

I hope you bring the lost priestess back to his family.

The heartbeat of the cloth against his own heart thumped. Lost family. Where on earth was Pamela? It was time to join forces with his English friend, Bram Stoker, to find her. He quickly made his way out of the train station and across the street to the Midland Hotel.

CHAPTER THIRTEEN

Pools of Magic

Aleister materialized in the dark cavern's main chamber. Getting his bearings, he took in the phallic forms of stalagmites and stalactites, poking out at slight angles from the floor and ceiling. The dank air tasted of metal and bat shit. To the left side of the wall, a torch lit the entrance to a passageway.

This passageway led to his Elbana, his rendezvous spot with the god who called himself Thoth. Would Thoth materialize today or not? Before he could recite a spell to invite the god in, he looked for the afrit that was bound to him. It was to report on how his captive was faring.

The afrit was hard to spot here in the cave, its body of blue dots blending in with the veins of malachite lining the walls. Other afrits, thralls, demons, and spirits, waiting for their masters and mistresses to arrive, rustled against the stalagmites and pillars of lava in anticipation. This chamber was a train station, a threshold of slaves waiting for their masters to command new orders.

Aleister felt the heaviness of his body pitch forward. He was now fully transported. The skyring session from his flat had been successful but regaining his sense of balance had not, and he plopped onto the stone floor. His transmit vibrations to float still tingled, but now gravity held sway. His threads of energy circled him, giving off a faint pulse.

He sat up and incanted, "Where is my god, my guide?"

The assorted spirits in the room scattered.

"Where is the one who calls me servant?"

No voice, no flame, no Thoth today. Sometimes the god did not answer. Well, at least Aleister knew that his slave spirit would be here. And he needed it for his next phase of taking over the Golden Dawn tarot project. But now, where was it? Aleister had conjured the spirit a week ago through a magical spell and knew he had limited time to bid the spirit to obey.

Cursing the absence of both god and servant, Aleister stood. He took the torch from the wall and walked along to the passageway leading to the sacred pools. "Where are you, damn spirit?" Aleister bellowed at the ghostly forms quivering behind rocks. "We have a god to attend!"

Wispy fumes in the shape of question marks floated toward him, but he batted them away. *Playing dumb, all of them!* Afrits weren't known for their honesty or ability to stay focused on a task, but they did know how to distract an assigned target. And Pamela's concentration was to be the prey while she was in the captivity that Aleister had arranged.

Aleister whistled sharply, and the piercing sound brought the afrit, shaped in the form of a half devil, half goat, more satyr than monster, and it bowed in submission at his feet. "You'll come when you're called, or you'll answer to Thoth," Aleister snapped.

He signaled the spirit to follow him into a room where deep pools glittered in the semidarkness. Aleister turned back once with the torch to make sure the afrit trailed behind him as they made their way into the chamber of pools.

Each pool was filled with luminous turquoise water so clear that their depths appeared to be seen through glass. The floor of each pool revealed hills and valley, some with dark entrances to underwater caves. Here, the stalagmites and stalactites were crystal, not the muddy-colored stone seen in main hall.

In the sputtering torchlight, Aleister spied four men huddled around an almost-empty pool. He silently snapped his fingers and motioned the afrit to sit, and it slumped near his heels.

Aleister noticed that one of the men had moved near the lip of the pool and was dipping his ghostly hand into the water. The man's spirit body had no substance with which to hold the water, so the shadow of his hand only passed through the water.

"Hallo there, Westcott!" Aleister called out. "I thought it was understood that we are not to touch the waters."

"As a man of science, I am entitled," Dr. Westcott responded, standing up nonetheless. "And if there are repercussions, I believe I'll be able to find the antidote."

Scratching noises of spirits scuttling into corners reverberated. The shaking afrit heeled behind Aleister as though it were a dog that had been beaten.

Westcott joined the other three men, and they all made their way over to Aleister. Tall Dr. Felkin, mousy Samuel Mathers, and Archer Prince in his cape trailed behind Dr. Westcott. Like Aleister, they had each used a magic spell to travel to this spot, and their bodies were now pale tracings of corporal figures. Each tracing had a separate pulse surrounding it, its own beat of energy a different hue. Prince had a gangrenous rope of clots shadowing his cloak. Aleister noted that this one, exhibiting the darkest energy, had grown more feral: his overgrown black eyebrows and snaggle teeth were more wolflike than human.

The four men stood and stared at Aleister and the twitching spirit near his feet.

"Now look here," Aleister said. "Until we stop that Pamela Colman Smith child from draining our pools, the waters mustn't be disturbed any further."

"You've sequestered her, but still the water levels continue to drop," Mathers said, squinting and pushing his glasses back up his nose. "Maybe your magical mutt there can restore our enchanted water that has disappeared."

"Nonsense," Aleister snapped. "The afrit I've recruited is here on the business of our latest captive." The afrit flattened itself against the ground so that it resembled a toy that had been run over. "A note to you all: I hope you don't try to conjure a cave spirit—they are wildly unreliable."

"I would like to conjure a cave spirit," Felkin mumbled from his great height as he motioned toward the sounds of the scampering spirits in the rock. "But then, I suppose, it's hardly likely that you would help us get one. You won't even share your grimoire with us, even though we all have certainly shared our magic with you."

"Gentlemen," Dr. Westcott said. "Before we discuss the idiot-savant tarot artist that Mr. Crowley has captured, we need to discuss our progress with the Carlists. It has been almost a year since our last attempt with them. I bring good news about our next possible strike."

"What have you heard, Westcott?" Aleister asked, settling down on the largest rock nearby. "You and your Carlists did a miserable job trying to get rid of the old queen at the Windsor military review. Any progress on the plans to solicit the prince?"

"We have one last chance to r-r-recruit Prince Edward," the stuttering Mathers said. "One of my clubs promised a rendezvous where I could talk to him."

Archer Prince barked an unpleasant laugh that echoed off the stone walls. "You talk to royalty, Mathers? You can't get a whole sentence out. And you think that the spoiled boy-king will promise we can 'naturally' remove his mother?" Archer's eyes glowed. "Highly unlikely. Prince Edward is only good at removing husbands from their wives during country weekends."

"We might convince Edward that she's at the end of her time," Aleister said, watching the caped one get up and pace. "If he could see that her removal could be a natural development, and that he might finally be able to reign, he might sign on."

Archer swirled his ridiculous cape. He looked like a moth in its death throes. "How?" he said, as he stopped turning. "Our last plans came to nothing."

"It didn't come to nothing," Westcott said, coming closer to Aleister. "Blowing her up in her carriage at Windsor may not have worked out, but it has given those who were unwilling to see her corrupt reign a reason to join us. And since that incident, the queen has made almost no public appearances. People are beginning to see Edward as the rightful ruler."

"Really, Westcott," Aleister said, turning to the doctor. "How do you plan to convince the prince? And at what price?"

"I'll start with the 1410 treaty that our Henry IV made to the French," Westcott replied. "Then, I'll bring up Napoleon's directives about the male ruling head. I know that Edward is partial to the tales of Napoleon. From there, I will stress how brilliant the House of Hanover was in making sure that the queen didn't rule Germany. I'll point out that if the Salic Law, which outlaws females rulers, had been applied here, there would be no doubt that Edward would have been governing over both England and the Germans the moment he came of age."

"Do you think that goading Edward over his inability to rule will draw him to our campaign?" Felkin asked.

"I think historical stories of men who took the crown away from female heirs will sway him significantly," Westcott said. "If we stress our belief that women have no place on the throne, especially during this intolerable age of suffragettes, I would think we could forge a very sympathetic link."

"What is the plan? Murder an eighty-year-old grandmother?" Aleister asked.

"Or just aid the natural process," Westcott said, his eyes shining.

Several of the men shouted.

"Calm yourselves," Westcott said as Aleister lowered the torch to shine in his face. "We of the Golden Dawn have discovered an Egyptian spell that may prove useful. It's not a poison, per se."

"What is it?" Aleister asked, raising the torch higher.

"It's an extract that hurries the demise of decaying bodies," Westcott said. "It only needs the added boost of magical intent from a quorum of magicians. And the sacrifice of a young girl of knowledge."

"The sacrifice of a young girl, you say," Aleister repeated. He held up the torch, shining it right over his afrit, a dusting of blue sparkles shining on the goat satyr's fur.

A throb of energy bubbled from the afrit's mouth, and a shiver of blue motes spewed out into the air.

"Interesting," he said. "My afrit seems to be telling me that Miss Smith's concentration has not yet been broken. She would be the perfect sacrifice."

CHAPTER FOURTEEN

Afrit Reveals

Pamela shuddered awake. Was the visitation by William a dream? Or did she really fly outside? The metal door slid open. There was a loud clank; then the sound of something dropping echoed and the door slammed shut. Getting to her feet, she found a bowl with a stew of some sort, bread, and a flask. The flask of water tasted sour, and the only recognizable food in the stew seem to be a potato, but hunger clawed at her stomach. She sat on her haunches and ate the rest of the stew in the bowl quickly. Dim light leaked in from the door hinges. There must be a torch outside her cell. Her watch said six thirty. She had spent one day in the cell. The watch was wound, so she could keep track.

She reached into her pocket for her handkerchief and discovered that her beaded coin purse was missing. It must have dropped at the Holy Names Church. She had learned long ago to wear an inside pocket. It tied around her waist, accessible only by the skirt's inner workings, an old stage trick for costumes. Pulling out her handkerchief, she held it up to the weak light. The cloth was still a vibrant blue, but the formerly colorful embellished strawberries were now dulled.

She spotted something moving on the curved turret wall—more precisely, it seemed to be crawling. An azure shadow crept toward her. Pamela crab-walked as far away as possible, her back up against the wall. The shadow grew until it took the shape of the goat-like satyr form that had appeared on Pablo's wall.

"Who are you?" Pamela asked, her voice ragged.

The shadow rose up from a crouched position and loomed over her. It then stepped forward, detaching itself from the wall.

No sound, no smell—only the shifting shape of blue darkness hovering over her. In the eyes of the spirit, pools of cerulean blue shimmered.

"Ahmed said that you might be an afrit," she said.

The shadow nodded its head.

"You've been given a task by Mr. Crowley?"

It nodded again.

"Do you intend to harm me?

It shook its head: no.

What had Ahmed said about afrits? They transformed into different shapes. But he had also said that if an afrit had died a natural death as a person, it would not be violent. So far, this one had only drawn "666" on her train window and scared her as a shadow play on Pablo's walls.

"Did you draw on my train car window?"

The shadow sat down across from her. *We're going to have a conversation?* As it settled down, it crossed its goaty legs. Despite her fear, Pamela almost giggled as the afrit's goat horns swiveled around as it attempted to get comfortable. For a moment, it occurred to her that its hooves were almost adorable. In the dirt on the floor between them, the numbers appeared:

666

"The sign of the devil!" Pamela exclaimed.

The afrit shook its head.

"No? In the Bible, '666' is the sign of the beast," she insisted, as she sat down in front of it.

The afrit shook its head and wrote on the dusty floor:

Book of Revelations 13

Shrugging, Pamela answered, "Sorry, I was raised Swedenborgian. I don't know Biblical phrases."

Was that a sigh? The long finger of the afrit appeared and continued to write on the floor. The afrit took a while to write out its message, giving Pamela time to study it. It seemed to be a him, not a her, because there were no breasts. He seemed smaller than the form she'd remembered seeing at Pablo's. Blue rays of dotted light dripped from his fur. Was he shedding? His blue-dotted hand wrote a long phrase in front of Pamela's crossed legs.

Let the one with understanding reckon
the meaning of the number of the beast, for it
is the number of a man. His number is 666.

"'Let the one with understanding reckon'? Is this a riddle?" Pamela asked.

The afrit nodded. She could see through parts of the afrit's body. He seemed more like a shaggy ghost than a terrible beast. Maybe he wasn't here to torment her after all.

"Oh, I love riddles," Pamela said, bending forward to inspect the inscription. An afrit who liked riddles? This couldn't be all bad. "Well, let's see, '*Let the one with understanding reckon.*' So, you mean, let the one who has knowledge figure it out. And, 'the meaning of the number of the beast.' Beast. Well, the Bible doesn't exactly say 'devil,' does it?"

The afrit clapped his hands together, sprinkling little shards of blue across the surface of the floor.

"Well then, so it's not necessarily the devil. But it is 'the number of a man.' So this beast is a man." Pamela laughed. "At least we have it narrowed down—this beast is a man."

The afrit wrote again:

Hebrew geometry

"Oh no!" Pamela cried. "I hate math. How am I supposed to figure this out? You really have come to torture me."

The afrit hit his head with his hand, and more gritty motes fell from his fingers. He scribbled symbols that Pamela couldn't make out:

רסק ןורנ

"Is this '666' in Hebrew?" Pamela asked.

The afrit nodded.

"But I'm supposed to figure out the identity of the beast by translating Hebrew and using geometry?" Her exasperated sigh echoed in the room. The afrit crossed its arms.

"Yes, very well, I will try. So, say these Hebrew letters add up to 666 . . . ." Pamela paused. "Does the beast's name add up to 666?"

The afrit wriggled like a puppy.

"Good. Glad to see I'm getting warmer. All right, so who would have been a beast back then? I may not know the Bible, but I know about John, who wrote the Book of Revelations. The number '666' has to mean Judas, the traitor, right?"

The afrit shook his head.

"Damn."

The afrit recoiled and hunched over, rocking back and forth. Pamela put out her hand to comfort him, but her hand went straight through the creature's outline. The afrit's fingers tried to join with hers but dissolved in midair, as more blue flecks fell to the ground.

"Oh, I'm sorry. Is it because you are damned that you hate that word?"

The afrit raised its head slowly.

"Yes, that must be it. I'll be more careful with my words. Shall we carry on?"

The afrit lay down on its side and looked up at Pamela.

"So, your clue is: 'A man who seemed like a beast to John, but who was not an apostle.' Ah. Can you help?"

The afrit stood and pantomimed clawing at his heart. From her seated position, Pamela got to her knees and watched the blue shape thrash around. The afrit was trying to pantomime something, but it only seemed as though he were writhing on the floor. Pamela tried to guess what he was doing anyway.

"Tear. Remove. Slash."

The afrit stomped his foot, only to have it dissolve. He held out one stubby arm and, using the other, seemed to place something on the elbow.

"This is entirely different. So, to share, to give, to donate . . . . Pay! Render?"

The afrit jumped up and down, clapping its stubs together.

"Good! Render. Well then, where in the Bible is "render" mentioned? Oh, wait, what is that quote—'Render unto Caesar things that are Caesar's.' And . . . 'God gets his own things.' Or something like that."

The afrit crouched down and patted Pamela on the head, a gesture she could not feel. He then settled down on the floor, making himself comfortable.

Pamela glanced down at her handkerchief: it was now white.

"You're the blue marks in my pocket handkerchief?"

He nodded.

"And you drew '666' on my train window to warn me about Caesar?"

The afrit sighed, little blue motes of dust escaping his mouth, his goat hands going back and forth as if to indicate a so-so manner.

"Sort of," Pamela interpreted. "But it's a Caesar-like person. But you can't mean my Sir Henry. He's not a Caesar."

The afrit nodded in agreement.

"Caesar," Pamela murmured. Her head shot up. "But which Caesar?"

The afrit leaned forward, his eyes now a dark-blue sapphire. Was he smiling as he scrawled?

Guess

"Let's see, who would be the worst Caesar to John?" Pamela stood and paced, twisting the handkerchief in her hand. She froze. "Wait. It would be the crazy one. Nero Caesar, the madman."

Blue dust covered her hands. The afrit dissolved into dots and crawled into her handkerchief, dying it back to its previous color. She held the material to her face. "No, wait, I need to talk to you! Where are you? Beware Nero the madman? What am I to render to Caesar?"

She stared down at the motionless blue cloth in her hands.

CHAPTER FIFTEEN

Knight from Nowhere

Bram peeked into Henry's dressing room. The anemic fire in the stove barely illuminated the actor staring into his round mirror on the table, surrounded by makeup brushes. Bram turned to Ellen standing by his side in the hallway, her eyebrows arched. He clutched Pamela's discarded purse that Brother Timothy from the church had given him and prepared to give a warning knock. He hesitated. The actor had issued an iron-clad edit that he was not to be bothered after the half-hour call for performers.. Disturbing the artist while he did his makeup for Shylock, especially on an opening night, would be a powder keg. Would an update on Pamela's disappearance throw him into a fit about his preparation for *The Merchant of Venice*?

Bram rapped at the door and motioned to Ellen to enter as Henry picked up putty for Shylock's hook nose and began to knead it. A small, furry blur raced past them to jump up on Henry's lap.

Mussie gave several licks to Henry's grease-painted chin and settled down. Bram stood silently next to Ellen, trying to gauge the actor's mood. Henry looked at them in the mirror and stuck a lump of putty on his nose.

"Well, she's not here, so what's the word?" Henry asked, his eyes not leaving Bram's face in the mirror.

Bram held out a small purse. "This is Pamela's," he said.

Henry stopped fussing with the putty and stared at the object. "No other sign of her at the church?" he asked. Bram shook his head. "I presume it's been picked clean by pickpockets," he continued.

"We've both looked through the purse, and there is only her hotel room key and a few coins," Ellen answered, taking the purse from Bram's hand. "There was always a special stone she carried with her that is missing."

"That was a stone I gave her," Bram said, and Ellen gave him a quizzical look.

Before she could ask Bram more, Henry interrupted. "If she'd been robbed," Henry said, "I doubt there would still be money in it. Or that they robbed her for a special stone."

"But Pixie wouldn't just leave her purse with her hotel room key lying around," Ellen said, sitting down in the only other seat in the darkened room, the armchair near the fire. She gently opened the drawstring purse and took out a small card. "There's also this prayer card from St. Saviour's church."

The lines running alongside Henry's mouth, emphasized by grease paint, turned downward. He turned around in his seat and squinted at the card.

"Perhaps the prayer card is a talisman against the would-be magician from the Golden Dawn, Mr. Crowley," Henry said, swiveling around and pinching the putty on his nose to a more crooked shape. "Doesn't this Aleister have issues with Pamela's tarot-deck commission? He's just another Oscar Wilde pretender, with none of Oscar's talent or charisma."

Bram stared at Henry. This was all the concern he had about Pamela's disappearance? That she was mixed up with an Oscar Wilde pretender?

Lovejoy rapped on the door and stepped in, trailed by a young boy of about twelve years of age. Lovejoy handed Henry a telegram.

"Guv'nor," Lovejoy said, "This just came express for you."

Henry motioned to Bram. "Pay the messenger."

Bram bridled—after all these years, to be still treated like an office boy by Henry! *Tip the porter, pay the restaurant bill, buy flowers for the patronesses*. Still, he took a coin out of his waistcoat and made a mental note for the syndicate office to reimburse him. Pocketing the tip, the boy doffed his cap and stared at Henry.

"Is it true, sir, that you're the Knight from Nowhere?" the boy asked.

Henry turned around in his chair, eyes blazing, and asked, "Who says so?"

In a small voice, the boy answered, "My grandad and the newspaper."

"Tell your grandfather that I am from nowhere and everywhere," Henry said in his grandest Shakespearean voice, hitting the consonants. "Nowhere he could imagine and everywhere he hasn't been."

"Well, he's only ever lived here in Manchester," the boy said. "But he saw *The Bells* and always says he can't hear bells without thinking of that damn Irving."

"Mr. Stoker, give this lad another coin," Henry said, clasping the boy on the shoulder.

Bram sighed. He took out another three pence and delivered it to an open moist hand.

Lovejoy took the boy by the shoulders. "I'll be right back," the stage manager said, ushering the boy out to the hallway.

Ellen pressed in closer to Henry as he put on his glasses and turned the envelope over in his hands.

"Well, look at that," Henry said. "This has already been opened."

Bram almost blurted out, *You are surprised the syndicate*

opened your mail when they own everything now? but held back. Henry pulled the flimsy piece of paper out and read it.

"Is it news of our Pixie?" Ellen asked, twisting her hands together.

"No, but this news is just as troubling," Henry said, handing the telegram to Bram.

Bram scanned it. "It's a royal decree for a command performance! No wonder the syndicate opened it."

Ellen inserted herself between Bram and Henry and snatched the telegram from Bram. She read, "The honor of your company and its play, *Becket*, is requested by her most Gracious Majesty for Tuesday next, December twelfth, at four p.m. at Windsor Castle."

Lovejoy came back in just in time to hear "Windsor Castle" as Bram squeaked out a weak, "Hurrah." He knew that this expedition would take away from the search party he needed to start up for Pamela. It was also a hideous expense for a theatre company facing possible bankruptcy.

Henry and Ellen had performed before the queen at Sandringham years ago, an expense and tribulation Bram never thought to repeat. Who on the royal staff knew that the company's tour schedule would include Liverpool, then Edinburgh? This would make Windsor a feasible stop. But Windsor Castle was over two hundred miles away! Bram already had his work cut out for him dealing with the logistics of the tour, Pamela missing, and the syndicate taking over. This detour to perform for the queen would be more than a headache.

Bram felt Ellen's reassuring hand on his shoulder. Henry slumped and put his head in his hands. Time to bolster up their leader.

"This is short notice for next week Tuesday, eh?" Bram asked. "Good God, in the middle of the Liverpool engagement? Well, this won't be easy. Just arranging the scenery will require several trips to London, but it can be done."

In his mental reckoning, the costs began to mount up. They would need a few pieces of furniture and costumes that were in storage, and to rehearse three new cast members. But one did not refuse a command from the queen.

"Their wish is our command," Henry replied, getting up to refill Mussie's food bowl.

"But Henry, how?" Ellen asked. "How can we leave Manchester when Pamela is still missing? We can't just continue the tour as if she were a prop we left behind."

Henry turned and addressed the room. "I am aware that Miss Smith is not a prop and that she is still missing. You know her almost better than any of us; where do you think she went?"

It was rare for Henry to snap at his leading lady.

"Pamela rarely went off on her own," Ellen said. "She was either at the theatre or going somewhere to perform her Jamaican folktale stories."

Bram kept his jaw from dropping. Did she really not know? Pamela was always "going somewhere." Either to the Golden Dawn Headquarters, the British Museum, off with W. B. Yeats to mumble his poetry, drawing costume renderings at Edy's costume shop, or protesting with the Suffrage Atelier. Now that Pamela no longer boarded at Ellen's house, Pamela's whereabouts were no longer tracked by the leading lady. But who here in Manchester would Pamela have spent time with outside the theatre? Bram knew she lived here as a child; perhaps there was still family here.

"Sir," Bram said, "I propose we open tonight here in Manchester and continue our tour, leaving one of the syndicate's private detectives to track Pamela from this city. These dicks must have better things to do than open your correspondence."

Henry plopped down in his chair and finished smoothing the putty into Shylock's distinctive hook nose.

"Lovejoy, is the syndicate's private investigator still here?" Henry asked.

"Yes, Guv'nor," Lovejoy said, lowering his voice. "In the office now, done going through the books, just packing up. The local detective wanted to attend tonight's opening night but didn't buy a ticket. I told them we only had complimentary tickets for investors."

"Excellent," Henry said. "We will hire that local investigator to find Pamela here in Manchester."

Bram leaned in. "And pay him with the best box-seats tickets we have left."

"Very well," Henry said. "Lovejoy, yes, let's not seat him in the gods." Lovejoy left, sighing at one more task to do on opening night.

Ellen exhaled. "Yes, I would wager our chances finding Pamela would be nil if we were to give him those terrible seats in the last rows. The stalls here are pitched at an awfully high angle."

Henry clapped his hands together and called out, "Walter! Time to dress! Where's the call boy? He should have come by with the time to places already." Walter, Henry's longtime dresser, arrived with his tea, and Henry relaxed. "The game's afoot."

"'The game is afoot'—why does that line remind me of Pixie?" Ellen asked.

"She illustrated the poster for the play that line is from," Bram said.

"Oh yes, that's right, *Sherlock Holmes*. Our Pamela, jack of all trades," Henry said, filling his pipe bowl with tobacco. "But *is* she master of any of them?"

"Pamela shows great promise with her posters and artwork," Bram said. Having been the one to introduce her to Henry and Ellen, he hoped she might have a career as a designer with the Lyceum. But, so far, her career never progressed beyond press brochures and bit roles for the Lyceum.

Henry leaned back and looked up. Above the mirror hung Pamela's poster of Henry as Shylock, the one that the locals had doctored with devil horns.

"Perhaps she'll turn up later on tonight," Ellen murmured.

"She always loved an opening-night party," Walter uncharacteristically offered as he sorted Henry's costumes out on the quick-change table.

Ellen sat on the edge of the dressing table and fidgeted with Pamela's purse. "Henry, do you think I should telegraph her relatives in New York to tell them she is missing?" Ellen asked.

"No, let's wait and see if she just took an impulsive day trip and lost track of time," Henry said. "No need to worry them unnecessarily."

The callboy in the hallway shouted, "Fifteen to places! Fifteen!" Mussie jumped down from Henry's lap to bark at the door.

"Henry, it's almost six o'clock," Ellen said, scooping her dog up to quiet him. "Even if we send a telegram to her family in New York now, they won't receive word of Pamela's disappearance until tomorrow."

"And I have a show to carry!" Henry answered, turning away from her to Walter, who was holding a tunic up. "Out! Out!"

Bram caught Ellen's hurt eyes. Portia was said to carry *The Merchant of Venice*.

Walter cleared his throat and motioned to the door with his head.

"And Mr. Stoker," Henry added, "don't let the company know that our errant child is missing. It will only worry them." He ducked as Walter held the tunic over his head.

"Where shall we say she is? She runs the props for the second act," Bram replied.

"Tell them she was afflicted with a fairies' 'stray,'" Henry said, putting the final touches on his hook nose. "Being Irish, you can explain this to them. Now, go!"

Bram ushered Ellen out of the room, and they stood together at the bottom of the stairs leading to the other dressing rooms.

"We're to say she's gone because of an Irish stray?" Ellen asked in a whisper. "What is that?"

"It's a curse by the fairies," Bram said. "If she is under this stray, this spell, she could have gotten lost near a river or a stream, but if she kept a stone to echo in the waters it will let her know where she is and she can soon make her way back to us."

"Pamela is too fond of us to leave without a word," Ellen said. "She must be lost. Or kidnapped." Mussie whined as Ellen's eyes filled with tears. She set the dog down and raced up the stairs to her dressing room, her dog whimpering as he followed in pursuit.

Fantastic—another star and her dog who'll need coddling while I have a command performance to plan. Bram made his way to the backstage door to make sure that Ellen's flowers were there, ready to go to her dressing room. Bram came to the guard at the door and was struck by the sight of all the bouquets ready to be delivered. Typically, flower delivery on opening night was Pamela's job—a task she enjoyed. Who or what would give her more delight that an opening night with the Lyceum? Was she out seeing someone? Where on earth could Pamela be? He'd get the call boy to arrange a telegram to summon Ahmed in Liverpool. Perhaps he'd have some ideas from his time with Pamela at the museum about where she might be.

CHAPTER SIXTEEN

Blue Knight Attack

Pamela had fallen asleep, her shawl tight around her to keep the chill out, the handkerchief draped over her head to keep her ears warm. Her watch's ticking let her know it was eleven o'clock, the end of her second day imprisoned. She examined the blue motionless handkerchief.

"Afrit, are you all right?" Pamela asked. A corner of the cloth disintegrated in her hands.

Pamela held the square tattered cloth up to the only light, the slot in the door. Small patches of blue writhed and wiggled within the cloth, falling on her wrists like flecks of dried paint. Was the afrit dying?

"Are you still in there, afrit?" Pamela asked, leaning her head closer.

Like a sleepy bat turning over, the cloth roiled between her hands.

"Oh, you're all right," Pamela cooed, stroking it gently as it gathered around her thumb.

The cloth shuddered side to side and then stilled, shedding more of its motes. A pile of dust gathered in a mound at her feet. A form spun together, and then the goat-devil afrit pieced himself together in front of her. This was a much smaller version of the goat satyr she had seen earlier. Major pieces of it were now missing. The fearsome face was now more billy goat than monster; his wings had merged into a hunchback, and his two great ram's horns had shrunk to the size of sprouting antler buds on a young deer. Altogether, the afrit looked more like a moth-eaten version of the god Pan—part deer, part satyr—rather than the frightful Baphomet. How had he ever had the power to whisk her from the church in Manchester?

"Hello there, kidnapper," Pamela said, in spite of herself. Perhaps it was the pitiful brown eyes training on her, but she no longer had the urge to throttle him.

The goat devil looked down and then held both of his wrists out to Pamela. They were frayed and lined with scars.

"I see you too are a prisoner," Pamela said. "Is it Aleister who's binding you?" The afrit held his hands up to his goat chest. "I see you're frightened. So am I. We can help each other, but you have to tell me: Who is this Nero devil joining Aleister?"

A buzzing sound came from the dark reaches of the bricked cell. Above them a small light blossomed into a golden circle, the yellow of William Terriss's Fool tunic. The orb drifted downward. As it settled before Pamela, the tunic disappeared, and all that remained was William's beautiful face.

"William!" she cried, scrambling to her feet.

"Aren't you going to introduce us?" William asked, motioning to the afrit, a smile spreading across his free-floating head.

"Afrit," she said, motioning to the undulating head, "this is Mr. William Terriss, god of the gallery girls. He is also the muse for my Fool." The goat devil raised his arms as if to protect himself. "He won't hurt you. William, this is the afrit who captured me in Manchester. He can't talk, so I still don't know why Aleister has arranged this."

The afrit hung his head.

"He's forced to do Aleister's bidding," Pamela said.

"Well, I can't say I'm pleased to make your acquaintance," William said. His head bobbed up and down as he inspected the afrit, who had shrunk back from them. "This chewed-up toy kidnapped you but can't speak? Is this thing friend or foe?"

Taking the scarred afrit's hands, Pamela said, "I think he started out as a foe. Now I think we're both fighting against Aleister's power. Aleister wants to crush me so that I give up on my tarot creations." The goat devil looked up and batted his long goat eyelashes. "I don't know what good it does to keep me here. I didn't do anything to make him hate me."

"You don't think that being able to conjure magic that can engrave initials on ears has anything to do with it?" William asked, his voice hardening as he turned his floating head. Pamela's initials—"PCS"—were clearly in view. "You'd best believe that symbol had everything to do with marking me for murder."

"I had nothing to do with that, I swear!" Pamela said, her hand over her racing heart. "My other muses—Sir Henry, Ellen, and Florence—told me about the tattoos appearing afterward. I didn't conjure them! In fact, I was only told about my initials on their ears much later.." Pamela sat on the ground and looked up at William's head, now swirling back and forth.

"Why was I marked with your initials?" William asked, his voice cold.

Pamela's stomach puddled. She remembered the day when Ahmed had given her access to the British Museum's Egyptian Sanctuary's Monumental Room. Ahmed coached her into an astral trance, where she saw William falling from a beam backstage at the Lyceum Theatre. The tools of the Magician, the wands, stars, swords, and cups, manifested out of thin air and cushioned William from falling to the stage floor. After that, Pamela's initials, "PCS," appeared on William's earlobe.

"I had a vision that you were marked with my initials after you fell from the upstage catwalk during *King Arthur*."

"But *why* are your muses being marked with your initials?" William asked, his head finally coming to rest on her knee.

Was she creating magic, or was magic being done unto her? Now William blamed her for marking him. Because of Aleister's jealousy over her tarot creations, William had become the target of a deranged murderer who was said to be a mentally unbalanced and jealous actor. Pamela now realized that it was all of Aleister's doing. So far nothing had happened to Sir Henry, Ellen, or Florence, thank the gods.

"My muses," Pamela murmured as she stood. William grudgingly settled his head on the afrit as Pamela paced from one curved wall of the cell to the other. "How and why could something mark my muses? If Aleister marked them, it could be because he hates the fact that I'm creating them." Pamela stopped walking.

"Let's start with your next two cards. Who are they?" William asked.

"The Emperor follows the Empress," Pamela replied. "The Emperor is Uncle Brammie. He understands what it is to obey and enforce the rules of the day, but he lives in the world of his own making."

William laughed, his head bouncing up and down on the afrit's leg. "Of course, Stoker is all about outward compliance, meanwhile living in his own macabre world. And the next?"

Pamela crossed her arms. "The Hierophant, Mr. Kamal. Ahmed Pascal Kamal. My friend from the British Museum. He's the pope of antiquities. William, do you know if they have been marked?"

"I don't," William said, levitating away from the afrit, who turned away from them both. "Well, spirit? Have they?"

The afrit shook his head. He turned and looked at Pamela. Sighing, he beckoned to Pamela to come closer. The shabby goat devil positioned Pamela in front of him with his ragged arms as though she were queuing up in a line at school. The afrit reached out and repositioned William's face so he was above Pamela's head, facing out, like a beacon. Pamela felt a light hand rest on her shoulder. The cell darkened to pitch around them. The only light was William's yellow head, emitting a yellow beam. Within that ray, a tiny spot lit up midair. Inside, a disjointed scene manifested itself. Pamela recognized something.

A sign: Windsor Royal. A train station. Her Miss Jones in Jamaica had told her train stations and shipyard docks were the thresholds where magical lines crossed. She had warned Pamela that she needed to pay attention to their magic. The train depot grew bigger and bigger until Pamela recognized people milling about: Lyceum Theatre company members. Under the station's gingerbread- and cream-colored columns, hundreds of people waited, roped off beyond the "Arrivals" area. In the middle of a train platform, Uncle Brammie bustled among crew and cast members, directing them where to go.

Oh, to be with him and the rest of the "reduced players" of the Lyceum Touring Company again. Pamela reached out to grasp Uncle Brammie's hand, but her hand only floated through the scene in front of her.

She watched the company exit the train car, staggering out in exhaustion but still teasing and joking with one another. Ellen jauntily stepped out onto the platform, seemingly exhilarated by the morning air. She was a theatre beast, her energy and verve always besting those years younger. A man thrust a portmanteau-size bouquet of flowers into her hand and escorted her down the platform. Pamela's heart clutched a little. She was usually the one the flowers were handed off to on such occasions. Now Ellen had to juggle them on her own. Uncle Brammie stepped into the last train car, calling out, "Last stop Lyceum Company."

Henry finally exited, his royal slouch distinguishing him as he stood apart from everyone. Bruno, Mussie, and Trini, the three company dogs, barked, keeping the swarms of fans on the platform at bay. Lovejoy admonished the porters to fetch the luggage trolleys. A lump came to Pamela's throat. It was a scene that played out at every arrival.

"Where are they?" Pamela asked.

"Windsor. To perform *Becket* for the queen," William's husky voice replied.

This all had to have been arranged since Manchester. How long had she been locked up? Oh, if only she had been back with the company and part of this!

"*Becket*! Who is playing your part, the Henry II role?" Pamela asked.

"Sidney Valentine," William answered. "This will be a fresh hell to watch."

The afrit jostled them from behind. Was it laughing or mad that they were talking?

Five oddly dressed men elbowed their way through the crowded passageway, attracting the crowd's attention. The tallest man wore a black velvet cape to dramatic effect. Pamela's hand went to her mouth to stifle a cry. It was Aleister! He was just as Pamela remembered: tall, alabaster skin, dark eyes, and floppy hair, his upper lip curled in a sneer. Even though the bubble was reflecting a scene far away, Pamela's breath caught as his coal-dark eyes turned to her directly. She jolted—even at this remove, she could feel the hatred he directed toward her.

Turning his focus back to the train station, Aleister strode toward Sir Henry. The crowd fell silent and watched. Four men followed him, and Pamela recognized the ousted Golden Dawn chiefs: Dr. Westcott with his elaborate waistcoat and topcoat, Dr. Felkin with his goat's-head walking stick, and Samuel Mathers, wearing a Scottish tartan. A fourth man, wearing an inverness cape, was unfamiliar to Pamela. He stayed behind Aleister.

"Who is the man in the hunter's coat?" Pamela asked.

"That is Mr. Archer Prince. He murdered me at the Adelphi stage door," William said. "Declared insane and released all within a month's time."

"No!" Pamela cried, shaking off of the afrit's hold of her arm. The afrit stepped back, and William drifted above her. William's murder was only mentioned to Pamela once, and she was told by Sir Henry and the others never to ask after it again.

"This is your murderer?"

"It is," William said, his ghost eyes trained on the man in the cape before them.

"And he's there to kill someone else? Sir Henry? Uncle Brammie?"

The train-station scene waivered in the air, as though it could hear her. Sir Henry's hand shot up, as if his stage gesture would command all minions to cease and desist. Aleister and his group barreled toward him. As they neared, the dogs put themselves between Henry and Aleister's group, barking and snarling. Aleister extended his hand to Henry, prompting Ellen's Jack Russell to jump up high enough to snap at Aleister's face, sending him whirling backward.

Pamela stood as William's head flew upward. "Get him, Mussie!" she shouted as the diminutive pup snarled and leapt up at Aleister over and over.

The five men huddled in a circle around Henry, chanting, "*Adiuro vos*," over and over.

"Uncle Brammie, look out!" she cried as she saw him running toward the chanting magicians. The Golden Dawn chiefs surrounded Sir Henry, continuing their chanting as the agitated crowd jeered. The dogs whimpered. Lovejoy shouted at his company, ordering them to clear the path. Uncle Brammie finally made his way to Aleister, put up his clenched fists, and dropped into a boxer's stance. The magicians surrounded Uncle Brammie, and he fell to the platform.

Pamela edged closer to the floating projection. Where were the police? They were usually at every train stop on tour.

Aleister brushed his cape backward and reached his right hand out to Sir Henry. Pamela felt an icy breeze surround her.

Miss Jones's sign of an evil presence. Within the bubble, stage hands and carpenters ran to join the actors now at Bram's side, helping him up. The rest of the crowd circled around Sir Henry.

Pamela's stomach tightened. Aleister fluttered his hands in front of the actor's face, fingers spasming open and shut as he continued to chant. A bright, cerulean blue ash spread from his fingertips, in a fine spray that dusted the air in circles. As Sir Henry struggled to wave the fumes away, a blue cloud enveloped Sir Henry's face and hands. He tilted his head back and collapsed on the platform. Screams went up as Uncle Brammie tried to make his way from the crew that held him up, but the magicians kept him back with palms held out in front of them.

"Sir Henry!" Pamela called. She tried to lurch forward into the mirage, but the afrit held her tight.

William's voice was low and strong. "Call your muse to power!"

"Bram Stoker, as my Emperor," Pamela said, shaking off the afrit's blue paws around her. "I command you: Rule the day!"

Henry and Bram's figures faded, but the man with the large cape whirled until Aleister and the rest became a black top. They spun until the entire vision wavered and the scene dimmed.

Pamela shot her hands through the space where Uncle Brammie, Ellen, and Henry had stood before her. They disappeared.

"Uncle Brammie!" Pamela shouted. Feeling the afrit's grip lessen, she jerked around. Only William's face flitted before her, with an expression of sorrow. She tried to grab hold of William, but he was out of reach. "Is Uncle Brammie all right? What's wrong with Sir Henry?"

The afrit tried to reach out to her with his blue hands, and she batted them away.

CHAPTER SEVENTEEN

SEARCH PARTY

Bram glued the paper with a sloppy stroke of his brush to the lamppost on the Manchester Victoria Station platform.

Information wanted on an English young female approximately five foot two, dark hair, last seen the morning of December 1 near the Midland Hotel. Contact management at Manchester Royal Theatre. Reward.

Just over a month ago, he and Pamela had disembarked from the London train here, and now he was posting fliers for her return.

The poster Pamela had designed for the *Merchant of Venice* was glued above it: Ellen's Portia in the foreground and Henry's Shylock covering the background.

"Pamela's artwork is lovely, isn't it, Bram?" Ellen asked, taking the brush from his hand and putting it in the paste bucket. Her dogs, Mussie and Trin, lay at her feet despite the chill in the air. "Here's hoping that detective will find her."

"I have little confidence that this local investigator will find any leads on Pamela, especially once we leave for Liverpool."

The sounds of a horse's whinny startled them both, and Bram spotted Little Beda's ebony head bobbing outside a freight car bearing the sign "World's Smartest Horse" on the side. Striding over to the horse, Pablo brushed straw off his hands as the giant reached her long head toward him. Pablo's red bandana on top of his shoulder-length hair, a large gold hoop earring, and big black boots made him look every inch the circus owner.

"Ah, Mr. Stoker, pleasure to see you again," Pablo said, as the horse nibbled Bram's beard.

"Pablo, this is Ellen Terry. Miss Terry, this is the one and only Mr. Pablo, owner of Little Beda," Bram said.

Ellen extended her hand, and Pablo removed his work glove and held out his hand to Ellen. She shook it and smiled. "An honor to meet the owner of the world's smartest horse."

"Nobody really owns Little Beda," Pablo said. "Honor to meet you, Miss Terry. Sorry to cut our visit short; we have a lot to do before we arrive in Dublin for our winter tour." He grabbed a stack of hay on the platform and chucked it to his sons who were in the railcar, barely missing Bram and Ellen.

"Here, before you level us with another bale of hay," Bram said, "I have a favor to ask. We're missing a company member." Bram pulled out a stack of the missing-person fliers from his coat and handed one to him: "Miss Pamela Smith"

"Oh, no! Not the little miss!" Pablo cried, standing closer to Bram. "Has she been gone long?"

"Since yesterday morning," Ellen said.

"She seemed so fond of your horse, I was hoping that she had run away and joined your circus," Bram said.

"Yes, Beda here took to her and her sugar cube immediately," Pablo replied, rubbing Beda's nose. Pablo leaned forward, cupping Little Beda's ears as though she were not to hear. "And she never forgets a sugar cube."

Bram began to hum the "Argyle Polka," the song Pamela had sung to Beda the night she rode her. The horse eyed him and her ears swiveled. Immediately, the horse turned to him and did the same dance-like steps she had done when Pamela rode her.

Bram murmured, "Where is she, girl? Do you know?"

Ellen cleared her throat. "Mr. Pablo, while you're touring, would you mind putting up some of these fliers along your route? There's a reward for her safe return."

Ellen took the fliers from Bram's pocket and handed them to Pablo.

Mussie started to whine, and the trio turned their attention to a figure with a walking stick and a dog coming down the platform.

"Isn't that Sir Henry, your famous thespian?" Pablo asked.

Henry and Trin, his Eskimo dog, approached at a fast clip as Trin and Mussie greeted one another with yips.

Henry came up to the trio. "The ticket office has not seen Miss Smith, neither buying a ticket nor boarding a train here," Henry said.

"Mr. Irving, this is Mr. Pablo and the world's smartest horse, Little Beda," Bram said.

The men briefly shook hands.

"And where are you off to, Mr. Pablo?" Henry asked.

"Liverpool, and then the ferry to Dublin," Pablo replied. "We'll be entertaining at grand houses these next few weeks, until the New Year. I'll be posting these fliers along the way, and if I see or hear anything about your Miss Smith, I'll get her home to you."

Pablo's sons loaded the last of the bales of hay into the train car and whistled for their father.

He turned to the men. "Well, time to get back to work. Beda, say goodbye."

The horse nodded her head up and down to the laughter and applause from those gathered around her. Pablo led her into the open boxcar and disappeared.

On the opposite train track, a train chugged into view. As Bram, Ellen, and Henry watched it pull up and stop, the passengers on the departure side began to queue up in the cars further along from Little Beda's train car. As soon as the arriving train stopped and doors flew open, chaos engulfed the platform with the mingling crowd jostling suitcases and packages.

Bram noticed a tall man with a clutch of men exit the arriving train; they fell into lockstep with one another as they walked toward them. He suddenly realized who they were: Aleister Crowley and his rebel magicians from the Golden Dawn. There was Dr. Westcott, Dr. Felkin, Mathers, and a man in an oversize cape. As they came closer, Bram noticed the odd, determined scowl on Aleister's face.

Aleister was just feet away from Henry when the actor raised his walking stick as though he were conjuring with a wand. Growling and baring their teeth, the dogs inserted themselves between the two groups,

"Mr. Irving, the magician," Aleister called, bowing and extending his hand.

Henry hesitated and then extended his free hand in greeting. As he did so, a blue hue enveloped his fingers. Aleister took Henry's hand and bowed his head, leaning forward as if he were kissing the actor's hand. Mussie charged at Aleister, leaping and biting him on the chin.

Aleister yelped and cradled his bleeding chin while his cohorts swirled about Henry. Bram tried to control the dogs, now menacing everyone on the platform.

The magicians gathered around Henry, their cloaks spreading out like mantling eagles ready to shred their caught prey. As the circle drew tighter, Sir Henry held up his cane as though to banish them.

"*Adiuro vos*," Bram heard them say. *I bind you*.

A searing pain shot through Bram's earlobe, and he stopped midstep to grasp his ear to see if he had been shot. There was nothing, no blood. Just pain as though he had been cut with a razor or bullet.

Bram saw Henry crumple within the circle of men. He ran to him as Pablo and his sons raced from the train. Kicking the men out of the way, they lifted Sir Henry up, his face a strange blue tinge. As the assaulters tried to slink off, Bram raced after them and grabbed the collar of Aleister's coat, pulling him close. Aleister's blue hand waved in protest as Bram punched him in his already-bleeding jaw.

"A table for six, please," Bram said, his fist still throbbing from the earlier altercation. Toby stood at entrance of the Midland Hotel's Peacock Dining Room and was about to lead them in when the maître d' took Toby aside. After a whispered scolding, the sour-looking man pointed to a table in the back. Toby led the party past tables with fancy wicker chairs adorned with peacock feathers from India until they arrived at an alcove behind a pillar. At a worn round table with short wooden chairs sat a fatigued Henry between Florence and Ellen, with Satish Monroe opposite. The maître d' set a screen around them, so they would be barely visible to the other diners.

Bram wondered if the screen had been set in place to conceal Henry's blue face, the dogs lying at Ellen's feet, or the man of African descent in their party. *Wait until Ahmed arrives wearing his fez. They'll seat us in the hallway.*

Ahmed, escorted by the glowering maître d', arrived minutes after they ordered. His attire did not disappoint; his fez was firmly affixed to his head.

Bram stood. "Mr. Kamal, welcome! This is Mr. Irving, Miss Ellen Terry, Miss Florence Farr, and Mr. Satish Monroe."

"Mr. Irving, Miss Terry, Mr. Monroe, a pleasure to meet you," Ahmed said. Before sitting next to Satish, he looked at

Florence and said, "Miss Farr, delighted to see you again." Ahmed peered over the screen. "Very kind of the restaurant to give our table a semblance of privacy."

Florence, Ellen, and Satish exchanged a bemused look with Ahmed while Mr. Irving drooped even more in his seat.

"I'm glad you're here, Mr. Kamal," Bram said.

"My apologies for being late," Ahmed answered. "I just had time for prayers."

Heads swiveled from the nearest table, but Bram continued. "Mr. Kamal, we were just beginning our plans for Pamela's rescue party." A waiter sidled up to take Ahmed's order.

"There is still no word on Miss Smith's whereabouts?" Ahmed asked. The ladies shook their heads while the blue tint edged around Henry's jaw and spread upward. Bram noticed tears delicately wiped away by Ellen.

"I'm afraid we've received no word on her whereabouts," Bram said. "Her paperwork for a missing-person report was just today submitted to Scotland Yard."

"Didn't Miss Smith sometimes call you the 'Emperor of Paperwork' because of your expertise?" Satish asked.

"Her nickname for me was 'Emperor of Arranging,'" Bram said.

Bram noticed Henry grimace. *Iis he jealous that I am in charge of anything at all?*

A bellhop came to the table, asking for Mr. Stoker. After a telegram was delivered, Bram sat sideways in his seat. The weak light from hissing gas jets in the overhead chandelier made reading the telegraph's blurry words difficult.

"Excuse me while I see to this," Bram said. "Perhaps someone has responded to our notice in the papers about our reward for Pamela's location."

Bram quickly scanned the missive. It was signed by a Reverend Thompson. Ah, he must have been the one who was to blame for Pamela's recent enthusiasm for churches across the Thames.

St. Saviour's Church, Southwark
To Mr. Stoker:
Subject: A matter of concern for Miss Pamela Smith.
Miss Smith visits St. Saviour's Church to sketch. Count Vladimir Svareff warned us today Miss Smith creates art used for black magic and sorcery. She has been seen at her Chelsea studio. Could you see the reward is sent to D649 Mercury Office London.
Yours in Christ, Reverend Thompson

Bram felt his blood pulse in his temples. How dare anyone accuse Pamela of black magic! It's just the sort of name-calling a man does when a woman has something he covets. Of course, this message had to have come from Aleister.

"Pixie's at her studio in Chelsea?" Ellen cried. "Thank the gods and goddesses! I'll telegraph Edy that she must let bygones be bygones and go at once to check on her."

"If Pamela is really there at all," Florence said. "This telegram could just be a trap from Mr. Crowley. Your daughter should go with company for safety."

Satish slapped his hand on the table, starling the dogs and causing them to yelp. "Count Vladimir Svareff—what a name! Anyone heard of him?"

Bram folded the letter. "Aleister Crowley's alias was Count Svareff when he first came to London."

Ahmed picked up the telegraph's envelope. "This accommodation address for the payment of the reward money is at the Mercury Office, a tailor shop near the British Museum."

Henry motioned to Bram to hand over the telegram. He scanned it quickly and said, "Now why would Mr. Crowley be impersonating this Reverend Thompson?"

Florence snapped, "To tarnish Pamela with the words 'black magic.' It will stop Annie Horniman from providing funds for a search party if the Golden Dawn has someone in the dark arts."

Bram lifted his head. "Well, it won't stop us— "

A line of servers made their way past the screen and swarmed the table, delivering plates of steaming food. The dogs began to rustle and yawn. Boiled potatoes, roast beef, chicken pie, and a veal stew were settled at the right place settings. Bram cut into the blood-red roast beef, cooked to his preference, and almost groaned with delight. The ladies also ate with relish, something that was not common in Bram's household. He felt a warmth come over him as he watched his comrades eat. It was good to be with people who appreciated him and the food he liked and who understood his capacities, even if he wasn't recognized as a writer.

As they ate, Henry asked Satish about his upcoming performance in Hull, a one-man presentation of Shakespeare's villains and heroes. Henry chewed his food slowly as he listened, and the ladies concentrated on avoiding one another. The glum scene was only relieved by Ahmed's eyebrow arching at Bram, acknowledging the diners' awkward strain.

As soon as Florence's plate was clean, she threw down her napkin and rested her elbows on the table. "Now let's talk about getting Miss Smith back. Who took her and why?"

"I can't stop thinking about Pixie being abducted without us realizing it," Ellen said. "Why would Aleister do this, and why over a tarot deck?"

"Perhaps he sent someone else to do it," Ahmed said. "He seems to be a very angry man."

"If he recently threatened her again, perhaps she is still here with friends or family in Manchester," Bram said. "She may still have friends or relations here."

"Yes, she does—in Didsbury," Ellen said. "She went there in a hired car; she wanted to see her old house."

"And did she meet any family members there?" Bram asked.

"We really didn't have time to talk," Ellen replied.

"You didn't see her when she came back?" Florence asked.

"We were in technical, Miss Farr," Ellen said. "I'm sure you know how all-encompassing that phase is during the run of a show."

Florence turned and looked at Ellen with pursed lips. "I'm sure I don't know how all-encompassing a Lyceum Theatre technical is."

"Miss Terry," Bram said, moving his chair closer to Ellen. "Might your daughter, Edy, know the names of Pamela's relatives here in Manchester?"

Ellen turned and looked at Bram, her tears making a reappearance. "Edy, as I have said, is no longer close with Pixie or her friends. I recently heard her mention a Miss Baillie and a Japanese artist—I think his name is Yoshio. They were looking to lodge with Pixie in London after the tour."

"Who are these two new friends?" Florence asked.

"They are friends of Miss Smith from the art world," Ahmed said quietly. "Rosa Baillie's brother, John, shows Pamela's artwork at his art gallery in Bayswater, and Mr. Markino is a regular haunt at her 'Bohemian Nights' soirees."

"It seems that none of us really knows Miss Smith very well," Henry said. "Except for you, Mr. Kamal."

"I know that Pamela's grandfather was the mayor of Brooklyn," Ellen offered. "A Mr. Smith, I think."

"Not really helpful," Henry retorted, stretching his legs. "Smith is a common family name."

"Where I come from, family is everything," Ahmed said, his eyes burning. Bram could feel the table leg next to Ahmed tremble. Was he afraid or furious? Ahmed continued, "If someone were missing, we would first contact every family member for help."

"That's actually a good point," Satish said. "If her grandfather was a wealthy mayor in Brooklyn, maybe someone kidnapped her for a bigger ransom than what a struggling theatre can offer. The sooner we check her Chelsea apartment for clues, the better."

"She may have been taken, or she may be ill and not know where she is," Henry said, looking through the outdated tour brochures on the table. "Or Miss Smith may have decided to leave behind this theatrical life entirely."

Bram blurted: "She wouldn't leave without telling me." His heart clutched. *Not always. I made sure of that recently.*

"You've always been Uncle Brammie to her," Ellen said as she clutched her hands together and sat as though in prayer.

Florence crossed her arms. "This report of Pamela doesn't sound like her, to leave all her friends behind."

"Granted, Miss Farr," Henry answered, "but none of this behavior seems to be characteristic of the Pamela we knew."

Ahmed sighed. "Is this what happens here to young women without family?" he asked.

"Even with family, Mr. Kamal, a woman's safety is not guaranteed," Florence snapped.

"Miss Farr," Ellen said softly, looking past Henry at Florence, "I'm afraid you are right."

Florence reached out to Ellen, and the two women clasped hands as Henry squirmed.

Bram felt his face flush. Had he neglected Pamela? *Ahmed must think theatre people have no morals, that they abandon one another at the drop of a hat.*

Ahmed placed his hands on the table as though steadying himself. "I do not mean to insult you all. I know you are her friends. What can I do to help? I am on my way back to London, and soon afterward I have a commitment out of town. But I can surely do something."

Bram cleared his throat. "If you could visit this Reverend Thompson at St Saviour's Church and ascertain whether he wrote this letter, that would be helpful. That way, we will know if Aleister is trying to slander Pamela to keep her from creating her tarot deck or get the reward. For now, during the rest of our stay here in Manchester, we will pepper the stations with missing-person posters. Since the police here in Manchester have been less than helpful, I will contact Scotland Yard."

"I'll do better than that," Florence said. "I'll go to Annie Horniman's house. She's Pamela's patron for the tarot cards, and I'm sure she's concerned about her investment. I'll see if she won't also fund a search party for Pamela, based in London."

"Excellent!" Henry said. "Now for the sake of our entire payroll, we must continue with this tour. We'll keep the Lyceum Theatre staff on alert to see if there has been any word of Pixie. If Miss Smith hears we have a command performance after our Liverpool engagement, perhaps she will appear at the train with us. Let us hope for the best."

Bram tried not to snort. Just like Henry to carry on with plans for his command performance and hope for the best that others find Pamela.

Ellen cried out, "If she's captured, how will she even know of a command performance?"

Bram reached over and patted her hand. "If there's one thing Pamela is good at it, it's tracking every opening night and cast party. She'll find her way back to us. Meanwhile, Miss Terry, could you contact this Miss Baillie and Yoshio to see if they've heard from her? Miss Farr, could you check her studio?"

"I'll stop by her Chelsea apartment tomorrow when I arrive in London," Florence said. Bram saw Ahmed flinch, and Florence lowered her voice as she added, "I'll take Edy and Annie Horniman with me for protection. They don't call Annie a battle axe for nothing."

"Good plan," Bram said.

Satish leaned in. "I'll take Pamela's missing-person fliers with me on my tour to Hull."

A trio of waiters approached the table and started to clear plates.

"Let us stay in touch during these next few weeks while we are separated," Henry said, rising. "I depend on all of you to contact Bram when you find out anything."

"*If* we find out anything," Ellen said, staring at Henry. "We're looking for unloosened tears in the ocean."

"Now, now," Bram said, "let's not give up the ghost. Here are the tickets for our next stop on tour." He took train tickets out of his waist pocket and passed them to Henry and Ellen as Satish started to hum the "Argyle Polka." The dogs howled as they gathered around. Instead of adding mirth to the room, their moans echoed the anxiety of the dining party.

The next morning, Ahmed ignored the stares directed his way by fellow passengers on the train platform. He bought the *London Times* morning paper from a young boy and tipped him generously.

Florence hurried toward him carrying a suitcase and a case of equal size that resembled a hat box. Two men flanked her, trying to engage in small talk.

"Your hatbox has a most unusual shape," said one. "I could carry it onboard for you."

"I'm quite capable, thank you," Florence said as she sprinted toward Ahmed. "Ah, Mr. Kamal, shall we find our seats?" she asked with a slight grin. As she passed him, she whispered, "Quickly, or we shall be besieged!"

Florence bustled down the aisle in front of him and opened the door to the first empty compartment. She motioned to him, and he followed her in. In the corridor, a woman and child stopped and gazed into their car.

"Mr. Kamal," Florence said. "You don't mind sharing this car, do you? We women are always in need of a safe spot to sit."

The girl of about five years of age stared at him. It was usually his fez that stopped people in their tracks. He bowed, stood aside, and held his hands out to store their luggage. He stowed it above just as the two men walked by, registering their car's occupants with grunts. Florence smiled at him for the first time—their fight at Thornton Manor was forgotten—and Ahmed motioned to the women and child to take a seat.

"Yes, women, children, and presidents first," Florence said in a low voice, claiming the window seat.

"Presidents?" Ahmed asked, sitting next to her. "Who is the president?"

"I am now," Florence said. Ahmed blinked. "Of Pamela's group," she continued. "The Golden Dawn. They just voted me in."

"Congratulations, Miss Farr," Ahmed said. *Were Women elected presidents?*

She tucked her harp's case further under her seat. The mother across from them took out a child's book from her satchel and began to read to the child in a slow, steady tone.

"Speaking of the Golden Dawn," Ahmed said in a low voice. "Where do *you* think Miss Pamela is? Not at her Chelsea studio, as the letter suggested?"

"She is somewhere not of her choosing," Florence answered just as quietly. "She may be impulsive, but she's not irresponsible. As president of the Golden Dawn, I shall make it a priority that we use all of our resources to find her."

"How ever did you come to be president?" he asked.

She tilted her head and smiled. "I find your disbelief somewhat insulting."

"I intend no disrespect, Miss Farr," he answered, "but that group has always appeared to be led by men and populated by women servers. Tell me how you were elected, please?"

"Mostly because the scandals involving past presidents eliminated everyone else, of course," Florence answered. She gave a small sigh. "We have needed new leadership for a while. Samuel Mathers, one of the chiefs in Paris, is linked to the Carlists. Scotland Yard has come by several times to interrogate Miss Horniman, who is not pleased. She is the one who nominated me; she also pays the rent for the group's headquarters. So, I won—by unanimous decision."

The train's whistle drowned out any chance for a reply, and the car lunged forward. The daughter gave a little squeal and cried, and the mother spent several minutes apologizing for the outburst. When all was calm, Ahmed set aside his newspaper and reached for his valise.

"Mr. Kamal," Florence asked, her voice in a sweet register. "Would you mind if I look at your newspaper? There is a court case I am following."

Ahmed kept his mouth from dropping open. *Well, perhaps she will not crush it too terribly.* He handed it to her and extracted his correspondence. There were many reports of recent auctions to go through, but all he could think was, *Where is Pamela?* His museum associates certainly had no way of finding a young woman between Manchester and London. He didn't know any of her family members. Pamela had told him she was the friend of Ellen Terry's daughter for a while but that they were friends no longer.

He looked up. Florence was staring off into the distance.

"You've been very kind to me, Miss Farr," Ahmed said softly. "May I thank you for your help in retrieving the papyrus and your recommendations for the other museums?"

"You are welcome, Mr. Kamal, but the whole idea of helping you was Mrs. Lever's."

"Yes, Mrs. Lever did arrange for an exchange of artifacts at the North Hampton museum," Ahmed said. "I will be glad to have some antiquities to take back to Cairo."

Florence stared at him. "You are going to Cairo?"

The mother jumped in her seat at the word Cairo. *Ah, such a fearful word.*

"I leave in two days," Ahmed said, his stomach roiling. "I hope we find Miss Smith before I sail, but my employer at the Antiquities Division in Egypt has ordered me to return immediately. I anticipate being gone for at least three weeks, three months if things go badly."

Florence turned to him. "Three weeks is ridiculous. You'll be gone a month or more. And right when Pamela has been kidnapped."

"If she was abducted, that would truly be the worst scenario," Ahmed said. "But so far, as Mr. Stoker pointed out, there has been no ransom demand—only a possibly bogus claim to the reward."

So far. But young women with means to support themselves don't just go missing.

When Pamela had first shown up to share his office space by order of the British Museum director, Ahmed was annoyed to be saddled with an inquisitive young woman, who asked him a constant stream of questions. But after a time, he'd come to be fond of her. He no longer found her appearance strange nor her earnest ways bothersome. Her interest in his work was refreshing. And she had been one of the few acquaintances who asked questions about his family and background.

"Miss Smith is unique, I give you that," Ahmed said. "Despite her unscholarly approach of using intuition for some tarot cards, when she finds a historical image that resonates with her, she researches its source fastidiously. Day or night, if an image caught her imagination, she would stay engrossed in its history for hours, but she would always report to me when she was leaving. I am afraid something foul has happened to her."

The newspaper in Florence's lap fell open, revealing the *Times'* headline. Florence gasped and picked it up before Ahmed could make it out.

"Good God!" she exclaimed.

The mother stopped reading to her child, and both stared at Florence.

Ahmed tried not to spy, but his curiosity was burning. Finally, Florence noticed him and delicately shared the front page.

"GOLDEN DAWN MADAME HOROS
IS A REAL-LIFE MADAM"

Swami Laura Horos and her son, now known
as her husband, are charged with imprisonment,
false representation, fraud, and rape.

"Rape!" Florence whispered.

The mother stood. "If you will excuse us, this conversation is not fit for us."

She pointed to their luggage on the rack above them, and Ahmed retrieved it. She threw open the door, juggling daughter and suitcase, bolting out to the car across from them. The ticket taker was just coming down the aisle, took their tickets, and ushered them into the other compartment. The conductor then entered their car, punched Florence's and Ahmed's tickets, and closed their door with a smirk. Was it proper to be alone with her? Florence seemed to tolerate this change. Ahmed sat in the seat across from Florence.

"Well, I didn't mean to upset the woman," Florence said. "But at least now we can talk." She motioned to the newspaper. "This criminal charge is a very bad turn for our group and for the funding for Pamela's search party."

"What does this rape case have to do with Pamela's disappearance?" Ahmed asked.

"Three years ago, a Fräulein Sprengel from Stuttgart sanctioned the creation of our Hermetic Order of the Golden Dawn," Florence said. "Recently, she tried to form her own order. Some in our group championed her because years ago, she passed on Rosicrucian magical rituals to us."

"The men in your Golden Dawn claimed their magical order was founded by a woman?" Ahmed asked.

He watched Florence's blue eyes narrow. "Yes, Mr. Kamal. It is curious, but our Golden Dawn believes in female magicians," Florence continued. "Countess Fräulein Sprengel was mentioned in some decoded secret manuscripts and reputed to be a powerful sorcerer. She is the one who authorized our charter, agreed to through correspondence."

Ahmed choked in spite of his attempt not to react. "Your magicians' group was given authority to organize solely through letters?"

"Yes," Florence answered. "You can ask our Dr. Woodman; he handled the correspondence."

"But how is sorcerer Fräulein Sprengel connected to the criminal Madame Horos?" Ahmed asked.

"Swami Madam Horos and Fräulein Sprengel are one and the same," Florence said, leaning over the paper and pointing it out in the print.

"The use of 'swami' with a woman should have been a clue that something was wrong right away," Ahmed said.

Florence glared at him and read from the newspaper: "'Golden Dawn chief Mathers met swami Madame Horos and her son in Paris and suspected nothing. Later, she stole secret order papers from the Paris office, so that she could present herself here in London as a Golden Dawn chief."

"To what end?"

"It seems she set up a Golden Dawn order to lead rituals, and to lure young women to give up everything to join her faction. Awful. Madame Horos is charged with aiding and abetting rape, theft, and imprisonment."

"This is very bad for the Golden Dawn's reputation," Ahmed said.

"More than bad," Florence replied. "Annie Horniman may not fund Pamela's search party now. No wonder I was elected president! The men in the group probably knew all about this brewing scandal when they voted for me."

Sunlight dimmed in the train's compartment. "Do you believe in magic, Mr. Kamal?"

"I have my own experiences with the unworldly," Ahmed answered as the handkerchief in his breast pocket beat loudly in time with his own heart.

"That answer is evasive at best, Mr. Kamal," Florence said, frowning.

Ahmed lifted his palm up in a conciliatory gesture but didn't answer. She was not entitled to know more. His own struggle to draw boundary lines with spirits that lived in antiquities was not to be shared.

Florence gasped and pointed at something above Ahmed's head. He craned his neck but couldn't see anything, so he switched seats to sit next to Florence.

A translucent, quavering five-pointed yellow star danced on the wall. It shimmied and twisted, casting no shadow or reflection, but it was clearly a living object. The star somersaulted inside the shape of a shield. The image shone brightly as it performed its somersaults.

In a querulous voice, Florence asked, "What is that?"

The train rounded a sharp turn, and the last of the day's light poured into the compartment. The sun perched above the horizon, and a lake appeared next to the train.

"Miss Farr, possibly it's just a reflection of the sun over the water."

Ahmed knew the sun wasn't strong enough to be casting that sort of reflection. The star had five points: this was not the reflection of water. On the way to Manchester, he'd seen "666" written on his train window. Now, on the way back, this image had appeared. Was Pamela's afrit traveling back to London with him?

The train whistle shrieked, and the *whoosh* of the tunnel swallowed them. They were submerged in darkness. However, a small prism of light burst into view, dancing once again above Ahmed's head. He craned his neck and watched the star bounce and burn. Ahmed had seen this star before: it was a pentacle.

"That star reminds me of Pamela's Magician tarot card," Florence said, as if she were reading his mind. "That pentacle is on her Magician's table. What do you think it is trying to tell us?"

"I am guiding you. Come find me," Ahmed said.

They sat for a moment watching the star waver. The black handkerchief in Ahmed's pocket thumped wildly.

The star fluttered one last time and then flattened out.

"It's not a star. It's King Brian's shield," Ahmed said, sitting up straight.

"What? Who?" Florence asked. "Why did you say that?"

"I don't know," Ahmed answered.

CHAPTER EIGHTEEN

Demon Hunters

Bram took the train from Liverpool to London the next morning, and it was as frustrating a journey as he had ever taken. Much more so than any train travel during their American tours. But then, he knew when he returned home from a successful tour that his reception by Florrie and Noel would usually involve a coming-home supper out at a restaurant. But today, Bram discovered at the ticket office that he had bungled the tickets not only for himself but for the entire company transferring to Windsor for the command performance. Chaos and bad tempers reigned during the entire trip, and he arrived home in a foul mood.

There he was met by Florrie, standing in the hallway with her arms crossed over her neat, tidy waist. He kissed her briefly and told her that he had to make a quick run to the theatre before he could settle in. He walked swiftly up the stairs with his valise, and when she followed him, he knew he was in trouble.

"Mr. Stoker, is this your career? Nursing the succubus Irving?" she asked as they entered his bedroom.

"Now, Florrie, this succubus has given us a fine life," Bram said, unpacking his suitcase.

"I could have had a much finer life if I had accepted Oscar Wilde's proposal instead of accepting that of a traveling secretary for an actor/manager."

Florrie knew how to wound. It took everything Bram had not to ask her how much finer her life would have been with Oscar after he emerged from two years of hard labor for buggery.

"You'll be staying to sup with our son at least, before you run out the door again. Or is that too much to ask?" Bram gulped a yes and was about to take her hand in apology, but she hurried to her bedroom and slammed the door. At least their son hadn't arrived home from school yet to witness this exchange.

Dinner was a stolid affair, Bram asking Noel and Florrie questions about their lives and school and receiving grunts and sighs in return. Fourteen-year-old Noel appeared indifferent to any of the stories Bram offered up of the tour, and the boy asked to be excused before the dessert. Florrie fled immediately after.

It was late afternoon by the time Bram entered the stage door of the Lyceum Theatre, closed to the public on what was called a "dark night." Dark, indeed. Ancient Mrs. Cornford opened the stage door holding a lit candelabra, a prop from *The Corsican Brothers*.

"Mrs. Cornford, all is well?" Bram asked, trying to ascertain her mood while she barely let him through the door.

"Ah, yes, busy, busy," Mrs. Cornford replied. "You know, my tasks are heavy with responsibility. Collecting all the posts that come while you're all out trotting the globe. And taking care of the cats that take care of the rats."

"Did the business people from the syndicate come by?" Bram asked, trying to see into her heavy-lidded eyes.

"Just once. With a lorry. But all is quiet, only us old-timers, us granny workforce workers, who toil away in the sewing circle," grey-haired Mrs. Cornford said. She stood in the middle of the hallway, barely making way for him to go to the stairs. She held the candelabra as though she were prepared to challenge him in a duel, although she barely came up to his elbow.

Bram heard muted talking coming from the Beefsteak Room, the greenroom and social area for the acting company. The penny dropped. The dozen or so elderly women who mended the costumes must be here sewing after hours—probably altering costumes into ball gowns for fancy dress balls. That would explain how the Duchess of Marlborough appeared in a newspaper wearing Ellen's *Much Ado About Nothing* costume.

"Ah, the sewing circle," Bram said, trying not to smile. "Mrs. Cornford, is the granny force supplying ball gowns as rentals, by any chance?"

Her mouth opened and shut.

"I'm sure I wish I had thought of such a venture back when I was in charge here," Bram said, taking a lantern from the prop table in the hallway. "It might have put the Lyceum in black ink."

"I climbed the stairs all the way up to your office and put the mail on your desk, Mr. Stoker," Mrs. Cornford said, turning away from him.

"Good night, Mrs. Cornford."

The new syndicate could track their newly acquired inventory of costumes. Not his headache any longer.

The electricity had been shut off as a cost-saving effort. Bram lit the lamp and carried it with one hand, the other holding his valise, as he trudged up three flights. He drew a breath. As his office door swung open, the sight that greeted him was a gut punch. His best rug had been rolled up and the bookshelves plundered. The syndicate had been here. The merger had officially closed only last month. *They couldn't wait until the tour was over to pack up my belongings?*

At least his touring trunk was still there, sitting in the middle of the room. He rushed over and opened it; there were his books and writing, stacked to the brim. Half a dozen rulers lay on top. That was one of his eccentricities, collecting rulers from every city on tour. He was the "Ruler of the Rulers," according to Pamela. He felt a twinge as he thought of her and took out the rulers from Manchester and Liverpool from his valise and added them to his collection.

Strewn on his desk were telegrams, letters, and records of phone calls to every conceivable "castle" from Manchester to Liverpool. The quest, costly and time-consuming, so far had not resulted in any leads on Pamela's whereabouts. Instead, there were piles of unsolicited scripts, books, bills, invitations, and mail. But there on the top was a telegram envelope. He tore it open.

> *Recieved mystical message in newspaper "she's in the castle." Will look for PCS at Windsor Castle. Bring her tarot drawings. Expecting you Tuesday the 11th by noon at the latest. HI*

What could that mean? That Pamela was at Windsor Castle? *Bloody unlikely*. Before he could ponder Henry's message, a woman's voice, not one of the ancients, rose up from the first floor. He went out in the hall to look down and spotted Mrs. Cornford on the landing, guarding the stairs. Florence Farr stood below, with her hands on her hips.

"What's going on here?" Bram called.

"Trying to get up to see you!" Florence yelled up to him. "I have some leads on Pamela."

"Come on up then," Bram shouted.

"No, let's head to Mr. Kamal at the museum," Florence replied. "There's news!"

"Mr. Stoker," Ahmed said as Florence and Bram entered his office. "I was pleased to receive your call and to hear that there is news about Miss Smith."

When they were all seated, Bram began. "It has been three days since Pamela has been missing. Meanwhile, Florence has received two pieces of mail concerning her." Florence took a small book out of her bag and removed a postcard from it.

"This postcard was mailed from Manchester by Pamela the day she went missing and was waiting for me at my sister's house," Florence said.

> *Being followed by a spirit that was on the train with Bram and Ahmed. Going to the church here in Manchester to get rid of it. If you don't hear from me in a week, bring my Emperor and Hierophant together.*

"She also sent along this sketchbook. You need to see it." Florence held up a small book and shuffled through a few of the pages, each one filled with artwork.

Ahmed picked up one of the pages that fell out. Pamela didn't think to ask him to keep her sketchbook while she was on tour? Even though she didn't work for him, Ahmed had given her keys to his desk so that she might lock up her belongings—a privilege he had never extended to anyone else. Perhaps she just didn't trust him or anyone to keep her sketchbook.

Florence slid the book across the desk over to Ahmed. He paged through it. There were primitive sketches of skeletons, demons, and angels. Ahmed stopped at one page and drew in his breath.

It was the image of a king who looked exactly like Bram. Ahmed held up the book so both Florence and Bram could see the sketch.

"This would be Emperor Stoker, I believe," Ahmed said.

"I am certainly not Pamela's Emperor," Bram said, crossing his legs. "What was the second letter?" he asked, gruffly.

"Miss Horniman received an anonymous letter," Florence said, retrieving a letter from her same purse as before. She opened the envelope and read the letter:

"Thoth has instructed me to ensure that only his symbols live on in my version of the cards, 'Crowley's Tarot.' Be warned that any meddling in these resources will directly impact Miss Smith's safety, as well as yours and that of the Golden Dawn. A.C."

Ahmed sighed. "Warring Golden Dawn chiefs—lucky us! Given these threats, especially in lieu of Miss Smith missing, isn't Miss Horniman likely to rescind Miss Smith's job designing the cards? That is, *if* we're able to find her and return her back to London?"

Bram grimaced. "Mr. Kamal," Bram said, "My latest telegram from Mr. Irving stated that a newspaper spelled out, 'She's in the castle.' Do you have any ideas about why we would have a message about Pamela being in a castle?"

Ahmed's eyebrows shot straight up, and he sat back in his chair. "She's in a castle? Well, Miss Farr and I had an experience in the train coming back here. We witnessed a five-pointed star and a shield that looked like it was floating above a saint on a castle."

"A saint on a castle," Bram said. "In this country, that doesn't narrow it down by much."

"What about the letter sent from Southwark Cathedral?" Florence asked. "Mr. Kamal, you said you would look into that.

"I met with Reverend Thompson in Southwark this morning," Ahmed said. "He knows nothing about this letter he supposedly sent, warning us about Pamela and her tarot cards. His church does have plenty of saints depicted in its stained glass windows, though. He is concerned that our Miss Smith may be mixed up with what he called the 'dark arts.'"

"That is disappointing news," Bram said. "Both in his reaction and the fact that he knows nothing about the letter."

"At least Miss Annie won't be swayed by the Reverend," Florence said. "If anything, she's more determined to fund her tarot project with Pamela and Waite. She's sponsoring a search party for her now."

"Where?" Bram and Ahmed said in unison.

"Well, it seems Miss Horniman had a dream," Florence said, "She said she saw that Pamela was in a castle with a lot of heads."

Ahmed blinked. "A castle with a lot of heads?" he asked. "Do you mean there were heads on pikes?"

"I only know it was a castle, Mr. Kamal, and heads were involved," Florence replied. "But in this dream, she saw Pamela being tortured in a castle's dungeon. And she also said she heard Penryhn Castle and Giza Castle mentioned by a furry spirit."

"Miss Farr, there is a Windsor Castle and a Dublin Castle, but I don't believe Miss Smith has ever visited either," Bram said, looking at Ahmed as though he were hoping for agreement on the subject.

Ahmed reached for an atlas of England on his bookshelf and handed it to Bram. "Mr. Stoker, Dublin Castle, Windsor, and Penrhyn Castle—how much distance is between them?"

Bram paged through the atlas until he found Windsor.

"It is a good two hundred miles from Windsor Castle to Penrhyn Castle," Bram said. "From Penrhyn, one must cross the Irish Sea to Dublin Castle—a distance of maybe one hundred miles. I can't recommend sending search parties on a three hundred–mile goose chase because of a rich society lady's dream."

Florence leafed through the sketch pad. "If Miss Horniman is willing to fund this excursion, I would think we should go along with it." She stopped at a drawing of a holy man on a throne. "This looks Egyptian, Mr. Kamal. What do you make of this?" She slid the book over to him.

Seated on a throne, Ahmed saw an official holding a triple-crossed scepter. Two officiants knelt before him, raising a staff between them. On the margin was written:

Hierophant Ahmed Kamal—
no beard or fez—holds papal scepter.

"What is the meaning of a pharaoh holding an ankh scepter in his right hand and a globe in his left?" Florence asked.

"It seems to be an Egyptian emperor, not just a king," Bram said. "What is the scepter on the floor?"

"Wait, where is that other drawing?" Florence asked, standing and turning the pages. She found the emperor drawing again. She pointed to Pamela's handwritten note sprawled on the side margin.

Ahmed let out a breath and read, "'Uncle Brammie—his orb/cross scepter and ram's heads.'"

"It seems Pamela's Emperor is you, Mr. Stoker," Florence said, turning back and forth between the drawings. "And her Hierophant is you, Mr. Kamal. Of course, it is odd that she has given you the Egyptian symbols, Mr. Stoker, and Mr. Kamal the papal staff."

Ahmed studied the sketches. "Yes, I've seen some versions of these before, but I never recognized any of them as renditions of Mr. Stoker or myself."

"The scepter the emperor holds, that is the Egyptian symbol of life, isn't that right, Mr. Kamal?" Florence asked.

Ahmed nodded. Yet, it made no sense why Pamela would give Bram Egyptian symbols. Or that he would be cast as a hierophant or pope: she knew he was Islamic.

Mr. Stoker stroked his beard and in low voice said, "Actually, this staff is a drawing of a prop we used in *The Cups*. Pamela knows I would recognize it; I commissioned her to design it."

Ahmed stared at the two keys on the Hierophant card. He had forgotten that he had given her the two keys to the archive room. "As the muse for Pamela's High Priestess, she sometimes confided in me about her drawings," Florence said, staring out the window. "Sometimes, she complained about Waite's insistence on using some random symbol or another. But I remember that she was adamant that these two cards, her Emperor and Hierophant, each have a scepter," Florence said as she leaned back in her chair. "Now I understand. When these two scepters are crossed, they create a sundial, a sort of compass to help the Emperor and the Hierophant find her. We need two scepters, one for each of you as you search for Pamela."

"Currently, there are no scepters in the acquisitions I curate," Ahmed said wryly. "And I hope you aren't thinking that we can take some artifact from the museum to make a compass?"

Florence gathered her coat and handbag. "You are both very resourceful; I'm sure you'll come up with something. Now, Mr. Stoker, Mr. Kamal, I'm going home to pack for a search-party trip to Penrhyn Castle. If we find nothing, then on to Dublin Castle. I hope you will join me, Mr. Stoker, after your command appearance before the queen. Have a safe journey to Cairo, Mr. Kamal."

Ahmed and Bram stood up.

"Is it safe for you?" Ahmed started.

"It's not so very late, not even eight o'clock, but thank you for your concern," Florence said. She let herself out of the room.

Ahmed and Bram both sat with a sigh.

"Mr. Stoker, let's go over what know we know about Miss Smith's disappearance," Ahmed said. Bram's eyebrows creased. "Yes, I'm sorry: she is Pamela to you, not Miss Smith."

"And please, call me Bram," Bram replied. "Otherwise, I feel as though I am still at work."

"Very well, Bram, please call me Ahmed. I'm sorry I cannot join you at Penrhyn Castle, but I hope to join you as soon as possible in Dublin," Ahmed said, placing an ashtray on his desk.

"How long will it take you to reach Egypt?" Bram asked.

"Five days to reach Cairo by transcontinental train and ship," Ahmed said. "Once I arrive, it will take me another day just to organize transportation to visit my employer in Giza. I anticipate being there a week. Then it will take me another five days to sail back here, then on to Ireland."

"Any chance that Pamela is captive in Egypt?" Bram asked, taking out his matches and cigar. "Maybe you could rescue her there? I know that is far-fetched. But perhaps these visions Miss Horniman had of Pamela walled up are a signal sent from a tomb in Giza?"

"Not at all. Unless her captor flies like a bird," Ahmed said. "And if Pamela is walled up in a tomb there, as she was in Miss Horniman's dream, I could begin to guess what vault she is in."

"I hope to be in Dublin within the day after the Windsor commitment," Bram said, as he held a trembling hand up to light his cigar. "My main questions remain: Who kidnapped Pamela? And why? She has no money. But she does have magical knowledge. My bet is on Aleister Crowley."

Ahmed sat up. "While you and I and Pamela were on that train to Manchester, that appearance could have been an afrit sent by Aleister. It could have been accompanying us, spying on us. You remember the '666' drawn on the window? That could have been a tactic used to frighten Pamela. Feeling insecure, she went into the Manchester church for protection. And finding her separated from her usual friends, Aleister decided to have her abducted there."

"But how on earth did this afrit have the power to abduct her from a church?" Bram sputtered, tiny clumps of cigar leaves crumbling between his thumb and finger. "That's sacrilege."

"The sanctity of the church couldn't protect her," Ahmed answered. "As with the tombs in Egypt, many churches sit atop tunnels that are underground, where the currents of spirits are very strong."

Bram hit his head with his palm. "Of course! Ley lines!"

"Ley lines?" Ahmed asked.

"Like the lines used to guide the sun into the darkest reaches of Celtic or Viking burial grounds here on certain days. Ley lines are the same across the Ireland and England," Bram said.

"I know of certain tombs in Egypt where the lines of the sun reach the innermost chambers only twice a year," Ahmed said, waving away Bram's smoke that was stinging his eyes. "I believe our tombs trump your Viking burial mounds."

"Very well," Bram continued, "even before the Vikings, these lines or conduits ran through underground tunnels. Later the thralls, the Vikings' slaves, traveled through them, snatching children. Maybe the spirit of one of them snatched Pamela. The ley line tunnels the thrall spirits are said to use have been found as far away as Liverpool and Manchester." Ahmed watched Bram sit straight up as the ash from his cigar fell down his vest, and he continued. "The lines also run up under the ocean to Dublin Castle." Bram looked at Ahmed, his blue eyes wide. "Dublin Castle. Where the heads of saints are perched on spires outside on the church."

"This afrit may have used a thrall tunnel to kidnap Miss Smith," Ahmed said. "But how would her physical body be transported to Dublin?"

"I have no idea," Bram replied, smashing the cigar's embers out in the ashtray on the desk. "That would be the ultimate conjuring in Golden Dawn magic, I would think. Well, if there is such a thing as underwater travel, we can divide and conquer: you take Egypt, and I'll take Ireland."

Ahmed stared at Bram. Could he be serious? Ahmed didn't doubt the spirits of the gods could transport themselves at will. But mere mortals? Pamela? Well, sometimes magical tokens gave magical powers. A magical token. He knew just the thing for Bram. An antiquity that he recently bought from a peddler. He would make a friend to find a friend.

Ahmed rose and unlocked his desk drawer, then took out a jeweled case and opened it. Inside was a small medallion. He would have to trust that Bram would not abuse the power that might be in this artifact. "Here is a miniature scepter, as it were."

Ahmed lifted a bronze-colored orb: it was about the size of a pocket watch. In the low light, the metal braid glimmered, and the surrounding eight jewels embedded around the edge cast prisms around them. Ahmed clicked a knob on top and handed it to his friend. In the center of the disk, eight prongs rotated, revealing faint symbols. Bram gasped.

"This is a Viking amulet, also used as a compass," Ahmed said, handing it to him. "I bought it from a mudlark. The Vikings considered these compasses excellent tools for searching for lost souls."

"What a thing of beauty!" Bram said, holding it up to the overhead light.

"We've seen these markings before!" Ahmed said, and he motioned to the tarot sketches on his desk. "You can see in them in the Emperor and Hierophant that Pamela drew. Look—the scepters! Both have exactly the same shape as the prongs on the Viking compass."

Bram picked up the Emperor drawing. "Somehow these two tarot cards caught the attention of the afrit. It's possible we can use the items in her drawing to track her down."

"Pamela drew scepters in her Hierophant and Emperor cards," Ahmed said. "Is it possible that she intended to arm them so that they might to rule and command over future battles?"

"Perhaps Pamela realized that she needs rulers in the tarot deck mix—not just magicians and high priestesses," Bram said, setting the Emperor sketch down. He picked up his newly acquired compass. "Yes, the Magician and Fool start the path. The High Priestess and Empress give the journey spirituality and sexuality."

"But the next steps of the Emperor and Hierophant involve decision-making," Ahmed added. "The ability to rule, depending on philosophy and loyalty. Egyptian, Viking, and Christian symbols . . . these symbols on this compass and in her tarot cards all tell the same story."

Bram shook his head. "But how can these Egyptian and Viking symbols help us find her?"

"I believe that these symbols may present themselves when she is near," Ahmed said.

"Like an energy field?" Bram asked.

"Like energy lines," Ahmed replied.

"Ley lines," Bram replied, looking out the office window. "Our unseen energy river." He tilted his head and raised the compass to inspect it more closely. "Won't you need this compass in Giza?"

Ahmed gathered up Pamela's tarot-card drawings and the sketchbook of hers that Florence had brought. He locked them all in his desk. "Thank you for offering, but that is your gift. Besides, since I am supposedly an Egyptian Hierophant, I prefer to use an Egyptian compass, not a Viking one. Speaking of Giza, though, I must be packing this evening."

Bram pocketed his compass. "Thank you, Ahmed, for this exquisite present. As the Emperor to your Hierophant, it is my hope that we find Pamela before Aleister Crowley can do any harm to her."

"A safe journey for all of us is my fervent hope as well," Ahmed said. "May we avoid all demons and their like!"

"Yes—and telegram me at once if you find anything," Bram said. "Especially any demons."

CHAPTER NINETEEN

Spires of the Royal Chapel

"Uncle Brammie!" Pamela shouted to the evaporated vision. "Sir Henry!" The goat devil was gone. Only William's face still flitted above her out of reach, with an expression of sorrow. "Is Uncle Brammie all right? Why did those men attack Sir Henry at the train station"

"You've commanded your Uncle Brammie to be your Emperor, but Sir Henry is no longer your Magician. He is the Blue Knight," William said, gazing down at her.

"The Blue Knight?" Pamela cried as she lurched around her prison cell, hands out in front of her. "What is a Blue Knight? Help!"

"Pamela! Miss Smith!" William said, using his deep Robin Hood voice. "Stop. I will tell you, but you must settle down."

Pamela threw herself against the stone wall, trying to catch her breath. "Will Sir Henry be killed, as you were? If I can command Uncle Brammie, how do I tell him to get me out of here? Where is my afrit?"

"Calm, calm. Breathe," William said, circling above her, his eyes fixed on the last place where the vision had appeared.

Pamela looked up and tried to see if the vision was still there, but only darkness remained. "Go on," she said. "Sir Henry is no longer my Magician."

"Alfred, Lord Tennyson, have you heard of him?" William's disembodied voice asked, moving about the room. "Author of *Morte d'Arthur*."

"Of course I know him. It was his *Death of Arthur* that Sir Henry asked me to read before he let me illustrate the *King Arthur* poster." Pamela knelt, trying to get a fix on William's orbit.

"Well, if you truly read the book, you would remember the story of the Blue Knight."

"I said he asked me to read it," Pamela answered, her face burning. "I haven't read it yet. It's on my list of books to read."

William grunted as he flew by her head. "Well, Miss Smith, Sir Persaunt was the Blue Knight, beaten in battle by a nephew of King Arthur. In his defeat, the Blue Knight tendered an invitation to his victor to stay the night."

"So, the Blue Knight was a good loser?" Pamela asked, getting a crick in her neck trying to keep up with the swooping head.

"He was more than a good loser. He also offered up his eighteen-year-old virgin daughter to bring the king's nephew good cheer in bed."

"And did she bring cheer to the king's nephew?" Pamela asked, her face burning. William Terriss talking to her about virgins being offered up was a conversation she had never envisioned and was not comfortable having now.

"No, Gareth sent the virgin back to her father, undefiled."

"So, Sir Henry as the Blue Knight means what?'" Pamela asked, trying to keep the peevish tone out of her voice. "That he is giving up his virgins?"

"It means he is being asked to sacrifice for others. But Sir Henry's pride may not let him. Unless it adds to his legacy, he will not contribute, like most Magicians. They are selfish about sharing their gifts, their love, their ideas."

"Sir Henry isn't selfish," Pamela said, a frog catching in her throat. "He hires hundreds of people. He takes care of all of us with his gifts!"

"You must see it, Pamela: As long as we serve his idea of who he is, he is generous. But when the Guv'nor is no longer popular, he's not willing to hand over the reins. Aleister knows that Sir Henry is prideful enough that he warrants being cursed as the Blue Knight. Spells only work where there is fertile ground. The Guv'nor is willing to sacrifice his own offspring if it means bringing glory to himself."

"So that's to be his legacy? Selling the Lyceum Theatre rather than sharing the leadership with his sons or Uncle Brammie?" Pamela asked. "Not his fame as the premiere actor of the age?"

William harrumphed. "We can't see into the future, now, can we? You now have an Emperor, your Uncle Brammie, at your call. Just remember, Stoker has always been a strong advocate of rules, regardless of the outcomes for others."

"Yes, he's my 'Ruler of Rulers.' But how do I call him?" Pamela asked.

Plinks of dripping water echoed in the hallway. Pamela knelt and peered through the slat. She couldn't see anything but the empty stone corridor. When she turned back, William was no longer there. "Did my afrit turn Sir Henry blue?" Pamela asked, her voice tremulous. "William? My Fool? Are you there?"

The only answer was the sound of something grunting outside the door, its reverberations shuddering the stone walls of her cell. It was a familiar call, like a horse or cow in heat perhaps? Where had she heard that? It was that "Ow, ow, ow, ow" moan again. As the last tones faded away, she felt movement in her palm. Her handkerchief was back in her hand—and even in the dim light, Pamela could see that it had turned back to its bright sky-blue color.

She began to run in circles; the air was fetid and damp. She was being kept alive, mentally tortured for a purpose. She sent a thought message to Bram and Ahmed: *Come find me!*

Nothing. No, wait.

A whistle. The forbidden whistle from backstage. William's call that he was in place? No, it was the stage crew's signal to lift a scrim. Two sharp blasts and a low one.

Make your own magic. Time to try to fly. She stood up and jumped. She landed in a heap and groaned. How could she get out of here if she couldn't fly on her own?

"Magic doesn't need a body," she heard William say.

"William?" she answered back. "This body needs some help!"

"Fly!" he commanded.

A jolt hit Pamela's midsection, and she catapulted through the air. She was a ray of light, weightless, yet—propelled upward. Once out of the enclosure, she floated along a tunnel and was spit out. Gasping, she was suspended in space, bathed in fresh night air. She gulped it in, trying to expel the fumes of her cell. Dangling midair, she made out a profile of stacked stones meeting the sky. It took a moment for her to realize what they were. The stones were a chapel's spire, all within arm's distance. She looked down and realized that she was hovering thirty feet up from a bricked courtyard.

Being up high in the air felt like a natural thing to do, and she soared up, bobbling in front of the church's pinnacles. She righted herself to face the looming spires. She was flying on her own!

Directly in front of her was a head molded into the base of a spire. Not William Terriss on the catwalk at the Lyceum Theatre backstage but a bearded king with a fine mustache, part avenging angel, part gargoyle.

"Are you Mad Nero?" Pamela asked.

The face glared at her. "You ignorant girl, I am Brian of the Tributes."

He sounded a little like Bram, but his name did not ring a bell. "I'm sorry, who are you? I'm terrible at most history. You do sound like my Uncle Brammie."

The stone face turned a darker shade of gray. "I am King Brian, and I happen to be the last great king of Ireland, who freed the Irish people from the Vikings."

A brush of wind at her side caught her attention. There he was, William Terriss. Not on the catwalk after all but floating with her. He drifted alongside her, laughing and shaking his head.

Winking at her, he nodded his head to the statues on the spires, and she tried to steady herself by grasping the base of King Brian's. Her hands couldn't catch hold. Her breath came fast and shallow. Her eyesight was dimming. She tried to grab William, but he had no substance.

"Is he Nero?" she asked, trying not to panic as she flailed.

"No, Pamela, he's King Brian," William replied as he soared below her and blew back up. "Slow your breath, slow your thoughts. I'm here to help, but you must help yourself first."

Fighting back tears, she breathed more deeply. Her lungs felt very heavy, and the air she gasped felt meager and thin. Her body dragged downward.

"Where am I?" she asked. She looked up: stars emerged from a purple night-sky quilt. She looked down: she was hundreds of yards up in the air. "How can I get out of this?" she asked William, gulping for breath.

"I'm not sure, Pixie, but we can manage this," he answered, soaring next to her.

William's outline became clearer. He wore the stage beard she had constructed for him. Yes, and on his head was the crown from *The Cups*. But his clothes—that was his Lancelot costume from *King Arthur*. Why the mishmash? No, they had been part of her job to check off as wardrobe staff. One of her most mundane tasks was to chalk an outline of William's body on the floor and lay each article of clothing on top of it for the quick changes. Here they were, still part of William's dress.

She felt a strong bubble of air buoy her up.

"After all," William said as her body began to tilt upward. "Did we not survive a falling off the bridge and a dunk in the Thames and climbing up the embankment? Did we not do all that, us two? We fly through danger."

That terrible accident—her falling off the Waterloo Bridge and William jumping in after her—still haunted her dreams. For years, she had relived the sensation of pitching forward and feeling the river drag her under. Her first experiences of flying with Maud as a child had devolved into a nightmare of falling. Fear of falling, fear of being left alone.

Pamela tried to muffle a sob. "But I'm no one. I have no family, no help," she moaned.

The crowned head on the spire snapped at her, "And do you think Brian Boru, the last great King of Ireland, came from wealth and power? No! From common folk I came, and yet I forced out the Ui Neill king. I ousted the Scandinavians! It was my destiny to fight against the vicious rulers of the day."

"Yes, King Brian Boru," Pamela said, "but I don't think I can hold on to this ability to fly. I can only fall. I know I'll fall! I feel it!"

William bobbed over to the king and threw his arm around his neck, chuckling. "Pamela Colman Smith, afraid? The young girl who flew in the air with Maud Gonne? Who painted magic into the set pieces at the Lyceum Theatre before the paint crew without asking permission? Drove her own horse cart in Jamaica before she was twelve? Went to school in New York City, lived on her own, and had an exhibit at an art gallery? Went on tour with the Lyceum Theatre and made them all love her? Pamela, afraid? Go on!"

She felt a laugh percolating under her ribs. Her back began to ache as she tried to remain upright.

"You're right, Mr. Terriss, I'm not a goner."

"No, you're not," William said.

"Then act like it," groused the stone face of King Brian.

Pamela whipped around to the statue. “I command you to help me get out of here!”

King Brian’s eyebrows fluttered, a smile curling under his beard. “There she is, at last. I will be first in your clan. Call in the others, and we’ll strike.”

She wafted toward King Brian’s head. Propelling herself forward with her hands as though she were swimming, she whooshed through the twilight sky. Coming closer to the rows of statues, the head next to King Brian turned to her.

Pamela knew right away from his tall ceremonial hat that this was Saint Patrick. The bearded saint looked jolly, his bushy eyebrows sticking out like two marble caterpillars. His eyes were so intense that he looked almost crazed, and his archbishop’s miter was tilted at such an angle that Pamela gasped. Recovering, she hovered bent over until she righted herself, waving her arms up and down until she was balanced.

Saint Patrick’s lips parted. “Well, lass, according to Brian Boru here, we are to be your tribe. Is that right?”

King Brian’s face swiveled toward them. “As the last great king of Ireland, I have decreed that we are to serve you,” King Brian said to Pamela.

“Oh, you decree it, do you?” Saint Patrick asked.

William appeared at her side, almost dawdling as he drifted. He whispered, “Command your troops before they become ungovernable.”

“I would be most grateful for your help,” Pamela said. “But I’m not sure what you can do for me since you are stuck all the way up here.”

Both stone faces groaned.

“If I’d known you were going to be this helpless, I would have stayed at the crypt’s entrance,” King Brian said.

“You’re not usually up here on this spike?” Pamela asked.

“It’s a pinnacle, girl,” another head snapped. “Didn’t you study anything at art school?”

Pamela gasped as she looked closer. It was Queen Elizabeth the First, her pinched face framed by a crown nestled in tight curls.

"Why is the English queen on the outside of an Irish church?" Pamela asked William in a low voice.

"English money paid for this Royal Chapel," William answered.

Next to Queen Elizabeth was a familiar face: Nera of Connaught, the hero of Irish fairy tales, the one who had taught her to fly during a bedtime story long ago.

"Nera!" Pamela cried.

"At your service," Nera answered. King Brian and Nera nodded at one another.

She looked at the four heads, each of them staring back at her in a critical way. "You're all here to help me?" Pamela asked. "You'll get me out of here?"

Queen Elizabeth's eyes narrowed. "Only you can get yourself out of here. We're here to fight alongside you. We await your command."

How could speaking stone heads on a church's spires help her? Pamela began to flail as she looked around. Whatever or whoever was she supposed to fight? There were no armed flying monsters nearby—there was nothing on the horizon.

"Where am I?" Pamela asked. "Who am I supposed to battle?"

"Where do you think you are?" Saint Patrick asked.

Pamela looked below her. There was a stone courtyard made up of an assortment of mismatched adjoining buildings. The courtyard square was anchored by two round towers, the bigger of the two adjacent to the church atop which she floated. Scanning the neighborhood, she could see that the castle enclave was surrounded by three-story buildings. Shops, theatres, and stables lined the streets extending to the warehouses piled up next to docks along a river. The river lapped the port, and the ocean's fresh smell wafted up to her. For a moment, she was in

St. Andrews, a child smelling the Jamaican salt air, the chimney smoke, and fish.

She studied the bigger turret beneath her. "Why does that round tower look familiar?" Pamela asked William.

"It's where your Uncle Brammie toiled away as a clerk for twelve years," he answered.

Now she recognized it. The tower was in the sketch Uncle Brammie kept on his desk. She had asked him once what it depicted, and he had answered, "A prison."

"This is Dublin Castle?" Pamela said. "But it doesn't look anything like a castle."

"Not all castles have to look like Windsor Castle," King Brian shouted to Pamela.

"Steady on there, Irish King," Queen Elizabeth said. "We don't expect your castles to come up to our level."

"As a cohort to the King of the Fairies," Nera added, "I've seen you don't need grand castles for a kingdom."

"There is only one kingdom, the Kingdom of God," Saint Patrick said. "He rules the realm now that the Druids have been expelled."

"Ah, yes, your big boast," Nera said, wagging his head back and forth in agitation. "You braggart, thinking that running the magical ones out of Ireland was a holy act. But we're all the poorer for it."

"Yes, thanks be to God that I drove the pagans and their blasphemous magic out," Saint Patrick said, his eyebrows knitting together like intertwined snakes. "It's kept the Druids' magic out of the hands of the devil!"

"It seems you didn't keep all the magic, Saint Patty," King Brian said. "Otherwise, we wouldn't all be stuck up here on Royal Chapel."

"Any chance you memorized an incantation for a battle with flying spirits?" Queen Elizabeth asked.

"A battle with flying spirits?" Pamela asked, flitting closer to them. "I'm to battle something midair? Is that why I'm here at Dublin Castle?"

"It's built on Viking ruins," King Brian said exasperatedly, as though everyone were familiar with this fact. "You must have troubled a Viking slave, or thrall, with your magic, and now you're called out to battle the others."

"Now, King Brian, remember that not everyone was brought up in your faith," William said, putting a protective arm around Pamela to balance her. "Miss Smith may not recognize Viking ruins or the Royal Chapel of Dublin Castle, even if it's familiar to others."

"What others?" Pamela asked, trying to swim toward the king as a breeze pushed her away.

William drifted up and away from the church spires. He called down to her, "I may not be with you all the time, but as your Fool, I will guide when I can."

Pamela tried to swim up to him, but the outline of his body disappeared, leaving only the yellow color of the fool's tarot card. In the dark night sky, the golden hue soon ebbed away. The last splashes of yellow burned her eyes like the sun. He was gone. She looked back at King Brian. His silhouette settled, and then it was still. The sharp pain in her back intensified, and she tumbled backward. The wind whistled past her ears as she fell, head first.

The tunnel opened. A swirl of light, a short tumble, and she was once more sitting on the floor of her tower prison.

As she tried to get her bearings, she heard sounds outside the door. The grate at the bottom of the door opened: a food and water bowl were plunked down, and the door was shut. She tried to get up in time to see who or what was there, but by the time she was at the door, there was no one there. "Who are you? Where are you?" she asked.

Once again, she heard the chirping sound, the *ow*, sounding off in the distance. Why was that sound so familiar?

PART III

Emperor and Hierophant Storm the Castle

CHAPTER TWENTY

AHMED'S NILE

From the deck of the *Nitocris*, Ahmed spotted a bask of crocodiles sunning themselves in the waning light on the banks of the Nile. Their teeth showed through their partially closed mouths like diabolic pearls. The scales of their backs, a matte mud color, made them almost invisible against the brown-gray grasses of the shore. The sun dipped another notch while, on one of the luxury boats next to them, a group of men played music to Indian tourists, seated women in saris and men in turbans. The lilting drumming of a tabla and sitar music cast a spell on the rowers in the cluster of adjoining ships, and Ahmed nodded in time to the music.

It had been over two years since he had been aboard a *dahabiya*, and as he looked to the sails fluttering above, he breathed in the familiar perfume of these banks. But the scent of reeds, fish, and salt air was mixed in with the exhaust of the newer steam engine of the boat. As the *Nitocris* slowed, Ahmed saw the new tourist stations and private homes dotting the riverbank. This was not the river of his youth. How odd to moor here overnight, flanked by the luxury steamers forged in Scotland full of English and Indian tourists. On the deck of a ship passing them, he could see men wearing turbans and tunics as they leaned against the railing. Indian and European visitors traveling to experience an exotic vacation were creating an entire new industry along these shores.

Pamela had once shown him a photo of herself wearing a turban, part of her costume as she recited her Jamaican folktales. When he asked why she was wearing it, she flippantly answered she was "dressed as a genie not a swami." When he told her that he didn't think she understood either, she sulked for a few days and then told him she was going to only wear her Jamaican crow-feather crown from then on. Where was she? Was her crow-feather crown protecting her where she was? How could she just disappear off the face of the earth? Had evil spirits whisked her away?

His boat stopped as outbuildings of the pharaoh's village came into view, just as the lowering rays of the sun momentarily blinded Ahmed. When his eyes adjusted, violet and pink hues infused the sand, stone, and limestone buildings along the shore. Everything looked lit up from within. A contagion of colors simmered among the rocks until the tilting rays drew up a riot of deep-hued purples and gold that overtook the last light.

Ahmed glanced over to his English traveling companion, Mr. Griffith, standing with his mouth agape. "Not quite the sunsets you are accustomed to on the Thames, are they?" Ahmed asked.

"No, this makes our sunsets but a smudge of light," Griffith said, sitting back in his chair and putting his feet up on the railing. "And what a view: wild animals, ruins, and heathens!"

Mrs. Griffith sitting next to him gently nudged his feet off with her parasol. "Dear, take your feet off the railing, we're not quite heathens yet," she said through terse lips.

Her husband turned away from the setting sun, a ray of light bouncing off his bald pate, and pretended to shoot some of the crocodiles. Granted these two had probably only ever seen wild animals in the London Zoo in Regent's Park, but Ahmed felt a wave of revulsion.

So far, the burden of having to travel with the Griffiths was bothersome, but at least they hadn't interfered with his travel for work, which was his first concern when he was asked to take them. But these English representatives of the Thomas Cook & Son travel agency were connected with the board members at the British Museum, and Ahmed had no choice in the matter. They had sailed together from the sodden shores of England to Paris, taken a train to Rome, boarded another ship to Alexandria, and, by the most auspicious stars, would be deposited at the Shepheard's Hotel in Cairo six days after departure from London. It would offer Ahmed enough time to meet his direct supervisor, Émile Brugsch, and report on the missing statue, Sekhemka.

The largest crocodile perched on the rock pile in front of the pharaoh's village roared, rousing Ahmed from his thoughts. He watched it flick its tail. As if on cue, twenty or so crocodiles thrashed about as they positioned themselves to dive, a frenzy of lashing jaws and tails. Once they had thrown themselves into the water, the tops of their heads barely grazed above the surface. They were swimming up to the *Nitocris.*

Ahmed recognized it, or rather her, right away. It was one of the smaller crocodiles with a more of a U-shaped jaw than the others. Then he realized it wasn't a crocodile at all but an alligator from the West Indies.

Pamela traveled with her stuffed alligator, a former pet from her childhood in Jamaica.

She'd brought it to the museum once when she had a performance after work. She took it out and held it up to him.

"This is Albertine, my reptile guardian," Pamela added. "My solo performance piece depends on her being with me." Ahmed could have sworn then that the alligator's glassy, green-marble eye rotated to fix on him.

Now, it seemed that the same alligator was swimming right up to the boat's side. The dying sun's last rays caught the jade color in her eye, and the green swirl of color gave him an instant vision. He saw her at last.

Pamela was in a stone cell, reaching out, her arms breaking free from bricks in a wall. Where had he seen this scene before? Yes, it was like the chamber where he discovered the Deir el-Bahri mummy cache. Both rooms had light filtering down from tiny cracks in the ceiling and water-soaked floors inset with stones carved with reptiles and dragons. But the Egyptian crypt had a secret entrance at the top with a grate adorned with outlines of swords in a geometric pattern. Before Ahmed could see if Pamela's cell had the same secret entrance, the alligator once again appeared before him in the water, opening its teeth-lined jaw. She emitted a pitiful, high-pitched call. Pamela's voice called from far away. The creature propelled itself through the water with its stout legs and turned in a flash to submerge into the churning depths, its tail leaving waves of figures on the surface. The images ran together and folded out into the waves, creating a blurred likeness of Pamela in a tower, holding an alligator.

His left ear started burning and snapped him out of his reverie. The vision was gone. He panted, trying to catch his breath. His hand went to his ear, clapping it so hard he almost brained himself.

Mr. Griffith, standing next to him, said, "Good God, man! What was that? Something's bitten your ear!"

Ahmed didn't need to look in a mirror to know Pamela's initials, "PCS," were embedded in his left earlobe.

CHAPTER TWENTY-ONE

Turning Heads

Pamela tried to hang on to the fluttering image of Bram at the train station. As the particles of William floating above her began to dissolve as well, she felt a new sense of determination. *Time to conjure my muses!*

Pamela stretched out her arms. "Uncle Brammie, Emperor, I command you, appear to me!" The sounds of dripping water were the only reply. "Ahmed, my Hierophant, where are you? I command you to appear!"

She kicked the ground, "How can you conjure spirits when they're unreliable?"

The sound of the slot in the door creaking open got her attention. The blue handkerchief erupted through the slot. It crashed in the middle of the floor, rocking itself back and forth.

"I'm having nothing to do with you, traitor," Pamela said, turning her face away.

The cloth came into her sight line, puffing up and flattening, as though it were sighing.

"Sir Henry is attacked by your blue powder, thanks to you and Aleister. I want no more of your dumb shows."

The handkerchief hopped along the floor until it was at Pamela's feet. She kicked it aside. It flew in the air and landed right next to her. She grabbed it and wrung it out. Blue speckles from the cloth fell into a pile of light-blue dust beside her.

From the dust, the goat devil began to assemble into a tangible shape, albeit even shaggier and more pathetic than his last incarnation, one goat leg being supported by a crutch. Pamela felt no fear as she approached him and stared into his face. "How could you? You poison Sir Henry at Aleister's bidding? You'll torment my friends until I refuse to draw more tarot cards?"

The afrit's eyes were no longer sparkling sapphires but the light-blue color of robins' eggs. The ghost hung his head. He then reached down, struggling to support himself on the crutch, and wrote in the dirt.

Fly to your friends.

A whoosh of air and she was jerked upward, out into the upper reaches of the sky, dangling above the earth. Was this her power, or was it due to the afrit? It was twilight, and the birds sang their evening-tide song. In another time and place, being this high up would have terrified her. On her transatlantic crossings, she had a petrifying shortness of breath and she clutched the ship railings, feeling dizzy just looking down from the deck.

But here, as purple shadows outlined the silhouette of Dublin, she was unafraid even though the city of Dublin was unfamiliar to her. She would see if any of it was recognizable. Her heart pounded as a fortress wall came up fast in her path. She tried to go higher, over the castle wall, but she bobbled to a lurching halt just as she reached a hard surface. As she came into contact with it, she slapped her hands before her to break the collision. *Be calm, like William Terriss advised.* She positioned herself so she could kick off from the stone wall.

Come on now! Fly!

She managed to propel herself upward. So, she could control this flight, even if she couldn't activate it. She stretched out her arms like a tightrope walker. No longer teetering, she stabilized in the air currents. She looked down at the blurry ground. It was so far away, but still her heart beat steadily. Looking out, that must be Dublin Bay leading out to the ocean, gulls making their last rounds in the upper drafts. The shoreline lapped gently at the city docks, city streets branching out from them past the center of the town.

At the fortress's left, she spotted a river only blocks away. *That must be feeding the underground stream in the embankment.* She propelled herself nearer the church, then landed on the roof's spine, right next to the bell tower at the entrance.

Yes, this was the church from the last visit with the stone heads on spikes. At this height, she had a better view of not only its roof but the entire contents of the walled-in fortress. There was a Restoration assembly hall and a regency courthouse with private apartments and halls, all connected by the outside wall. The total effect was more of a medieval fort than a castle, especially because the corners were anchored by four towers, two of them almost ruins. Four towers in a castle—Uncle Brammie told her a story once about haunted castles towers. *Was it his story about Dracula?*

In the lowering light, she noted the courtyard's four walls were from different time periods. Underneath the biggest tower, she spied a small stream meandering around the fortress's circumference, the remains of a moat. An underground river—that must have been what the sounds of water dripping in her cell were from.

She willed herself to fly higher. Rather than flapping her arms like a bird, she lifted her arms up, chest out. Soon, she was clumsily circling around the church's roof, examining the spires with the stone heads on it, the scene of her last encounters. The spires ran the entire length of the roof, and on each one four stone heads were speared. Unlike her last visit, they were currently inert. Were these supposed to be gargoyles or grotesques?

Looking toward the horizon, she saw the sun start to dip. In the other direction, the exhaled breath of dusk came over her, with smells of the sea and peat smoke. Evening was coming. Could she stay afloat in the dark? Could she get down and escape?

She caught sight of the four familiar heads on the church spires, Nera, King Brian, Saint Patrick and Queen Elizabeth. "Are you just going to stare at me? Why don't you help me? Pamela called.

"Use your talents to help yourself," Nera called back.

"The world is waiting for them."

"The world doesn't want my talents!" Pamela said.

"What was the lesson the Fool taught you?" Nera asked.

Pamela's heartbeat paused. "To start, to take risks, to let go," she replied.

"And your magician, Sir Henry," King Brian said, "Taught you to transform into something bigger than yourself, yes?"

"Yes, but I had to ask for magic from outside to help me," she said. "There was no magic inside of me."

"You have enough magic to take risks," Nera said, his eyebrows undulating with every other word. "Without waiting for the outside's blessing. Own your gifts."

"Very well, I own being a risk-taking fool and a magic-making magician," she said, twirling in midair.

The scenery shifted and spun, and Pamela almost fell over, then steadied herself.

"I will use the tricks of the Magician to right myself!" she cried. "I will ask all my muses to share their gifts!"

The world stopped twirling. They were at her disposal, all for the asking!

"High Priestess is the Magician's companion. What can you claim from her?" William asked.

"Florence Farr, wherever you are as my High Priestess, your astral travel will be my gift." A warmth bloomed in her face as she spread her arms out and felt the oncoming night breeze envelope her. "Flying is so much easier now!"

"Easier said than done," the dour Queen Elizabeth chimed. "You haven't lived up to your responsibility of being an Empress."

"Ellen has taught me to mother my creations," she said, whirling around, spinning like a top in the breeze around the spire.

"Excellent! Brava! That's it!" the stone heads cried as she spun around them. Slowing in her circling, she focused on William's face as he swiveled around.

"The Emperor will give me my earned power—that'll be Uncle Brammie," she said, placing her hands first on William, then King Brian. She reached out to touch Queen Elizabeth's stone face. "Ahmed is my Hierophant—my access to wisdom."

"Not wise enough yet," the queen snarled.

Pamela fell through the air until she was sitting outside a wooden door. It was the door to her cell, only now she was on the outside in a corridor, three open windows in the stones letting in late-afternoon light. Heavy wooden doors were at the end of hall. She ran to one door and tried to open it. Locked tight. She ran to the other door. It was shuttered as well.

Damnation!

Standing, she shouted, "I command you to release me!"

Nothing.

"By the power of my Fool and Magician, I will be free!"

She was whisked back into her prison cell.

"Oh no! I didn't mean to be free of the corridor! All my muses unite to rescue me," Pamela said, her voice losing strength. There were no signs of the afrit. "Afrit, I command you, appear!" Nothing.

The small metal flap in the door to her cell rattled, and the crashing sounds resonated outside the door. Pamela dashed to the door of her former prison cell and crouched down. The thrashing sounds from the other side stopped. She craned her head down and peered through the small opening. What had been inky blackness in her prison began to lighten from the yellow glow pouring in. A mist poured out from the cell into the hall, surrounding Pamela. A smell of dank water, fetid and pungent, assaulted her. A form began to pillar in front of her, and Pamela scrambled to her feet. It was brown, then green, then emerald green. It had claws and a snout. She gazed into the gray marble eyes of her alligator, her first pet.

"Ow, ow, ow!" it cried.

"Albertina!" Pamela gazed into her reptile's eyes. The yellow green surrounding the pupils lit up. The rest of the creature's body snapped into being. She was huge, at least fifteen feet long, and her stubby paws skidded on the corridor floor as she positioned herself to be stroked.

"Ow, ow, ow!"

It was the baby alligator sounds Albertina had made when she was first hatched. When Albertina first came to her in a dream as an adult, she could talk.

Pamela stroked the beast's massive jaw. She massaged it as far as she could, from underneath Albertina's chin to the top of her head. The rubbery and pliant scales moved as one as Pamela continued to scratch the fine places between her eyes. The eyelids fluttered upward to shut, and the "ows" came in earnest. This was their ritual twenty years earlier, on the beach in Jamaica. Pamela would harness her pet and take her along to Albertina murmured soft ows. *There must have been a spell to keep me from remembering her call.*

"Oh, ow, ow, ow, my friend. Here you are. Here we are. Aleister broke my memory of you but we can talk now."

The two chirped together, almost as if humming or singing, as tiny rays of light seeped in between the looser stones.

"I know if I command you to free me, you will, won't you?" Pamela said in the singsong voice she she had commanded her pet in the past.

Albertina's lower eyelids suddenly flew open, and her marble eyes glowered. A thought appeared in Pamela's mind in the Jamaican accent that Pamela once heard from her.

"Aleister broke our talk magic. But me, Dragon of Wormingford, not to be commanded," the message said.

Pamela laughed and shook her head. "Who called you the Dragon of Wormingford?"

Albertina jerked her head away from Pamela's hand and her tail thrashed back and forth until she turned around. Her great jaw snapped and, as her body crouched even lower over her stubby legs, she growled a slow, ominous, deep thrum. As Pamela pulled her hands back to keep from being hit, the reptile's call grew in volume until it became a tremendous bellow. Her beast slithered near the slot in the door and her body began to diminish, growing shorter, smaller. Her stubby legs disappeared and her obtuse body became sleek and dolphin-like, making herself thin enough to squeeze through the opening flap back into the cell. Once the other side, sounds of water splashing echoed.

"Albertina!" Pamela cried. "Please come back and mind talk with me!"

Pamela knelt before the opening and imagined herself a tiny wisp of smoke. Perhaps she could follow Albertina like a fume. The flap opened, and a shovelful of ash sprayed all over her face and hands.

This magic was going to take some doing to tame.

CHAPTER TWENTY-TWO

Possession of the Pools

Aleister awoke from his meditation with a jolt. Another pool must be nearing a dangerously low level. Thoth fed on these magical pools to communicate with him, but who would dare to vandalize Thoth's meeting place? It couldn't be Pamela—she couldn't access the pools from where Aleister had locked her up. Or could she? He stood up so quickly, he felt dizzy, the walls of his flat spinning around him. If only he had access to the Golden Dawn's damn Vault, he could be there immediately. He could astral travel to the pools instead of using time-consuming spells that stipulated that his spirit wander to other places. But without the Vault, he had to use almost all his energy, which was the very reason the pool levels needed to be replenished.

Time for a new tactic. The vial of white powder he kept in his curiosity cabinet called to him. After inhaling it, he lit a candle, his hand barely shaking, and held it high, greeting the four corners of the room. He sat on the hand-drawn pentagram on the floor, watching the flame of the candle dance. Next came one of the most potent spells he knew, taught to him by his former flatmate, Allan Bennett. He had been warned that conjuring Elbana, the magical meeting place for Thoth, would always come at a price. Summoning a god was easier than directly appealing to the god, but still, there would be costs. Aleister stomped his feet at the thought. A banging from his downstairs neighbor thumping in response distracted him for a moment, but then fury at the disruption inspired him to roar, "I am a glowing ball of compacted force! I transcend space! I command flight!"

A blue circle appeared above the pentagram and throbbed. The light dissolved in and out, hues running from sky blue to the deepest cerulean. Good, the Blue Magic's energy manifested. Now, he could travel to the other dimension. His heart thumped wildly, an effect of the portal opening and the healthy dose of cocaine. This trip would be over quickly.

In the blink of an eye, he was in the main cavern still holding the candle. That was new. Usually the candle stayed behind. He ran along the pathway, dodging low ceilings, almost hitting a stalactite, then running into a stalagmite, still holding the flame as straight as possible. There was the main pool, or the remains of it. He gasped and stretched out his light far out over the edge. The level had fallen feet since he'd last seen it. There it was, scratched into the sides of the now-exposed wall: "PCS."

Damn her! How dare Pamela Colman Smith leave her initials in triumph! How could she siphon away this precious liquid? Who had broken through to Pamela in prison and helped her get access? The spirit of a Hanged Man? A Star? He needed to corral these entities into his tarot deck before the Waite Smith tarot universe claimed them. Waite Smith—what absolute cloying dreck they espoused for their proposed deck. Selectively picking from all times and eras using the most simplistic of Christian archetypes for the most simpleminded.

He sat down at the pool, his legs dangling over the edge. The sound of dripping water and the flutter of bats soothed him.

The metallic perfume of the sacred waters washed over him. Who was this vampire sucking up the pool of transformative magic? Time to find out who was inspiring her.

He peered down into the water and murmured, "Come to me of your own free will."

The echoes of seeping rivulets and rustling wings answered. Grit got into his eye, and he coughed. Even conjuring the images of muses was a trial.

He needed Thoth's belief in him so that together they could create magical icons, so that followers would worship him. The only sure way to lure the public was to enthrall them. In order to do that, he would need to dazzle them with feats of sorcery and enchantment, transforming himself into an owl and all the other expected tricks. This scientific age incited the imagination, stretching tired laws and rules to limitless boundaries. Aleister knew he only had a short window of time for people to think for themselves. War would soon break out in Europe, perhaps if they were lucky, not for the next four or five years, but it was imminent. The bright minds of the age would be drafted to fight another sham grab for power. With Thoth leading him, he could inspire a generation to think for themselves, to resist the moral judgements of the age. His followers would resist the comfort of being sheep, of being constrained by the supposed virtues of religion and society's expectations. Damn these virtuous tyrants. Funny to think it was rumored that he, the supposed incarnation of the devil, could damn anyone. There was no devil, only the selfish, fearful nature of each person. And it was mostly women who insisted on these insipid rules to chain free will to their limited ideals of morality.

Well, this pool was too depleted to use. Aleister stood and walked further down the narrow path until he reached one of the smaller ponds. Good, this one was almost restored, the water level within reach of the brim. During his last visit, it too had been almost drained.

Concentrating on the candle reflecting in its waters, he whispered, "Matter with spirit, knowledge with wisdom, logic with emotion, light with dark. Appear to me, newborn muse."

He repeated it several times. The currents within the pond agitated. An inky image of a man began to assemble within the swirling eddies. Finally! Aleister had performed several incantations here but to no response. Now he might find out if it was Pamela or her muses sucking up the cavern's elixirs. A man in a renaissance tunic waivered just below the surface. The Fool. The first card in Smith's tarot deck. That Robin Hood actor, who worked in Irving's Lyceum Theatre. This was the muse Thoth insisted on being sacrificed to keep these waters safe. Aleister threw a rock at the Fool. It faded, and the image rippled away in waves. The trade for a Fool for magical waters wasn't exactly an even trade: a buffoon for power. If Thoth had insisted on the life of an explorer, a scientist, or an adventurer, that would have been different. Pamela, the mutt-child, didn't have the imagination to use them as muses for her cards, relying on actors and stage managers instead.

Aleister rushed to the next pool, smaller but with more current swirling within its depths. He offered up the same spell, and up came Henry Irving posing as King Arthur. Ah, yes, the precious Magician, the queen's pet, riding for thirty years on the country's insatiable hunger for King Arthur stories. Jesus Christ without the religion. Or miracles. On the water's surface, Irving transformed into a red-suited devil—his Mephistopheles in *Faust*. How like an actor to think that he could be both heaven and hell without being compelling as either. It sank into the turquoise blue, fading away before it hit bottom. The spell to conjure up this rendezvous allowed Aleister to see who was still feeding here. If they disappeared, they were no longer active.

He scrambled onto the pathway until he came upon the bronze flowers of crystalized sulfur bordering the outlines of the smaller pools. Florence Farr appeared in one. She was the current president of the Golden Dawn, who had excommunicated him. Picking up a large stone, he chucked it right into her comely reflection and watched her face fragment into waves. The royal bitch. Their loss. How ironic this High Priestess muse believed in free love but not free magic. He'd make her pay, even if she was currently draining this reservoir.

In the waters next to her, Ellen Terry bobbed up and down, costumed in a white toga adorned with pomegranates, a twelve-star crown on her head. Of course, Pamela would use the whore of the London stage to suggest fertility. A poseur available to any man's fantasies for a price. Yes, yes, he knew all about the High Priestess and Empress Pamela had created. Another tossed rock, and another mirroring shattered. Who was next?

Bram Stoker, the Golden Dawn chief who groused endlessly about his unpublished horror book, appeared in the next pond. Within any group, he was the stickler for rules and regulations, a tireless Emperor, a fanatic devoted to obeying doctrine. How unoriginal of Pamela to pick him—not a true leader like, say, himself. With extra vigor, a stone was chucked into the center of Bram Stoker, the waves slapping back and spraying Aleister's pant leg. He stretched the candlelight out over the settling surface. Stoker's likeness stayed. Found one! Here was a parasite syphoning off Thoth's feed.

Aleister scrambled to the last pool. A man wearing a fez appeared. Aleister didn't recognize him, but he heard the hum of Thoth trembling in the cavern's floor. A scene unfolded around the man, who was on the deck of a boat, pyramids floating by in the background, feeding an alligator in the river. Now he was standing in a tomb's entrance, a ribbon of hieroglyphics encircling his feet. Hieroglyphics. The Hierophant. She had activated this muse for the Hierophant card. Was he in touch with his spirit of the tombs?

No, this muse was the Hierophant, who lived a life of servitude. In this card, the querent who would be having a tarot reading would have recourse if he appeared. Aleister crouched down and dipped his hand into the water.

"Come to me," he whispered to the man now petting the alligator.

The man turned and looked straight at him. Aleister was motionless, his hand now in the water, his astral fingers feeling the cool and oily liquid. He shivered. Of all the elements, water was the one he disliked the most. Dark, unstable, evasive in revealing its true properties. Aleister motioned in the water for the man and alligator to come to him. He would get these bottom-feeders bound to him. They drifted lower but didn't dissolve. How dare they disobey him!

Standing, he bellowed, "I call upon you all to do my bidding!"

From the depths, the man in the fez thumbed his nose at him.

A fury coursed through Aleister, and he found himself carried upward and out. His next awareness was being thrown down, landing in the middle of his apartment, dripping with water. Thoth must have been angry with him for failing to ensnare the trespassers. The chalked pentagram ran, the ribbons of color spreading on the floorboards like blood. He shook himself.

Enraged, he stomped his feet. When he could pound the floor no longer, he centered his thoughts, panting from the effort.

"Spirit, reach into the corners of my mind, retrieve and utilize my intent," he said.

An icy knife cut into Aleister's brain. A green, festering blob spit out in front of him on the floor. This would be his failed attempt to capture the Emperor and Hierophant at the well. The green mass levitated and spun until it became a beam of light. Aleister placed his mind within its sphere, and they soared up and out. They landed in the prison cell, hovering over Pamela.

Crouching down next to her, Aleister saw her eyes dancing under closed lids, deep in sleep.

"Time to pay another price, Pamela."

Her eyes opened, but he disappeared before she caught a glimpse of him.

CHAPTER TWENTY-THREE

Ahmed in Cairo

In a private meeting room in Cairo's Shepheard's Hotel, Ahmed watched the stern lip of his supervisor grind into a grimace. By that expression alone he knew that Émile Brugsch would not be granting him permission to sail to Liverpool tomorrow to join Pamela's search party. Despite the two recovered artifacts on the table before them, Nectanebo's *shabti* and the *Book of the Dead* papyrus, the German's puckered mouth did not indicate any pleasure in Egypt's returned artifacts. The statue of Sekhemka was still missing.

Ahmed was distracted and had difficultly following what Brugsch was saying. If only Miss Farr or Mr. Stoker would contact him to say they'd found Pamela! Until then, he was consumed with worry. It tainted the happy remembrance of last night's reunion with the extended family. Fatima was in her glory with their recent happy, healthy baby boy, who was adored by his older brother and sister. But his older children were now shy around him—being gone for six months in London had made him a stranger. He would have to come back to Cairo again sooner than later.

"So, the statue of Sekhemka is still somewhere in England?" Brugsch spit out, in his heavily German-accented English.

"Yes, I believe Sekhemka is still in England, possibly at the museum in Northampton," Ahmed said.

Ahmed had first met Émile Brugsch twenty-five years ago when he served as an assistant at the biggest dig of his career: the finding of the mummies at Dayr al-Bahri. Ahmed had been one of the few Egyptian apprentices allowed at the dig at Montu, where the magnificent "Monastery of the North" was being dug out. The monastery comprised a collection of mortuary temples on the Nile's west bank, opposite the city of Luxor, and Émile had been in charge. Ahmed served as the "local" contact at Montu. The grave-robber brothers, Mohammed and Rasul, had disclosed the location of a deserted air shaft to Ahmed, and they arranged to investigate.

With the brothers in tow, Émile and Ahmed had lowered themselves into the tomb and discovered the great cache of royal mummies. They found unequaled treasures: funerary offerings, alabaster vessels, draperies, treasures, and royal bodies. So many mummies were discovered that the team didn't believe they were bodies at first. In all, they discovered an astonishing fifty kings, princes, and courtiers and almost six thousand objects. Afterward, Émile and Ahmed were assigned to transport all the artifacts to Bulaq to be presented in the new museum in Cairo.

From that accomplishment, Ahmed had been promoted to his current position as a visiting Egyptologist in London, locating looted Egyptian artifacts taken out of Egypt and not necessarily retrieving them but at least identifying their whereabouts.

"I personally have not laid eyes on Sekhemka yet," Ahmed continued, "but Mr. Griffith, who accompanied me here, has contacts in England who might help. In exchange, however, he wants permits for his explorer group to dig here."

"Are you sure that Sekhemka is even in England?" Émile asked. Even though Ahmed had worked with him for years, Émile's brusque manner still rankled him.

"I believe it is still possible," Ahmed replied, his breath unexpectedly giving out. He shook himself slightly and rallied. "But in order to be sure, we will have to raise more funds for me to stay in England. I can now claim that I am the British Museum's authenticator for Egyptian artifacts. I can be useful to British collectors."

Ahmed swallowed. So, far he had only spent two nights with Fatima and the children. Seeing Fatima run the household, tending to three active children and her parents, was a revelation. It was then that he realized much he missed her and how much the children had grown over the past six month. But if his position was not funded again, he might not have a job at all. And he would never see Miss Pamela or Bram again.

"If you had returned with the Sekhemka statue, the khedive would have been very willing to provide funds to return to London," Émile answered. "Your employment is dependent on the number of permits for excavations sold here, not setting the value of artifacts already taken out of Egypt. You say that Mr. Griffith's group is petitioning for the permit digs here?"

"Yes, and Mr. Griffith will book digs with his group, and I can arrange it, as long as I have a job with the department," Ahmed said, his stomach roiling. Not having a job with three children and a wife would be untenable. "There are English enthusiasts who want to apply for permits. They channel funding through the travel agency Thomas Cook & Son."

"The steamboat agency?" Émile asked, his eyes trained on Ahmed. "Mr. Griffith has a sponsor within the cruise ship company?"

"Yes," Ahmed said. Émile settled back in his chair.

"Very well," Émile replied, reaching for his tea. "It may be that your stay in England has steadier legs than we thought. Bring him to supper tonight."

Ahmed's breathing returned to normal. Maybe providing for his family and a passage back to London wasn't out of the question.

After an afternoon of cuddling with his youngest son, telling stories of London to the eldest, and practicing the writing of letters with his daughter, Ahmed was exhausted. Fatima let him sleep for an hour, and then he arrived back at the Shepheard's Hotel.

In the lobby, taxidermized lions and Nubian ibex heads lined the damasked walls, with couches and small tables set out for guests to collect themselves before checking in. Ahmed peered past the men in tunics, Egyptian and British soldiers, and British tourists until he spotted tall, skinny Mr. Griffith.

They shook hands, and Mr. Griffith surveyed the lobby and its inhabitants. "This is a little different from our voyage on the *Nitocris*," Mr. Griffith said, "but what a view of the Nile that was: wild animals, ruins, and heathens!"

Ahmed noticed glances from the soldiers who understood English. "Not too many ruins in here, I would think, Mr. Griffith. Or heathens. But," Ahmed said, motioning to the snarling lion over them, "here are some ruins of wild animals."

Mr. Griffith peered at Ahmed's ear. "I don't see a scar from that bite on your ear. Never saw anything like that bite out of nowhere."

Ahmed's hand automatically went to cover his left earlobe. He hadn't checked to see if the traces of "PCS" that had appeared were still visible or not.

"No, I'm quite recovered," Ahmed said. "Is this your first visit to the Shepeard Hotel?"

"Yes! And the atmosphere here is so delightfully English," Griffith confided to Ahmed as they made their way down the carpeted hallway to the restaurant. "Mr. Kamal, I am determined to arrange future permits for the Egyptian Explorers Club, and I am hoping to receive a telegraph back from my London group tonight, agreeing to my proposal of arranging more tours here to visit actual digs."

What Griffith's future English tourists didn't know was that, yes, they would be granted their dig sites, but most locations had been picked over by other looters and archeologists for decades if not centuries. The typical digger would be lucky to find even a fragment from an autopsy jar.

As they stepped into a dining room guarded by two Egyptian soldiers, Griffith stood still.

The private dining room was as elaborate as any at London's Savoy Hotel, but service here involved a line of waiters standing against the wall. Ahmed knew that hotel jobs were greatly prized by the locals. The main requirements were to fit into the uniform white pleated pants, red sashes, and short jackets with red caps—and to be able to stand at attention for hours on end. The curved knife that was tucked into the uniform's sash was only worn when English guests were dining. The total look was thought to enhance the amount of the bill.

Griffith took in the oak paneling and damask tablecloths. "What a delight to find some of England here in Cairo!" He seemed more impressed with the dining room than he had been with anything that he had seen on the boat with Ahmed. The headwaiter took them to the table in front of the open French doors where Émile and another man already sat.

As Griffith, Émile, and Mr. Kneely settled in, Ahmed breathed in the night-blooming jasmine in the garden below and took in the moonlight bathing the terraces. Bill Kneely, a Thomas Cook & Son travel representative with an East London accent, had made sure that the wine flowed at the table. He was experienced in what wines Émile was fond of and knew that, with enough of it, permits would be dispensed for anyone who could afford the fee. When a bottle of German wine was on the table, Émile smiled for the first time since Ahmed's return. Ahmed's job was safe for now.

This business meal would last for hours. How he longed to be back at the house with his aunts and uncles around Fatima, telling stories of his time among the foreigners. A stabbing in heart pricked him—had there been any progress finding Pamela? Ahmed couldn't recall the date for the Lyceum's command performance that Bram was managing. Had they left for Dublin yet? Ahmed had instructed the hotel staff to bring any telegrams addressed to him immediately. It was not a good sign that no one from the search party had sent any updates.

Griffith and Kneely told one story after another about the insistence of the British middle-class travelers who came in droves, intent on experiencing Egypt's exotic allure. Many, Ahmed knew, would prefer never to speak, look at, or deal with a "native." He caught a glance between two of the servers attending them and felt his heart beat faster. Did they think him a traitor to sit here and negotiate away the rights to their treasures? Egyptian, Turkish, Greek, African—they were all natives in these men's eyes.

After the meal, as they sat smoking cigars and drinking, Kneely, flushed from drink, leaned forward and rapped the table.

"Gentlemen, I have a story for you," Kneely said, pouring yet more wine for Émile. "Recently, a most peculiar fellow from London contacted me. He says he wants to translate our catches from the Dayr al-Bahri dig, specifically from the Stele of Revealing. He claims Thoth has spoken to him and that only he can interpret the meaning of the Stele's text."

Ahmed sat up. The Stele of Revealing? There was one person in England said to be channeling Thoth, and that was Aleister Crowley, Pamela's nemesis. He swallowed hard and motioned for more tea.

"Has this person seen the Temple of Thutmose III?" Ahmed asked, trying to keep an even tone to his voice. "Those guides are the ones most likely to talk about the Stele of Revealing."

"This fellow, a Mr. Aleister Crowley, has never been in Egypt before," Kneely answered. "But he claims to have visited it astrally, and he follows the progress of the digs here."

Émile laughed. "Well, I astrally visit my homeland in my dreams, is that the same?"

"He also writes that if we allow him private time with the Stele, he will arrange many more tours from England," Kneely continued. "These excursions would be for seekers of religious experiences. However, he was most adamant that only he would be granted access to the Stele ahead of these proposed tours."

"More tours?" Mr. Griffith asked. "We could help with that."

"This dilettante communes with Thoth? Did he say after which libation?" Émile snorted.

Ahmed attempted a curious smile. It would not do for them to suspect he knew of Aleister. Let Kneely be the one to introduce Aleister and his wayward group of misguided magicians.

"We should believe that this would-be magician Crowley wants to study the Stele of Revealing because the god Thoth suggested it?" Ahmed asked. "He's anxious to learn spells, but should he should be allowed to see it or be alone with it?."

The Stele of Revealing was a plaster-covered wooden tablet depicting Ankh-ef-en-Khonsu as a priest offering gifts to the falcon-headed god Re-Harakhty. The symbol for the place of the dead was behind the god, and, above, the sky goddess, Nut, stretched her wings. Chapters from the *Book of the Dead* had been inscribed on both sides, each with five lines of exquisitely detailed drawings of hieroglyphics.

This precious tablet was discovered by Ahmed's mentor, Auguste Mariette. Ahmed was with Mariette when he had discovered this tablet at Dayr al-Bahri. Their excitement in finding it had shaped Ahmed's dreams of conserving hidden treasures. And Aleister wanted to be alone with it? No.

"I would love to drum up some religious experiences for

our English tourists," Kneely said, reaching for the hookah pipe now being set up in front of him by the waiters. "We'd make a fortune. If this Aleister Crowley can actually channel Thoth at the Stele, what a bonanza! Think of the tourists it would bring. I say more power to him."

A table of Egyptian officials sitting next to them had fallen silent. Glancing at them, Ahmed recognized military attachés. Scores of soldiers could earn money escorting boatloads of tourists to the complex temple mazes. But the higher-ups in the Egyptian ministry cabinet would not be pleased to hear about plans for visits to sacred tombs—not unless the ministry controlled the entrance fees.

"So this astrally enabled Mr. Crowley from England insists on visiting the Stele alone?" Ahmed asked. "How did he even hear of it, if he has never been here?"

"Well, Mr. Crowley is quite determined," Kneely said. "He says he was visited by a 'being' who described the Stele to him. He claims that he can create a whole movement, a whole cult, around what he can channel from this piece of antiquity. I would imagine that Crowley is qualified. After all, he says a god confides in him. We could create whole seasons of tour groups based around lectures for this."

An astral visitor. A cult. The men around the table chortled as more hookahs appeared at their feet. This would be the time to propose that Aleister's proposal be denied. Kneely seemed the most receptive at the moment.

Ahmed turned to Kneely, who was having difficulty drawing on his hookah. "Mr. Kneely, let me help you." Ahmed took the base of the hookah and gave it a gentle shake to settle the water in the base. He handed the smoking cloth blade back to Kneely, who grabbed the hose and greedily inhaled, his eyes closing."

"Much better," Kneely said. "When I return to London, I'll be the one showing my club how to work one of these."

Ahmed smiled. "Mr. Kneely, why do you English need so many clubs to belong to? Is their government and their church not enough to give them a sense of belonging?"

Kneely's eyes darkened. "I don't expect you to understand, Mr. Kamal. Mr. Crowley belongs to the ranks of Trinity-educated scholars. From that, we assume that he is a man of intellect and morals. Our 'clubs,' as you call them, define who we are. Mr. Crowley knows all about men's clubs in London." Kneely's last words slurred as he almost dropped his hose.

Émile arched one eyebrow and turned to Ahmed. "Would it be a crime if Mr. Crowley had access to the Stele?"

Ahmed sipped his tea in reply. If Aleister wanted access to the Stele because he thought he was a prophet of Thoth, perhaps he intended to channel the god's power. And since he had sworn to destroy Pamela's tarot creation, this would be an unfortunate development for her safety.

"Why should the Egyptian government give this Crowley person access to our treasures just because he attended a university?" Ahmed said, keeping his voice light.

Kneely smiled and pushed up his glasses with his thumb while still holding on to his hookah pipe. "Well, if he's a university man, I can see why that lifestyle appeals so much to so many. I never heard of more plush living than being away at university."

"Clubs and orders are very important for us," Griffith finally said. "They give us a community of like-minded fellows to pursue our interests outside the walls of the academics."

"I say we vote on whether Mr. Crowley has access to the Stele or not," Émile said, staring at Griffith and Ahmed. "I'm not sure we want to muddy the water with more inquisitive amateurs." If Mr. Griffith wanted any permits for his club back in London, he would have to follow Émile's lead.

A waiter approached Ahmed with a telegram on a silver tray. At last! He tore it open.

Mr. Ahmed Pascal Kamal—Pamela still missing but may be siphoning off Aleister's magic pools at astral Elbana. King Brian shield on train was pools spirit asking for help. Search party meeting at Dublin Castle as soon as possible. —FF

Pamela had access to Aleister's magic at Elbana? How could she even know if Aleister went to Thoth's astral rendezvous place to get magic? And that King Brian's shield had appeared to them on the London train—how did Florence know that was a sign from the pools? So many questions. The one thing Ahmed did know was that he had to make sure Aleister didn't get access to the Stele. If he did, he might be able to access Thoth's power.

Ahmed folded his telegram and put it away as more wine was delivered to the table. Émile winked at him. A few more rounds, and Émile would let Ahmed sail for Dublin tomorrow.

Griffith's Thomas Cook & Son travel agency could arrange transport. Ahmed would join Pamela's search party in Dublin in a week and a half, if the winds were with him.

His left earlobe burned, and he cupped his ear as the initials "PCS" rose to the surface and throbbed.

CHAPTER TWENTY-FOUR

Penrhyn Castle of Wales

Bram's nerves were shattered. He and the company members, exhausted after giving the command performance for Queen Victoria, had collapsed in the Windsor Castle holding room next to the theatre.

Prince Edward took his royal time coming in to compliment them and excuse his mother's inattention. "Her Majesty falling asleep during the Becket scene was a sign that it was 'reassuring' for her," he said. "Your pleading scene in *Becket*, instead of the shouting in *The Bells*, was an excellent choice for her."

After damning Henry with faint praise, the prince left the actors to change out of costume and ready themselves for the train. Lord Penrhyn, the most generous patron of the Lyceum Theatre, had extended an invitation for Pamela's search party, Bram, Henry, Ellen, and Florence, to stay at his country estate in Cornwall on their way to Dublin. Lord Penrhyn was notoriously exact, expecting punctual arrivals for supper. It would be a tight race to get there on time, and they still had to pick up Florence and Toby, the waiter, and some of the other boys.

As soon as they were dismissed, the staff for the Prince of Wales whisked them to the Windsor train station. The prince had arranged for them to travel in the new Royal Family Train, and they were to stop in Manchester to pick up Florence and Toby. It was Ellen's idea to bring Toby.

"Think of the weapons he hides in his clothes," she insisted. "They might prove useful." Bram offered to pay for Toby and friends to come along for two nights to provide "protection." He hoped he wouldn't regret it.

As the train pulled up to the Manchester platform, Bram spotted Toby herding two dozen boys, all wearing red scarves, barbaric haircuts, and metal-studded shoes, the Scuttler gang uniform. Bram jumped down to greet him and Toby saluted him, handing over a telegram.

"Arrived at the hotel for you, sir," Toby said.

Bram tore it open: it was an update from Ahmed on his expected Dublin arrival. No mention of Pamela's whereabouts, but something about a coin. He would give it closer attention later.

Whoops and hollers from the boys on the platform brought Bram back to the business at hand. He directed them into the smallest of the three train cars. Piling in, they gasped and shouted at the sight: six rows of four fancy chairs, tables with drinks and ashtrays already set up with cigarettes. Bram threatened them with the police if they damaged one royal item in the train car. They sat, properly cowed, twisting their heads to gaze at the embossed wallpaper, running their hands over the upholstered chairs, and cautiously lighting cigarettes.

Florence came into the club car.

"I've come to keep you company, Mr. Stoker," she said, though Bram suspected it had more to do with Henry shutting her out of his private conversation with Ellen. The adolescents boasted about the knives sewn into their caps, sang filthy songs, and shouted puns for two hours. By the time they arrived in Holyhead, Cornwall, Bram was knackered.

Toby and the boys were set up in a hotel on the main street. Bram paid a local policeman to keep them in line and make sure they didn't harass anyone. A car sent by Lord Penrhyn pulled up in front of the hotel, but Henry and Ellen seemed to have vanished in transit. The hotel clerk explained with a smirk that Henry requested a hired car to take just him and Ellen to Penrhyn Castle. Bram gritted his teeth. The two stars had better show up before supper, or there would be no more donations to the Lyceum Theatre coming from Cornwall.

Florence had showed patience with the boys on the train, but once they were in the chauffeured car en route to the castle, she leaned her head back and let out a long sigh.

"Boys with weapons are so tiring," she said. "Why did Ellen insist they come?"

"They might be a help when we find Pamela." This was all Bram could offer. He patted his vest pocket to make sure the telegram Toby gave him was still there. He would read it privately once they arrived at the castle.

"Mr. Stoker," Florence said in a lowered voice, "I had word from Yeats. He's working on Ptolemy's Greek manuscript for the Golden Dawn, and he believes that Elbana, mentioned in this manuscript, may be where Pamela is."

"Really, Miss Farr?" Bram asked, trying not to snap at her. She should know better than to talk about this in a chauffeured car. In a lower voice he added, "A Greek manuscript has a clue to Pamela's whereabouts? When did you and Mr. Yeats discuss this 'Elbana'?"

Florence concentrated on the darkening roads and replied, "Let's just say, Yeats appeared to me last night. He told me that Pamela could be siphoning the magical pools of Elbana, and possibly that's where Aleister has taken her."

"Good God!" Bram said despite himself. "Magical pools seen during astral travel? That's our big clue?"

Florence turned and looked at him with steady eyes. "All

I know is during this astral experience, Yeats cited Elbana as a battleground of magical pursuits. Pamela may be held near the conduit of this astral entrance."

"The Elbana astral entrance—not a very helpful road mark," Bram said. He noticed the driver glancing back at them.

"We'll discuss it later, when you've had some rest," Florence said.

"Or coffee," Bram answered.

The car took a sharp turn at the top of a drive, and they passed ancient walls. In the rays of the setting sun, a castle appeared in the shape of a long line of ancient buildings shouldered side by side. Bram gasped. The first impression was a twelfth-century Mediterranean castle of towers, turrets, a chapel, stables, gardens, and a guard tower—all within a massive stone wall. The car stopped. Bram's second impression was that this was a fortress run under a tight hand, as a flurry of servants and porters ran from the hallway and assumed straight lines to greet them.

A tall gentleman with a white beard and ramrod posture emerged, flanked by barking Irish wolfhounds. Lord Penrhyn was known in London as a bereaved widower and as the conservative politico of the day, the perfect English lord. Tonight, he wore a red silk head wrap, a blue velvet jacket, white riding pantaloons, and tall black boots. Bram grimaced: a country-manor look by way of Egypt. At least Ahmed wasn't here to see this would-be pasha.

Florence hummed a low exhale. "Why do they all want to look like a version of Apollo?" she whispered to Bram. He almost replied, "He looks Egyptian, not Greek," but stopped himself.

The car door opened, and dog noses probed Bram and Florence's faces.

"Hercules! Achilles!" Lord Penrhyn commanded. *Perhaps he does have a Greek fetish*, Bram mused. The dogs resumed their places next to him. "Mr. Stoker," Lord Penrhyn said, jutting his hand out as though it were to be kissed, not shaken.

"Yes! Pleased to see you again, Lord Penrhyn," Bram said, shaking his host's hand. He introduced Florence, whose presence Lord Penrhyn barely registered.

"Sir Henry and Miss Terry should arrive any moment in another car," Bram said as they walked toward the front door. He noted Lord Penrhyn's pursed lips.

Porters trundled Bram and Florence's suitcases to their rooms while Lord Penrhyn motioned them to a parlor entrance. The brilliant marble floor shown, but it was the medieval staircase that caught Bram's eye. Florence jumped slightly at the sight of the many sinister faces in the white columns of the staircase. Bram pointed to the fabulous beasts with snakelike tongues staring down at them from the ceiling.

"Ah, my grand staircase," Lord Penrhyn said. "One of the many triumphs of the castle. I'll give you a quick tour.

Bram spied French doors down the hallway leading to the back. An unearthly trumpet blasted.

"Trumpets at sunset?" Bram asked.

Lord Penrhyn frowned. "There are no trumpets here."

Something or someone was trying communicate with them.

Lord Penrhyn continued wearily down the hall toward the glass-paneled door leading to the outside. On the other side of it was an exquisite garden. In the dimming light, Bram could make out, farther down, an assembly of cottages, stone barns, and stables surrounded by garden terraces. A huge tree stood against the encompassing stone wall.

As they stepped out onto a gravel path, Florence whispered to Bram, "Castle, fortress, palace—what is this place?"

"Welcome to Penrhyn Castle," their host boomed as he led them onto a lower level. There was no sign of a bugle player.

Trailing him, Bram murmured to Florence, "Distract him for a moment? I want to check out the energy here."

Florence approached a circular herb garden and asked questions about the local soil and the hardiness of shrubbery in salt air. Bram would have a moment to investigate. That sound could have been a portal signal.

Walking away from them in the direction of the tree, Bram recited a Golden Dawn incantation under his breath, asking to identify energy. He had never tried to do an incantation before. Perhaps he could feel a ley line—a conduit to the unseen magical world. England was thought to be striated with them. *It's time I practiced some magic myself.*

He held out his hands, palms down. Bram felt nothing. Perhaps the castle itself held off connecting energies. He reached into his vest pocket, opening his Viking compass, the gift from Ahmed. He turned it to the left, in the direction of the tree. The dial spun wildly. He held it to the right: nothing. Perhaps this Viking tool was tapping into a ley line—or, according to Yeats, an unseen energy pool that Pamela was sapping. Bram pocketed his compass and rejoined Florence and their host.

"Mr. Stoker, you and Miss Farr here are on your own until Sir Henry and Miss Terry show up to sup with my daughters and me," Lord Penrhyn said. "In an hour," he added, heading back inside.

"There's an energy coming from that tree," Bram said. They walked toward it.

Florence found a stick near the wide trunk. "Fabulous! Hickory. Let me try."

They both glanced up at the windows of the great house and turned their backs toward it, trying to achieve as much privacy between them as possible.

"Mr. Stoker, interesting energy blockage here on the grounds, wouldn't you say?" Florence said softly as she waved her stick.

"This castle certainly brings to mind a 'pile of bricks,'" Bram replied, looking at the long assembly of mismatched buildings.

"If you could hum while I incant that would be helpful," Florence said. She turned away from him and mumbled to herself. Bram hummed a few phrases of "Spanish Ladies." After a moment, she sighed, threw the stick on the ground, and rubbed her earlobes.

"Well, this is not an entrance to Elbana," Florence said. "No magicians could conjure the god Thoth here."

"Damn!" Bram answered, shading his eyes to see if there were any faces from the castle watching them. "So, there are no invisible tunnels built by thralls linking Penryhn Castle with Dublin. Still, I did sense something, an energy of some sort when that trumpet sounded. You heard it, felt it as well?"

"Yes. But there's no connecting energy here now. I don't know what was here before. Maybe one of your undead is following you."

"Or an afrit," Bram said.

"Yes, I heard from Ahmed that an afrit might have followed you to Manchester," Florence said, looking at Bram intensely.

Is she trying to blame Ahmed's knowledge of afrits on Pamela's disappearance? Bram almost replied, *Singing to mummies at museums could have invited them to follow you*, but he opted to remain friendly. "Yes, Ahmed and I also discussed whether a mummy spirit from the museum could have possibly attached itself to our party."

Florence dusted dirt from her hands. "Speaking of not feeling alive, I need to go ready myself for supper."

They made their way indoors, and a maid brought Florence up to her room. Bram found the butler near the front door.

The butler's Welsh accent made conversation difficult, but eventually he answered Bram's question: "What lies south of the Penryhn estate?"

"Oil Aide," was the answer. Bram repeated "Oil Aide" back to the butler several times, growing increasingly irritated. The butler excused himself and came back with a housemaid.

"Sir," the young girl said. "I was told you were asking about Holyhead, south of here?"

Bram exhaled. Her accent was thick, but at least she was understandable.

"Oh, Holyhead!" Bram answered. He turned to the butler and said, "Thank you for making sure I understood."

The butler nodded.

"I know a woman from Holyhead who is above wise in the ways of history here," the maid said. "She lives not five minutes away—in one of the cottages outside the walls. She advises the gardeners, all about herbs and medicine plants. Even His Lordship respects her."

"Could the woman be brought here now?" Bram asked.

The butler drew a long face. "A visit like that needs permission from Lord Penrhyn."

Well, at least Bram understood the butler now. "Can you take me to him so that I might ask?"

He was escorted to an immense study, where Penrhyn sat in a large chair before a fire, reading a newspaper. Bram approached him.

"Sir, I was wondering if I might speak with someone who lives nearby who knows the history of the area?" Bram asked.

"As a rule, I am not inclined to permit strangers access to my estate, although I have made an exception in your case." Lord Penrhyn rattled the pages of his newspaper. "I am currently under attack by the London press. There have been exaggerated reports of working conditions at my slate quarry. Allowing any stranger into my castle is out of the question."

"Begging your pardon, my lord. It seems your staff knows a local woman who is an expert on local herbs and such. She doesn't seem to be a stranger to the household."

"Oh, the witch lady," the lord said, going back to his paper. "Very well, I give you leave to see her in the great room, as long as she doesn't hex anything. Good luck if you can understand her! The staff here seems to understand her, though."

The lord dismissed him with a wave of his hand, and the butler escorted Bram to the great room. He could certainly feel a great amount of energy in the room. At least twenty clocks perched on various shelves, none of them working but all of them adorned with bits of amber as top ornaments or on their hand dials.

As he perused the shelves, Bram inhaled the perfumes undulating in every corner: old wood, fireplace smoke, book bindings, and leather topped off with the scent of lemon and vinegar. In addition to the stacks of books, the shelves contained glass domes covering natural miracles: a blossom, an insect, a flower in mid-bloom encased in amber.

Bram studied the one clock working adorned with a winged creature in amber: A dragonfly? Or was it a butterfly? Whatever it was, the insect was trapped in perpetuity in the hour hand, encased in an amber resin. Set before a gilded mirror, the hapless creature cast a double image as the hour hand rotated around the dial.

A lump rose in Bram's throat. Was this relic a sign of what had happened to Pamela? No, Annie Horniman told them she had received news that Pamela might be in Dublin. That was where, he hoped, they would find her.

Gazing at one captive relic after another, Bram awaited the arrival of the local seer. Was he himself an insect, embedded in this dour castle's energy?

He fished out Ahmed's battered telegram from his pocket. The return address—the Shepheard's Hotel, Cairo, was smudged. Bram had constantly folded and refolded the telegram ever since he'd received it from Toby.

EBLANA MAY BE AT DUBLIN CASTLE. NEED DEINIOL COINS FOR AFRIT RANSOM. NOW HAVE PCS TATTOO MYSELF. AHMED

Elbana was at his old workplace, at Dublin Castle? Bram knew an old river flowed beneath the ancient fortress, but he never suspected that an Egyptian god could roost there. How did Ahmed come up with that idea?

And Ahmed recommends paying an afrit with Deiniol coins? What use could a spirit have with currency? The coins, Bram knew, were mined in honor of Saint Deiniol centuries ago and were sold for protection. Dublin Castle was supposedly where the first ancient coin was discovered, but Bram knew from his twenty years of working there that a lot of relics lay beneath the moat. The castle itself had been built on Viking ruins. Why give an Irish Deiniol coin to an Egyptian afrit?

And now Ahmed had the "PCS" tattoo on his earlobe as well as William, Henry, Florence, and Ellen. Whatever magic Pamela had, she seemed able to mark her muses. A proper tribe for whatever magic she was amassing. Or was she? Was she even alive?

Bram watched the hour hand of the clock rotate with the embedded creature. Had this trip been a fool's errand?

The maid entered the room, curtseying. A wizened old woman appeared behind her. The maid announced, "This is Bethesda from Holyhead," and then she left.

Bethesda could have been forty years old or she could have been 140. She had the curly black hair and black eyes of the Welsh women from the area. The skin around her eyes was so deeply lined, she could have been a relic herself. Several protrusions—warts and moles—stuck out on her chin, and her woolen cloak could have been centuries old.

"*Rydw I wedi bod yn eich disgwyl chi,*" the ancient said.

Bram couldn't understand a word. "I'm sorry, madam," he said. "I fear I do not speak your language. I wanted to ask you about Deiniol coins."

She held out her palm. "*Gadewch imi weld rich dyfais,*" she answered.

A soft cough by the doorway caught Bram's attention. The maid had not left; she was dawdling outside the crack in the doorway.

"Do you know what she is saying?" Bram asked, motioning the girl in.

"She says she wants to see your magical device," the girl answered, holding one hand out flat and making a spinning motion with the other.

"My compass?" Bram asked. "Why, of course!" He took the compass out and opened it up. Both crone and girl crept closer to him to peer at it. The needle jumped from place to place, spinning as though possessed.

Ah, the compass was picking up the pull of telluric lines now. Here it channeled a cosmic crossing, an intentional energy that called to him.

The woman hummed a tune while the girl oohed and aahed over the whirling dial. After a brief moment when the older woman's eyes fluttered open and shut, she retrieved a cloth sac from under her cloak. Tugging its strings open, she took out a green-tinted disc, the size of robin's egg, one side depicting a cloaked man with a curly beard. She held it out for Bram to see the other side. Swords rimmed the entire piece, like minute hands on a clock, and one long sword transected the entire length of the coin. A Saint Deinol coin.

The woman motioned for Bram to hand her the compass. Holding it with one hand, she set the Saint Deinol's coin inside it. The entire compass buzzed and vibrated, clicking. The swords on top spun so quickly the image became one blurred line.

As the coin settled within the compass, the long sword in the middle pointed in one direction: west.

The one working clock with the amber insect went off, emitting a deep thrum of its chime. The girl screeched, and the old woman pointed at him.

Bram's hand shot up to his burning earlobe. He stood before the gilded mirror. There they were: "PCS." The initials were now tattooed into Bram's fleshy left earlobe.

The muses for Pamela's Major Arcana tarot card progression now made sense to him: Magician, Fool, High Priestess, Empress, and himself as Emperor. As well as Ahmed, as the Hierophant. The crone and the young girl followed his reflection in the mirror and gasped. The letters fluttered and shimmered.

"*Castell Dulyn*," the woman whispered.

Bram didn't need the young girl to translate for him. He knew what the woman was saying: Dublin Castle.

CHAPTER TWENTY-FIVE

KING OF DEPRAVITY

"King of Depravity!"

"Cannibal at Large!"

"Wickedest Man in the World!"

"Beast 666!"

"Most Popular Club Member?"

Aleister burst out laughing at the last contribution. His four companions joined in and resumed smoking as they clutched the railing of the steam yacht, *The Devil's Plank*. The early morning water was rough in the Bristol Channel. Even though the ship was built to endure these conditions, it was more of a cruiser than a racer. The crew dashed about the railings, stabilizing the sails as the steam engine thrummed away.

"Is that the best you can come up with?" Aleister asked. "The nickname my mother came up with, 'The Beast,' still bests all of yours. Surely, you can come up with a more despicable crown."

The chugging of the engine grew louder as they motored against the increasing headwind. Aleister took a breath. Here on this deck, he was captain of his domain; there were fellows to do his bidding and there was magic to their advantage. The only problem was that he was surrounded by water, not his favorite element, as the threat of drowning was always in the back of his mind. Fire, air, earth—those were the fundamentals where he thrived. Not water.

As they left Bristol, the winds picked up. As a last wisp of brume evaporated, the harbor lighthouse came into view. This lighthouse tower served as a goddess of light giving benediction to the sailors.

Dr. Westcott, the most dapper member of the group, moved down the railing to stand next to Aleister. "I've always been partial to 'Your Maleficence.' It has a nice ring to it."

Aleister smiled. "Maleficence—it does seem to suit our Abremelin system."

"The Abremelin system," Mathers said. Whenever he memorized something, he tapped the side of his jaw with two fingers, a grating habit that Aleister came to detest.

Noting the tic, Dr. Westcott said, "Oh, for heaven's sake, Mathers, feed your ideas into your mouth with your brain, not with taps."

"It's a system," Mathers said, drumming his chin even more furiously, "and one that with adequate practice and knowledge can compel a large body of demons."

"Ah yes, demons," Aleister said, trying his best not to swat the fidgeting magician. "Your specialty."

"It should never be forgotten," Felkin added, adjusting his spectacles, "that the essential work of the Magician is to attain the knowledge of and communications with the Holy Guardian Angel."

Every coven had a blowhard, and Felkin fit the bill. A shadow passed overhead. It was an attractive sailor swinging by on a rope on his way to secure the flagpole. Felkin gawked like a starving dog seeing a flying steak.

"Felkin!" Aleister snapped. "Discretion, if you would?"

Bespectacled Felkin turned away, feigning that the watery churn below was fascinating. Aleister observed the sailor from the flagpole disappear into the wheelhouse. They didn't need a suspicious sailor reporting them to the captain. But what could he tell him? That there were magicians aboard? That might get them kicked off or at least monitored.

"Sometimes our Guardian Angel is the Fallen Angel," said Archer Prince, slumping in a nearby deck chair. "An angel who is thirsty to drink at the pools of renewal."

With his deerstalker hat tilted over his head and his rumpled inverness cape, he looked like a drunk, possibly deranged, uncle on holiday. Yes, every coven also had to have one of those in the ranks—the lunatic. Archer Prince was the loose cannon in the group. Recently released from the Broadmoor Criminal Lunatic Asylum for the fatal stabbing of William Terriss, he was the group's Fool. Prince was at least a would-be magician, a higher standard than Pamela Smith's muse, a lowly actor.

The fact that Archer murdered Terriss on Aleister's orders meant that he was the coven's responsibility from here on out. The security constraints on Prince on this released trip were minimal. He was out on leave "to take a restorative seaside trip with family." Eventually he would be missed. He was the conductor for the prison orchestra. The prison warden confided to Aleister that the musicians followed Prince's lead more out of fear than his conducting prowess.

"Magic is thirsty. I thirst for magic," Prince crooned, closing his eyes and rocking back and forth.

Aleister slapped Prince on the arm. "Come on, fellow, act like a human being."

Prince jumped up and kicked the side of the wooden railing with such force that he dented it. He spun around in a circle and fell flat on his back. As the others helped him up, Aleister checked to see where the crew was stationed. The captain's lack of motions within the wheelhouse suggested nothing was seen. Aleister pushed Prince back into the deck chair.

"Not that human being!" Aleister snapped. "You are with

us on strict terms, and our trip to Dublin mustn't be in the press in any way."

"Speaking of being in the press," Dr. Westcott said, lowering his voice, "the court case against Madame Horos and her son will begin soon. When it does, she will claim to be associated with us. So, it seems, our days are numbered, whether we practice in the open or the dark. Or rather, in society or out."

Mathers turned around from the railing. "How are we to apply our collective magical pressure? The pools are shrinking, and that idiot Smith child is unaware that she is creating magic to siphon off the pools' energies."

These men cannot keep their mouths shut about magic. Aleister sat down next to Archer and motioned the other three to stand closer.

"All right, let's have quick, private conversation," he said as they drew their deck chairs closer. Aleister brushed his hair back from his eyes with a rough hand. "This Madame Horos will ruin our reputation and that of anyone associated with the Golden Dawn. This is what happens when you allow women to advance to the upper level—they adore the notoriety and the press. The scandal of Horos only strengthens our need to limit Smith and her access to the pools. Women should not have access to magic."

The sun glinted through the clouds. A spray of water came up and splattered the deck. For a brief moment a prism hung in the air above them. The other magicians watched as Aleister reached out his hand, his Viking ring sparkling. The center of the ring sucked the rainbow into it, leaving a blue coloration swirling in his palm. It dissolved. Aleister shook water off his hand, a droplet falling on each one of his magicians. Mathers, Prince, Westcott, and Felkin all flinched as the water hit their faces. Aleister clenched his hand, then hugged it to his chest, as though feeding new blood to his heart.

"You have just been given a little something to help you do battle with the Blue Magician," Aleister said.

"Since when do you have access to a Blue Magician?" Dr. Westcott asked. Blue Magicians were temporary incarnations that could destroy inspiration and creativity and even undo any spells that were fully cast.

Aleister towered over Dr. Westcott. "Yes, I have created a conduit to a Blue Magician." He turned toward the sea and said, half to himself, "You should have figured that out from the train-station attack. At any rate, an entire tarot deck will be created around this entity."

"It will?" Felkin asked. "And will your Blue Magician tarot deck have twenty-two major cards? Suites of pentacles, cups, wands, and swords?"

"Oh, yes, and a baboon," Aleister said, relighting his cigarette. Felkin would hate to hear that any animals would be in a tarot deck—they didn't fit in with his notion of magical symbols. Hearing the men behind him chuckle, Aleister turned around. "But now, you see, our next step is the destruction of the Smith Magician, Sir Henry. Our Blue Magic spell at the train station should have weakened him by now. Soon Irving's magic will dissipate like a leaky air balloon and he will have no audience or followers. But it's essential that Prince dispatch him in the proper way so that we can funnel his gifts."

"This dispatch of Sir Henry Irving will be private?" Prince asked, his glinting eyes narrowing.

"No, unlike Smith's Fool," Aleister replied, "this killing needs to be a public performance to convert the masses."

"Yes, the pools drained as she created her High Priestess and Empress," Archer said, looking off toward the watery horizon.

"She knits magic from sources we can only imagine," Mathers added.

"No, she's greedy, like Terriss was greedy," Prince said, looking at Aleister. "He took all the acting roles and wouldn't share them with me. Killing a greedy person feeds the universe."

Aleister glared at him, then motioned everyone to lean in.

"The fact is, the symbols she uses are haphazard and circumstantial. Just a child's gathering from Waite's tutelage. She seems to have several spirit guides protecting her. We don't know what attributes she has assigned for each card, and until we do, we can't prevent her from creating her next tarot card."

A boat whistle shrieked as the vessel passed from the bay into the sea.

"You've tried isolating her without success," Felkin said, wiping off his misty glasses.

"Yes, thanks for summing it up like that, Felkin. You, Prince," Aleister continued, "will be on call to do the heavy lifting in Dublin. When I give the signal, it's up to you to remove Irving from his mortal coil. By the way, nice work getting Miss Smith into Dublin's crypt."

Prince looked at the others and smiled. "When you have the collective energy of a madhouse, the magic of the ley lines appears easily."

"Easily at first," Aleister said. "But I'm sure there will be a price to pay, as all magic demands. And, in fact, there might be more than one mortal in Dublin we'll need to dispatch. If Miss Smith has called in more of her associates, we'll have more weeds to pull."

Dr. Westcott started to pace and then came back to the group. "The power that Miss Smith manifests is astounding. How will we be able to transmute it to us?"

"We could use the Abremelin system. That could syphon off her energies," Felkin said.

"We've never tried to transmute another magician's magic," Dr. Westcott said, rubbing his hands together. "This could be fantastic larceny. But we shouldn't depend on Archer's Broadmoor Asylum for collective energy. It's the height of unstable magic."

Archer sprang up and planted himself in front of Dr. Westcott as though he were about to strike him. A giant wave slapped up against *The Devil's Plank*, tilting the deck at such an angle that Prince plopped back into his chair.

"Gentlemen!" Aleister said. "Let's make one thing clear. Archer Prince transported Smith to Dublin because of his access to lunatic energy. He performed this in a perfectly orderly fashion and managed to transport her body to another destination from a distance."

"Your afrit did the transporting," Prince mumbled.

Felkin stomped his foot at Alesiter, "You still haven't shared the magical spell on how to find an afrit and bind him to your will, Crowley."

"The afrit found me, but point being, as leader I don't have to disclose every one of my incarnations or conduits," Aleister said, taking another drag on his cigarette. "We have to use every spell we can to claim our pools; that is the only way to stop Smith. After that, we can worry about stealing wizardry from others. But let me be clear on one point: I keep my own magic. But never fear, it's only a matter of time before the world is ours."

"The world beyond seems to be all yours," Dr. Westcott said.

For a brief period, it seemed as though the "beyond" world was theirs for the taking. Aleister was set to assume leadership of the new order of the Golden Dawn. Prince Edward would be their patron and, as the newly crowned king, would work with them so they could assume a privileged place, behind the scenes of course. The prince didn't need to know about their thwarted attempt at Windsor Castle last year, to bring an early demise to the queen to hasten the process.

Aleister looked at the rough horizon before them, battling a wave of seasickness. He hoped Edward's first order of business would be instituting Salic Law. This would prohibit women from ruling, and, after what Edward had suffered waiting for the crown, they were sure he would be sympathetic to their cause. Women should know their place: in the bedroom, kitchen, and laundry.

Aleister would be put in charge of the Golden Dawn's London office—goodbye Florence Farr and Annie Horniman. *I could be appointed as an ambassador on the continent. Free to preach on independence, free love, Sex Magik* and *the freedom to do whatever one wants, regardless of society's norms.* It would be a man's world once again with the pool's sustaining waters only available to him and his chiefs.

"You see, Dr. Westcott," Aleister said, "some of us assumed that this would be an easy assignment. I have been willing to explore every means of claiming dominion over my magic."

A tugboat pulled alongside the sleek yacht as they moved into the main part of the channel. Aleister leaned over the railing to take it in. On the deck of the tug, two people stood next to an elegant bearded man.

"Who's that?" Mathers asked, planting himself next to Aleister on the railing.

"Mr. Kamal," Aleister said. "Miss Smith's Egyptian museum friend."

Aleister stared at the other passengers. It was Mairead Jones, the mudlark from London, who sold him his Viking ring, standing next to her father, Davy Jones.

"What the devil are they doing here with the Egyptian?" Aleister said.

He motioned his magicians together, and they stood together on the deck peering at the smaller boat. Aleister raised up his ring. The wind kicked up. *The Devil's Plank* skimmed past Flat Holm island. A massive row of waves began pounding the disappearing shore, booming as though cannons were on the attack. Black clouds gathered, and rain pummeled the deck. The yacht threaded nimbly between the growing waves, while alongside the tugboat struggled, twisting and turning among the pounding walls of water.

The sailor raced out from the wheelhouse and shouted, "Captain says everyone below!"

While the sailor's back was turned, guiding other crew members to the quarters below, Aleister raced over ropes and booms to reach the wheelhouse. He threw open the door to the captain's quarters, who was struggling to maintain control of the steering wheel.

"What in God's name do you think you're doing here?" the captain shouted. "Get below with the rest of them!"

"I'll stay out of the way," Aleister said, plastering himself against the wall. The captain was too busy to do more than to curse at him, as Aleister breathed deeply.

On the faltering tugboat, the mudlark, her father, and the Egyptian made their way to the captain's perch. In between squalls, a huge wave heaved up and crested over the boat. Bodies were flung across the boat's floor.

"Christ save the ship!" the captain said, trying to steady the helm.

Struggling sea travelers on the smaller ship tried to make their way to the two rescue rowboats strapped to the side. Another wave reached over from the sides and smashed a foamy fist over everything.

As the captain in *The Devil's Plank* furiously spun the wheel, Aleister lifted his hand. The Viking ring hummed. Through the window, he saw the dark clouds so low they almost touched the top of the main sail. A thrum of wind set the sails furiously slapping. The ring glowed with a blue pulse. A crack of thunder exploded, and a streak of lightening bounced off the main mast. Fragments of blue light zigzagged all over the deck like gruesome dancing spiders. One splintered off and spread to the captain's wheelhouse, and it jagged off Aleister's ring to the sea. A blue ball bounced off wave tops until it reached the tugboat. A flash of cerulean blue illuminated the entire boat, and then darkness swallowed it up.

After two enormous waves, the tug slowly came back into view, tilting badly. When it righted itself, Aleister saw that the rowboats had been swept off.

There was not one person left on deck.

CHAPTER TWENTY-SIX

Dublin Landing

"Pick up your pace, we haven't all day," Bram barked to the young Scuttlers ambling down the Dublin Dock in the gathering dark. The two-dozen boys from the Manchester gang were mostly rangy adolescents. Only the two ringleaders, Toby the waiter and John-Joseph, were tall enough to pass as adults.

As Bram went to safeguard Henry's luggage—tossed ashore from the ferry—Ellen, Florence, and the dogs descended the gangplank. Bram had sequestered the women, along with Lord Penrhyn and Henry, away from the hooligans in a separate compartment on the ship. But now a roar of hooting and whistling broke out as Florence and Ellen walked down the plank. Curbside, the horses hitched to the triple-decker buses reared up. Cabbies swore at the boys, the Scuttlers swore back, and it looked as if a fist fight were about to break out. Bram ran to restrain one boy about to charge a cabbie—he took care to steer clear of the boy's cap, and the blade hidden in the brim, as did all the Scuttlers.

Having succeeded in distancing the boy from the impending melee, Bram watched the cabbie stagger, holding a bottle of

Crowley beer. The Dublin Bay smell came over him now—beer, fish, salt air, chimney smoke, and linseed oil from the factory. Add on to that drunk cabbies and armed gang members—this was not the most auspicious beginning for rescuing Pamela.

The boys started singing:

At last, quoth she, saving your tale,
Give me some more of Crowley Ale,
Ah, good sir, full well I know,
Your ale, I see, runs very low.

Wouldn't you know Aleister would make an appearance here, too, if only in song? Bram almost said to Florence. He thought she was at his elbow, but when he looked around to confide in her, he saw that Lord Penrhyn was steering her to one of the waiting cabs. Torn between going to the rails to assist the women or staying with the Scuttlers and preventing a riot from happening, he opted to stay with the Scuttlers.

The Scuttlers screeched their song at top volume, and as they circled around him, Bram felt his temper almost get the better of him. Fortunately, after two sharp whistles from Toby and John-Joseph, the Scuttlers came to order. The boys formed a queue, and Toby herded them aboard a horse-drawn bus.

"Nine o'clock tomorrow morning, without fail, we all meet at Dublin Castle," Bram shouted out.

A chorus of "nine o'clock" roared back.

The horses jerked the bus down the dock, then careened toward the street. Bram exhaled his breath, forming a soft cloud in the gathering twilight. They only planned to stay two nights, but he knew there could be no shenanigans or cutpurses on the streets or at the hotel. Bram wondered if he would be held to his promise to Toby that he would employ Toby's eleven Scuttler brothers in London if they stayed out of trouble.

Now to load the last four members of the search party—well,

four plus Lord Penrhyn, who was now stroking the muzzle of a cabbie's horse. Bram had found the lord to be invariably drawn to horses and women. At least Penrhyn wasn't wearing his red turban here in Ireland.

"I must say, I am surprised at the quality of this horse for hire," Lord Penrhyn said as Bram hastened over to him. "Amazing haunches. This cab will do nicely to take the three of us to the State Apartments."

That wasn't quite Bram's plan—he'd intended to assign the smartest cab to Sir Henry, but Penryhn was already directing the porter to load not only his luggage but the ladies' as well. As Bram gave the address in State Apartments address to the cabbie, Ellen and Florence climbed in. They tried to coax the dogs to jump in, but it was up to Bram to lift them up. Once Florence had placed a dog on either side of her, she motioned Bram to come closer to them.

"It's very complicated what we're attempting tomorrow," Florence said, looking back to make sure Penryhn was still at the back with the cabbie.

Ellen added, "Yes, there's a lot to juggle here, Pa."

Bram took a hand of each. "Complicated? Miss Farr, you sing Yeats's poetry exquisitely, and, Miss Terry, you excel at managing Sir Henry's moods while performing Shakespeare. This will be as easy for you both as stealing focus onstage."

Ellen burst into laughter while Florence petted both the dogs. "Well, Pa," Ellen said, "if I see Aleister's cloven hoof in the crowd tomorrow, I'll play up my part." Lord Penrhyn climbed up and sat next to Ellen. *Ah*, Bram thought, *that's why Florence surrounded herself with dogs on that seat.*

"Your host, Mr. Glencairn, is expecting you," Bram said. Lord Penryhn slung an arm around Ellen's shoulders, and she tilted her head back enough so that the large feather in her hat nearly gouged his eye. The cab rattled down the dock, their chatter gradually fading.

"All ashore who's going ashore," rang out from the ferry.

Henry ambled down the gangplank with the aid of his cane, Mussie padding alongside. Bram tried not to sigh. The ferry trip had been exhausting. It was late afternoon, and Bram's stomach was growling. Henry approached, his face still slightly blue from his altercation with Aleister at the Windsor train station. Bram motioned toward one of the last two cabs waiting. A cabbie jumped down and retrieved Henry's suitcase.

"I'll take this to the Clarence Hotel, yes?" Henry asked Bram, clenching a cigar between his teeth. "I hope it is far away from those loud ruffians."

Bram smiled. "Yes, sir. The Scuttlers' hotel is across the river. The Clarence is holding your usual room."

"Where is the rest of the search party planning to stay?" Henry asked, not looking at Bram. *Did he spot Penryhn sitting next to Ellen in the cab?*

"Lord Penrhyn, Miss Florence, and Miss Ellen will occupy the lieutenant governor's State Apartments at Phoenix Park. Everyone is to gather at the Royal Chapel on the grounds of Dublin Castle tomorrow morning."

Henry made a clicking noise with his tongue and nodded, his blue complexion blending in with the shadows of the wharf. Approaching his carriage, he turned to Bram. "Well, Mr. Stoker, it's been twenty-five years since we met here during my *Hamlet* tour. Do you think we'll find Miss Smith in the bowels of Dublin?"

"Every indication we have is that she is here," Bram answered.

"I haven't always done right by her talents," Henry confessed, stroking Mussie's head.

Bram almost said, *Nor by mine*, but he bit his tongue.

Henry picked up Mussie, settled himself inside the cab, and banged on the ceiling with his cane. The carriage jerked forward, and the clip-clopping of the horses' hooves echoed and waned as the cab joined the cacophony of the street.

As Bram made his way to the remaining cab, a poster on a gas lamppost caught his attention:

Royal Dublin Society's Winter Horse Show.
Little Beda, the Amazing Thinking Horse

The poster's artwork featured Pablo standing on Little Beda, executing her famous "Spanish Steps." That night in Manchester when Pamela stood on Little Beda's back in Pablo's courtyard—how long ago was that? Two months? Bram approached the poster to read the schedule. The first performance was scheduled to begin that night at the Merrion Road Hall.

Had he known, perhaps he could have tried to take the Scuttlers with him—a show with horses might keep them out of trouble. They had been fairly well-behaved on the train, but given their antics on the wharf, he knew those high spirits needed exercise or the boys would channel their energy into trouble. For now, Toby and John-Joseph would have to keep them in line. For some of the boys, it would be the first time they'd had a warm bed in an age.

The driver yelled, "Oy, are we leaving or not?"

Bram grabbed his bag and jumped in. "Clontarf, but drive by Dublin Castle first," he shouted to the cabbie, surprising himself. This detour wasn't on the agenda, but supper could wait. It would be good to see his former workplace before tomorrow's performance. The cab followed the street alongside the river. After two or three turns, they were next to Dublin Castle's underground moat. Bram's Viking compass whirled and clicked in his pocket. *We're here, Pamela. We'll find you.*

Bram squinted, trying to see past the entrance to the courtyard, his former workplace that was both official palace and prison. He thought of those first few years when he and the boys in the patent office explored the castle's many secret passageways after hours. Some of those hidden entrances led to Viking tombs, though very few knew what they were. But the office boys knew. Tomorrow the boys from Manchester would have to help distract the crowds, so that he and Ahmed could get into two of the towers.

As he viewed the Royal Chapel, his stomach roiled—it was a combination of homesickness and the memory of the years of his dead-end job at the castle. He knew the layout of the castle and adjoining chapel like the back of his hand. Who was better equipped to find the entrances to the two secret staircases?

The horse's pace hastened as they passed the hundreds of plaster heads decorating the Royal Chapel's exterior. There they were, the heads from Annie Horniman's dream. *I should have known.*

Plaster and wood had been used to build the Royal Chapel instead of stone and granite. Traditional materials were too heavy, it was said, to construct a palace over an ancient Black Pool—a source of water from the time of the Goths and Vikings that fed into the River Poddle and then out to sea. Ever since he was a boy, Bram had heard tales of spirits coursing through the caverns under Dublin Castle.

Sure, Dublin Castle didn't look like a castle, at least not compared to Lord Penrhyn's feudal country estate. Dublin Castle was a bricked-in fortress, updated to be a Georgian palace for the English to reside in and rule from. The cab passed the remaining tower—the Record Tower.

The cab turned onto the main street as it headed to Bram's parent's house in a northern suburb in North Strand, an hour away. Back when he was a student at Trinity College, he could barely afford the trip to school and back. It wasn't until he was in his late thirties that Bram had the means to afford his own room. And for over two decades, he had been in charge of the employment and travel of the Lyceum Theatre's cast and crew.

So far on this trip, there was only one person he never had to plan for: Ahmed Kamal, due to arrive the next day. Bram patted his pocket to make sure he had Ahmed's latest telegram. In the dimming light, he took it out to verify the time stamp.

Boarding boat at Bristol. Have Talisman.
Will arrive Saturday, my friend.

Were he and Ahmed truly friends? They certainly had spent affable time together lately. He sensed courteous curiosity on the part of the Egyptian but not an overwhelming fondness. Other than Ellen and Pamela, Bram didn't have many close friends. Ahmed was one of the few people who knew enough about mummies to hold an intelligent conversation with him. And he would certainly be a great help in attempting to infiltrate the castle.

As the hansom approached the suburb of Clontarf, the Stokers' family home appeared, a neat, three-story stone house. After paying his fare, Bram looked up. There it was—his bedroom window on the top floor. How often as an isolated child had he gazed out that third-story window to the Irish Sea and imagined himself a world traveler?

It had been a year since he'd last seen his mother. She was tender, talkative, and nurturing. *Yet her views of the world are definite and fixed.* Bram had gotten his need for order from her, not from his accountant father, who made sure that he inherited the mindless clerk job here in Dublin. Yet, Bram's mother had a wild imagination. While he was bedridden for his first seven years due to an undiagnosed condition, it was she who read him terrifying stories. Gory Irish folktales activated his imagination while his body lay inert. But once he was able to run, he ran headfirst into the world. He was now obsessed not only with the legends his mother passed on but with all sorts of monsters and the cholera survivors. Every type of horror story was enthralling, then and now.

And here he was, quietly letting himself back in the house after hours. The gate still squeaked and the door still stuck as he opened it. When visiting for the first time, Florrie commented that the Stokers didn't want you in and once you were in, they didn't want you out. *Ah, Florrie.*

Florrie was the prettiest ingenue in Dublin, pursued by many eligible bachelors, including Oscar Wilde. Bram had originally told her that he knew that he was "ugly but strong." Regardless, he promised that he would always provide for her. At the moment, she was firmly ensconced amid London Society. She had declined to accompany him on this trip, professing she was neither fond nor proud of her Dublin origins. *She still resents my commitment to Henry and to the Lyceum Theatre.* Their son, Irving Noel, was studying to become a clerk. Noel, as he preferred to be called, detested theatre and the arts. The Stoker men had also traveled full circle, from clerk to artist to clerk. Bram hoped that he would prove to Florrie that he was a man of action, not just an "answer boy" serving Sir Henry Irving.

The faint smell of beeswax and lemon furniture polish greeted him in the foyer. Home. In the kitchen, a plate had been set out for him—roast beef and soda bread.

Well, this is a comfort. Good to note that Mother's hired help was reliable. The coal bin was full, the kitchen lamp wick was trimmed, and there was ice in the icebox.

Padding down the hall, he noticed that the pocket door of the parlor was open. Peeking in, he spotted his mother sleeping in the big armchair before a dim fire, her mass of gray hair piled up like a silver tiara on her head. Her lined face was nestled against her shawl, and her chest rose and fell in a steady rhythm as she gently snored. The sleep of the dead, as she would call it.

As a child, when he was finally well enough to go outside to play, his favorite playground had been the graveyard. Suicides were often dumped there, hidden in a stack to be buried at a later date, so there was always something new on the property. He'd asked Mother why the poor killed themselves if it was a sin against the church. His mother's only answer was to enlist

Bram to come along on her next charity visit in the worst slums in Dublin to see the "vast suffering of the poor."

A stack of books sat before her. One volume was propped up, as if on display. Bram picked it up. A slip of paper inserted in the pages revealed his mother's shaky but beautiful handwriting:

For Bram, my scholar, remember Abhartach

Bram did his best not to make a sound, but he couldn't help gasping. His mother startled briefly in her sleep but drifted off again.

He leaned over her to make sure she'd fallen back asleep. He sat in the chair closest to the fire. The book was the fairy tale collection his mother had read to him from during his years as an invalid. His favorite story was marked, the tale of the Celtic dwarf chieftain, Abhartach. A tyrant, a vicious politician and fighter, was murdered by an opponent, but through magic, he was able to rise from the dead and drink the blood of his conquered subjects. Not until he was buried, standing up, under an enormous stone, was his spirit finally crushed.

Working all those years at Dublin Castle, Bram became obsessed with crypts, tombs, and mummies. Would his rescue team succeed in crushing malevolent spirits who might have kidnapped Pamela?

He closed the book. Thinking on his own literary child, *The Un-Dead*, he sighed. After musing how Pamela hated the title, Bram had recently changed it from The *Un-Dead* to *Dracula*. And it had been judged "dreadful" by Sir Henry and "unimportant" by the critics. Now, without a publisher, it would remain inaccessible to the public. A failure and doomed to be forgotten.

He raised the book of fairy tales to his nose, inhaling the scents layered into the old burgundy leather: the sweet cherry tobacco of his father's pipe, the grassiness of the paper, the sour vanilla of the leather, and the heavenly aroma of aged must. Oh, the people and places he'd experienced through books, the old, new, male, female, "others." Books were a drug that transported him.

Bram felt a slight burning in his left earlobe. He stood before the mirror above the fireplace. The letters "PCS" appeared, slightly raised, a translucent snake writhing from the surface of his flesh. Bram touched the spot lightly. Ah, yes, he was a marked man now, like the great Irving, Ellen, and Florence.

Would they succeed in finding Pamela? Bram reached into his waistcoat pocket for the Viking compass. In the semidarkness, the two coins on the surface were almost impossible to see. He rubbed his thumb over the circle of swords, set in so finely they seemed flush. He turned it over in his hand.

His mother's eyes fluttered open and, without turning her head, she murmured, "Ah, Bram. Tomorrow, bury the demon headfirst, my son."

CHAPTER TWENTY-SEVEN

Cursed Leg

Pamela awoke with a lurch, the clang of metal ringing in her ears. The stone castle floor of her cell gradually came into focus. *Did someone just leave her cell?* The disgusting bucket she had used to relieve herself had been switched out while she slept every other night, but she had yet to catch sight of anyone. What day was this? She had counted fourteen days of stew and bread or porridge and bread; had it been two weeks? She listened for new sounds, and then she realized her watched had stopped. She forgot to wind it yesterday! Desperately, she turned the stem to six thirty, her usual time of waking. The sharp sounds of a whistle pierced the air, and her vision clouded.

Brammie was next to her in sawdust, center stage, blowing a whistle. Ellen, Sir Henry, Florence, and Ahmed were in the audience, watching her. She tried to call out, "My muses," but the word came out as "amuses."

Blinking, Pamela felt the dreamscape drain away as she watched a wisp of twisted shadows undulate toward her in midair. The afrit appeared in the center of the fumes, now more pathetic looking than ever. His fur was matted; one eye hung out of its socket. The afrit stood on only one of his satyr legs, holding the other in his sorry, tattered claws.

"What on the green earth is going on with you?" Pamela asked, sitting up on her cot. "I command you to tell me what is happening!"

"I've come to make amends for your mother's leg," the creature said in a low voice, offering its severed leg.

Pamela startled at the specter's voice. "How long have you been able to speak?" Pamela asked, her heart thumping in her chest.

"Since you commanded me to. I speak only when asked," the afrit responded. He wobbled slightly as he pathetically propped himself against the wall with a trembling claw.

"All I had to do was command you and you would have spoken to me?" Pamela said, jumping up and reaching to steady the faltering afrit. His fur was rough. She could feel his bones poking beneath.

"I don't know *everything* about your magic," the afrit snapped as Pamela sat him down next her.

"Well, I'm only now learning myself," Pamela said, leaning against the cold wall.

"I'm on my last leg. Here, this one's for you." He tried again to hand her his haunch.

"What are you doing? I don't want your leg!" Pamela said, recoiling.

"I owe you this. I am the spirit who entered your mother's coarse soul when she died."

"My mother's coarse soul?" Pamela asked in a daze, backing away. Her mind race back to the night of her mother's funeral in Jamaica. The funeral was in a pocket of memories buried away from her everyday mind.

Four years ago, at her mother's gravesite, Miss Jones, Pamela's minder in Kingston, told her of an altercation that occurred, but Pamela had been too overcome at the time to absorb the information.

In Jamaica, burials were carried out according to very strict rules. The island's obeahs—women of magic—believed there was a price to pay if all of the burial rituals were not carried out correctly.

"Afrit, tell me how you know about the soul's journey after death," Pamela said, crouching down to sit on the cot. "What happens?"

The afrit rolled his one good eye and leaned on his haunch as if it were a crutch. "Well, you see, I took over some of your mother's soul—at least the part of her soul that was in her leg."

"What!" Pamela screeched.

"Your family forgot to put the island's requirement payment in the coffin. It was missing the cotton silk branches and coins, and the duppies kicked up a storm."

"So that means you got her leg?" Pamela cried.

The afrit sighed. "You know that people own two souls: there's the spiritual one that flies up to heaven and the coarse soul that has to be tamped down. If the body isn't properly prepared and planted in the earth for the Nine Nights, the coarse soul can be taken over by duppies."

"Wait! Are you a duppie? I thought you were Aleister's afrit?" Pamela asked.

"Think back to your mother's funeral," the afrit said.

Darkness engulfed Pamela's vision. She heard pounding, the sound of men banging on a front door, then her father's voice, soft and pleading, barely audible. The darkness lifted, and Pamela was looking out her father's bedroom window. Torchlights danced in the front yard. A crowd of angry men—railroad workers who'd laid the mountains' train tracks for her father's company—milled about, cursing and yelling. She recognized, mingling in their midst, some of the family's household staff. The very ground seemed to tremble. There had been a small earthquake two nights ago, the night of Pamela's mother's funeral. Could this be another?

"Miss Jones, what is happening?" Pamela asked, as she pressed her hands against the frame of the open window. Kingston windows had no glass, only shutters and curtains to keep out the night. Now, the sound of breaking glass echoed from the kitchen below.

Miss Jones ran to Pamela's side. Her wide face, framed by a white headscarf, glowered in the dim room.

"Is it another earthquake?" Pamela asked.

"No, Miss Smith. Your pa's East India Company violated the magic of the earth. The men have come to settle debts."

"Who? And Pa would never violate magic!"

"Well, you know they ripped open the ground to place those steel rail tracks. Without any asking or potions."

A gun went off outside. Like a whirling angel, Miss Jones grabbed Pamela and pulled her across the hall to her bedroom, locking the door behind them. Throwing open the wardrobe, Miss Jones hurled Pamela's clothes into a pile while Pamela stood in a daze.

"You find out what is what. Your pa insulted the spirits with your ma's coffin," Miss Jones grunted, pulling a valise out from under the bed and handing it to Pamela. "No silk branches, no coins left inside for the spirits. Your people thought it was fine to put your ma in the earth without paying for it? Well, the duppies showed them."

Pamela was crying. Opening the valise, she found her old velvet hat, the one she had smuggled from London when they first moved here, when she was ten. It was now faded and matted, like a furry toy animal left outside in the sun.

"What's going to happen now?" Pamela asked, sitting on the floor and wiping her tears with the musty velvet hat.

"The village is scared. The big obeah had a vision of your ma's leg floating in the street," Miss Jones said, stuffing clothes into the suitcase and slamming it shut. "But a floating leg's not the work of a duppie; it be some other spirit. Your people, they're going to have to dig up your blessed mother's body and separate the leg from it."

"What!" Pamela cried, holding the hat to her heart.

"Yes, my child, they'll be amputating that leg and shipping it off the island. It's time for you and your father to go. And by go, I mean you run to the governor's house through the back path—now!"

Miss Jones yanked her up and hugged her harder than Pamela could remember her ever doing. Once released, Pamela looked at Miss Jones's face. Her eyes were filled with fear. Pamela had never seen her like this before.

"You must beware now—this spirit that's offended by your ma's funeral will haunt you at all thresholds. You must take care at all trains and bridges, all crossings. You are your father's daughter, and now all trains are cursed to you. Remember that."

"But they are my father's trains," Pamela cried. Before she could say more, the bedroom door shook violently. She and Miss Jones froze.

"Pamela," her father's voice cried, "open the door!"

Her father stood there surrounded by his secretary and two men from the stables who took care of the horses. The next hours were a frenzy as she and her father ran through the back paths to the governor's house and hid beneath the stairs.

The next day they took a ship to join Father's family in Brooklyn. A month later, she and Pa stood in Uncle Teddy's parlor. They were both shaking at the letter that had arrived from Jamaica in Pa's hand. The local community had determined that Mrs. Smith's body was contaminated by "other forces" and that Mother's leg would be arriving in New York City later that year, in care of the East India Shipping Company. Miss Jones was right: the townspeople had "separated" Pamela's mother's leg from her body.

Five months later, the shipment arrived. There was a blurred memory of her uncles and her father standing next to her as they stood before a small metal slate in the ground. Mrs. Corrine Serena Colman Smith's leg was buried under an unmarked plaque in Brooklyn's Greenwood Cemetery.

Pamela's consciousness returned to the prison cell. Rising to lean against the wall, she stared at the beast on her bed. His fur was like that of her velvet hat, all patchy and musty. Was this creature her hat?

"Are you the duppie who ate the soul in my mother's leg?" Pamela asked with the little breath she could summon.

"I am bound alongside other spirits," the little beast said. "I belong to a tribe of lost souls, shadows known as *qliphoth*, and sometimes afrits, sometimes duppies, and we all wait on Master Crowley. He knew that someday you would be a force to be reckoned with."

"How?" Pamela asked.

"Magical projection, or so it is said. His spell sent me from Egypt across the ocean to be with the duppies here in England. We work together to keep the curse on you and your family alive. Aleister's minions want to block your magic so that they can serve their master, Aleister, the more powerful magician."

"And you joined forces against me because you think Aleister will rule my magic?" Pamela cried.

The afrit hung his head. "I've limped along between worlds for years, not wanting to harm you. But I'm losing spirit energy in dribs and drabs. Master Crowley promised me a reincarnation if I obey him."

"Where is he now?" Pamela asked.

The afrit raised a pathetic claw, two of his three nails missing, and held it in front of Pamela's face. "Look into the sphere."

Pamela gasped as she saw a miniature world blossom, like a peony unfurling, in the creature's palm.

In the vision, the Golden Dawn chiefs stood on the prow of a ship, gathering around their leader, Aleister. He who towered above all of them except for a blond magician with glasses—Dr. Felkin, who Pamela had met in London. Aleister peered at the horizon as a spray of water sprang up, dampening the huddle of men. As Aleister's dark, long locks plastered against his face, he pointed to something in the distance. Then the scene evaporated.

"What are they looking for?" Pamela asked.

"Your friends from the theatre and the Golden Dawn are on their way here. Aleister's magicians hope to cast a spell to extract your magic first. I was to keep you disorientated until they arrive." The afrit's one good eye teared up.

"But will you help me now? How do I get out of here?" Pamela asked. "I'll reciprocate by helping you to enter a much better world, if I can. It will be a world of my own making, not a reincarnation. I may not know how to create it now, but I will learn. What do I need to do?"

"Command your mother," the afrit said, as one of his goat horns fell off. "She came to you in Manchester and almost saved you there."

Pamela remembered the incident in the park across the street from her childhood house in Manchester. It was after she first arrived with Brammie and had taken the car to visit where she'd lived with Father and Mother. Mother appeared as a winged statue and saved Pamela from a mob. Could her mother have been by her side all along?

"When you commanded me to speak, I spoke," the afrit reminded her. The dark, furry afrit stared at her through his thicket of strangeness. "Crowley is afraid of you. Call for your mother."

"Mother?" Pamela whispered. Her palms began to sweat and her heart thumped louder than before. "I command you to help me."

The statue from her childhood park in Manchester materialized above her. It was the same angel, with fluttering wings, a fierce gaze chiseled into her eyes, and the same extended marble hand.

Pamela reached out and grasped the smooth palm. It gently enfolded her hand, its coldness shocking Pamela.

In a breath, Pamela catapulted out of the cell.

CHAPTER TWENTY-EIGHT

Castle Performance

Bram and Florence wrangled the Scuttlers into the choir room of the Royal Chapel, trying to shush and direct the twenty some boys, unaccustomed to full breakfasts or travel to Irish castles.

"Toby Dolan," Bram called out.

"Here," Toby answered, sitting straight up.

"John-Joseph Champion," Bram continued, scanning the room for the gang leader.

"Yeah," John-Joseph replied, his insolence prompting giggles from the younger Scuttlers.

Bram watched Florence stand behind the seated John-Joseph and rest her hand on his shoulder. Florence looked quite attractive today, dressed in a form-fitting black coat with a feathered hat perched over her curls. At her touch, John-Joseph blushed a shade of ruby.

Bram had to bite the insides of his cheeks to keep from smiling. *The lady conquers the tiger.*

"We're so glad you're present, Mr. Champion," Florence said in a soothing tone, half seductress, half schoolmarm.

Encouraged, Bram continued the roll call, all boys accounted for. Now he would rehearse them as though they were at the Lyceum Theatre for a put-in. They were issued typed pages of sides at the beginning of the train trip, and they now had to prove that they knew their lines and blocking. Bram asked each in turn: "What do you say?" "Where are you when you say it?" "What do you do next?"

He was pleased with their performances, even if some had learned their roles by rote because they couldn't read. The thick Mancunian accent of others made them a little difficult to understand, even with simple lines such as "Reporting for duty" or "No, sir."

"Act like you know what you're doing, and the Dubliners will leave you alone," Bram advised at the end of the run-through.

Manchester lads appearing at an Irish horse show would escape the usual Dubliner scrutiny if they presented themselves with purpose. Florence did a final check on the ten boys wearing uniforms, making sure cuffs were straight and belts tightened. When she went to straighten a cap that was askew on a boy's head, he swatted her hand away.

"Sorry, ma'am, there's sharp edges there," the boy stuttered.

Bram approached the boy and then looked at all the boys' plaid caps. Focusing on the caps on the other boys' heads, Bram realized that the brims of the caps were dotted with razorblades. A memory of the wardrobe mistress in Manchester warning him the Scuttlers wore razors rousted in Bram's brain.

John-Joseph was by his side and whispering in Bram's ear. "The blades won't glint, Mr. Stoker. They're pushed down low so the sun won't catch 'em. We only use 'em when we're caught."

Bram turned to the boys. "There will be no street fight with these caps. Is that understood?"

The boys murmured yeses until John-Joseph answered back with a strong, "Understood," and the room followed his example.

"Don't forget," Bram said, "I want you to melt into the crowd at the entrance to the courtyard. The castle's locals will pick up if there's a gang afoot."

Bram looked at his pocket watch: eight o'clock. The Winter Royal Performance of the Horse Regiments would start in an hour. And still no Ahmed.

"All right, my boys, do me proud! And don't get hurt or hurt others!" Bram called out, feeling both proud and worried about his hooligans.

As the boys bolted from the church's back chamber, Florence came up to Bram. She was unusually pale. Would she be up to her role today?

"Mr. Stoker, I'll keep an eye on the boys before I join you in the stands. Any word from Mr. Kamal regarding his arrival?"

Bram was accustomed to her brusque manner, but today he noticed worry in her voice.

"No telegram from Ahmed yet. He was scheduled to arrive with the first ferry, which gets in presently. He'll be here soon. My biggest concern at present is the musician you'll be replacing. The horses may be unpredictable while we infiltrate the crowdthe musicians' promenade, and he may be injured."

"Yes, may the gods forfend that the musicians and horses have minimum impact," Florence replied. "I won't play my harp well if I know someone's been hurt on my account. Will all this distraction succeed in finding Miss Smith?"

"I'm hopeful," Bram answered, batting away his own doubts. He wasn't certain that Pamela was here in the compound. If they were to execute this plan without finding her—well, he couldn't entertain that possibility right now. "We'll do our best."

"That we will, Mr. Stoker," Florence answered, nodding as she headed out. At the door, she turned and added, "I think your plans are excellent, Mr. Stoker. My visions say we will find Pamela."

Bram exhaled as she closed the door. *Well, at least someone thinks my plans will work.* He glanced around the choir room to make sure that the boys hadn't left any telltale items behind.

A knock on the door was followed by a man's voice: "All set, Mr. Stoker? If you're done, I'll lock up after you."

"Thank you," Bram replied, momentarily alarmed at the man's voice until he remembered the plan. Opening the heavy door to the chapel, he saw no one around, and he exited quickly. *So far, no need to worry.* Many favors had been called in to arrange this day's events, and they were unraveling right on cue.

Bram walked up to the Palace Street Gate and entered Dublin Castle's grounds under gray clouds, dulling the color of the brick street. *My old stomping grounds.* He slowed his pace until he stood before his old office at the Cross Block—an unimposing, three-story brick building. His decade of drudgery here seemed like a long-ago nightmare, but it was recent enough that he laughed with shaky relief at not having to enter the building. Yes, his days of drudgery publishing *The Duties of Clerks of the Petty Sessions of Ireland* were over.

Today, he would be battling different demons in order to save Pamela. Did he risk being buried headfirst, according to his mother's warning last night?

He approached the ticket booth: it was surrounded by loitering British police. Glancing inside the courtyard, he saw that there was a large police presence lining the walls. Switching out the Scuttlers with guards would be more difficult, and the time Bram had to escape undetected to the inner sanctum of the castle would be extremely limited. But they had to pull this off if they were to search for Pamela undetected. *And where is Ahmed? It's not like him to be late.*

Bram scanned the crowd streaming in: there was Florence on the other side of the ticket booth, mingling with the crowd. Ellen, Sir Henry, and Lord Penryhn were due in forty-five minutes. They would provide a distraction for the Scuttlers to filter inside the State Apartments. Bram knew the castle's intersection of staterooms, apartments, jail, spirit channels, and magical waters inside and out. There was a chill in the air, and Bram picked up his step to the castle entry.

Arriving at the booth, he glanced at the ticket taker: it was Eyre from the old days, a former Cross Block office boy. He was grayer and wider than Bram remembered. They nodded at one another. Money was exchanged for a packet and single-entry ticket. Bram turned his hand sideways so that the envelope Eyre palmed him couldn't be seen. Without exchanging a word, Bram presented his chit and entered the courtyard. He glanced back from time to time, to make sure that he wasn't being followed.

The stands in front of the State Apartments were beginning to fill, even at this early hour. A small stage in front of the Viceroy Stand had been decorated with paper garlands and banners, crafted not to survive any December rain. So far, the weather held.

Across the courtyard, Bram could see a line of horses queued near the guard box: it stretched almost all the way around the massive brick square. There was Pablo with Little Beda, the horse pawing the ground in anticipation, the circus act queued up with the white military horses. Little Beda's sleek black coat stood out against the rows of white steeds, the horses of Hanover favored by the British Army. Bram waved to Pablo, who saluted back before returning his attention to his jittery horse. An involuntary breath escaped Bram. *So far, so good.* He jostled though the crowd to claim his seats in the royal box. A banner—*Reserved for Stoker Party*—had been draped across a row in back of the viceroy and vicereine's flower-bedecked seats.

Bram glanced at his watch: eight thirty. Another half hour before the viceroy and his wife would arrive. Bram, Ahmed, and Florence would have an hour between the horse show and the Lyceum Theatre performance inside the castle to penetrate the Record Tower.

After making sure that no one was behind him, Bram opened Eyre's envelope. Nestled amid the stack of passes for the reception and a small key was a hand-scrawled note.

VLL @ DCSA no PP.
OTR sf, hw=sohw.
IMT rec ha.
wbyob

Eyre's Cross Block Office code, Bram thought as he easily decoded the message:

Viceroy lord lieutenant staying at Dublin Castle
State Apartments, not Phoenix Park.
Old throne-room stone fireplace, same old hallways.
International military team for reception on high alert.
Welcome back you old bastard.

A knot in Bram's stomach tightened as he read the warning about the presence of "international military." That would complicate their efforts getting into the Record Tower. Bram stashed the note and the key away in a pocket of his coat, making sure to keep them separate from the passes he would be dispersing later.

More uniformed soldiers swarmed the stands. Saffron-colored robes from Africa, scarlet kilts from Scotland, and the horsemen from India wore ivory turbans that stood out against the dark blue of the British Lancers' military regalia.

In the row in front of Bram, to the side of the royal box, two ladies sat. Each had fur blankets on their laps and hats piled so high with feathers that Bram was relieved he wasn't sitting directly behind them. One lady turned around to him and asked loudly in an elegant English accent, "Excuse me, sir. We were wondering where the castle would be?"

"Dear lady, this wonderful array of historical buildings *is* our castle," Bram replied. "In the Pooley River alongside us, there are signs of an old Viking route."

"Old Vikings. How quaint," the woman replied flatly, turning back to her companion. Bram was glad his mother hadn't arrived yet. She would have had some choice words for anyone calling their castle "quaint." Her joyous response last night when Bram told her that she was to come today with Bram's brother made Bram more on edge. *Golden Dawn kidnappers and family—not the optimum combination.* There were so many mixed emotions about being back at the castle.

True, disappointment was usually newcomers' first reaction to Dublin Castle: a series of buildings set in a square and incorporating ruins of medieval towers. The landmark lacked a true castle and held no displays of armor or weaponry. Bram recalled Oscar Wilde, his onetime friend and competitor here in Dublin, quipping, "The Irish needed no weapons in their castle, as their wit was in constant display." Now Oscar's wit was recovering in France after his conviction of gross indecency. Bram hoped that today the rescue party's wit would prove sufficient to win the day.

As Bram scanned the courtyard, the piles of Gothic, Norman, and Georgian buildings sitting side by side now seemed chaotic. Perhaps his two decades in London had colored how he viewed the history of Ireland, slice by slice.

Breaking out of his reverie, Bram spotted Florence approaching a cluster of Scuttlers socializing among themselves rather than being on the lookout. She escorted the four boys in household uniforms to the door to the State Apartments. They would be ushered inside to guard the Apollo Room entrances. He had checked all five outdoor entrances to the State Apartments and deduced they would need access to the one nearest the Record Tower. Yes, the boys were all at their posts near the exit doors. Once the assigned inside crew was in position, he and

Ahmed could find the hallways leading to the ancient prison. Provided Ahmed arrived in time!

At last he spotted his mother and brother, William, coming through the main entrance. The crowd had grown to at least four hundred spectators. His mother approached the stand, and as she took in the fact that they were to sit behind the royal box, a girlish smile spread across her face. As they sat down, the viceroy, George Cadogan, and his wife, Lady Beatrice, approached the stairs to their seats, and the immediate crowd stilled.

As the vicereine and viceroy sat, Bram's mother beamed at him.

"I'm so glad I wore my new bonnet," she said, her eyes crinkling as she pointed to the rosettes on her hat's bill. Tucked among the ribbons was a bejeweled Celtic cross. His mother loved to see the royals but still wanted them to know Fenians were on the grounds.

A trumpet blasted, and two columns of horses, bearing musicians, streamed into the center of the courtyard, their lines dissolving as the horses milled in formation. Bram saw Florence wrangling a couple of boys in the crowds to stand apart and stop conversing. For the briefest of seconds, the sun peeked out of the clouds and flashes of light streaked across the bricks. Toby's Scuttlers, with the razors in their caps, twinkled like demonic stars. Bram glanced around the stands; no one seemed to have noticed the reflections. The boys stood along the far back wall and mixed among the stable hands. Bram had arranged for two of the largest soldiers from India's regiment to stand guard over them. When Bram lifted his chin in his direction, Toby waved back with a subtle brush of his dark, curly hair.

Sir Henry, Lord Penryhn, and Ellen entered the courtyard. *For the love of God, they brought all three dogs with them.* The dogs were supposed to be left at their lodgings. At least they were leashed. Bram stood and waved, then fought his way down the stairs to lead them to their adjoining seats.

As they were getting settled, the viceroy and vicereine turned and nodded to Henry and Ellen. Bram noticed that Lord Penrhyn's nose seemed somewhat out of joint, but the lord made sure that he was seated next to Ellen.

Bram scrutinized the crowd again just as a new horse entered the courtyard to perform. He spotted Ted, astride Little Beda, looking directly at him. Bram touched his brow, in acknowledgment.

Little Beda abruptly cantered out in front of another horse, one of the white Hanoverian steeds, which promptly bolted. Rider and horse crashed into a military band horse, causing its rider, a French horn player, to fall off while still holding his instrument. Most of the horses were quick enough to shy away from one another, but a pair of musical equestrians and their mounts collided into one another. A tuba and trumpet rained to the ground even though the riders held to their mounts. Just when the flute player seemed to be in control of his steed, he tumbled off to cries from the stands. Bram was glad to see Little Beda move away as the police ran to the grounds to sort out the two fallen riders and horses. Bram smiled, as Pablo and Little Beda waited at the side, innocent bystanders to the chaos.

"There goes our musical entertainment for the reception," the vicereine Lady Beatrice said, turning to her husband.

Florence appeared and slid into the seat next to Bram. He exhaled. *First steps to the plan gone off without a hitch.* "Just in time," Bram said. "Everything settled?"

"The boys are all in place, and I just met Pamela's flatmates coming in," Florence said quietly. "I haven't spotted Mr. Kamal yet."

Bram handed reception tickets to Florence as a young couple dashed up the stairs and sat in the last two seats of the Stoker row. It took Bram a moment to recognize Rosa and Yoshio, Pamela's friends from the London art scene. Bram gave two more reception tickets to Florence, who subtly passed them along them to the newcomers and then sat back in her seat next to Bram. She patted his arm in a motherly way. *Florence is as nervous as I am.*

Down below, the lord lieutenant made his way to the dais on the courtyard. "As your viceroy opening our Dublin Winter Performance, I commend our riders and musicians, who endured perhaps just a few bruises during our equine ballet entertainment. Thanks to all for your participation. Now, I give you Miss Ellen Terry, celebrated star of the London stage."

Ellen stood in Bram's row and made her way down to the stand, and a buzz from the spectators followed in her wake. Bram knew that not every Dubliner would be familiar with her stage career, but most would have read about her in the London newspapers. Wearing a dark-green velvet riding suit with feathers at the shoulders and a matching feather-plumed hat, Ellen looked like Winged Victory ascending the dais.

"Dear celebrants of Dublin Castle," Ellen said, projecting with her best stage voice. "I am honored to be here in Ireland, home to my dear friend, Mr. Bram Stoker, a former employee at Dublin Castle and now second in command at the Lyceum Theatre London."

A roar went up from the local sections. Out of the corner of his eye, Bram noticed that Henry flinched. It never went well when Henry was not the most celebrated guest.

"And now, it is my honor to present to you Mr. Ted Pablo and his amazing horse, Little Beda," Ellen continued. "You will be delighted by their performance of Irish dancing!"

The military band, now on the ground to the side of the courtyard, played "The Argyle Waltz," the song that Pamela had hummed the night she rode Little Beda. Hopefully, if Pamela was within hearing distance, she would know that they were here.

Little Beda burst from the sidelines with Ted firmly latched onto her back. They raced in a furious circle, then stopped to execute sidesteps and kicks. The crowd clapped and exclaimed as the beautiful ebony beast leapt in the air, kicking both back legs behind her. The black steed didn't miss a step as three other horsemen tore through the open gates and joined them in the dance. Two of the men wore white turbans and had slung curved blades across their chests. The third rider was familiar to Bram: Satish Monroe.

Could it only have been two months since Satish, Pamela, and Bram had met Little Beda at Ted's house in Manchester? When had Satish learned how to ride horseback so expertly while performing his solo *Othello*?

Satish's horse balanced on his hind legs and Little Beda circled him, prancing. The audience broke out in wild cheers as the four horses concluded the dance by lining up and bowing to the royal box.

Exiting, Satish rode by and waved toward Bram without looking at him. The signal for the next step was in order.

A bugle blasted as an Irish division regiment rode in, performing their routine of precise high steps and exact turns. The home crowd acknowledged their boys with whooping and clapping. After several minutes of high spirits and shouts exchanged between the riders and the audience, the horses and riders cleared out and the English lineup entered to perform the closing portion of the show. Even before they completed the first round of the courtyard, spectators started descending from the stands.

Bram took a mental roll call: Henry, Ellen, and his mother were nowhere to be seen. They must have gone down the aisle in the opposite direction for the reception in the royal apartments. Now an entirely new group of soldiers stood guard at the entrance, each one a Scuttler from Manchester. Bram glanced over at William, glad that his brother opted to stay by his side.

Bram could feel his Viking compass spinning in his waistcoat pocket. Perhaps it was locating Pamela—or a demon.

Peering into the crowd, Bram caught sight of Toby, who now wore his red scarf around his neck—the signal for trouble.

"Look what the devil dragged in," Florence murmured through clenched teeth.

He glanced to where she was staring and caught his breath. Five men, wearing similar black cloaks, snaked their way through the crowd. He recognized them as the Golden Dawn chiefs: Aleister, Samuel Mathers, Archer Prince, Dr. Felkin, and Dr. Westcott.

So they did have something to do with Pamela's kidnapping.

Bram studied the Golden Dawn chiefs, now busy talking among themselves, Aleister the center of the group. Toby had moved closer to them, and Bram nodded his head at him as John-Joseph also planted himself by Aleister's side.

A limping man making his way through the assembly had a familiar face. It was Ahmed without his fez, carrying an unconscious girl.

CHAPTER TWENTY-NINE

Pamela the Magician

Pamela exhaled as her body crystalized above a packed reception. Bobbing like a sea buoy, she found she was levitating near a ceiling. She grasped the wall's crown molding to keep from swaying. Her hold seemed tenuous at best. No one in crowd below looked up. That was good; she must be invisible to them. The plaster roses on the railing brushed against her ghostly fingers—a sensation of touch! She stared at her hands—they were translucent. *Where was her mother who rescued her? Were they now both spirits tucked between worlds?*

Looking down at her floating ghost body, she realized that she was wearing her violet day dress; it too was filmy, just like her hands. It was the dress she had been wearing when she left the Midland Hotel before she landed in the cell.

"The Argyle Waltz" played in the distance as the dignitaries entered the queue at the bottom of the stairs. Little Beda's music? Was it a coincidence that the horse's performance song was playing? Letting go of the knob of plaster roses, she hovered awkwardly above a crowded ornate staircase. It was filled with women and soldiers jostling to make their way up into a stateroom. With swords strapped to their waists, the soldiers wore uniforms of red coats and gold sashes that stood out from the white ballgowns of the ladies next to them. From the staircase, the din of conversation was punctuated by the cries of the young ladies as their dresses were trod upon by soldiers. Pamela maneuvered herself lower by paddling her arms to get a closer look.

Ah, dance cards. So, this was a ball, not a play. *How like my mother to deliver me to a ballroom.*

Pamela floated above the debutantes and patronesses. Mothers and sponsors shimmered in colorful ballgowns, and the young women wore white satin. Their hair was piled up and laced with tiaras and small veils topped with white ostrich feathers, complimenting their pale, powered décolletages adorned with jeweled necklaces.

"Watch it, you battle-ax!" a soldier protested as a huffy matron tried to navigate around him on the stairs. Pamela felt a ripple of joy. To be back among the living, and at this grand reception, having been cooped up for so long was almost more than she could bear.

She willed herself upward and found herself gliding higher, almost holding a steady course. Soaring near the ceiling, she was relieved she was no longer bouncing about like a balloon in the wind. She didn't wish to attract any attention. She drew near the three windows at the first landing outside the entrance to the stateroom. Looking out, she saw a bricked courtyard teeming with swarms of people and soldiers on horseback. Turning back toward the hallway, Pamela watched a flood of people charge up the stairs on either side of the landing. Pamela reached out her ghostly fingers and clung to the nearest crystal chandelier to steady herself.

Taking one last look below, she spotted him! It was her Magician! Her heart skipped a beat. Sir Henry stood talking with what looked like a royal couple on the floor below. He was wearing his best evening dress, but his face was absolutely blue. In fact, Cerulean blue, but the couple and the people around him acted as though nothing was unusual about his appearance. Propelling herself away from the molding, she waved her arms in his direct line of sight. No reaction. She almost shouted but thought better of it. Sir Henry hated a scene. That is, he hated it when others created a scene.

Sir Henry left the couple and climbed the crowded staircase, his blue face huffing. Was this unnatural blue a result of illness or makeup? None of the people pressed in around him reacted at all to his complexion. *Am I the only one seeing his blue face?* It was illness—she could now see through his body to the disease. It was eating away at him as though he were a rotten fruit.

If he was so ill, why was Sir Henry here, if this wasn't a theatre? *This must be a benefit for the Lyceum Theatre*, Pamela thought. Sir Henry rarely went to large events outside of Lyceum Theatre openings.

She launched herself past the chandeliers and found that she slipped through the glass inset above the arched door into the ballroom. *I can pass through glass!* She was still wobbly on the other side in the crowded room as she soared lopsided near the high ceiling. On the canopy, she noticed a painting depicting several royal figures seated below a blue-robed angel, who was blowing a trumpet. The blue angel soared loftily in the painting, surrounded by putti. The angel made flying look so easy.

Pamela sailed in a crooked flight above the packed room. Soldiers leaned against the Corinthian columns and called up to a musician's gallery, demanding "better music." A line of people stood before two grand, empty thrones set on a stage. The volume in the ballroom grew louder as more debutantes and mothers rushed in. The soldiers took notice and fixed on the latest arrivals. Near them, a group of men dressed formally in black huddled together. English tailoring, possibly Saville Row. Another group of men wore white dinner jackets embroidered with Celtic symbols and images of horses, and they loudly jostled and teased one another as the ladies drew near. Judging by their white outfits and the number of gingers in the group, Pamela guessed this cluster to be Irish horsemen. The men in the black clothes studiously ignored them.

Conversation in the room came to a halt at the arrival of two regal figures wearing capes and crowns. An equerry called out, "The viceroy and vicereine of Dublin," as the pair made their way toward their thrones, tossing their capes back with a flourish before sitting.

Murmurs of "Lord Cadogan" and "Lady Beatrice" coursed through the compact lines of people waiting in the queue before the thrones. The coterie of Englishmen whom Pamela had been tracking made their way to the front of the line, and the lord steward formally introduced each person to Lord Cadogan, a clean-shaven, pleasant-looking man with a large forehead and an impressive head of hair. Pamela soared closer to Lady Beatrice. The vicereine was an imperious beauty, her head titled back possibly to balance her large crown. Her voice had a tinkly lilt. After the Englishmen had made their introductions, the women waiting in line pushed forward to be greeted.

Out of the throng, a familiar face appeared. Ellen! Pamela almost cried out to her. Ellen was escorted by an elderly gentleman whom Pamela didn't recognize. But how perfect Ellen looked, her green velvet dress embellished with bows and arrows, her tiara shaped like a laurel wreath. She looked like Diana the Huntress. *Perhaps she's looking for me!*

With that thought, Pamela tried to shout out, *It's me, Pixie!* But nothing came out of her throat. She hated the nickname Ellen had given her: it made it sound as if she were a house cat. Now she felt a longing for Ellen to look up and call out her pet name.

Spectral tears stung in her eyes. Pamela tried to soar down

toward Ellen but only managed to spin about like a dog chasing its tail. By the time she had righted herself, Sir Henry had entered the room.

How can I get down? Pamela flitted and floated at awkward angles, her head coming perilously close to the chattering guests.

Do as the afrit said: command yourself. I command, down!

Sure enough, the next thing she knew, she was drifting alongside Sir Henry as a surge of people traversed right through her ghostly body. So, her body was but a vapor here—not so different from standing by the stage door on opening night, where she was invisible to everyone who'd come to rub elbows with the stars.

A butler came by, bearing large crystal glasses. Pamela gasped. They were exact replicas of the cups Pamela had designed for Sir Henry's production of *The Cup*. She had fashioned the prop to be outstanding, as the play's plot centered around the cup being handed to an evil ruler, leading to his death by poison. Bram had suggested a late-Roman vessel as a possibility, but Pamela was inspired by a Viking model.

A tall blond man wearing pince-nez glasses took two off the tray and offered one to Sir Henry; he seemed oblivious to Sir Henry's blue coloring. "What do you think of our royal Dublin goblets?" he asked, his Irish accent shining through.

"It's more than substantial," Sir Henry replied.

"It's our royal cup!" the blond man cried, slurring a little. "Designed after the Ardagh one, buried to save it from the Normans."

It wasn't the Normans; it was the Vikings who created the Ardagh chalice, *not* cup*!* Pamela almost shouted at the man.

As if he could hear her thoughts, Sir Henry turned his blue head in her direction, his eyes open wide. The markings on his face weren't the blue greasepaint or watercolor makeup she had suggested to him for the role of Mathias in *The Bells*. Now that she was closer, she could see that blue outlined his decaying flesh.

They heard a shout from outside the room, and a crush of soldiers stumbled in. The mob parted and, from their midst, Aleister Crowley swaggered out. Pamela felt her ghostly body recoil. She soared up to the highest point of the ceiling.

His long dark hair was no longer plastered against his face as it had been when the afrit showed him during the vision in her cell. Aleister now looked every inch the society dandy in his form-fitting evening clothes. His dark eyes flashed as he strolled through the crowd, drawing attention to himself by staring back at the partygoers with an insolent sneer.

Three men accompanied Aleister, the Golden Dawn chiefs Westcott and Mathers, and one man Pamela didn't recognize.

Aleister and his minions inserted themselves into the circle of Englishmen gathered around Sir Henry. The man who had escorted Ellen in earlier seemed to be the unacknowledged leader of clustered Englishmen.

Aleister introduced himself to the group. Then he introduced his chiefs—Dr. Felkin, Dr. Westcott, and Mr. Mathers—and he named the fourth caped man, a Mr. Prince, who barely lifted his eyes from the floor. Aleister made conversation confidently, but he kept looking about the room. Pamela drifted closer. *Was he looking for her? Or the afrit?*

"I would like your opinion, Lord Penrhyn," Aleister said to the man who was escorting Ellen. "Should I introduce myself to these gentlemen next to us?" he asked, motioning to the Irish horsemen.

Clicking his tongue, Lord Penrhyn led the group a short distance away. Pamela dove low enough to hear Dr. Felkin murmur to Aleister, "'Tis best not to make acquaintance with the local horsemen. The Irish—especially Ballsbridge half-breeders and Kildare smut—are not to be trusted."

"Ah, be careful how you disparage the Irish," Aleister said, flicking his hair away from his brow. "My name Aleister is Irish for Alexander, and I'm rather fond of Dublin and those in it."

So, Willian and her stone heads were right, she was in Dublin. But she was last in Manchester with Henry's tour. How did she get here?

Despite the slur that had been voiced, Sir Henry strode over to the Irish group and was greeted by surprised exclamations and hearty handshakes. Aleister's English contingent turned their backs and talked among themselves. Pamela flapped her arms, trying to get closer to Sir Henry.

To the ground: command yourself there.

Pamela pitched herself downward and almost crashed on the floor. She straightened herself up and wobbled to Sir Henry's side. Aleister turned from the English cluster and stared right at her. Doing her best to shrink herself, Pamela squeezed in between Sir Henry and an Irishman in uniform. Aleister strode over and stood so near that she could feel his human breath.

Could he see her, sense her? She peered around to gauge how close he'd come to her. He was an arm's length away, his eyes squeezed shut. When he opened his eyes, his pupils were vertical and slit-shaped, like a lizard's. He seemed poised to strike. Mesmerizing and yet threatening. Was he about to cast a spell to siphon off whatever magical powers she now held?

Aleister turned his head to Sir Henry, interrupting his conversation about a horse show they all had just seen. "Sir Henry, I was just discussing with our English compatriots what seems to be the Irishification of this Winter Horse Show."

An Irishman standing next to Henry stuck out his chest and stood right before Aleister, his face flushed. "In Dublin, you'll see that we know a lot more about the spirit of a horse than any Englishman."

"Well, what do you know?" Aleister asked the red-faced man. "Are the Irish fairy kings to be the judges for the race? I'm not sure our English Viceroy and Vicereine would approve."

Florence elegantly sauntered into the ballroom wearing a diaphanous pale-blue Greek-styled gown. Pamela clapped her hands together in delight. Her High Priestess of the Golden Dawn was here in Dublin too?

Pamela spun around. How could she break out of the invisible shroud covering her? She sailed over to Florence just as a butler wheeled a large harp into a corner of the room. It moved right through Pamela's body, as though she were a fume. It didn't even hurt. *Am I dead or just floating in another world?* Here her physical spirit body couldn't stop things or people, but she could touch things like ceilings. Spirit life was confusing. She hovered over Florence as she sat down on a chair and splayed her long fingers across the harp strings.

"Florence, it's me, Pamela," Pamela whispered into Florence's ear. Her head jerked up. *She heard me!* Florence had studied astral travel with the Golden Dawn, so maybe she did hear her.

Pamela waved a hand in front of her. No response.

Henry strolled up to Florence and kissed her hand as Pamela drifted aside, just in case she could be perceived. From across the room, Ellen's head whipped around, clocking the gesture. Pamela felt a happy burning ache: some things had remained the same with her loved ones.

"Do you think the viceroy would like a jig?" Florence asked.

"Do you know any Scottish sword dances?" Sir Henry asked. "'I Will Break Your Head,' perhaps?"

Florence pivoted to her harp, mumbling to him under her breath, "Yes, 'Breaking of Heads'—very apt for now."

Florence began to play. Pamela placed her fingers on Florence's harp strings to feel them vibrating, but her fingers had the same weak hold as when she tried to anchor herself on the ceiling's plaster roses. "I'm here, Florence!" she said. The strings held a flat tone when Pamela held on, and Florence's eyes widened. With a smile, and despite the flat note, she continued to play the lively music.

Florence's harp music was soon overwhelmed by chatter. Pamela caught sight of Aleister crossing to stand face-to-face with Sir Henry, who stood by the harp, listening. Almost of equal height, Aleister bowed to Sir Henry.

Sir Henry bowed his head as Florence embarked on a lively stream of arpeggios.

"Hello, juggler," Aleister said to Sir Henry. Aleister stood back a bit, his eyes half shut as though bored. Florence steadfastly ignored Aleister and passionately continued playing.

Ellen threaded her way through a swarm of soldiers in order to get closer. Did Ellen know that "juggler" was a slur to insult magicians? This confrontation wasn't going to end well.

Pamela floated near Ellen. Turning so she could see, Pamela rolled over in midair as Aleister grabbed a goblet from a waiter and was toasting Henry. "We've actually met before," Aleister said. "Or rather, I've bested you before."

"Let bygones be bygones, Mr. Crowley," Henry said, reaching out as if to offer a handshake.

Aleister snorted, "Ha, imposter!"

Henry held his chalice to his breast. An actor wants to be known as the real thing, not an imposter. Then Pamela spotted it, the tell. Sir Henry tapped one shoe continuously on the floor. That was the telling gesture that signaled to the Lyceum Theatre that Sir Henry was nervous, a rare event. From across the room, the crowd surrounding the viceroy and vicereine went silent. Florence's harp music died down, and an icy breeze wound through the room.

Pamela was swept up and away. She fought to descend but could only remain a haze drifting in the air. She willed herself to the ground to protect Sir Henry, but she remained bobbing near the ceiling. *Damn, damn, damn! This magic is hard to learn!*

Aleister downed his drink and tossed his goblet over his shoulder. In midair, the crystal shattered into tiny silver arrows, all trained on one target: Sir Henry. A wave of the small projectiles flew through the air, a few soaring up through Pamela. No one in the room followed the paths of the tiny arrows—the crowd was frozen in place. Pamela's spectral form wavered for a moment, as if the lines that connected her had been severed. But her ghostly body still held its own as the arrows passed through her.

Sir Henry cried out as his throat was peppered with arrows. Blood dripped down and dyed his white shirt collar red. He buckled briefly but remained standing upright.

The crowd came back to life. A woman's scream reverberated through the dense room. Ellen stood by Henry's side and tried to hold him up as he staggered; she was barely able to keep him from collapsing. A rush of men surged to Sir Henry to support him.

I command myself: down!

Pamela anchored herself in front of her bleeding Magician. Sir Henry's blue hands clutched the gashes pooling in his throat.

Aleister sidled up to Henry as if to tend to him while Ellen held Henry's arm. The Irishmen in white waistcoats took over holding Sir Henry up. Women used their dainty handkerchiefs to stem the flow of blood from the puncture wounds along his jaw and throat, but Henry's eyes rolled back in his head as they sat him down.

Pamela heard whispers of dismay and disbelief from the bystanders. How could one glass do so much damage?

"Juggler," Aleister hissed. "We'll stop if you give us your minor gifts from Miss Smith. We know she is here with us now."

Henry tried to speak, clutching at his throat. Onstage, he would have turned the blood into a red scarf or a dove that flew out into the audience. Here he could only collapse on the floor, panting.

Pamela dove down to him, and Aleister swiveled his head right to where Pamela hovered over Henry's body. Aleister put a hand out in the air: he could sense her presence.

Flying away from him, she stabilized in midair and stretched out her arms, flexing her palms. She would need to harness her Magician's power. One of the courses of the Golden Dawn had mentioned it—if only she had truly studied it. Time to try this spell instinctively.

The Magician's tools materialized around Sir Henry as he lay on the floor: cup, sword, wand, and star. Pamela felt a puff of pride. *I can conjure at will after all!* Those attending to Henry paid no notice to her magical manifestations, and the rest of the ballroom seemed unaware as well.

The tools floated up as though on a current of air, and Pamela reached out for the royal cup, the Ardagh chalice. Before she could grasp it, it fell and smashed into pieces at Sir Henry's feet. The wand wobbled in the air and levitated near the group kneeling around Henry. Aleister made a grab for it. The drifting sword sliced through the air, keeping his hand from clutching the wand. Aleister tried again and, this time, the star counter-attacked by cuffing him on the ear.

"I own these magician's tools in service to Thoth!" Aleister roared.

There was a tickling at the back of Pamela's neck.

Command your gifts, Corinne!—Corinne, the nickname that Mother used when she was cross with her!

Pamela took a deep breath and intoned: *Down now!*

Pamela swooped down and settled in front of Aleister. His dark eyes widened, no longer serpentlike.

"These tools aren't yours to command, Crowley," Pamela said.

A rush of cold air thrust Pamela into a dizzy tumble, and she was no longer in the throne room but tossing about above the church. When she caught her breath, she braced herself by hanging on to the nearest church spire, as 103 stone heads turned to look at her.

CHAPTER THIRTY

Underground Channels

Bram trotted after Ahmed and William as they carried the young woman into the butler's room on the upper floor of Dublin Castle. After Bram flipped the lock, he turned to see the ailing woman on a cot, writhing in pain. *Another delay in our search for Pamela*, Bram realized.

"Gentlemen, this is Mairead Jones," Ahmed said. Bram noticed a bruise on his cheek, as he adjusted the pillow under her head. *Did Aleister get to Ahmed, or was the channel crossing brutal?* "Outside of the Bristol Channel, a rogue wave tossed our boat up. Miss Jones's arm may be broken."

The young woman, about twenty years of age, clutched her right elbow and softly moaned.

"Miss Jones," Bram said, tenderly patting the young miss's good shoulder. "Dr. William Stoker, my brother, is a surgeon. May he examine your arm?"

She nodded. Ahmed and Bram stood off to the side.

"What part of Dublin Castle are we in? Is this throwing our plan off?" Ahmed asked softly as William attended to the whimpering Mairead.

"State Apartment butler's station number one," Bram whispered back. "We can still make it to the Record Tower on time if we moved quickly."

Mairead cried, out and William turned to them. "Her arm is broken in at least two places," he said. "I will need to set it."

"Not until I see my father," Mairead sobbed, her voice breaking.

"Miss Jones," Ahmed said in a calm voice, "the authorities are still looking for him and will telegraph us as soon as they know anything."

The door rattled as a key scratched at the lock. A butler surveyed the scene with raised eyebrows. Bram stepped forward to greet the white-haired man with open arms.

"Niall Dolan!" Bram said, embracing him.

"Mr. Stoker, the junior?" the older man asked, holding Bram at arms' length. Niall noticed William and held out his hand. "Dr. Stoker, as well! Your father would be pleased to know that his two sons were here at Dublin Castle. Who is this?" he asked, spotting Mairead on the cot.

"Niall, this is Mairead Jones," Bram said, putting his arm around the older man's shoulder, "and this is Mr. Ahmed Kamal. My brother will need a private operating room to set Miss Jones's arm. Would you be able to take them to the operating theatre downstairs?"

"Yes," Niall answered. "We'll see to her, Mr. Stoker." He went to the door and glanced down the hallway. "Follow me."

William helped the girl stand upright. With an arm around her waist, he swiftly walked her out. As Niall patted Bram's hand in goodbye, something metal slid onto Bram's palm. Niall gave him a wink before exiting. It was a large iron key. Bram pocketed it next to the smaller key Eyre had gave him when he entered the courtyard.

Bram took out his pocket watch. Ahmed glanced at the dial.

"Eleven o'clock, Bram?" Ahmed asked. "Now we're behind schedule."

Bram took out the Viking compass Ahmed had given him. The dial settled to the southeast. He took a deep breath.

"According to this compass you gave me, you'll take the southeast stairs." Ahmed retrieved a ring from his pocket and put it on, adjusting its snug fit. "What is that, Ahmed?" Bram asked.

"A demon detector," Ahmed said. "I have a feeling we're going to need it."

When the chaos of the reception in State Drawing Room died down, getting to the Record Tower without being noticed would be a challenge. They had less than three hours to find Pamela.

During his time as clerk here, there had been rumors of an underpass connecting the Record Tower, one of the oldest parts of Dublin Castle, to an underground Viking fortress. Secret closets, stairways, and rooms remained hidden even from the most educated Dubliners who claimed to know the entire layout of the castle. Few were fully aware of all the hidden tunnels and pathways layered on top of remains of moats, river channels, and pools.

"I'll take the tunnel," Bram said. "I doubt they're holding her captive in the old dungeon, but you never know. As planned, you take the path along the underground river, and we'll meet in the Record Tower."

Bram and Ahmed peered out the door. Seeing the coast was clear, they quickly strode down the State Drawing Room passageway. Threading themselves through the excited mobs of military and the society types, they walked with heads down. There they spotted some of the Scuttlers in oversize uniforms, trying their best to pass as military guards. The rehearsals had paid off: none of them attracted any second looks.

Taking Ahmed by the elbow, Bram turned into an ante room, and they hurried along a narrow corridor before halting before gothic doors. Bram ushered Ahmed inside the turret, and he smiled in spite of himself. It was the same all these years later: the most beautiful turret in Dublin Castle.

The gorgeous domed ceiling was reflected in the floor's mosaic of purple and green stones. "Welcome to Bermingham Tower," Bram said, turning just in time to note Ahmed's wide eyes taking it all in.

"This reminds me of the temples of Cairo," Ahmed said.

Bram glanced out one of the gothic windows. The crowd in the courtyard was thinning out from the horse show. They were losing time.

He crossed next to the turret's unlit fireplace. A landscape painting hung over the mantle. Bram tilted the frame and motioned to Ahmed to hold it. Ahmed peered at the wall behind the painting. Bram found a faint outline of a door amid the chimney bricks. There is was: the keyhole.

Bram used the larger key to open the lock. A door popped out. Ahmed stepped back as Bram swung the creaking door open. Ahmed squinted into the dark as Bram motioned down to steep stairs. Bram put the key back in his pocket and, reaching down to the top step, picked up a folded map, matches, and a small lamp. The Cross Block Office boys had done their job. He handed the map to Ahmed and lit the lamp. Bram pointed to dotted lines around the outline of the castle.

"We are here, in the Treasury Building Conduit staircase. Descend quietly—sound is very alive here. The dotted lines are the former moat, as well as the Viking river route. Since you're skilled at channeling former waterways, you'll be able to follow the path to the Record Tower. We don't who or what is down there." Ahmed put the map in his vest pocket as Bram handed him the lamp. "My friend, we'll meet in the Record Tower's lower level, in half an hour. Hopefully, one of us will have found Pamela by then."

Descending the ancient circular stairway, Ahmed grasped the rusty handrail. With every step, the ring on his hand tightened until his finger throbbed. The stairs creaked, despite Ahmed's best efforts to move soundlessly. No sign or scent of water. Also, no sign of Pamela.

After two more turns down the circular stairs, he was struck by a pungent layer of air. It was reminiscent of the scents he'd encountered in the tombs of kings. He inhaled a dry mustiness, an odor of corroded iron, cinnamon, wet clay, desiccated flesh, and the traces of cedar, juniper, and cypress oil. All were found in the formula for *antiu*, the embalming potion. When he had described what tombs smelled like to Pamela, she renamed the scent "Ghost Water." And Ghost Water was a conduit for spirits.

Ahmed spotted the floor below the last swirl of steps. He held up his lamp. Embedded in the earthen floor was a wooden trapdoor. He bent down and flipped it open, revealing the glint of a dark, slow-moving, gurgling river. Taking out Bram's map, he studied the Dublin Castle compound. This had to be the Pooley River right beneath his feet, the site of old Viking crypts and a natural artery for spirits wishing to evade detection. *Yes, this could be the spirit conduit.* Ghost Water never forgets its former channels, where kings commanded and spirits obeyed.

A single drop of condensation hit Ahmed on the head. Without his fez, he felt it acutely. He crouched down and thrust out his hand into the inky river. Another foot below the surface, he felt an even more frigid brew. Unseen watery spirits brushed against his palm, like invisible jellyfish, then pulsed away in spasm, rejoining the current. Just as he'd thought: *spirits in the waterway*. These entities could follow this feed into the sea, perhaps finding their way back home. *Did the Vikings curse or charm the water spirits?*

Another glance at the map told him that he was near the base of the Powder Tower. He took out a small crystal stone, red and gray, and turned around, placing it near the lowest rung of the staircase. It lit up the chamber, revealing a very low ceiling extending over the water. Squinting past the stairs, Ahmed could make out a small boat tied to a dock. *What did spirits need with boats?* The Golden Dawn chiefs must have been using this as a rendezvous point. Time to breach the ruins of this tower and find a channel to Pamela.

The boat was similar to the skiffs of his childhood on the Nile. It had only one oar and no mast. He lifted his hand and licked a forefinger, confirming there was only a slight breeze above the babbling current. Ahmed shakily placed the lamp at the far end of the boat and settled in. The walls were sheer stone: no banks or niches. He would need to make his presence a surprise. He began to work the oar noiselessly.

Is the Pooley a river, stream, or mudflat? While I am on the river, can a spirit swallow me whole? So many questions.

He noted there were three engraved prongs on the oar's handle that glimmered in the candlelight. The carvings resembled the shape of one of Pamela's drawings: the Hierophant's staff. How many people knew that he was Pamela's muse for her Hierophant tarot card? Was the afrit leaving clues of her whereabouts on the oar? Was this afrit obeying Pamela or Aleister?

Ahmed noticed that downriver in the dim light, the roof appeared darker. He lay on his back and cleared the low arch, one hand paddling through the biting brackish river to keep himself moving, the other pushing against the black ceiling. Once he'd passed through the arch, a whisper of air blew out his lamp. It was pitch-black. The current pushed the boat slowly along.

Ahmed was startled when a splash of water hit his face, caused by a clumsy positioning of the oar. Cold water felt unnaturally harsh to him; he was accustomed to the warmth of sunbaked water, not this freezing black churn. His throat grew tight.

He knew not to panic when in complete darkness: his time in the tombs had taught him that. Still, he felt terror rising. He tempered his breath with slow exhalations. The boat, quickening, rocked back and forth, and soon a small shaft of light appeared ahead.

He was thirty feet away from the light when he saw that the river split in two. Approaching the divide, he veered to the right. As he passed through under the shaft, he heard heavy breathing and a splashing echo behind him. Had someone or something followed him? The boat bobbed more gently as the passageway grew darker. He craned his neck and looked behind him. A familiar shape barely broke the surface.

Crouching on all fours, Ahmed turned around. The green slits of a crocodile's eyes blinked back at him as its great head lifted from the water.

Ahmed stifled a gasp. This was Pamela's familiar, not the afrit. There was a world of difference between a spirit and a familiar. And her familiar would lead him to Pamela!

Bram dodged around a line of bejeweled guests coming up the staircase. Coming into the sparsely populated Presence Chamber, he quickly made his way to the connecting State Drawing Room. He exhaled when he spotted the two tallest Scutters dressed up as military guards at the drawing room's entrance facing the corridor. His relief soon turned to annoyance. The Scuttlers were supposed to deter anyone from following him, but right now they were taking in the parade of celebrants with open mouths. As Bram walked by, he gave them a hard look. They stiffened into the military pose they had practiced in Manchester.

Bram hurried on to the Record Tower and dashed to the door, closing it behind him. Here was the passageway to the second staircase. The door, connecting the servants' corridor, was unlocked. Bram listened for a moment to make sure that no one was coming down the corridor. Once he was inside, his eyes adjusted and he looked up toward the top of the landing, where he found the ancient wooden door in the stone wall.

He climbed up. Eyre's small bronze key fit perfectly, and the creaking door swung open to a tiny anteroom. He shut the door behind him and looked out the small window onto an air shaft between the Record Tower and the State Apartments. The room was bare but for a round iron grate in the floor. Bram groaned at the thought of fitting through the narrow opening.

Crouching, he hoisted the heavy grate to the granite floor. He peered down. *Terrific. A ratty little iron ladder.*

The sparce light from the window allowed Bram to just make out the spiral handrail. He was a large man, and he hated squeezing into tight spaces, but this had to be done. Breathing heavily, he arrived at the bottom, where the light was barely enough for him to find a lamp and matches that had been stored under the last rung. The lamp barely illuminated a hatch in the dirt floor. The door's ancient, battered oak boards had aged to the color of silt. Reaching down, he grasped its iron ring. The door wouldn't budge. He noticed a small lock in the center of the door. He set his lamp down on the ground and tried the small bronze key. It didn't fit.

Holding up the light, he almost hit a row of keys on the wall. All around the ladder hung keys of all sizes. He reached for the largest one. A cold hand came out of nowhere and grasped his own.

With a yelp, he flung the hand away and knocked some of the keys off their hooks. Turning to see who was in the stairwell with him, he found he was alone. The echo of the keys ringing on the stone floor and his yelp reverberated in the tower.

So much for the element of surprise.

"Unless this is a friend visiting, I'm going to ask you to leave," Bram barked. His words bounced off the walls.

Inhaling slowly, he calmed himself. He stooped down to pick up the keys. A yellow stone in the floor, lighter in color than the surrounding stones, caught his eye. He gasped. It was the stone that was missing from Pamela's purse after she disappeared – the stone that Bram gave her for joining the Lyceum Theatre company. Using his large key, he pried the golden-hued stone out of the floor and pocketed it. Underneath it, in the loose clay, lay an ancient key, its large stem engraved with the initials "BB." Bram recognized the key at once. He chortled, despite trying to keep quiet.

The Corsican Brothers was a Lyceum Theatre production that William Terriss, Sir Henry, and Bram had worked on. "BB" was engraved on all of William Terriss's props during the run: it stood for "Breezy Bill," Terriss's nickname. Bram loved to kid Breezy Bill that a man could never have enough keys and that when the run was done, he must keep the prop key with his initials. *But how did the key get here? William is dead. His spirit must be guiding me. Or pranking me.*

Saluting the invisible Breezy Bill, Bram used the key engraved with "BB" to unlock the hatch. He patted one waistcoat pocket to make sure the Viking compass was still there; in his other pocket, he grouped Eyre's, Niall's, and Terriss's keys. *A man can never have enough keys.* Bram lifted the trapdoor open with one hand and, holding the lamp with the other, climbed down a short ladder.

There was a small dirt landing lined with stones next to the burbling Pooley River. Examining the stones, he remembered the stories of fairies using stones to curse humans. He picked out a flat stonewithout depressions in the middle—a depression was a sure sign that a stone had been cursed—and put it in his pocket with the other stone. Lifting his lamp high, he tried to gauge how deep the river was and in which direction it flowed. There was no other passageway. Without a boat, this channel was useless.

"Pamela," he whispered to the dark waters. *Perhaps magic in the walled stones and the water of this Viking fort will carry my voice to her.* If Pamela couldn't hear him, maybe she could feel his presence through the water. Bram had only studied two spells during his brief time with the first order of the Golden Dawn: letting in imagination, and focusing on vibrations. Water spells weren't included until the second order. He would have to use his imagination and vibrations to find Pamela.

He climbed back up and dropped the door back into place. It fell with a thud. He placed the lamp on the floor, and the flame cast shadows on the stairs, etching elongated shapes around him. There were no crypts, no tombs, no dungeons to be found here, as rumors suggested: only steps in a curved tower.

Bram placed one hand on the wall's ancient stones and held the Viking compass with the other. How could he get to her?

Moving the lamp closer, Bram noticed for the first time that his Viking compass had a rod crisscrossing other prongs on top. That was a familiar shape: the staff of Pamela's Emperor, the ankh. Ahmed must have known about this when he gave it to him. This symbol of eternal life was there to protect him. As he stared at the compass, the ankh rose up from the other prongs. Smoke streamed from the metal rods. The compass was heating up.

Bram waved the compass to cool it down. The prongs all pointed to his left. Putting his hand on the weeping stone wall, he felt the jut of a door in its curves. *Was this door here before?* He looked more closely. A wooden staff about half Bram's height was jammed into the latch. He grabbed hold of it and pulled it loose. The staff was shaped like the ankh in Pamela's Emperor tarot card.

He tried to open the metal door, but prongs in the ground anchored it into the floor. He looked down to spot a lock in the middle. He took out Terriss's engraved key and inserted it: a perfect fit. As he turned the key, the prongs clicked and the door unlocked.

"Pamela?" He whispered louder, "William?"

No response.

He pulled the metal door open, its rusty hinges squeaking. He picked up the ankh-shaped staff. *Well, this will make a good weapon to ensure eternal life.*

From his days working here, Bram knew this must be the Viking section of the Record Tower. He thrust his head into the black open space. The faintest outline of an immense cavern opened before him, and cool air blew on his face. The entire time he had worked in the Cross Block Office, he'd had no idea that a huge cave lay below.

He heard something scuttling along gravel, somewhere in the darkness. He stuck his lamp out into the blackness. *What was that?* He heard it again, something scuttling along the wall.

It was Pamela—or something that resembled her. She was crawling up the sheer stone of the Record Tower like a lizard, grasping the corners of the stones with her fingers and toes, propelling herself upward. And she was moving at considerable speed. Then she was gone.

Holy Mother of God, an undead!

Monstrous! It couldn't be. It had to be a hallucination from his novel *Dracula*. Could it be Aleister using a decoy? Or a demon reading his mind?

Bram stared at the dark wall, trying to make out any shapes. A tumbling stone bounced several times beneath him. He held his staff in front of him. The falling stones could be just an accident—or they could be the work of the fairies trying to confuse him by tossing stones to make him lose his way.

Holding the lamp in front of him, Bram gasped at the cavern's expanse. The river continued on about forty feet below him. On a ledge just below Bram, a person stood perfectly still.

It was Ahmed. He looked up and nodded at Bram.

Bram lifted a finger to his lips and took the stones from his coat pocket. He tried not to shiver. They didn't need to be fairy-struck, where you lose all sense of direction, and fall into the river. Best to get his bearings where this river really was.

He looked at the river below and determined where to throw the stone.

He threw the Pamela's gold stone wide, out to river's middle. *Not-Here,* the river gurgled. So, the river really was below them and didn't lead to Pamela. *But is it also right in front of me?* He stepped forward and threw the flat stone down to Ahmed's ledge. It landed with a clunk. Solid rock—it was safe to bring Ahmed up.

Bram lowered his staff to Ahmed. It was long enough for Ahmed to grab and hoist himself up. Bram anchored himself on the ground and pulled his friend up to the platform's edge. As they faced one another, Bram watched Ahmed yank an oar out from the folds of his coat. Bram tapped Ahmed's oar with his staff.

"En garde, monsters around us," Bram whispered.

"Pamela's familiar is here as well," Ahmed said, tilting his face to the rustlings in the cave. He stepped closer to Bram, keeping his eyes peeled on the walls. Bram stared at him. "Her crocodile," Ahmed continued.

"A crocodile in the Pooley?" Bram shook his head. "You're seeing things."

"I also saw that thing on the wall. Is that Aleister?" Ahmed asked.

"Aleister changed himself to look like Pamela," Bram murmured.

Ahmed placed a reassuring hand on his shoulder. A hissing sound from below the cavern prompted both men to widen their stance. Shuffling noises grew nearer. From the interior of the abyss, a low moan rumbled.

Ahmed pounded his oar on the rocky ledge, and it grew to a tall staff, leaving chalky marks on the ground. Snaky rivulets streamed from the marks, circling until a desiccated human dressed in tattered wrappings stood before Ahmed. It raised its black eyes. A mummy. It turned into a whirling dervish dressed in rags and lunged at Ahmed, its white ragged form swirling all around.

"*Totototo*," the mummy moaned as it slowed. It stopped spinning, and one boney hand reached out to Ahmed. Bram started near them, but Ahmed motioned him back.

Ahmed pointed his staff at the monster and said, "In the name of our gods, the merciful, the compassionate, we remember you." He raised the staff over the white-bandaged apparition and paddled it as if it were still an oar. "We will find you and honor you! Basmala, in the name of God, the Most Gracious, the Most Merciful!"

The mummy convulsed, as though pierced by an arrow, and writhed. To the sound of shattering pottery, it dropped to the floor. A twisted cotton cloth thrashed before Ahmed and then spread out, blood seeping from the center. Ahmed and Bram bent over to inspect the bloody bandages.

"Is that blood?" Bram asked.

"Ghost Water," Ahmed said, crouching further. "A reminder that I am not an embalmer but a mediator to the spirits."

Bram straightened up when movement behind them caught his eye. It looked like Sir Henry—only much ghastlier and bluer. "Sir Henry?" Bram asked. "How did you get here?"

Henry resembled an archangel and held a staff in front of him as if he were warding off a devil. Bram lifted his own staff as Henry transformed into a blue skeleton, blue skin peeling away from his face.

The apparition of Sir Henry swayed before Bram. "You talentless hack, you are doomed to ignominy," the spirit sneered. "No one will recognize you as they recognize me! You will be forever unknown!"

Bram was stung, knowing that his real-life Sir Henry believed this to be true. A rush of adrenaline coursed through him. *I've had enough!*

Bram swung with his staff and smashed the skeletal blue Sir Henry Irving. He swung over and over, pulverizing the bones as they crashed onto the floor, the echo pinging off the cavern's walls. The blue skull lay among a pile of shattered, rotten bones. "We've found and vanquished our monsters," Bram panted. Ahmed patted Bram on the back.

Bram placed the skull upside down in the loose clay and threw some dirt over it. He made the sign of the cross.

"Where is Pamela?" asked Ahmed.

Bram caught sight of a door above them in the wall. "Let's find out," Bram said.

CHAPTER THIRTY-ONE

AIR AND WATER

Gasping for breath, Pamela was jostled above the castle compound among the sainted church spires. She waved her arms to keep her balance. Almost tipping over, she felt something brush her ribcage—*was it a hand or a claw?* Florence was floating in front of her, her blue-gray eyes boring into Pamela, her hand around Pamela's waist. "Excellent skyring for someone who never made it out of Level One," Florence said as she floated them nearer the church's roof.

Am I skyring? Doesn't the Golden Dawn teach that you can't skyr until Level Two? Pamela's questions were half out of her mouth when Florence's firm hands released her from her side and tossed her to one of the spires adorned with a saint. Pamela clung to the chest of Saint Patrick.

"Holy Jesus Christ," Saint Patrick sputtered as his beard grazed Pamela's head. Fourteen other stone heads and torsos swiveled. Florence seemed unperturbed, floating among the spires.

"Sir Henry, is he alive?" Pamela asked Florence, who was treading lightly through the air as though pedaling a bicycle.

"He still has his mortal body," Florence said, patting Pamela on the shoulder. "One can't fight Aleister and his Golden Dawn chiefs alone. Your muses are here to rescue you and destroy Aleister's path to your magical pools."

"What pools?" Pamela asked.

Florence's feet stopped spinning. "Your magical sources, Pamela. We'll go over why you need more schooling from the Golden Dawn later, but for now, your Magician, Henry, is recovering in the Octagonal Tower with Ellen. However, Mr. Kamal and Mr. Stoker are not yet in position in the Record Tower. Your London flatmate, Rosa, is in the Bedford Tower, and Yoshio is in the Bermingham Tower to keep the energy of the castle contained." Pamela tried to hold back a choked sob. Florence shook her gently by the shoulder. "Pamela, you need to focus. When Aleister and his magicians arrive here, you must fight them until we can destroy the river conduit to the pools. You can't kill their earthly bodies, but you can destroy their current magical state. You only have moments to prepare." Florence pointed to a pile of bricks in the courtyard next to the church. "Keep your eye on the ruined tower. And find the magical pools."

"What tower?" Pamela asked. "What pools?"

A light breeze picked up, and Florence dissolved. Pamela crawled up Saint Patrick's torso, ignoring his protests, and made out the adjoining brick courtyard, with not one but two round towers. *Which one is the ruined tower?* Pamela tried to spot any entrances. So far, no sign of Aleister and his followers.

Something scratched her legs, and she yelped. Something—no, *someone* the size of a person was climbing up her body. She cried out when two green eyes filled her field of vision.

It was Albertina! Pamela wrapped her arms around the beast's scaly neck and mounted her back. Albertina grunted.

"Ready for war of firestorms," the mind-talk of Albertina said to Pamela.

Trying to stifle the fear that rose up in her throat, she stroked Albertina behind the ears. Her beast's ever-alert eyes rolled from side to side. They had ridden in the magical worlds, and this felt as familiar to Pamela as riding her childhood pony in Jamaica, but Albertina always told the truth.

She reached into her skirt pocket to make sure she still had Ellen's *Othello* handkerchief and Florence's cigarette-paper butterfly. She would need all her tokens. "I command you to protect us, Albertina," Pamela said. A light-green film washed over them and ballooned out into a bubble. Pamela felt something nudging at her side. It was an even rattier version of the goat devil, her one-legged afrit. This sorry incarnation of an afrit was barely a goat and certainly not devil. The tattered toy was the size of a puppy.

"This may be my last incarnation," the afrit said. "But I'm here to fight on your behalf."

Pamela exhaled. This was not going to be a fair fight, even with Albertina and the decrepit afrit here to help. At least all three of them were in the bubble together.

A stir rippled among the stone heads as they twisted to peer down the church's belfry. It was a small steeple supporting a bell, with a stone Celtic cross adorning the top.

Pamela looked down the ladder to the steeple's base. Stone faces shouted and yelled, calling Pamela's name. "Pamela! Pamela!" It hit her: they were rallying her to fight.

Before she could think, four figures slithered onto the deck of the church's roof, and they raced to the four corners. Pamela dug her knees into Albertina's sides, and they floated nearer the church's rooftop. She recognized the men. They were Golden Dawn chiefs: smarmy Westcott; freakishly tall Felkin, his glasses glinting in the fading sun's rays; bad-haircut Mathers with his plaid cape; and William Terriss's murderer, Archer Prince.

The afrit yipped and Pamela hurled him out of their green

bubble toward Saint Patrick, who let go of his staff long enough to catch the afrit by the remaining leg.

"I command you, afrit: fight from this spire," Pamela said as the green bubble around them wobbled. The afrit saluted. Commanding was easy!

The sun was beginning to set behind gathering clouds. Pamela saw that Westcott and Felkin were on the east side of the church's top deck, and Mathers and Archer Prince were on the west. But where was Aleister?

Pamela guided the rumbling Albertina near the front of the church as the magicians floated toward her chanting, "*Taphthartharath.*" It was the name of the god Mercury's spirit, the one who executed the earth's malevolent forces. Not good news.

Pamela spotted something in the air and plucked it as it twisted in flight. It was a feather. Once grasped through the green film around them, it undulated and grew in her hand until it turned into Sir Henry's old sword. She clung to Albertina's neck with one hand and held the sword with the other.

The stone heads from the spires began to chant, "Fight! Fight! Fight!" Pamela felt a tightening around her throat. Was she being choked? Her necklace lifted away from her skin—the garnet Satish had given her backstage many months ago—and began to rise off her neck. A gold ray of light emanated from her chest.

Shouts of "*Taphthartharath!*" from the chiefs mingled with "Fight! Fight! Fight!" from the stone heads.

"Fight, girl!" the head of King Brian howled. A rush energy hit her, and Pamela and Albertina dove downward.

They neared Westcott first. As they swooped by him, he lunged, and Pamela felt acid brushing across her face as he scratched a swath from her ear to her cheek. The pain melted at once, and she kneed Albertina to circle around to get closer. Approaching Westcott again, she took a deep breath and swung

Henry's sword with both hands as Westcott came closer. Recoiling upward, Westcott bumped into one of the spires. An array of animated stone faces turned toward him, screaming, trying to bite him. Pamela threw her sword up into the stone face of an ancient Viking warlord, and the sword set in the statue's mouth. As Westcott spun in midair, the Viking head opened his gray mouth and, using the sword as teeth, devoured Westcott. A wave of nausea hit Pamela. She gritted her teeth.

One down, three to go.

Mathers leapt up to her as she settled near the stone heads, his Scottish cape billowing behind him like a sail. He whipped it around as he sailed above her, preparing to attack. The statue next to Pamela held out his stone cup, shaped like her Ardagh chalice. Reaching through the protective green bubble, Pamela grabbed it. Mathers dropped out of the sky like a plunging bird of prey. When he arrived at eye level, Pamela tossed the contents of the chalice into his face, blinding him. He fell on a low spire and was impaled. A bearded statue pulled Mather's body off the spike and devoured it. Pamela thought she ought to feel horrified, but she was relieved to see Mathers's blood oozing on the stone jaws. Panting, she turned back to the spires.

Saint Patrick swung the afrit onto his breastplate and beckoned Pamela. He handed the long crook of his papal cross to her as Felkin raced across the edges of the roof. King Brian tried to bite Felkin's legs as he darted close to Albertina and Pamela, but Felkin jumped on top of the stone head of Queen Elizabeth I and vaulted over toward Pamela. As he propelled up to her, his glasses turned into two pinchers, ready to cut her in half. The green orb surrounding her provided a barrier, and she twisted back on Albertina. Righting herself, she kicked Felkin sideways, whipping his body within King Brian's reach. Felkin tried to fight his way out of King Brian's grip, but Queen Elizabeth reached out and got hold of one of his long legs. The monarchs chomped down on him, tearing him in half. Felkin's two halves fell into the courtyard, his curdled magical remains smeared across the stones like wet ash.

Pamela looked up to see a shape resembling one of Bram's vampires circling her. It flew above the tower next to the church, its inverness cape spreading out like the mantle of a dark angel. It was Archer Prince, the man who had killed her Fool and her first love, William Terriss. He circled near her, and Pamela could make out his flat, hate-filled eyes.

The stone heads shouted "Fight!" once again. Pamela and Albertina pivoted away to ready themselves, but all at once, Archer was in front of them. He kicked Albertina with such force that the green bubble surrounding them exploded and Pamela was knocked off her mount.

Archer's hands were around her neck, crushing her. She tried to pry them off, but his grip was like iron. Her windpipe closed up as he dragged her away on an air current. Hysterical, unable to breathe, she gazed at the spires of the church as snapping heads drifted farther away. Her vision closed in on the face of the murderer of William Terriss. Plastered black hair framed his face, his eyes were lit up like bonfires, and his breath came quick and frenzied. Archer ballooned into a blur, the whites of his eyes turning yellow.

Opening her eyes wide, Pamela saw that darkened clouds roiled around them. Summoning the last of her strength, she grabbed his hands as he choked her, but she was still held in his tightening grip. Her hands felt hot. She tried to spot Albertina. She looked to the heavens—everything was blurry.

Directly above her, she spotted the evening star, blinking. It was a silvery twinkle amid a celestial lavender field. The star fixed itself in line with Pamela's weakening sight. It blinked again and, along her collarbone, her necklace vibrated. She understood: *follow the star to use your star*. It blinked once more, and, letting go of Archer's grasp, Pamela pushed her now-scorching hands to Archer's jaw. His flesh burned and he winced, dropping his hands as she tore Satish's star necklace from her neck. She held the star out to him, and the heat from the necklace shoved Archer away. She kicked against him and twisted herself out of Archer's reach.

Lights streamed from the towers and streaked across her vision as she fell, her arms outstretched, her feet still kicking to keep Archer away. She saw statue-headed allies drawing closer to her as she fell.

Suddenly, she was pulled short by a jolt so severe that her teeth clamped together. A pair of hands clasped her waist, jerking her away from the sharp edges of the church's roof. A second later, she found herself propped on the roof next to the church's bell tower. A winged angel made of stone wafted before her. She had seen this angel before—it was the angel who had saved her from the mob in Manchester. She looked closer.

"Mother!" Pamela howled.

"Well, you're the one who commanded me," Mother replied, her stone wings still fluttering like a butterfly's. "If you're going to fly, you'll need guidance."

Pamela reached out to her, but Mother hovered away. "You have the gifts of the Colman women. Use them!" She up flew to the stone heads, settled near the head of Nera, and turned to stone.

Pamela clung to the bell tower as she saw Archer lurching among the line of spired heads. He came to Nera and kicked his head off and then turned to Mother's head. A great roar grew from below. A door at the bottom of the bell tower burst open, and a swarm of boys, each wearing a cap, emerged. The Scuttlers from Manchester were here! Boys raced along the roof, spreading out. The sun came out for a moment and caught a silver glint in each cap as they ran. They looked like glittering spiders racing to feast on prey.

Archer steadied himself between the head of Saint Patrick and her mother. The Scuttlers lined up along the edges. They removed their razor-edged hats and, as one, they threw them at Archer. Dozens of hats embedded themselves in Archer—in his face, his hands, and his plaid cape, tearing it to shreds. Archer howled in agony, clinging to a spine of the roof and almost tumbling off. His wounds oozed with a dripping tar-like substance; then his body dissolved into powder. All that remained was a pile of ash on his plaid cape. It fell to the rooftop, where the boys were cheering.

There at the center of the crowd was Toby, the waiter from the Manchester Hotel. He took out a handful of leaves from his jacket and threw them down on Archer's last remains. Nothing was left but wisps of ash. This incarnation of the demon would not come back. Pamela half sobbed to herself. *Four down.*

She heard a sound behind her on the bell tower. "Ow, ow, ow"—Albertina's call. She turned to see her tiny afrit riding Albertina to her like a miniature general.

"Even magic doesn't last forever, does it, my friends?" Pamela said, crushing the two of them into an embrace. For a moment, all three breathed as one.

A scream from the tower echoed, "*Taphthartharath!*"

"That has to be Aleister," Pamela said, clutching the afrit to her chest. She jumped onto Albertina's back. "Let's go!"

As the Scuttlers cheered, Pamela, Albertina, and the afrit flew down to the tower next to the church. At its top, a gap opened up. They flew down a narrow crevice until they came to an opening leading to a riverbank. "Ready yourselves," Pamela cried. "He's here."

Smoke rolled up from the river below. Foggy numbers formed above Pamela:

666

The numbers dissipated into a stream of ash. Aleister emerged amid the sifting ash that covered the landing. He looked as he had in the Throne Room, formally dressed, his pupils tiny pinpricks of yellow surrounded by black.

"Appear, oh thou mighty angel!" Aleister chanted, drawing nearer.

Pamela felt Albertina's snout digging under her arm, and she ran her hand along her mount's scaly back and held on firmly. "I'm ready," Pamela said, lightly kicking Albertina into place. The afrit jumped up from her chest and perched on Pamela's shoulder. The trio steadied themselves.

Aleister spun flames before them, approaching as a whirling dervish, his rant growing louder. "Angel who art lord of the seventeenth degree of Gemini, wherein Mercury takes refuge!"

Pamela extracted Ellen's handkerchief from her pocket and held it out. The cloth streamed blue smoke, creating a wall of azure soot around Albertina as her tail whirled back and forth.

Aleister laughed, extending his hands out in front of him, fingers splayed. "Send thou unto me that powerful but blind force in the form of Taphthartharath!"

A torch appeared in Aleister's hand as he ballooned to three times his mortal size. Immense horns popped out of his forehead; fur and hooves unfurled from his limbs. A devil's pointed tail thrashed from side to side. A five-pointed star grew between his eyebrows. But it was his eyes that struck Pamela as the most monstrous. They were a terrible yellow hue, with red irises. He had become Baphomet, the god that Pamela had sketched for her Devil card. It was a grotesque, exaggerated version of her afrit when she first encountered him.

"Aleister," Pamela shouted, "meet my magic!" She dug into Albertina with her knees, the afrit clung to her shoulder, and they soared to meet Aleister head on.

Aleister flicked his demon tail, snarling as they neared. A dim light poured from his bloodied eyes. Creatures and objects formed in the rays from his irises and barreled toward them—eagles, bulls, castles, swords, wands, stars, and cups—and all of them grazed the afrit and Pamela as they clung to Albertina. He was using her tarot images to attack her!

With one hand still clutching Albertina, Pamela used the other to rummage in her pocket for Florence's cigarette-paper butterfly. As she grasped it tightly, the butterfly transformed into an enormous flying wood nymph, its wings flapping ferociously as it spun out a howling current and Pamela grabbed its legs. The icons from Aleister's eyes bounced away from them.

Pamela thrust the fluttering creature toward Aleister. He screamed as a blast of wind from the nymph's wings blew out his torch. Albertina's tail snapped forward and ensnared Aleister's devil tail, pinning it in place.

The wood nymph's wings beat faster, and the wind howled as it stripped the fur off Aleister's devil body. His face became as bald as an Egyptian cat's. The yellow rays streaming from his eyes began to burn his own body, disintegrating his arms and legs. Reaching out amid the blinding, swirling stream, Aleister's skeletal hands swiped at Pamela.

She veered Albertina sidewise, but not quickly enough. His bony fingers plucked the one-legged afrit off Albertina's back.

"My afrit!" Pamela screamed, as Aleister opened his mouth to eat the little fur ragdoll dangling between his fingers.

Hot blood coursed through Pamela's veins. She leapt off Albertina, floating in midair, and snatched the afrit from Aleister as he opened his jaw. She tossed the small creature back toward Albertina. Facing Aleister, Pamela held out her hands to him, just as she did during Archer's assault. Her hands were now red-hot. Their heat reached him in dappled waves and toppled him to the ground.

Floating above Aleister, she kept her flaming hands over him, paralyzing him in place. "My monsters are not yours to command!" she said. "I will not kill you, but with the strength from my Emperor and Hierophant, I banish you from my pools of magic!"

Aleister rolled over until he reached the edge of the landing; then he fell off the ledge. As he was falling, a moat filled with shimmering water materialized. *The magical pools!* He shrieked when his body hit the water. Ripples radiated from his entry point, and a foam bubbled up. *It's water that dissolves Aleister's power, not air, earth, or fire!* Pamela floated to the church rooftop and looked down at the moat. It was changing shape, curling into itself; then it disappeared. Aleister and the moat were gone. *And is he now in my pools of magic for me to claim?*

From above, Albertina squawked and soared down to her. When she landed next to her, Pamela stroked the crocodile's tilted head. The afrit perched on Albertina's shoulder and appeared concerned. With one more soothing stroke, her crocodile grunted and dissolved into the air. The afrit fell on the church roof, unharmed, except for the missing leg and eye.

Pamela picked up the afrit and held him in one hand. "As a bound slave, you've fulfilled your terms of bondage," she said, caressing his one remaining leg as his one eye blinked. "You're free."

"Yes, I'm a free spirit now," the afrit answered in a raspy voice. "Crowley's spell is broken, and so are my chains, thanks to you and your flying crocodile." His little body flickered as a fluttering wind began to whip about. "Thank you for helping me to complete my service."

Pamela petted the afrit. With each stroke, the pile of fur shrank until a gust of wind blew the remains out of her hands.

The sainted spire heads nodded at her approvingly. She smiled at them and placed both her hands over heart. "I command my powers to restore me to my human best self."

She was plunged into darkness but awoke to a crowd surrounding her as she lay on a brick courtyard.

Bram, Ahmed, and Toby pushed through the crowd and rushed to her side. "We'll leave the castle with as little ado as possible," Bram said into ear, nestling her shoulder against his. Ahmed patted her hand, and Toby bowed and melted into the crowd. The three headed toward the gates at the end of the courtyard, Bram taking her arm.

"Were you at the battle in the air?" Pamela asked, trying to gather her strength as they walked.

"We arrived just in time to see Aleister fall into the hidden moat," Bram said. "No one else saw it."

"Let us discuss this among ourselves later," Ahmed said, steering her with the other elbow.

They reached the exit from the castle grounds. Toby reappeared, then saluted and ran off to join his gang of boys nearby—they were gathered around Ted Pablo and his horse, Little Beda. Across the street Sir Henry lay on a stretcher near the back of an ambulance with Satish, Ellen, and Florence at his side.

Ellen and Florence ran up them, and all five talked at once. Ellen hugged Pamela, peppering her with questions, while Florence grasped Pamela's left hand and held it tightly. Bram, ever the Emperor, guided the group over to Sir Henry, Ahmed trailing behind. Sir Henry, no longer blue, weakly raised a hand in greeting as a nurse tended to a gash on his cheek. Of all the tiny slashes Aleister had inflicted on him, only one remained.

Sir Henry motioned the nurse away as the group huddled together. Bram set out who would accompany Sir Henry to the hospital (Ellen, of course), who would work the timetables for ships so they could cross the channel (Florence's task), and who would determine the times of the trains to London (Ahmed's assignment).

"What should I do?" Pamela asked.

All five of her muses fell silent.

"Miss Smith," Sir Henry said, sitting up. "As your Magician, I encourage you to master your magic. You are on a steep learning curve. Practice and learn before you execute."

Florence leaned in and softly said, "And be sure to close the doors to whatever portal you are in—just a word to the wise from your High Priestess."

Ellen came close and held Pamela's right hand up to her own face. "Continue to follow your passion, Pamela, but don't forget to love the real people in your life, not just your art. Then you will be the Empress in your personal life as well."

"As your Emperor," Bram said softly, "my primary responsibility will be to keep your foes at bay. My battle was with a spirit of my own making—learn from that. Ahmed fought a spirit in battle as well."

"Ahmed—my Hierophant," Pamela said, turning to him as he perched outside the cluster. Drawing him close, she said, "Thank you for summoning my crocodile familiar from Egypt."

Ahmed tucked her hand into his and quietly answered, "Ah, but Miss Smith, your familiar was not from the Nile—she was from Jamaica. And as your Hierophant, I will provide you with connections to your many faiths. You will see: your Emperor and Hierophant will fight for you on many different shores."

She turned to looked at her muses. On either side of her stood Bram and Ahmed, and she squeezed their hands. "Well, Emperor and Hierophant, I have learned how to command some of my magic, thanks to you. All of you, thank you for coming for me."

The nurse called out to Sir Henry—if they didn't load him into the ambulance now, they would leave without him—and this started a whole new discussion of who was and wasn't going to hospital. Sir Henry, Bram, and Ellen began to argue among themselves and with the nurse, but the Irish nurse's voice overpowered all of them.

The palm of Pamela's left hand itched, and she raised it to examine it. Two tiny blue-etched grooves now ran alongside her life line. On her left ear, the letters "PCS" knit together and throbbed.

She turned to the gates to Dublin Castle across the street. She stood apart from her muses. She felt the dark energy in the church where she'd been abducted, a dark-purple essence trying to shroud her. She needed to make sure it did not follow her; she needed to close it off, as Florence suggested. Her hands now seemed to be the conduit to her magic. She held her left hand out.

"I command you, spirits, to close the portal to my prison."

Through a break in the buildings below them, the last rays of sun reflected over the sea, almost blinding her. Somewhere, a door slammed shut, startling her. In response, she heard the lulling sound of water lapping, and then it evaporated.

Her magical pools were calling her. She must find them and claim them. In their deepest waters, she would find her next muses and go on to complete her tarot deck.

Acknowledgments

I would like to thank Ashlyn Petro, my intrepid editor who helped me shape *Emperor and Hierophant*, this third book in the Arcana Oracle Series, into its final incarnation. Ashlyn's feedback dealt with the nuts and bolts of the novel's structure and overall. This feedback was made all the sweeter with follow-up comments such as: "to read your novel after a day of other work was a bit of a reward, rather than a job." How could you not want to rewrite like mad with an editor like this? Thank you, Ashlyn!

Barbara Lucas, Catherine Siemann, Gro Flatebo, Finola Austin, and Laura Schofer were also tremendous sounding boards as well as being fine-tuners, grammar guardians, and POV sensors. Thank you for all your notes, rewrite suggestions, and ideas. Also, the insightful feedback from the writing group with Kate Gale, Ellen Rachlin, Sandy MacDonald, and Loretta Goldberg made me step back and see the whole picture, helping to tighten the pace and focus.

At SparkPress, Shannon Green has been my editor on this book and the previous two books of the series, *Magician and Fool* and *High Priestess and Empress*. Thank you, Shannon, for your diligence and patience in birthing these books with me. Addison Gallegos, kudos to you for picking up the reins in keeping this book series going and holding my hand during the tribulations that a trilogy can foster. I am so grateful to you and your diplomatic and editorial skills. Barrett Briske provided excellent notes, grammar corrections and continuity in their edits of the book, helping me tie up loose ends. I also appreciated the talents of Crystal Patriarche, Lauren Wise, Julie Metz, and Megan Milton. Thank you for all your hard work, insights, and dedication. A special shout-out goes to Lindsey Cleworth for creating the book covers for the Arcana Oracle Series; Lindsey, your skills at summing up the world of tarot and Pamela Colman Smith are spot-on. And Brooke Warner, publisher at SparkPress, thank you for bringing new methods and ideas to help us get our books out into the world.

Thank you to Cynthia Wands, who ponders with me how best to bring Pamela's muses and arch rivals to life. And thank you, Robert Petkoff, my most patient and supportive of husbands, who has never asked, "Don't you have enough tarot decks?"

And to the spirit of Pamela Colman Smith, mother of the modern tarot deck, thank you for continuing to haunt my dreams with inspiration and light.

About the Author

Susan Wands is a writer, tarot reader, and actor. A graduate from the University of Washington, she has acted professionally across the United States and on Broadway, has written plays, screenplays, and skits, and has produced several indie films. As a cochair of the NYC Chapter of the Historical Novel Society, she helps produce monthly online book launches and author panels. Wands's writings have appeared in *Art in Fiction, Kindred Spirits* magazine, and The Irving Society journal *First Knight*. with the third book, *Emperor and Hierophant*, out May 2025. Susan lives in New York City.

Author photo © Robert Petkoff

Looking for your next great read?

We can help!

Visit www.gosparkpress.com/next-read or scan the QR code below for a list of our recommended titles.